EXTRAORDINARY ACCLAIM FOR
WILLIAM R. LEIBOWITZ'

"To call *Miracle Man* a 'medical thriller' or a 'political story' would be to do it an injustice. *Miracle Man* is about miracles, motivations, ethics and morals, and the influence of special interests in the work of genius minds. It's about one 'super' boy's devotion to solving some of medicine's greatest mysteries against forces that would divert these great talents to something darker; and it's ultimately about the ability to withstand moral and ethical temptations against all odds. Readers are treated to a plot with many twists and turns: it holds intrigue, describes compulsions and diversions, shows how a genius battles dark forces within and outside of himself, and generally paints a powerful picture of a search for privacy, as much as meaning.

—And so a gripping novel of psychological tension becomes much more than your usual 'medical thriller', and is a pick for any who want high octane action and emotionally-charged reading right up to an unexpected, gripping conclusion."

—Midwest Book Review

"The story of Robert James Austin proves the talent of William R. Leibowitz. Rushing like a river in a torrential rain, *Miracle Man* stuns and entertains, swivels and twirls above and beyond that which we know. Absolutely brilliant in plot and characters, I could not put this novel down for even a second. This novel pulses and throbs with a story that proves both vulnerable and heart breaking. Brilliantly written, utterly entertaining and un-put-downable, *Miracle Man* is one of those novels of the year that cannot be missed. STUNNING — 5 STARS."

—The Review Broads

"Once in a while, I come across a book that is just one of the most amazingly written works I have had the pleasure to review. *Miracle Man* is one of those books. Mr. Leibowitz' book kept me glued to its pages. I have to admit, the author would have had me convinced that this was a biography about a genius of a man, had I not known it was a fiction book. This is a magnificent story. *Miracle Man* by William R. Leibowitz is destined to be a best seller. I gave it one of my very rare A+ ratings. This is a dramatically superior novel."

—blogcritics.org

"The Only Book You Should Be Reading Right Now—*Miracle Man* by William R. Leibowitz. I had put off reading *Miracle Man* until my son left town for school because I had a feeling it was going to entrap me. There was something about the way the eyes on the cover kept staring at me that I knew there was no way I was going to put the book down. I was right, it was spell-binding from the very first sentence. *Miracle Man* began with a horrifying jolt that sent you on a page turning thrill ride that not even the ending could release you from.

William R. Leibowitz is a mastermind storyteller and his lead character, Robert James Austin, becomes so alive on the pages. The aching realness of him is what sets this book apart from other stories with superheroes or anti-heroes. His feelings of inadequacy, abandonment and betrayal are all too real to those of us who understand those feelings. And for some of us, what it feels like to get lost in the madness of our own mind and the inescapable nightmares we find waiting in the dark.

This book is incredible. It could have ended cheesy, it could have ended overdone or a hundred different things... but William Leibowitz ended it spectacularly. I was very pleasantly surprised and excited, so much so that I still haven't been able to get the story out of my head. Get this book!"

—outnumbered3to1 blog

"*Miracle Man* is a heartbreaking, inspirational and beautifully written story. I was absolutely consumed by this story the minute I started reading. Robert James Austin ("Bobby") is one of the best characters I have ever read. He is simple and genuine. He sacrifices his life for the betterment of mankind, and with it comes so many moments of heartbreak, you just want to shake him and hold him, and as the reader you can feel the other characters in his life who want to do the same. He is such a beautiful character. This is an incredible book. I give *Miracle Man* 5 Stars."

—Savannah Mae Blog

Well written? What makes a story well written? Heroes you cheer for, characters that you empathize with, and villains that you can loathe. All of that plus —plot and style. *Miracle Man* presents all this and more. *Miracle Man* is compelling."

—ReaderViews

"Underpinned by a clever and sophisticated plot, high voltage superhero action makes for a genre busting thriller in *Miracle Man* by author William R. Leibowitz. A highly original and absorbing read, he brings a unique literary voice. Writing with an acerbic pen and an exacting eye for detail, Leibowitz gives the protagonist, Robert James Austin, real room to grow. This creates a true sense of place and purpose into which Austin must ultimately decide where he fits and provides for some splendid twists to his tale.

Superbly written, and faultlessly executed, *Miracle Man* will raise much interest in Leibowitz and rightly single him out as an author to watch. Definitely deserving of a place on your bookshelf, it is recommended without reservation!"

—Book Viral

"Have you ever read a book that left you in a stunned silence? No? Then read *Miracle Man* by William R. Leibowitz.

As I sit here, I go back through what I have just read. If you haven't read *Miracle Man* than you probably have no idea what I am going through. What book has that kind of power? None besides this one that I have just read. *Miracle Man* is absolutely amazing and full of insight. I have no idea where to even start reviewing it. I feel like this book reviews itself in the title alone. This is a great story. I have been seriously stunned into silence by this book.

Miracle Man will have you look at life in general in a whole new way."

—feedmeinbooksreviewblog

"*Miracle Man* is a fascinating novel that explores intelligence, corruption, politics and the pharmaceutical industry. This is fiction, but it is timely and will make you think about the real life implications of the questions raised in the novel.

Miracle Man will leave you wondering "what if…"

—Sweeps 4Bloggers

"This book's got a great storyline and genius characters. The author has written a truly great novel. *Miracle Man* flows, it draws you in, and it finishes strong. *Miracle Man*'s a thriller —not just in the hidden agendas and motives— but also on a personal level, because you really start to care about Bobby, and want to see Bobby happy and succeeding in what he chooses. It really pulls you in — you just start to feel it. *Miracle Man* is perfect."

—Sunshine and Mountains Book Review Blog

"A perfectly wonderful read. Well researched and plausible, there is an intriguing spiritual element, one that is unique in such stories and an urgency, not often found."

—**Pacific Book Review**

"In his debut novel, *Miracle Man*, William R. Leibowitz puts a new twist on the thriller. Along the way, he exhibits a keen knowledge of science and medicine. Some readers will see in Robert James Austin (the protagonist), a leading spiritual figure for the modern era."

—**Palmetto Review**

"*Miracle Man* is a smart thriller that blends together suspense and science in a story of one very special young man's coming of age. There are enough twists in the plot of *Miracle Man* to keep things exciting, and Bobby Austin himself is a novel character —a genius who wants to work for the good of mankind, but is driven to self-doubt and bad decisions by his own demons and past. In fact, part of what makes this book so enjoyable is because unlike in many thrillers, the suspense isn't driven by action alone —it's also driven by the reader's wish for Bobby to find happiness and freedom for himself. It's suspense that arises both from dangerous situations and from the reader's personal investment in the character, who you watch grow and stumble and succeed from age four to adulthood. This book has emotional heart."

—**Penn Book Review**

"With a tremendous amount of medical knowledge included in its pages and a swift-moving plot, *Miracle Man* makes for a smashing debut performance by Leibowitz."

—San Francisco Book Review

"I only put this book down to use the bathroom, it had me reeled in very quickly. If you enjoy suspense and thrillers, then this one should be on your to-read list for sure."

—Confessions of a Psychotic Housewife Blog

"Mr. Leibowitz has truly created a masterful tale of scientific accomplishments, romance, and industry intrigue that will keep you in constant suspense."

"One word: Awesome. All I can say is that you need to read *Miracle Man*."

"My heart broke for Robert Austin. I wanted to jump into the story and just give him a big hug and be his friend. *Miracle Man* was very emotional."

"An honest to goodness thriller from start to finish. Characters jump off the pages and get under your skin so you cannot put it down. Topical and smart."

"It's quite a feat recently for me to find a book I consider a 5 star book. It is also quite a feat to discover a 5 star read which totally held my attention and took me only several days to finish. *Miracle Man* is that book. I was totally blown away by the story. I would love to see where the author takes the story should he do a sequel.

An amazing read from an author who draws you into the story in such a way you will find yourself rooting for Bobby to achieve everything he sets out to, and hating those who are out to stop him. The author shows his own talent throughout the whole of the story. A definite one to watch in the future."

"Robert James Austin deserves a place alongside the most compelling modern literary heroes. In fact, all of the characters in *Miracle Man* are multi-faceted and evolve as the story progresses. Skillfully paced, always surprising and cinematic in its imagery, I can't help thinking what an incredible movie this novel would make. And despite the darkness, the psychological tension, the intrigue and endless conflict (on so many levels), *Miracle Man* is inspirational and uplifting. This is a book for our times. We need a Miracle Man. Trust me —you haven't read a book like this."

"I was hooked after a few pages. It kept you gripped from page to page. A great story line from beginning to end."

MIRACLE MAN

WILLIAM R. LEIBOWITZ

Published By Manifesto Media Group, a division of ILP Limited MMG
Copyright © 2014, 2015 by William R. Leibowitz

ISBN-13: 978-0-9898662-1-7

Visit: miraclemanbook.com, and Miracle Man on facebook
Contact the author: wrlauthor@gmail.com

Book Cover Design and Formatting by Streetlight Graphics Copyright © 2014 by William R. Leibowitz

THE AUTHOR WISHES TO THANK:

My parents, Sidney and Lillian —who encouraged me to re-engage and persevere

My wife, Alexandria —whose insights inspired me and who challenged me to do better

My daughter, Tess —who was my skilled and tireless sounding board

My son, Sam —who solved the riddle

James S. Thayer —who edited the manuscript and gave me the benefit of his expertise

'To destroy one life is to destroy an entire world and to save one life is to save an entire world.'

—Rabbinical Scriptures

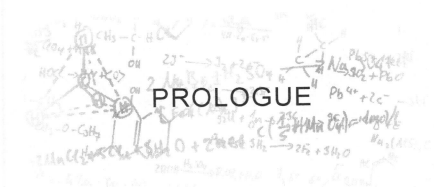

PROLOGUE

A TALL FIGURE WEARING A BLACK-HOODED slicker walked quickly through the night carrying a large garbage bag. His pale face was wet with rain. He had picked a deserted part of town. Old warehouse buildings were being gutted so they could be converted into apartments for non-existent buyers. There were no stores, no restaurants and no people.

"Who'd wanna live in this shit place?" he muttered to himself. Even the nice neighborhoods of this dismal city had more "For Sale" signs than you could count.

He was disgusted with himself and disgusted with her, but they were too young to be burdened. Life was already hard enough. He shook his head incredulously. *She had been so damn sexy, funny, full of life. Why the hell couldn't she leave well enough alone? She should have had some control.*

He wanted to scream-out down the ugly street, "It's her fucking fault that I'm in the rain in this crap neighborhood trying to evade the police."

But he knew he hadn't tried to slow her down either. He kept giving her the drugs and she kept getting kinkier and kinkier and more dependent on him and that's how he liked it. She was adventurous and creative beyond her years. Freaky and bizarre. He had been enthralled, amazed. The higher she got, the wilder she was. Nothing was out of bounds. Everything was in the game.

And so, they went farther and farther out there. Together. With the help of the chemicals. They were co-conspirators, co-sponsors of their mutual dissipation. How far they had traveled without ever leaving their cruddy little city. They were so far ahead of all the other kids.

He squinted, and his mind reeled. He tried to remember in what month of their senior year in high school the drugs became more important to her than he was. And in what month did her face start looking so tired, her complexion prefacing the ravages to follow, her breath becoming foul as her teeth and gums deteriorated. And in what month did her need for the drugs outstrip his and her cash resources.

He stopped walking and raised his hooded head to the sky so that the rain would pelt him full-on in the face. He was hoping that somehow this would make him feel absolved. It didn't. He shuddered as he clutched the shiny black bag, the increasingly cold wet wind blowing hard against him. He didn't even want to try to figure out how many guys she had sex with for the drugs.

The puddle-ridden deserted street had three large dumpsters on it. One was almost empty. It seemed huge and metallic and didn't appeal to him. The second was two-thirds full. He peered into it, but was repulsed by the odor, and he was pretty sure he saw the quick moving figures of rodents foraging in the mess. The third was piled above the brim with construction debris.

Holding the plastic bag, he climbed up on the rusty lip of the third dumpster. Stretching forward, he placed the bag on top of some large garbage bags which were just a few feet inside of the dumpster's rim. As he climbed down, his body looked bent and crooked and his face was ashen. Tears streamed down his cheeks and bounced off his hands. He barely could annunciate, "Please forgive me," as he shuffled away, head bowed and snot dripping from his nose.

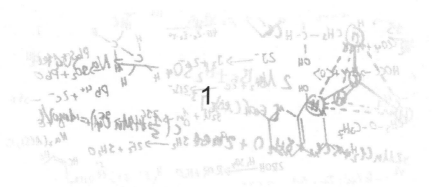

1

EDITH AND PETER AUSTIN SAT stiffly in the worn wooden chairs of Dr. Ronald Draper's waiting room as if they were being graded on their posture by the receptionist. Edith's round cherubic face was framed by graying hair that was neatly swept back and pinned. Her dress was a loose fitting simple floral print that she had purchased at a clearance sale at JC Penney. Their four year old son, Bobby, sat between them, his shiny black dress shoes swinging from legs too short to touch the floor. Edith brushed the boy's long sandy hair away from his light blue eyes that were intensely focused on the blank wall in front of him. Peter, dressed in his construction foreman's clothes, yawned deeply having been up since five in the morning, his weathered face wrinkled well beyond his years. Looking down at his heavy work boots, he placed his hand firmly on Edith's knee to quiet her quivering leg. When they were finally shown into Draper's office, the receptionist signaled that Bobby should stay with her.

Ronald Draper was the Head of the Department of Child Psychology at Mount Sinai Hospital. A short portly man in his late forties, the few remaining strands of his brown hair were caked with pomade and combed straight across his narrow head. His dark eyes appeared abnormally large as a result of the strong lenses in his eye glasses and his short goatee accentuated his receding chin. Glancing at his wrist watch while he greeted Peter and Edith, Draper motioned for them to take a seat on the chairs facing his cluttered desk. Draper had been referred by Bobby's pediatrician when Bobby's condition didn't improve.

"Describe to me exactly what you're concerned about," Draper said.

Edith cleared her throat. "It started about a year ago. At any time, without warning, Bobby will get quiet and withdrawn. Then he'll go over to his little chair and sit down, or he'll lie down on the window seat in the living room. He'll stare directly in front of him as if in a trance and then his lids will close halfway. His body will be motionless. Maybe his eyes will blink occasionally. That's it. This can go on for as much as forty minutes each time it happens. When visitors to our house have seen it, they thought Bobby was catatonic."

Draper looked up from the notes he was taking. "When Bobby comes to, do you ask him about it?"

Edith's hands fidgeted. "Yes. He says, 'I was just thinking about some things.' Then, when I ask him what things, he says, 'those things I'm reading about.'"

Draper's eyes narrowed. "Did you say, things he was reading about?"

Edith nodded.

"He's four, correct?"

Edith nodded again and Draper scribbled more notes.

"Do you question him further?"

"I ask him why he gets so quiet and still. I've told him it's real spooky."

"And how does he respond to that, Mrs. Austin?"

Edith shook her head. "He says he's just concentrating."

"And what other issues are there?"

"Bobby always slept much less than other children, even as an infant. And he never took naps. Then, starting about a year ago, almost every night, he has terrible nightmares. He comes running into our bed crying hysterically. He's so agitated he'll be shaking and sometimes even wets himself."

Draper put his pen down and leaned back in his worn leather chair, which squeaked loudly. "And what did your pediatrician, Dr. Stafford, say about all this?"

As Edith was about to reply, Peter squeezed her hand and said, "Dr. Stafford told us not to worry. He said Bobby's smart and imaginative and bad dreams are common at this age for kids like him. And he said Bobby's trances are caused by his lack of sleep, that they're just a sleep substitute—like some kind of 'waking nap.' He told us Bobby will outgrow these problems. We thought the time had come to see a specialist."

Tapping his pen against his folder, Draper asked Edith and Peter to bring Bobby into his office and wait in the reception area so he could speak with the boy alone. "I'm sure we won't be long," he said.

His chin resting in his hand, Draper looked at the four year old who sat in front of him with his long hair and piercing light blue eyes. "So, Robert. I understand that you enjoy reading."

"It's the passion of my life, Doctor."

Draper laughed. "The passion of your life. That's quite a dramatic statement. And what are you reading now?"

"Well, I only like to read non-fiction, particularly, astronomy, physics, math and chemistry. I've also just started reading a book called 'Gray's Anatomy.'"

"Gray's Anatomy?" Draper barely covered his mouth as he yawned, recalling how many times he had met with toddlers who supposedly read the *New York Times*. In his experience, driven parents were usually the ones who caused their kids' problems. "That's a book most medical students dread. It seems awfully advanced for a child of your age." Walking over to his bookcase, Draper stretched to reach the top shelf and pulled down a heavy tome. Blowing the dust off the binding, he said, "So, is this the book that you've been reading?"

Bobby smiled. "Yes, that's it."

"How did you get a copy?"

"I asked my Dad to get it for me from the library and he did."

"And why did you want it?"

"I'm curious about the human body."

"Oh, is that so? Well, let's have you read for me, and then I'll ask you some questions about what you read."

Smiling smugly as he randomly opened to a page in the middle of the book, Draper put the volume down on a table in front of Bobby. Bobby stood on his toes so that he could see the page. The four year old began to read the tiny print fluently, complete with the proper pronunciation of medical Latin terms. His eyes narrowing, Draper scratched his chin. "Ok, Bobby. Now reading words on a page is one thing. But understanding them is quite another. So tell me the meaning of what you just read."

Bobby gave Draper a dissertation on not only what he had just read, but how it tied it into aspects of the first five chapters of the book which he had read previously on his own. By memory, Bobby also directed Draper to specific pages of the book identifying what diagrams Draper would find that supported what Bobby was saying.

Glassy eyed, Draper stared at the child as he grabbed the book and put it back on the shelf. "Bobby, that was very interesting. Your reading shows real promise. Now let's do a few puzzles."

Pulling out a Rubik's cube from his desk drawer, Draper asked, "Have you ever seen one of these?"

Bobby shook his head. "What is it?"

Draper handed the cube to Bobby and explained the object of the game. "Just explore it. Take your time—there's no rush."

Bobby manipulated the cube with his tiny hands as he examined it from varying angles. "I think I get the idea."

"OK, Bobby—try to solve it."

Thirty seconds later, Bobby handed the solved puzzle to Draper.

Draper's eyes widened as he massaged his eyebrows. "I see. Well, let me mix it up really good this time and have you try again." Twenty seconds after being handed the cube a second time, Bobby was passing it back to Draper solved again. Beginning to perspire, Draper removed his suit jacket.

"Bobby, we're going to play a little game. I'm going to slowly say a number, and then another number, and another after that—and so forth, and as I call them out I'm going to write them down. When I'm finished, I'm going to ask you to recite back whatever numbers in the list you can remember. Is that clear?"

"Sure Doctor," replied Bobby.

"Ok, here we go". At approximately one second intervals, Draper intoned, "729; 302; 128; 297; 186; 136; 423; 114; 169; 322; 873; 455; 388; 962; 666; 293; 725; 318; 131; 406."

Bobby responded immediately with the full list in perfect order.

He then asked Draper if he would like to hear it backwards. "Sure, why not," replied Draper.

By the time Draper tired of this game, he was up to 80 numbers, each comprised of five digits. Bobby didn't miss a single one. "Can we stop this game now please, Doctor? It's getting pretty monotonous, don't you think?"

Draper loosened his tie. He went through his remaining routines of tests and puzzles designed to gauge a person's level of abstract mathematical reasoning, theoretical problem solving, linguistic nuances, and vocabulary. Rubbing his now oily face in his hands, he said, "Let's take a break for a few minutes."

"Why Doctor? I'm not tired."

"Well, I am."

Taking Bobby back to the waiting room, Draper apologized to Peter and Edith for the long period during which he had sequestered Bobby.

"Is everything alright, Doctor?" Edith asked.

"Why don't you take Bobby to the cafeteria for a snack and meet me back here with him in thirty minutes," Draper replied.

When the Austins returned to Draper's office, Draper had two of his colleagues with him. He advised Peter and Edith that his associates would assist him in administering a few IQ tests to Bobby.

Peter's eyes narrowed as he looked at Draper. "What does that have to do with the nightmares and trances, Doctor? We came here for those issues - not to have Bobby's intelligence tested."

"Be patient, please, Mr. Austin. Everything is inter-connected. We're trying to get a complete picture."

Draper and his associates, one a Ph.D in psychology and the other a Ph.D in education, administered three different types of intelligence tests to Bobby (utilizing abbreviated versions due to time constraints). First, the Slosson Intelligence Test, then the Wechsler Intelligence Scale for Children — Revised (WISC-R) and finally, the Stanford-Binet L-M.

By the time the exams were concluded, Draper's shirt was untucked and perspiration stains protruded from beneath his arms even though the room was cool. He brought Bobby back to the reception area, and took Peter and Edith into a corner of the room, out of Bobby's earshot. "Your child isn't normal. Are any of your other children like this?"

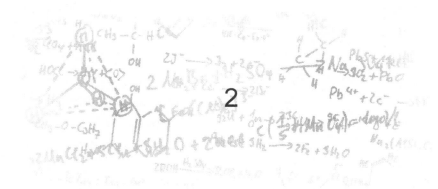

2

A T 2:00 THE NEXT AFTERNOON, Draper stood in the Austin's living room.

"So, Doctor, what exactly do you want to see? Although, I'm not sure why you need to see anything," said Edith, her brow furrowed.

"It would be very helpful if I could see Robert's bedroom and the family room you mentioned, the books in the house, and the items that Robert plays with."

"And the point of all that, Doctor? How does that relate to why we came to see you?"

"Mrs. Austin, as I told your husband—everything is interconnected."

First, Edith showed Draper the living room book shelves on which Bobby's college level text books were piled. Draper examined the stacks of treatises on astrophysics, mathematics and bio-chemistry that Bobby had printed-out from the internet which were strewn on a low table next to the computer. Draper photographed them as Edith described how Bobby would stand, surrounded by open books that he would read in an ongoing rotation, his concentration level so intense that he was oblivious to all household noises and activities.

Then came the family room where Edith showed Draper Bobby's Lego constructions and explained how in a non-stop frenetic four hours of unbroken concentration, he would construct, without directions or diagrams, Lego projects comprised of 5000 individual pieces that would perfectly replicate the pictures on the Lego box.

As he snapped a few photos of the Lego creations, Draper's face looked pale. "When did you first notice that your son was —shall we say — precocious?"

Edith smiled. "It started early. Bobby taught himself from the kids' DVDs that we played on TV while he was in his playpen. He loved when we read to him and showed him pictures. He starting talking at five months, and his vocabulary grew quickly. By eleven months, he was a good speller. When Bobby was one, Peter found out by accident that he could already read, and by fifteen months he was reading and understanding fifth grade level books. At two, he was doing complicated arithmetic, all in his head. He got better at it every day."

Examining Bobby's bedroom, Draper thought he was in a college dorm. Open textbooks were piled everywhere. There was a large blackboard leaning against a wall that was covered with what Draper recognized as lengthy trigonometry equations, scribbled in the immature hand-writing of a four year old. Draper snapped a photo. On the floor were a few open boxes of plastic molecule building models—the kind that are used by pre-med students in college organic chemistry classes. Taped to one of the walls was a life-sized color diagram of a male human body which showed every muscle, bone and blood vessel in medical school level detail. In another corner of the room, was Bobby's little five foot long junior bed with its railroad train-motif headboard, footboard, sheets and pillows, and a teddy bear dressed in a train conductor's uniform sitting on the bed waiting for Bobby.

As Draper walked around the room taking photos, he almost tripped on some long strings that were tightly taped to pieces of furniture, each string at a different angle from the other, with paper circles of varying sizes hanging from them. He found a ruler and protractor on Bobby's shelf and measured the angles and relative distances between the cut-out circles and the various strings from which they were suspended. Draper photographed it.

On the credenza, Draper picked up an odd looking home-made contraption that had instructions wrapped around it that were scribbled in a child's handwriting. "What's this?" Draper asked Edith.

"It's a perpetual calendar that Bobby designed. If you follow the directions, it will let you do what Bobby does in his head."

"What exactly?"

"It lets you figure out the day of the week on which any given date, past or future, would fall. Want to see how it works?" asked Edith.

"I can't possibly believe that it's accurate. I've never heard of such a thing." Draper tested it out ten times.

"Robert designed this? When?"

"About a year and a half ago," Edith replied.

Draper pulled out his camera and took a picture of it.

"Is there anything else I can show you, Doctor?" asked Edith.

"What I've seen is quite sufficient. Thank you for your hospitality."

Several days later, at the Psychology Department's weekly meeting, Draper said, "This boy, Robert Austin; there's something unusual happening here. It doesn't seem possible. But what I've recounted to you is fully accurate and not exaggerated, and Doctors Lewis and Mardin participated in the testing of the child."

Draper then projected onto a screen the photographs he had taken in the Austin house and his list of measurements on the 3-D mobile made from string. Everyone stared at the photo of the mobile.

One of the psychologists said, "This is just a play thing the kid made, nothing more than that. Arts and crafts." A part-time assistant of Draper, a graduate student in astrophysics, kept looking at the projection screen. He started to type into his laptop as he continued to view the projected photograph. He kept typing, looking at the projection screen, and pressing "enter" on his computer emphatically.

"Doctor Draper, with all due respect, I don't think that mobile is meaningless arts and crafts. I'll hook my computer up to the projection screen so I can show you something." He was able to position on one side of the screen, Bobby' mobile and juxtaposed on the other side of the screen, a scientifically accurate 3-D extrapolation diagram of the Andromeda Constellation which he had pulled off the internet. He super-imposed one side of the screen atop the other. There was a perfect match. Bobby's string mobile perfectly represented the Constellation down to the exact degrees of spatial relationships between its components. Silence overtook the room.

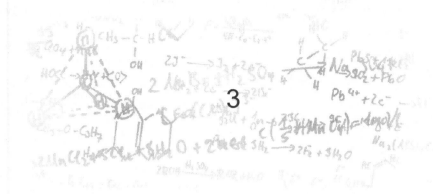

3

DRAPER CALLED DR. HERMAN KNOLL, the Chancellor of the city's Board of Education, a recognized authority on gifted children.

"Dr. Knoll, I've discovered a highly unusual young boy. I would like the Board's assistance in verifying the findings that my department has made."

Knoll said, "I've never received this kind of request from Mt. Sinai before, so am I safe in assuming that this situation is really that special?"

"You are, Chancellor. I'm confident your time will not be wasted."

"OK then. Send me your full report and I'll review it with my staff. Then we'll schedule an interview with the boy and his parents, and prepare to conduct our own tests."

Two weeks after receiving Draper's detailed report, Knoll called Draper.

"Well Doctor, Robert Austin does seem to be exceptional. But your conclusions appear extreme. Perhaps the Board's experience over the years has brought us into contact with more highly gifted children than your department has encountered. You know, there are more children who are gifted in mathematics and science than you may think, and photographic memories are not that rare, particularly among the gifted."

"But Robert isn't just a child who can do calculations in his head and has a photographic memory. He has theoretical problem solving and mathematical reasoning abilities that are extraordinary, with very high powers of abstraction, conceptualization and synthesis. With all due respect, Doctor, in twenty-five years of being exposed to gifted children, I've never met anyone who comes even close to this boy. I'm aware of the differences —and I believe we're talking here, not about 'highly' or 'exceptionally' gifted. I believe Robert fits into the category of 'profound intelligence' and we know how rare that is Doctor."

"Coordinate with the parents and my secretary, and make an appointment. We'll get to the bottom of it and see just how profound this boy really is."

Dr. Draper didn't have an easy time with Peter and Edith in getting them to agree to have Bobby tested by Knoll's experts. But he did prevail, and after Knoll's tests confirmed Draper's conclusions, Draper had an even harder time when Knoll brought the Austin case to the attention of Raymond Massey, the dean of the State Board of Regents examiners. Massey wanted his experts to also examine Bobby. Exasperated, Peter told Draper, "Look Doctor. How many people have to test Bobby to confirm what Edith and I have known since he was five months old? My son is highly unusual. That's obvious. He's been tested enough. And we still haven't gotten any answers to the questions we're concerned about. His nightmares persist and so do his withdrawals. Does anybody care about that? Is anybody testing anything to fix that?"

"Mr. Austin, please. I understand your frustration. But you are asking us to help you with a boy that we are trying to truly understand. Hasn't it occurred to you that his intelligence and these problems you are concerned about are products of each other—are interconnected in some way? The more we learn about Robert, the more likely we'll be able to help him."

Edith piped in, "You know, he's not a guinea pig or a circus oddity. He's our son and deserves to be helped."

Draper nodded. "But we're not hurting Robert. In fact, I think he somewhat enjoys these tests and interviews. He thinks they're games. He's entertained by them. The last thing he said to Dr. Knoll was, 'So when are you guys going to give me some tough questions?'"

Edith and Peter relented and the experts of the State Regents Board subjected Bobby to six different intelligence tests including those designed for the most rarified levels. Their conclusions were the same as Draper and Knoll. Dean Massey summed it up in his report when he wrote, "The boy's intelligence defies accurate measurement by any current means of testing. We can only determine Robert Austin's minimum intelligence—we have no way of measuring its upper reaches—his real intelligence—because he quickly 'ceilings-out' on all of our test scales."

Dean Massey knew what he had to do. In his thirty year career in education, he never had to even consider compliance with Intergovernmental Protocol 329. But it was obvious to him that he had to now. So Massey reported Robert James Austin to the OSSIS (the Office of Special Strategic Intelligence Services), a security agency of the Federal government. The discovery of profound intelligence is considered to be a matter of national security because such people are regarded as rare natural resources.

The director of the OSSIS, Orin Varneys, received from Massey, not only his report with copies of all the testing materials and results, but also the materials of Knoll and Draper. Director Varneys had more experience in these matters than any local or state authority, and he was quick to dismiss hyperbole. Intrinsically skeptical, Varneys was fond of saying, "Genius is a relative term and it's used too loosely. Every educator and psychologist wants to discover the next Einstein, but we're still waiting, aren't we."

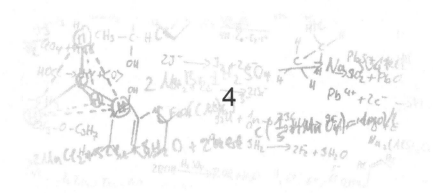

4

THE AUSTIN FAMILY WAS ENJOYING one of their favorite weekend indulgences, a bucket of Kentucky Fried Chicken with mashed potatoes, gravy, corn on the cob and coleslaw, when the phone rang. Edith picked it up.

A woman's voice said, "Is Mr. or Mrs. Austin there, please?"

Edith answered, "Yes, this is Mrs. Austin."

"Hold on for Director Varneys."

"Who?"

"Hello Mrs. Austin. Is your husband home?"

"Who is this? Is this a crank call?" replied Edith.

Peter motioned to Edith and took hold of the phone. "Who is this?" he asked with annoyance.

"This is Director Varneys of the OSSIS."

"We're not interested in buying anything, and you shouldn't disturb people on their weekends. I thought that became illegal."

"Wait—don't hang up. I'm not selling anything." Peter slammed the phone into its cradle, and then a few seconds later picked it up and left it lying on its side so it would ring busy.

On Monday morning, an envelope was delivered to the Austin's house by Fed Ex. No sender was indicated. Edith opened it. It was a letter on engraved stationary with the initials OSSIS at the top and a Washington, D.C. address.

> Dear Mr. and Mrs. Austin:
>
> I am sorry we were unable to speak when I telephoned you on Saturday. I can understand that my call was unexpected. I am the director of a U.S. government agency called the Office of Special Strategic Intelligence Services. We are, among other things, in charge of monitoring unusual intelligence assets. We have been advised by Drs. Draper, Knoll and Massey that your son, Robert James, may possibly be of importance to this office.
>
> I can assure you that it is in your son's best interests that you kindly cooperate with us.
>
> Please call me when you receive this letter.
>
> Very truly yours,
> Orin Varneys

Edith did something she virtually never did because Peter didn't like it. She called him at work. Edith's voice was shaky as she read Peter the letter and he was annoyed that someone had upset her. Telling her to calm down, he asked her for Varneys' phone number, which was printed on the letter, and said he'd call him during his lunch break.

When Varneys got on the phone, Peter said, "Mr. Varneys, we received your letter. I'm sorry I hung up on you the other day, but we get a lot of phone solicitations and you certainly sounded like one. What's your letter all about?"

"Mr. Austin. Let me ask you a question. What's the most valuable asset that the United States has?"

Peter replied, "A lot of things."

"No. One thing is the most valuable. Human talent. Superior human talent and intelligence. From this, stems everything— economic dominance, military security, our entire way of life."

Peter responded, "Well, we're not the only country with smart people."

"Exactly my point, Mr. Austin. Many of our competitors have extremely intelligent people. So all we can do is to try to keep ahead. That's why my agency exists. To identify extraordinary human intelligence. And to nurture and protect it. And that's why we're interested in your son."

"What do you want from us?"

"All we want is to fly you, Mrs. Austin and Robert to Rochester, Minnesota for a few days. All at taxpayer expense, of course. We'll put you up in the best hotel, deluxe rental car, fine restaurants, everything. It will be a nice respite for you and the family."

"Why Rochester, Minnesota?"

"That's where the Mayo Clinic is located. We want Robert to spend some time with a doctor who does work for us there. Dr. John Uhlman. He's chief of Psycho-Neurological Development at Mayo."

"More tests on Bobby?"

"I assure you that these will be the last. Uhlman is the biggest expert in the U.S. —-probably in the world."

"And what happens after that, Mr. Varneys?"

"Well, let's just take one step at a time Mr. Austin."

"Is 'no' a viable answer here?"

The silence lasted long enough for Peter to think the line had gone dead. Finally, he heard Varneys say, "It really is in your family's best interests to work with me on this, Mr. Austin."

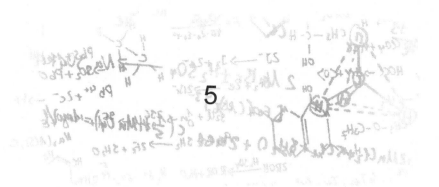

5

PETER WASN'T HAPPY ABOUT USING up a week of his vacation time for a trip to Rochester, Minnesota, but the "Welcome to Rochester" website touted the attractions of the city and the family hadn't been away together on an "airplane holiday" for two years, so Peter and Edith decided to make the most of it. They were candid with Bobby as to the purpose of the trip, but Bobby was excited by the prospect of the airplane travel and he loved airports. So two weeks after Peter had spoken to Director Varneys, the Austin family sat comfortably ensconced in business -class seats for the first time in their lives. After finishing a glass of red wine, Edith began to feel more relaxed. The alcohol had taken the edge off her apprehension over the trip. *It's all so weird*, she thought. *Director Varneys and his strange agency. And now the Mayo Clinic.* As she grew sleepy from the wine, her head sunk into the pillow. Closing her eyes, she thought back to how it began — a voice-mail on her answering machine a little more than four years ago. The call was from Natalie Kimball, a social worker at the Bureau of Child Health and Welfare Services.

"What did you want to speak to me about?" Edith asked, returning Kimball's call.

"Mrs. Austin—would it be possible for us to talk in person? I'll come to you so it won't be inconvenient. It's about an important matter."

"Well, is there a problem? Did something happen to one of our children?"

"Nothing like that. It's a good thing."

The next morning at eleven, Kimball arrived at Edith and Peter's home. A clapboard two story house with a small front yard in a tidy working class neighborhood, the house was built in the late 1930s and had that slightly crooked appearance that befalls old wooden houses as they settle in over the decades. Once through the door, Kimball's face lit up and she smiled. Although a few years had passed since the last of the foster kids had lived there, the living room walls and shelves still paid tribute to the changing mix of twelve children who had called this house their home over a period of two decades. Sports trophies, academic awards, little ceramic sculptures, watercolor paintings and diplomas from kindergarten through college were on display. Countless games, childrens' books and other juvenile treasures were piled high in open wooden storage boxes that Peter had built and decorated, which were stuffed into the corners of the room. Hanging in the dining room were numerous framed photos of Edith and Peter posing proudly over the years with each of the twelve foster children they had raised, a veritable time-line of Edith and Peter's adult lives.

Edith made a pot of coffee and poured two cups as Kimball sat down at the kitchen table. A 44 year old spinster of Norwegian ancestry, Kimball's frizzy grey strands were brushed tightly back culminating in an unflattering bun which sat like a meatball on her head. She wore no makeup and her face was prematurely aged. Dressing in dowdy clothing that would have been unstylish even if worn by a woman twenty years her senior, Kimball sipped her coffee and got right to the point.

"Mrs. Austin. Edith— if you don't mind. I need your help. I know that you and your husband really care about kids. That's so evident as I feel the magic in this house. A wonderful little infant who has had nothing but the worst of luck needs a break. Everyone's afraid to take him in, but only because of their suspicions."

"Ms. Kimball, Peter and I are too old to even think of taking in another child, let alone an infant. Pete's almost sixty. He's a few years away from retiring. We want to sell this house and move down south where it's cheaper to live. We just can't take on the responsibility. It wouldn't even be fair to the child. Someone else better will come along. You'll see. Be patient."

Kimball's eyes grew watery. "No there won't. No one will come forward. You're this baby's only chance. This is the child that was in all those terrible newspaper articles. You read them—didn't you? Doesn't he —- more than anyone else you ever had in this house—- doesn't he deserve a home?"

Edith's face drained of color. "Oh my heavens. That poor little boy. Nobody has taken him yet?"

"Not for want of trying on my part. Edith, we can't let this happen. Please. Think about it and talk to your husband."

As Edith showed Natalie to the door, she rubbed her hand hard against the back of her neck, her jaw clenched tightly. "I can't promise anything. Peter won't like this."

It was 6:15 in the evening when Peter walked through the front door and did what he always did. He hung his jacket on the wooden coat tree and went into the kitchen to get a cold beer from the refrigerator. But this evening, Edith didn't greet him when he entered the house. Instead, he found her sitting at the kitchen table drinking a cup of tea with a dour expression on her face. Peter said, "What's wrong? Why are you sitting here like that?"

"I have to talk to you about something. Sit down please."

"Can't it wait for later? I'm tired and I just want to relax and watch some TV before dinner."

"Peter, do you remember that phone message from a Ms. Kimball at the Bureau of Child Welfare?"

"Did something happen to one of our kids? Did someone get hurt?"

"It's not that. It's that we're not done yet. We're just not done. Do you remember those horrible articles about that newborn?"

"Yeah."

"Well, nobody wants him. Ms. Kimball says that we're his only chance. She's tried everything else."

"Edith, we agreed no more kids. We've done twelve and we did it well and it was great. But we're done now. Let someone else step up."

"I can't live with myself if we just turn away."

"You read the articles. You know what the experts said. He's an accident waiting to happen. That's why nobody wants him. They're not stupid. We don't need our lives complicated like this now Edith. Enough already. Stop feeling that you have to take in every stray."

Edith replied, "Let's talk to the pediatrician and get the facts. People say awful things all the time. It doesn't mean it's true. Look what they said about Phillip, and look how he turned out. We couldn't be more proud of him. And nobody was going to give him a chance."

Peter's eyes strayed to the dining room and to a photo hanging on the wall of the two of them proudly standing on either side of Philip in his college graduation robe.

"Peter, let's just look at the baby. You know how we can tell what he's really like just by looking. Let's just look. And we don't have to keep him forever. We can just get him started for a few years. Then, he'll be older and the stigma will be gone. People won't be afraid to take him then and we can still retire and move like we said we would."

"Why are you doing this to me, Edith?" replied Peter as he walked out of the kitchen.

The Austin's doorbell rang on Saturday at noon sharp. When Edith opened the door, there stood Kimball holding #2764, together with Dr. Edward Drummond, the chief pediatrician of the Bureau of Child Health and Welfare Services, whom Kimball had begged to accompany her. The visitors were led over to the living room sofa.

Edith called down to Peter who was in his basement workshop, "Peter, they're here. Come up please."

Peter appeared, his mouth twisted to one side and his eyes aimed at the floor. By this time, Edith was sitting in the easy chair cuddling the baby, and saying "You are such a beautiful baby boy. Just look at you. I never saw such pretty blue eyes on an infant."

Kimball was beaming. Peter groaned. He pulled up a chair next to Drummond.

"Doctor, I have to be honest with you and I'm asking you to be honest and straight with me. What's this kid's health risks? We don't need a train wreck in our lives."

Drummond replied, "This baby has had more tests performed on him than an astronaut. He's fine. Nobody comes with a guarantee, but all this media noise about him is just that—noise."

Peter shook his head. "Would you take him in?"

44

"I certainly wouldn't be afraid to, I can tell you that. Look at him, he's alert, he's active. He displays no problem signs."

At this point in Peter's life he didn't want to be a foster parent to any child—and particularly not to an infant. But Peter saw that look on Edith's face, that glow that had been missing for over three years since their home had become childless. Kids had been Edith's life for virtually their entire marriage. They were the only thing she was interested in talking about. Children were her calling, her mission. Peter asked Kimball and Drummond to give him and Edith a few moments alone. He suggested that perhaps they'd like to go downstairs and see his workshop. They quickly complied.

"Edith, is this what you really want?"

"He's so adorable. Look at those eyes. Look how alert he is. Look at those hands and feet. He's perfect, Pete. We can't turn him away."

"Haven't we had our fill, honey? And diapers and toilet training. Geez, Edith we're too old for this."

"I promise you. He's the last one. He'll be our lucky thirteen. You won't even know he's here. I'll do all the heavy lifting. You'll see. We won't be sorry."

Peter paced around the living room and then settled into his favorite chair facing out to the front yard. He was silent and just gazed out the window. Then he got up and walked over to Edith. "We'll try this out but only because I can see if we don't, you'll never forgive me. But at the first hint of trouble—that something's wrong with him—out he goes. I'm not getting involved in a melodrama with this kid. I'm doing this against my better judgment. So first sign of a problem—we're done. Is that a deal?"

"It's a deal."

"I'm asking you to promise me, Edith. Do we have an understanding between us here?"

"Yes, we do. Now let's tell them," Edith replied excitedly.

Peter called down to the basement, and Kimball and Drummond came upstairs. Edith's voice sounded years younger and her smile almost touched her ears. "Ms. Kimball—how long will it take for you to do the paperwork? I think we still have a crib and a lot of other baby stuff packed away in the basement."

Kimball's eyes closed as if she were in prayer. "You two are my angels. God bless you both. What you are doing is…" Her voice broke and her words stopped. She stretched out her arms to their full length as she walked over to the couple. She hugged Edith, who was still holding the infant, and then she hugged Peter. "Thank you. Thank you so much."

Dr. Drummond said, "Congratulations. I know you won't be sorry. I have a sixth sense about babies. I've seen enough of them that's for sure."

Kimball took 2764 in her arms. "I'll be back with the paperwork tomorrow. Will that give you enough time to put the nursery together?"

"Yes it will," replied Edith, as her eyes commanded Peter to get started on the job immediately.

As Kimball and Drummond were halfway down the path to their car, she turned and shouted back to Edith, "And don't forget; you have to think of a name for him so we can put it in the documents."

When the car pulled away from the curb, Peter muttered under his breath, "Here we go again."

"What should we name him? I want it to be something special," said Edith.

All of the twelve kids that they had raised had come to them with names. 2764 was the first child that they would have the privilege of naming. Edith knew that Peter had always wanted a son to be named after him, but given Peter's expressed reservations about 2764, on reflection she decided against that. The person she had always wanted to memorialize with a son of her own was her older brother, Robert, who had been killed in Vietnam at 19 years of age.

To Peter, the name James was special. He had first become enamored of it as a boy, voraciously reading Ian Fleming novels. "James" signified everything in life that Peter had fantasized about: an exciting career, sophistication, world travel, glamour, being a hero and an indisputable winner. James. That was the name for this infant who had had no luck so far. And so, when Edith and Peter sat down at the kitchen table to eat their roast chicken dinner, it was soon decided. The baby's name would be Robert James. Robert James Austin. They smiled, kissed, and toasted the choice with their favorite chardonnay that Edith had purchased in the supermarket.

———————

The impact of the airplane touching down at Rochester International Airport jolted Edith out of her recollections and back to the present. As they disembarked, a tall athletically built man about thirty years of age with short blond hair, dressed in a conservative dark blue suit and tie, was standing at the gate.

"Hello, Mr. and Mrs. Austin. And this must be Robert. Welcome to Rochester."

"How do you know who we are?" Peter asked, his eyes narrowing, as he looked the man over.

"Director Varneys asked me to meet you upon your arrival to be sure that everything went smoothly. I'll be here for the duration of your stay. My name is Ray McDermott."

"Where's our rental car? We're more than capable of finding our own way to the hotel," replied Peter with obvious annoyance.

"That'll be delivered to you at your hotel. Don't concern yourself. Everything has been taken care of. You'll be at the best hotel in Rochester and close to the Mayo Clinic. I'm staying there, too."

───────────◆◆◆───────────

When McDermott opened the oversized double-doors to the Austin's guest room, the two bedroom corner suite glistened. Its living room was three times larger than the Austins' own, and there was a stunning two hundred seventy degree view of the city from glass walls on all sides.

"I guess when Varneys said the hotel would be nice, he meant it," Peter said.

"This is amazing," Edith added.

"Awesome," Bobby said.

McDermott's green eyes sparkled. "I know the director will be glad you're pleased. On the desk, you'll find a note from him. The concierge will recommend the best restaurants and attractions for you—-just ask—and remember that arrangements have been made in advance so that everything is paid for. You'll also find Robert's schedule on the desk, and here's my card. If you need anything, just call me. I'm in room 317. Have a good day."

Peter went over to the yew wood desk that stood by the wall of windows. He picked up an envelope addressed to him. The letter was on the same engraved OSSIS stationary as the letter that had been Fed Ex'd to them only two weeks earlier. It read:

Dear Mr. and Mrs. Austin:

Thank you for accepting our invitation to visit Rochester, Minnesota for Robert to meet with Dr. Uhlman. Your cooperation is appreciated. We will endeavor to make your stay as enjoyable and memorable as possible. If during the course of your visit, you have any questions or concerns, please do not hesitate to contact me.

Very truly yours,
Orin Varneys
Director

Edith picked up another envelope from the desk that was labeled "Schedule." Inside was a piece of paper with the following list:

Monday—-10:00 AM —11:00 AM—-introductory meeting of the Austin family with Dr. Uhlman
11:00 AM-12:30 PM Robert/Dr. Uhlman
12:30 PM-1:30 PM Lunch recess
1:30—-4:30 PM Robert/Dr. Uhlman

The schedule for Tuesday, Wednesday and Thursday was the same: 10:00 AM-4:30 PM Robert/Dr. Uhlman, with only a one hour lunch break each day. Friday had only one item scheduled: 10:00 AM—Noon: Austin Parents/Dr. Uhlman

Edith frowned as she showed Peter the schedule. "Well, they sure are intent on getting their money's worth. Except for today, Bobby hardly has any free time."

Peter's face reddened as he took the schedule in his hand and read it. "That's a hell of a lot of time for them to want a four and a half year old to spend with a shrink."

"Don't worry," said Bobby. "I'll try to move this grand inquisitor along quickly so we have more time to have fun. It will be fine, you'll see. I'll bore him. He'll want to finish early."

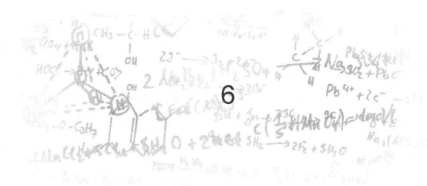

6

THE AUSTIN FAMILY ARRIVED AT the Mayo Clinic office of Dr. John Uhlman on Monday at 9:45 AM. To be sure that they didn't get lost on the huge Mayo Clinic campus, McDermott met them in the lobby of the hotel and delivered them to the doctor's office.

"I've never been in a doctor's office in which we're the only people waiting in the reception area. It's so quiet and private," Edith said to Peter.

"I guess Uhlman isn't on the HMO list," said Peter.

Bobby sat contentedly in a corner reading a copy of the *New England Journal of Medicine* which he found on a table with other publications. At precisely 10:00 AM, Uhlman's secretary brought the Austin family into Uhlman's spacious wood panelled office. As they made themselves comfortable on the three leather guest chairs in front of Uhlman's huge mahogany desk, Peter scanned the diplomas and other framed documents hanging on the wall. A bachelor of science from Dartmouth College, summa cum laude; Phi Beta Kappa certificate; M.D. from Stanford University; Ph.D in Education from Columbia University; Board of Diplomates Psychiatry; Board of Diplomates Neurology.

"Good morning, Mr. and Mrs. Austin. And good morning to you, Robert. It's a pleasure to meet you all," Uhlman said. He was a large heavy-set man with a particularly big head that looked all the more imposing shaved and shined as it was. He was wearing a stiffly pressed white lab technician's coat which gave him the appearance of a butcher in a gourmet meat market, especially since his hands were massive and inelegant. His oversized ears were blood red and protruded prominently and his large nose was flattened as if from a pugilist's blow. All of these imposing features were incongruous with his small closely-set dark eyes which peered out at the Austins from behind the thick lenses of his glasses.

Sitting on the biggest leather executive chair that Peter had ever seen, Uhlman studiously looked at the Austins, as he said, "Let me explain what we'll be doing here over the next few days. Robert is a special boy—we all know that. I'm going to spend a significant amount of time engaging Robert in discussions, games and other challenges. I've done this many times over the years with other children."

Peter interjected, "Doctor, do you have Bobby's records? There are a few items that Edith and I are looking for answers on."

"I'm very familiar with Robert's file. I'll be looking into those areas also. We're in no rush here. We'll explore everything."

"Doctor, I would appreciate it if we could move at a good pace as I'd like to finish early so I can explore Rochester with my parents," said Bobby.

"We'll see Robert. We have a lot of ground to cover."

"Doctor, what exactly are you looking to find out?" asked Edith.

"Mrs. Austin, there is so much that we don't know about the human mind. Children like Robert provide science with a unique opportunity. With children of this age, before they have been exposed to schools and other social influences, we have an opportunity to explore intelligence in its purest form."

"Robert, what's your favorite activity?" asked Uhlman.

"I like to learn about things, doctor," replied Bobby.

"And what's your least favorite activity?"

"Sleeping."

"And what do you spend the most time doing?"

"Thinking," said Bobby.

"Okay. There we have it. Mr. and Mrs. Austin — Robert and I are going to get started in a few minutes. He'll be ready to be picked-up each afternoon at 4:30 here in my office. I'll be seeing you at the end of the week, as you know."

Uhlman took some time to just look at Bobby. There he sat, all forty-seven pounds of him, feet dangling in his shiny black dress shoes. A cute but unremarkable looking four and a half year old, whose only distinguishing physical characteristic was his striking eyes. He would blend into any pre-school play-room without difficulty. Uhlman tapped Bobby's thick file. *Could this child really be so unusual or was he just another in the ranks of the top one or two percent of the population that psychologists and educators routinely encounter? Why would this little boy be so special—why should he be?* From what Uhlman had read, there was no reason to believe that this child had any extraordinary genetic inheritance. He was likely the progeny of, at best, mediocre genetic material—and very possibly sub-medicore. *'Nature or nurture?' What populist rubbish*, Uhlman thought. *There was no 'nature' here and no 'nurture' either.* Bobby's parents weren't brilliant avant-garde educators who had devised a revolutionary learning program starting in the child's infancy. Edith and Peter were ordinary people who provided nothing more than the average home environment.

So what was this child? A genetic mutation —like a two-headed horse or a child born with four arms? Uhlman scratched his head, wondering if he should start getting religious. Leaning forward at his desk, he cradled his chin in the beefy palm of his left hand. There was so little that he and the others really understood. The more he studied and the more research he did, the more he realized how little about human intelligence was known.

"Are you aware, Robert, that you've caused quite a stir, quite a bit of curiosity among people like me?"

"Yes Doctor, I am."

"Do you like being the center of attention?"

"I don't really care but I think it upsets my parents." "Do you know that you seem to be much smarter than most kids your age?"

"I don't socialize much with other kids. I spend most of my time alone."

"And why is that Robert?"

"Because I like to read and figure things out."

"What scares you, Robert?"

"I don't like to talk about that."

Uhlman handed Bobby a Tootsie Roll. Bobby's face lit-up like a jack-o-lantern.

"Robert, if the distance between two cities is sixty-five miles, how many steps must I take in going this distance, if each of my steps is three feet in length?"

Four seconds later, Bobby answered, "114, 400."

"That's correct Robert."

"And how many minutes are there in fifty-two years assuming that there are 365 days in each year?"

"The answer is 27,331,200 minutes and 1,639,872,000 seconds," replied Bobby almost instantly.

Uhlman reached for his scientific calculator. He hadn't previously worked out the number of seconds since that wasn't part of the question. The calculator confirmed Bobby's answer. "And what is the cube root of 413,993,348,677?"

"Seven thousand, four hundred and fifty three."

"Right again, Robert."

"And what is 98235 multiplied by 73268 and divided by 6482?"

"1,110,652", Bobby said.

Never in his life had Uhlman experienced what had just transpired. "How do you figure these things out in your head so quickly?"

"The answers just come to me, Doctor."

"Do you like to do this kind of thing?"

"Not really. It's kind of boring. I like to do real problem solving— you know, where you have to think a lot and figure something out."

The calculations that Bobby had just done in his head were amazing, but Uhlman knew that they in themselves were not proof of profound intelligence. Throughout history, there were examples of certain people who had an astounding ability to do highly complex number calculations in their heads within seconds. In fact, some of these individuals were autistic or had various types of learning disabilities, or were what are commonly referred to as "idiot savants." But what was unusual from a historical perspective, was that Bobby had this staggering calculating ability in addition to all of the other indicia of extraordinary intelligence that were documented in the reports of Draper, Knoll and Massey.

Uhlman then administered tests that were designed to measure a person's capacity to reason abstractly in mathematics, logic, spatial relationships and linguistics. Uhlman started with exams designed for eight year olds and worked his way up to exams that were given in educational research labs to graduate students at MIT. Bobby's mind danced through it all and he wasn't even straining. His energy level was prodigious. He didn't tire. His ingenuity and accuracy were uncanny. Uhlman had never witnessed comparable powers of focus and concentration. By the time 4:30 came and Peter and Edith arrived at Uhlman's office to pick-up Bobby, Uhlman was exhausted.

"Are you okay, doctor?" Peter asked.

"Just a bit tired. It was an eventful day. You've got quite a boy here."

"See you tomorrow, Doctor. Think up some good ones for me," said Bobby cheerfully.

The next day, Uhlman had three of his colleagues join him. He and his crew had compiled a regime of eight different types of intelligence tests including the Stanford Benet Form L-M, the Stanford Benet Version SB-5, the Wechsler WISC SB-IV, and five other exams that were proprietary to the Mayo Clinic that had been especially designed by Uhlman and his staff over a period of years for the purpose of distinguishing among different cognitive levels of the highly gifted. Unlike many IQ tests, these were aimed at measuring abstract and theoretical reasoning abilities and the capacity to rapidly absorb, process and integrate complex concepts. The time period allotted for completion of the eight exams was six hours of total exam time, divided into three sections of two hours each, with a thirty minute break between sections. Bobby finished all eight exams in two and a half hours. Uhlman had never seen anyone read and process complicated directions and questions so quickly. It was as if he were scanning the pages. What Uhlman began to realize was that just as classical music geniuses were capable of running as many as six or seven different complex melody lines in their heads simultaneously and plotting their development and interaction at the same time, Bobby could do this with reasoning problems.

At lunch, Uhlman asked Bobby, "So how do you like these games we're playing so far?"

"Better today than yesterday, Doctor. More interesting, but a lot of it is pretty obvious stuff. I guess you just want to be sure I can read directions accurately."

"Well, okay then. What's something interesting that you did recently?"

"A few months ago, I devised a new table of logarithms using a base of twelve instead of the normal ten. I thought that was fun," replied Bobby.

"You did that by yourself?"

"Yeah, I'll show it to you later if you want."

"Good, I'd like that. I never heard of anyone doing that," said Uhlman. "Have you ever done anything with the binary system?"

"Sure. I worked 2 to the 80th power. I used my blackboard. When it would fill up, I'd erase it and keep the figures in my head and start filling up the board again."

"How long did that take?" Uhlman asked.

"About an hour."

When Uhlman called an early end to the third day's events, Bobby jumped up and down like he was on a pogo stick. Peter and Edith picked him up at 2:30 and the Austin family headed off to see the sites of Rochester. Uhlman then corralled the senior members of his department for a strategy session.

"Here's what I want to do now with the Austin boy. He hasn't studied—and by that I mean taught himself—mathematics beyond advanced algebra and trigonometry. Jesus Christ, that sounds crazy, doesn't it? Anyway, tomorrow, I want to see if he can somehow solve problems that require knowledge of calculus, number theory, combinatorics and set theory. I think it's impossible, but I have to find out."

One of Uhlman's staff responded, "Doctor, it's not possible—-that's why those mathematical disciplines were invented. They're the only way to solve those kind of problems."

"Compile a test. I need 20 problems to give Austin tomorrow."

The following day, Uhlman sat with Bobby and said, "Robert, I know you like challenging games so I have 20 of them here. They're tough ones and you'll have to use a lot of ingenuity to figure them out. I want you to take your time, don't rush, and don't get discouraged." Uhlman passed the exam over to Bobby and then walked to the other side of the room and sat down to observe.

"Doctor, is there a blackboard I can use?"

Uhlman went into an adjoining room, found a blackboard, and wheeled it in to the room Bobby was in. He adjusted the legs so that the board was as low as it could go. Bobby stared at the page of questions. Uhlman walked over to Bobby and saw that the boy appeared to be transfixed, his eyes half closed. This trance like state continued for thirty minutes until Bobby grabbed the exam paper and walked over to the blackboard. He wrote #1 and underlined it. Then he began to quickly fill the board with numbers, diagrams and equations, none of which Uhlman could follow. To Uhlman, it all seemed disjointed and fragmented. Bobby worked at an intense pace. As the blackboard became too crowded with Bobby's notations, Bobby would erase what he had scribbled, and he'd fill the board again. Finally, he triumphantly circled something on the blackboard, put a check mark next to it and then copied the circled item on to the test paper as the answer to problem #1.

This same process continued uninterrupted for three hours as Bobby gradually worked his way through the 20 problems. Uhlman had no idea what Bobby was doing and whether or not the test answers would be correct, but he was astounded by the process and by Bobby's indefatigable energy level and ability to concentrate. Finally, Uhlman interrupted Bobby and said, "Let's take a lunch break. You must be tired."

"No Doctor, I'm not. And I really don't want to break now. I'm in the middle of this."

Four more hours went by. Bobby had filled and erased the blackboard fifty-five times. As Bobby worked, Uhlman photographed the notations on the blackboard each time before it was erased. Finally, Bobby wrote his answer to the last problem, number twenty, on the exam sheet and handed it to Uhlman.

"Here it is, Doctor. Now, those questions were really interesting. Is it too late to get something to eat?"

Uhlman tousled Bobby's hair, and then picked him up in his big arms. Holding him as they walked, he said, "No it's not too late, little fella. You're quite a guy."

Bobby's face flushed. "What did you just call me? You called me a name. What was it?"

"I called you 'little fella.'" Bobby's brow furrowed and he fell silent for a few minutes.

As they headed to the building's cafeteria, Uhlman gave the exam paper to his assistant. Bobby selected a grilled cheese sandwich, apple juice and cherry Jello with whipped cream. Uhlman poured his fifth cup of coffee for the day.

"So, Robert, why don't you like to sleep?"

"I often have very bad dreams."

"What kind of dreams?"

"Very scary dreams. They're horrible."

"What happens in these dreams?"

Bobby squirmed in his chair as he looked down at the floor. "I don't remember them in detail, but often I'm being chased in the dark. Then I fall and I continue to fall endlessly. And there are terrible odors. And people are screaming. And horrible faces are up against me." Uhlman noticed that Bobby was gripping his spoon so tightly that his knuckles were white.

"Oh, that's all? I have dreams like that every night, Robert. Don't let that bother you—-that's nothing. I thought you had really bad dreams." Uhlman laughed, and then Bobby did too.

As Uhlman was returning to his office with Bobby for Peter and Edith's pick-up, he was intercepted by one of his department heads.

"John, can I see you for a moment alone, please?"

Uhlman turned to Bobby and said, "Robert, you know where to go—through that door and you'll see your parents in my office. I'll be right there."

"What's up, Bill?" asked Uhlman.

"The twenty questions on the exam. He got them all correct."

"I want a meeting with full staff in one hour. Tell everyone it's going to be a late night," said Uhlman.

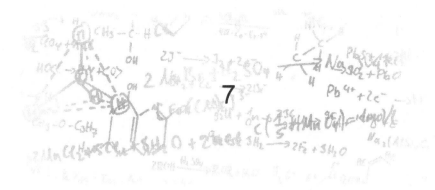

7

THE NEXT MORNING AT 8:30, Uhlman called Orin Varneys.

"Orin, I think we've hit the mother lode," Uhlman said.

"What do you mean?"

"The Austin boy. I've never seen anything like it. He makes the kids at the Institute look like they're retarded. I don't think there's ever been someone like this."

"This could be what we've been waiting for," said Varneys.

"He's not even five years old yet. All of his growth is ahead of him. There's no telling what he'll be capable of," said Uhlman.

"What's the kid's IQ?"

"I had the whole department work on it for days and we used computer extrapolations, but it doesn't get us anywhere. We can't get any kind of accurate figure. There's nothing to compare him to. So it's just a guess. But if you have to have a number, I'd say a minimum—and I stress the word —minimum—of 550."

"That's impossible. The highest ever on record—and that was presumed exaggerated—was 300."

"That's what I'm telling you, we're dealing with a first here," replied Uhlman.

"Is there any downside that you can see?"

"He suffers from very intense recurrent nightmares. That's unusual in a child of his age. I've also witnessed him withdraw into a prolonged semi-conscious state which could be indicative of a proclivity to reality detachment."

"Nightmares. What's he afraid of?" asked Varneys.

"It's hard to pinpoint, but he exhibits paranoid characteristics. All in all, he may be in the early stages of psychosis or dementia. It's way too early to tell. It depends on how he develops. But a mind that powerful can not only create. It can also destroy."

"Destroy what?" asked Varneys.

"Destroy himself," replied Uhlman.

"When are you going to speak to the parents?"

"In about an hour. We have a meeting scheduled."

"John, we can't let this one get away. Make this happen."

———— ••• ————

Right on schedule, Peter and Edith walked into Uhlman's reception area at 10:00 Friday morning for their "summation" meeting with him. Ray McDermott was taking Bobby around town to explore Rochester. It had been a pleasant holiday for them, staying in the luxurious hotel suite, ordering room service, watching the latest movies on "pay per view," and eating at the nicest restaurants in the city.

"Well, where should I begin?" said Uhlman, folding his large hands and leaning forward in his chair. My staff and I subjected Robert to a battery of examinations, which were beyond rigorous. I would say unprecedented. And let me say that Robert was patient, polite, cooperative and in excellent humor throughout the process. He's a real trooper, your boy. A delightful child."

"It's lovely to hear you say that," said Edith, beaming.

Uhlman leaned further forward and tapped his desk with his forefinger for emphasis as he spoke. "The results of the exams are nothing short of astounding. Robert is like the Grand Canyon; he's one-of-a-kind. I don't believe there has ever been anyone who possesses the magnitude of raw intelligence that Robert has."

"How can that be?" asked Peter as he shook his head from side to side.

Uhlman sat back in his chair. "Frankly, we don't know. There's no plausible explanation for something like this. The more we study human intelligence, the more we realize how little we know."

"Well, what does that mean in practical terms?" Peter asked.

Uhlman handed Peter and Edith a sheet of paper. "Here's a list of some of the great geniuses in history and their actual tested IQs, or comparative-history determined IQs, based on Catharine Cox' renown analysis. These are widely accepted in the scientific community as being accurate." Edith and Peter read the names and the corresponding number:

William Sidis: 300
Johann Von Goethe: 225
Leonardo da Vinci: 225
Kim Ung-Yong: 210
Nathan Leopold: 210
Hypatia: 210
Christopher Langan: 210
Emanuel Swedenborg: 205
Gottfried Leibniz: 205
Francis Galton: 200
Michael Kearney: 200

John Stuart Mill: 200
Hugo Grotius: 200
Thomas Wolsey: 200
Michael Grost: 200
Isaac Newton: 190
Albert Einstein: 180

Uhlman continued, "Now, in comparison, Robert's IQ is so high that we here at Mayo can't accurately quantify it, and Drs. Draper, Knoll and Massey reached the same conclusion. And I have to tell you, if you'll excuse the immodesty, that my staff and I are at the pinnacle of expertise in the field of intelligence measurement."

"Do you have any idea?" asked Peter.

"We can only begin to estimate Robert's minimum intelligence. This we put at 550-600, but I'm confident that this is inordinately minimized. Now in IQ terms, every fifteen points higher is a standard deviation off the mean, which means that a 200 or 300 point differential in IQ between Robert and the highest person on the list, William Siddis, represents not just twice, but a quantum leap in the intelligence level. A veritable different species altogether."

"How could this happen? It just doesn't make any sense," Edith said.

"We don't know. My guess would be some kind of genetic mutation. We're running DNA analysis from a piece of Robert's hair."

Peter shifted uneasily in his chair and pulled at his pants. "Doctor—is this a good thing or is there a dark side here for our son?"

"That's a very good question, Mr. Austin."

"The good, of course, is that Robert enjoys his intellect, as you know. He has an insatiable thirst for knowledge and loves to be challenged mentally. His potential is unlimited," Uhlman said.

"And the bad side?" Edith asked, sitting rigidly, her back straight and her hands pressed tightly together.

Uhlman intertwined the fingers of his massive hands in front of him as he looked squarely at Peter and Edith. "Well—there are a few things. So far, Robert has been sheltered from society. He hasn't attended school and he hasn't been exposed to the media. So he has been able to thrive in the private sequestered environment that you've created for him. That will come tumbling down the moment Robert steps foot in school. That will be the beginning of the pain and hurt for him. The isolation, the frustration, and the taunts."

"What are you talking about? He'll be the star in school." Peter flicked his right hand as if to brush away Uhlman's comment.

"That's not how it works, Mr. Austin. There are hundreds of treatises written on the subject. Robert will suffer mightily in a normal academic and social environment."

Peter's face was now flushed and his voice had grown louder. "Let's change gears here for a moment. Did you investigate what we originally went to Dr. Draper for in the first place? The nightmares and trances?"

"Yes I did. Let me give you some background. Children who have exceptional intelligence also have what are called "Overexcitability Factors". These were first identified and classified by the famed Polish psychiatrist, Dr. Kasimierz Dabrowski, who recognized five dimensions in which gifted children showed greater than normal psychic intensity. He called these intensities, OE's—which are heightened levels of awareness and sensitivity to various stimuli. The greater the intelligence level, the more pronounced the OE. This has been proven in countless case studies. Robert, being of extraordinary intelligence, is also prone to extraordinary levels of OE. Of the five types of OEs, the two that are most relevant to Robert's nightmares and trances are the ones which Dabrowski designated as "Imaginational" which are characterized by inventiveness, the ability to visualize clearly, dreaming, daydreaming, fantasy and magical thinking; and "Emotional"—an intensity of feeling and susceptibility to depression, anxiety and loneliness.

I believe that these OEs explain Robert's problems. However, the ramifications are uncertain. He's too young. Only time can tell."

"What do you mean?" Peter asked.

"I had several discussions with Robert about his dreams. They evidence strong paranoia and irrational fears. That, coupled with the trances, points to the possibility of early stage dementia or psychosis, perhaps even schizophrenia," Uhlman said.

"Oh, my God. Not my baby. Not my beautiful boy," said Edith, her eyes instantly welling up with tears and her hands clenched together.

Uhlman walked over to them, pulled over a chair and sat down close as he bent forward. "Don't assume the worst. There's an equally good chance that as Robert matures, he'll outgrow these problems and cope very well. We just don't know. But one thing I can tell you is that a negative environment will exacerbate the problems and cause Robert to withdraw more and more, maybe to the point of no return."

"This is awfully dismal. What do you suggest?" Peter asked.

"I heartily recommend that you place Robert in a special program that we have developed for extraordinary children."

"Who is 'we'?" Peter asked.

"The Mayo Clinic under my guidance and the OSSIS, working in conjunction with MIT and Harvard University. I'm talking about a private educational facility, by invitation only from Director Varneys. It's called the Institute For Advanced Intelligence Studies. All costs are fully covered. It's an education and social environment tailor-made for the most brilliant children in America."

"Where is this school?" asked Edith.

"Newton, Massachusetts -- just outside of Boston. That gives the students easy access to MIT and Harvard, but at the same time gives them their own sixty acre private campus. It's gorgeous. It's the finest for the finest. Even the school food is delicious."

"I wonder how Robert would do there?" asked Edith.

"Even there, he will stand-out prominently and dwarf all the other students. But the Institute's as good as you can get. It's the closest he'll ever come to fitting in."

Peter shifted in his chair, cocked a foot against the floor and glanced at the door. "Ok Doctor. Thank you for all of this. But we can't make any snap decisions. And we're also going to have to talk to Bobby."

Uhlman's voice was firm. "Think carefully about what I said—and do some research on the subject. I can promise you that no ordinary school—public or private-can handle Robert appropriately. And home schooling for a child of his resources is out of the question. Perhaps you should consult with Ms. Kimball."

Hearing her name, Peter shot an icy glare at Uhlman as he took that to imply that he and Edith lacked final authority on the decision. Rising from his chair, Peter extended his hand to Edith signaling that she should do likewise.

"Thank you for your time," said Peter, as they exited the office.

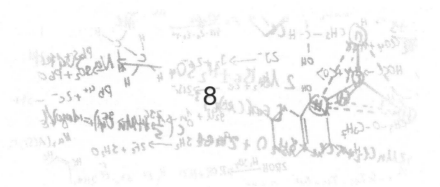

8

O NCE HOME, PETER WENT TO the library and took out every book he could find on the educational system's handling of highly gifted children. He combed the internet for articles and advice. There was no mention of the Institute For Advanced Intelligence Studies anywhere which bothered him. The materials that Peter read including those written by parents of gifted children were uniform in pointing out the inadequacies of public school systems in accommodating the special needs of extraordinarily intelligent students. Peter and Edith understood that these problems would only be compounded in Bobby's case as he was so much more advanced than any of the children whose negative experiences were analyzed in the articles. As one prominent author explained:

"From their earliest months, highly gifted children absorb information from the world around them at an astonishing rate. Outside the school environment, their learning and development may proceed naturally, encountering few obstacles. Though parents may not always be prepared to provide optimum learning experiences and materials, they aren't likely to actively work against the child's development. Once unusually bright children begin formal schooling, however, this open-ended learning environment almost always disappears. For the first time they are expected to conform to a learning curve that bears no relationship to their own. They are expected to stop learning and wait for other children to 'catch up'. In school the problems of boredom, lack of challenge, dearth of materials and adult failure to recognize the extent of the children's capabilities combine to short circuit learning. Boredom, frustration, listlessness, disinterest and hostility to school develops."

Peter and Edith were alarmed by a highly regarded article written by psychiatrist, Theodore Isaac Rubin, who said, "Failure to nourish the capacities these children bring with them thwarts and distorts their whole being. Much psychic pain and disorder is caused by deprivation of the resources and support necessary to fully develop their abilities. The stunting and crippling effect of deprivation is directly proportional to the innate capabilities and potential of the person in question." Peter and Edith interpreted this to corroborate the admonitions that Dr. Uhlman had given them about Bobby—i.e., that a negative educational environment would exacerbate and accelerate his mental problems. It appeared to them that enrolling Bobby in the Institute was the only responsible decision.

Standing at the kitchen sink, Peter seemed to be applying more concentration to washing the dishes than the job required.

Edith sat at the table barely touching her tea cup. "He's so young to be sent away to boarding school," she said. He'll only be five years old. He'll be so lonely. We're his whole life. How will he possibly adjust?"

"Honey, what's the alternative?" replied Peter. "We should be happy he'll be getting the best education money can buy with kids who are as similar to him as possible. The Institute will be a place that he can thrive in."

Edith got up and stood behind Peter. Putting her hands on his shoulders, she pressed against him and said softly, "Promise me we'll visit him every weekend."

Peter turned around and looked into Edith's teary eyes. Tenderly stroking the side of her face, he said, "You know that won't be possible Edith. It's an 800 mile drive to Boston. We'll visit him a lot and we'll talk with him on the phone every day. We can webcam with him. And we'll know he's also getting the best medical care if he needs it."

"I hate this," Edith said.

They decided that they would warm Bobby up to the idea of the Institute by first casually talking about the shortcomings of the local schools and showing Bobby the curricula that he would be forced to endure year after year. They wanted him to come to his own realization as to how torturous attendance at a regular school would be. To their great relief, this strategy worked. When Bobby finally in frustration asked what alternative there might be, they told him about the Institute and the invitation to attend that Dr. Uhlman had extended to Bobby. As part of their sales pitch, they explained that they would speak to him and see him every day by webcam and visit him a lot. Hesitant, worried, but also excited— Bobby asked if they could all visit the Institute to check it out before making a decision. When Peter called Dr. Uhlman, he got a return call in five minutes.

"Dr. Uhlman, we've thought about what you said about the Institute and we've spoken to Bobby. Can we all visit it? Any chance you could join us there?"

"Well, this is auspicious news. I was actually going to call you later this week to follow-up. I'd be delighted to show you all around the school. Does this weekend work for you?"

"Yes Doctor, that's fine."

"I'll have my assistant make the flight and hotel arrangements. I know Director Varneys won't have a problem picking up the cost."

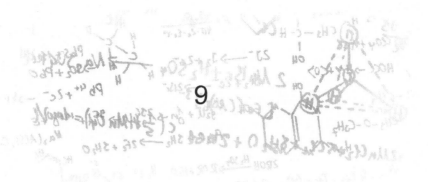

9

THE RIDE FROM BOSTON'S LOGAN International Airport to Newton only took about thirty minutes. As Ray McDermott's gleaming black Lincoln Navigator cruised down Newton's tony residential streets, Edith remarked, "My goodness. This must be what Beverly Hills looks like." The neighborhood got progressively fancier as the SUV continued its journey. Rounding a corner, Ray turned on to a street whose sign read, "Private Drive —Lindhover Lane." Another sign admonished, "Trespassers Will Be Prosecuted."

As the Lincoln cruised down Lindhover Lane, there were no houses on either side of the street for blocks. Finally, the vehicle pulled up to huge black ornate wrought iron gates which bore the elaborately scripted initials JD on them. The gates were attached to monumental limestone columns topped by five foot tall marble urns. Security cameras and flood lights were mounted on the sides of the columns. The gates opened automatically and after a quarter of a mile, the vehicle rounded a bend and came up to a stone gatehouse and imposing modern electric security gates. Two armed guards approached the SUV. One of them took Ray's ID into the gatehouse and could be seen calling someone. Finally, the gates opened and the SUV continued its trek.

"Pretty tight security for a school, don't you think Ray?" Peter asked.

Ray didn't answer. The tall trees soon gave way to beautiful open pastoral vistas of estate gardens on each side of the driveway.

"Damn, is all of this land part of the Institute?" Peter asked.

"Sixty manicured acres. It's a virtual botanical wonderland. Newton used to have some other estates of this size, but they're long gone. This is the only one left."

Around another bend, buildings finally came into view. A mansion reminiscent of Thomas Jefferson's Monticello, but five times as large, was fronted by a tremendous oval marble fountain with muscled Greek gods and voluptuous nymphs frolicking in its center. Quite some distance to the left were four modern looking single-story tan brick buildings. The Lincoln pulled up to the mansion edifice where Dr. Uhlman stood, together with a svelte fortyish blonde woman dressed in a Chanel suit. Chiseled into the marble overhang above the fourteen foot tall double mahogany doors was the inscription, *Institute for Advanced Intelligence Studies*.

Ray opened the passenger door, and Bobby jumped out. "Dr. Uhlman, good to see you again. Is this your weekend get-away cottage?" said Bobby. Uhlman bent down and lifted Bobby up in a smooth sweep.

"My boy, you're gaining weight or I'm getting weaker." He put Bobby down and faced Peter and Edith. "I welcome all of you to the Institute, a unique school with a unique mission and unique resources to accomplish it. Let me introduce you to the dean, Dr. Avalon Vanderslice."

Vanderslice's pale but flawless complexion accentuated her

high cheek bones, strong jawline and well sculpted nose. Her long arched eyebrows, notably darker than her blonde hair, framed light gray translucent eyes. The cold authority of her facial features was only partially attenuated by her surprisingly full burgundy lips. "Dr. Uhlman and I have so much to show you, but first, why don't we have some lunch. You must be hungry after your travels." Vanderslice led them all in to the mansion's opulent reception area.

"Who built this place?" Peter asked, craning his neck to take in the size of the structure. "It's a palace."

Uhlman replied, "John Denning, a partner of William Vanderbilt."

Vanderslice added, "We use the first floor of the house for administration offices, and for receptions and special events. The library occupies the entire second floor. The third floor houses a natural history museum which the students find fascinating. Much of its contents is comprised of Mr. Denning's private collection, but we have supplemented it substantially. You may have noticed the large rotunda. The fourth floor is our planetarium and I must say that it meets rigorous scientific standards." When Bobby heard the mention of a planetarium, his face lit up. Vanderslice continued, "Our class rooms, laboratories and dormatories are housed in the four buildings that you saw when you arrived."

"How many kids attend this school?" Peter asked.

"Attendance varies since we don't have a set curriculum or grade levels here. But I would say three hundred students are here at any given time."

Peter's eyebrows arched upwards as he shook his head. "All this for three hundred kids? I guess you're not exactly operating on a public school's budget."

"No we're not," replied Uhlman.

After lunch, Uhlman and Vanderslice led the Austins on a tour of the Institute's facilities. "All of our teachers have Ph.Ds and could easily find positions in leading universities. They recognize that the Institute provides them with a unique opportunity," explained Vanderslice. As they toured the physics, chemistry, biology and computer science labs, Vanderslice said, "No expense has been spared on these facilities. The natural science laboratories are comparable to those in the top colleges and our computer science lab is equal to that of any graduate school in the country, bar none."

The students of the Institute looked like ordinary kids going about the typical activities of students. There were no shortages of smiles, laughter and animated conversation.

"Let me show you our dormitories," Vanderslice said, as they entered another of the modern brick buildings. "For children of Robert's age, we have found that they are most comfortable with an "apartment style" set-up. This consists of a living room that is shared by three children, each of whom has a separate bedroom. This way the children have companionship but also privacy when they want it. As the children get older, or in certain circumstances where they express a preference, they can private accommodations. We carefully pair children to maximize compatibility—and we're sensitive to any issues. And also note that we have on staff a full-time pediatrician, nurse, and psychiatrist who also holds a qualification in neurology. So rest assured, Robert will receive the best care, and constant monitoring and sensitivity to all situations or issues."

Edith squeezed Peter's hand and Peter nodded.

Vanderslice ushered the Austin family and Uhlman into an oversized golf cart for a trip around the Institute's grounds. Two large swimming pools (one of them indoors), four tennis courts, six basketball courts, a baseball diamond, soccer field, track, gymnasium building, and a two acre pond were the highlights, interspersed between impeccably-maintained gardens and museum quality statuary.

"This place is like a resort," Peter said, shaking his head.

Uhlman asked, "What do you think Robert?"

Bobby's face scrunched up. "It's a bit overwhelming I guess. It's so big. You could fit the school near my house in one of the swimming pools."

Uhlman laughed as he patted Bobby on the shoulder. "You'll get used to it soon enough. Now let's get to the important stuff. Wait till you see the cafeteria!"

The golf cart whisked them away to the Copernicus Student Center. Inside, there was a video game room equipped with multiple units of all of the latest game consoles and a library of video games, an arcade, table-tennis tables, billiard tables, air-hockey tables, and beverage and snack vending machines (which Peter noticed didn't require any payment).

"The cafeteria is open twenty four hours a day. We find that often the students get hunger pangs at irregular hours because they stay up late working on a project and don't want to eat at the normal times," Vanderslice said. "Our kitchen staff will also accommodate any dietary restrictions or special requirements."

Peter, Edith and Bobby gazed at the array of food.

Waving her arms excitedly, Edith said, "This looks like the buffet at the Luxor Hotel in Las Vegas."

Bobby beamed as he looked in the direction of the desserts. "I'm going to get really fat here. Forget learning, I'm just going to eat."

The cafeteria was going a long way to clinch the deal, but the closer was coming. Uhlman gave Vanderslice a conspiratorial wink.

"Dean, is there any chance we could give Robert a demonstration of the planetarium?" Bobby's eyes gleamed. He had never been to a planetarium.

When the planetarium show was over and the lights came back on, Bobby looked as if he had been sedated. He sat motionless, staring straight ahead. Edith tapped him on his shoulder, and then shook him gently. Bobby snapped back to the present and said, "That was the most wonderful thing I have ever seen in my whole life."

"Well, Robert. For those students who display a particular interest and aptitude for astrophysics and astral mathematics, our planetarium is programmable to interface with our computer laboratory for real-world type testing of formulas and theories. It's a unique capability that we have here," said Vanderslice.

Uhlman smiled. The look on Bobby's face said everything. The Institute had a new enrollee.

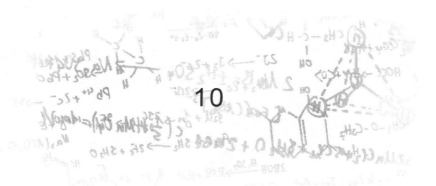

10

As Uhlman had predicted, Bobby was in a different league from all of the other students at the Institute. Even in this rarified environment peopled by the most profoundly gifted children in the country, Bobby, the youngest student at the Institute, was like an eagle among blind bats. By his seventh birthday, he had exhausted all of the Institute's teachers and Dean Vanderslice had shifted most of his daily schedule to graduate classes at MIT and Harvard. The time he continued to spend at the Institute was mainly under his own auspices, working in the computer lab and experimenting with the planetarium interface. Dean Vanderslice repeatedly had to admonish several of the Institute's teachers to stop interrupting Bobby to seek his help when they were stumped on their own research projects.

As was in keeping with the OSSIS' mandate for the Institute's students, three-quarters of their studies focused on mathematics, physics, chemistry, biology and astronomy. Bobby's facility in science and math was uncanny. The Institute's teachers and his professors at MIT and Harvard had never encountered a child or, for that matter, any student, who could conceptualize as Bobby could. His agility in the realm of abstract reasoning confounded them. He was a transcendental thinker, and his intellectual powers appeared to be growing with each passing month. His mind moved at a fantastic speed, sorting through, tossing out and deleting what he considered redundant information as he coalesced the essence of a problem. He became increasingly interested in the inter-relationships between the various sciences, and by nine years of age, expressed the view that all divisions among the sciences were artificial, and that mathematics should be the common language to express all scientific phenomena. The problem he said was that the vocabulary of mathematics had not yet been developed sufficiently to become the unifying bridge between the disciplines.

But just as Bobby's intellectual vision was intensifying, so were his demons. Within his first few weeks at the Institute, he had to be moved to private dormitory quarters because his fitful cries at night scared the children he was rooming with. Dean Vanderslice had him placed in a two-bedroom apartment, and the second bedroom was manned each night by a volunteer from a circle of grad students who were assisting at the Institute. When Bobby ran to the other bedroom sweaty and wild-eyed with fear, there was someone to calm him down. On a good night, he would get six hours of sleep, but when the nightmares were particularly bad, three would be all that he could sustain. Despite this, Bobby's energy level was prodigious. As for the trances, they usually took place in the computer lab as Bobby was feverishly engrossed in writing programs, and designing proofs for theorems. As had been the case since he was three years old, without warning, Bobby would just drift off. He would no longer be present—sometimes for as little as ten minutes, often for closer to an hour. The same thing happened in the planetarium with regularity. When Bobby would finally surface, he seemed refreshed and would plow-back into his work reinvigorated as if nothing had happened.

Bobby had a weekly appointment with the Institute's psychiatrist, Dr. Riaz Verjee. Verjee was under explicit instructions from Uhlman to refrain from prescribing any drugs to Bobby or engaging in hypnosis, regressive therapy, or any other form of deep analysis, so Bobby and Verjee usually spent the hour playing chess. Director Varneys had made it clear to Uhlman that he wanted nothing done that could possibly impinge on Bobby's lucidity or dull his intellect, and he didn't want to risk any form of analysis that could have negative ramifications. So all Verjee did was to monitor Bobby's situation and talk to him in general terms. Verjee vehemently disagreed with this passive approach, and told Uhlman, "The boy is a time-bomb. The fuse is burning and you're not letting me do anything."

Uhlman was unequivocal. "Robert's mind is a finely tuned mechanism that we don't understand at all. We can't risk polluting it. Meds are problematic enough on ordinary people, and I'm not going to involve him in an analytic therapy that might open a pandora's box in his head. You're not aware of it—and you don't need to know the details, but this child has a dark history."

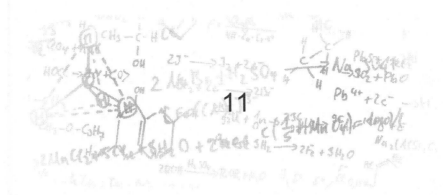

11

THE SUN REFLECTED OFF THE hard packed snow on the side of the highway. Peter sipped coffee from his travel mug as he steered the old Toyota Corolla while Edith passed him a donut.

Edith was beaming. "Bobby's going to be so surprised to see us."

Peter smiled as he accelerated to pass a slower car, his head bobbing to the country music on the radio.

Edith's eyes sparkled. "He's doing so well at the Institute. I guess we made the right decision after all."

His mouth too full of donuts and coffee to respond, Peter nodded his head enthusiastically as he navigated the car around a bend in the road.

Edith patted Peter's knee. She loved to see him so happy and relaxed. He glanced over and smiled.

"Oh my." Edith's voice sounded like she had seen the face of God. Her words stopped mid-sentence.

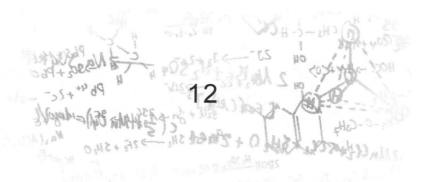

12

HARVARD YARD WAS BARREN, UNWELCOMING and monastic on a nasty March day. Frozen sleet pelted the ground as Bobby looked out the window. Sitting in the office of the head of the astrophysics department, Bobby was bored as he read a pre-publication draft of the professor's latest article. The inaccuracies were so evident to Bobby. They jumped off the page. Eager to be done with this task, Bobby made his corrections quickly, circling formulas and equations that he knew were wrong and scribbling revisions, as he had done many times in the past for his teachers. The renowned scholar sat next to Bobby, craning his neck to look at what Bobby was doing to his treatise, and asking Bobby to explain so that he understood what he had done wrong. That was the part that Bobby disliked the most, as it always took a lot of time for them to comprehend what he was saying. There was a knock at the door as Jason Winterthur, the dean of Harvard, walked in. *A reprieve,* Bobby hoped.

"Professor, can you please give Robert and me a few minutes?"

"Of course. No problem. I'll go get my nineteenth cup of coffee. Maybe then I can keep up."

Once they had privacy, the dean said, "Robert, I just received word." The dean placed his hand on the eleven year old boy's shoulder as he softly said, "Your parents have been in a car accident. Apparently, they were on their way here to visit you. A trailer truck jack-knifed and slammed their car head-on. The officers said they died instantly. I am so sorry, Robert."

Bobby's face drained of color as he crumpled to the old wooden floor. He lay there on his side sobbing and gasping for breath. Dean Winterthur knelt over him. As the pitiful sounds of the child resonated through the vacuous halls of the Jefferson building, students and professors rushed into the room to see what was going on. Despite everyone's efforts, Bobby was inconsolable. He lay there crying for fifteen minutes, and then he was gone, silent. The Harvard medics rushed the unconscious boy to Massachusetts General Hospital. Dean Winterthur called Dean Vanderslice who politely chided him for not having had Bobby brought to the Institute's own medical facility. Vanderslice called Uhlman who called Director Varneys.

Varneys slammed his fist against his desk as he barked at Uhlman, "I want Austin out of that public hospital immediately. This is outrageous. Get him back to the Institute now."

"I'll see how quickly I can get him released," said Uhlman. "Mass General has strict protocols."

"I'll take care of it myself," Varneys snarled. "Meanwhile, get Vanderslice over there and tell her to take security with her. I don't want anybody at that hospital touching Austin."

Within one hour of Uhlman's hanging up the phone, Bobby was in an ambulance heading to the Institute, accompanied by Vanderslice. Four security guards followed in a black Lincoln Navigator. Bobby still had not regained consciousness. Via webcam, Uhlman supervised Bobby's installation into a heavily equipped hospital room at the Institute. As he did this, he called Director Varneys.

"We have him back now," Uhlman said.

"Now what the hell happened?" asked Varneys.

"You remember we discussed Professor Dabrowski's Overexcitability Factors and how the magnitude of those are directly proportional to intelligence?"

"Yes, of course I remember," replied Varneys.

"Two of those OE's came into play when Robert got the news of his parents' death. 'Psychomotor' and 'Emotional'. He was overcome. His mind just shut him down."

"When will it power him back up again?" asked Varneys.

Massaging his forehead, Uhlman was hoping he could keep his headache from escalating to a migraine. "I don't know. But I can tell you that this will have consequences."

Varneys' mouth twisted in a sneer. "Well, it's your job to minimize them. The boy's officially now a ward of the federal government. He's in our hands. I'm having his background records sent to me. They'll be sealed."

———————————

Dr. Uhlman, Dean Vanderslice, and three professors accompanied Bobby to his parents' funeral. The twelve other foster children that Edith and Peter had raised were all there, as were their spouses and children, many friends, neighbors, Peter's co-workers and Natalie Kimball. The Austin's church, an unpretentious wood frame building with worn gray carpets and pews badly in need of refurbishment, was full. Because the accident had been so catastrophic, the caskets were closed. Never had Bobby felt so alone, except in his nightmares.

As Kimball listened to the eulogy and stared at Bobby, her mind drifted back eleven years. She remembered how she had visited him at least once a day in the orphanage, usually on her way to work. She could still visualize him lying in a tiny crib in the cavernous ward, one in a triple- line of identical metal cribs numbering over fifty. Mantra like, Kimball had repeated to the infant, "Don't worry. I won't let anyone hurt you." She recalled her conversation with Dr. Drummond of Child Welfare Services after he had completed his examination.

"The good news is that the little boy —#2764— is a healthy baby who's about two weeks old. Some antibiotics are needed as a precaution, but he'll be fine."

"Wonderful," Kimball replied. Is there any way you can speculate on what hospital he was born in?"

"Well, that's easy. I don't have to speculate. He wasn't born in any hospital. He didn't even have a professional home birth. This kid was born the old fashioned way."

"Are you sure?"

"There's no question about it. His lungs are congested by the presence of amniotic fluid due to the absence or improper administration of pulmonary suctioning following birth and the umbilical cord was left several inches too long when it was cut."

At the end of the memorial service, Kimball came up to Bobby. " I'm sure you don't remember me Robert, but I just want to say that I've heard so much about your accomplishments and I'm very proud of you. I'm so sorry that we meet again under these circumstances."

Bobby stared at Kimball, his mind racing to recognize her. The face didn't look familiar, but he recalled the voice. Just as he was about to start a conversation with her, Uhlman nodded to the two security guards who had accompanied them, and they ushered Bobby off to a waiting limousine.

Since his parents' death, Bobby had changed. He had become quiet, withdrawn, taciturn and joyless. His quick light-hearted banter and precocious sarcasm were gone. As the ensuing months rolled by, it was evident to everyone around him that he was suffering greatly. Dr. Verjee did his best to try to draw Bobby out and comfort him, but the boy had erected a barrier around himself, a fence to insulate himself from any more hurt. He buried himself ever more deeply in his work and it became his refuge. Most nights, the grad students in the adjoining bedroom heard him quietly crying. His trances became more frequent and lasted longer. Dr. Uhlman became increasingly concerned.

"Orin, I'm worried about the Austin boy," Uhlman said.

"He'll get over it. Everyone does. He's still working, right?"

"That's not the point. He's not headed in a good direction. Don't forget his proclivity for reality detachment. He could shut down and check out, period. We have to do something affirmative," Uhlman said.

"What do you propose?"

"We need to bring someone into his life who can rejuvenate him, help him get his spark back. His *joie de vie*. Someone who can be a surrogate parent, who he can relate to."

"I'm not starting up with any more foster parents if that's what you have in mind," replied Varneys.

"What I'm thinking of, is to find him a mentor. Someone on a high intellectual level that he can relate to — not just another professor, someone who would spend real time with him and bring him back to the world of the living."

"I'll support that in principle as long as that person keeps him focused where we want him, and doesn't waste time. I don't need some boy scout here. And I don't want anybody who's going to fill his head with nonsense."

"Let me work with one of your programming people and the database and I'll see what I can find," said Uhlman.

"Okay, but remember our priorities."

Uhlman made a list of the key search criteria. The OSSIS data banks were among the most comprehensive in the nation, and within fifteen seconds of the programmer's pressing "Enter," Uhlman had a list of prioritized names and contact details.

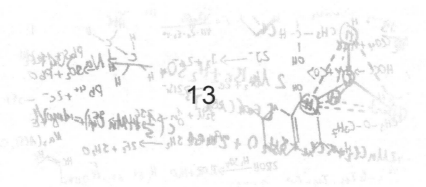

13

UHLMAN HANDED A THICK RED file to Joseph Manzini as they sat in the study of Manzini's rambling Tudor style house in Brookline, a Boston suberb not far from the Institute.

"Dr. Manzini, I can't leave this file with you as its contents are highly confidential, so please read through it now. Take your time, I'm not in a rush. That will give you the background on what I'm here to discuss," said Uhlman.

Joseph Manzini was of Northern Italian ancestry. Standing five feet ten inches tall and of average build, he had an olive complexion and short black curly hair that was neatly coiffed behind a receding hair line. His nose was too prominent and imperfectly formed for him to be considered handsome but a broad smile illuminated his face and his warm brown eyes twinkled playfully. At 58 years old, his outgoing, high-energy personality was what one would expect in a matire'd at a fashionable bistro, rather than a renown bio-chemist. Manzini had risen to a prominent position in a major pharmaceutical company by virtue of his brilliant discoveries. Tired of corporate politics, he resigned from the company at forty-six, cashing-out hundreds of thousands of highly appreciated stock options that he had accumulated over twenty years on the job. His retirement was derailed when he was quickly recruited by Tufts University to chair its bio-chemistry graduate school program. Manzini held this position for nine years but then left so that he could spend all his time caring for his ailing wife. She passed away when he was fifty-six from Amyotrophic Lateral Sclerosis— Lou Gehrig's disease.

Manzini put on his reading glasses and began to read the reports of Dr. Draper, Chancellor Knoll, Dean Massey, Uhlman, Dean Vanderslice, Dr. Verjee, and lengthy assessment letters from six renown MIT and Harvard professors (all of whom Manzini knew personally). An hour later, Manzini scratched his head, sat back and let out a deep sigh.

"This is incredible. Absolutely incredible. Hard to believe, in fact. But I guess this had to happen sooner or later. Einstein times 10. Thank God you found him. But what does this have to do with me?" Manzini asked.

Uhlman leaned forward in his chair and looked intently at Manzini. "Robert has always had serious issues. You read my report. But since his parents' death, I'm afraid he's extremely vulnerable to a complete breakdown. He's alone. He needs someone. He needs a mentor, someone with special qualities. We think that man is you."

Manzini's eyes narrowed as he stood up and walked toward the bank of windows that overlooked an impressive garden with a large pond. Gazing at the ducks swimming serenely on the rippling surface of the water, he seemed oblivious to Uhlman's presence. Finally, after a few minutes, he turned around and said, "This is all fascinating, Doctor, but I'm retired. I'm not looking for a job."

Uhlman's eyes locked with Manzini's. "This isn't a job. It's a unique opportunity to help a remarkable boy. You have no children, Dr. Manzini. Robert has no father. You can make your mark here.

Who knows what affect you might have? Surely, he's worth your time. And needless to say, a handsome salary has been authorized."

The words were barely out of Uhlman's mouth when Manzini shot back, "I don't need the money and I'd never accept a fee for doing something like this. God, if he ever found out, it would be devastating."

Manzini's attention shifted to a framed photograph of his wife that sat on an antique credenza across the room. He walked over, picked it up and seemed to space out as he recalled her tireless good works. After awhile, he put the photo down. Taking a seat next to Uhlman, he leaned over the coffee table and picked up Bobby's file and flicked through it again for over a quarter hour. "There has to be chemistry or it won't work. I'll agree to meet the boy."

Uhlman smiled. "Let me mention just one more thing. This is a long-term commitment. Robert can't get close to someone again, only to have them leave. So if you were to accept, you'd have to be in it for the long-haul."

Manzini nodded.

"Good. I'll arrange a meeting for you with him tomorrow at the Institute. He'll be most comfortable there—it's been his home for the last six years. But remember, the boy you'll meet is a shadow of the real Robert James Austin. It's going to be your job to bring him back."

Still holding Bobby's file, Manzini shook his head. "If I do this, I'm not going to do it to bring him back to what he was. I'll do it to move him forward —know that before you give me the job."

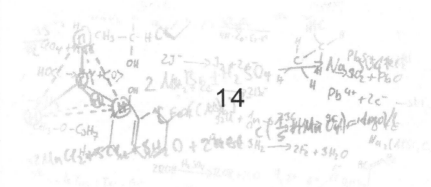

14

WHEN MANZINI MET BOBBY HE immediately sensed the child's extreme isolation. His despair and loneliness were apparent to him. Perhaps Manzini was particularly empathetic since only two years earlier, he had fallen into the abyss of depression when his wife passed away. Bobby could barely make eye contact with him. Manzini suggested to Uhlman that he leave the two of them alone while they took a walk.

"Can I call you Bobby? Robert sounds so formal," Manzini said.

Bobby didn't look up from the ground. "Sure. My parents called me Bobby. No one else does."

"I know how much you miss your parents."

Bobby glared at Manzini. "Why would you say that? You didn't know them and you don't know me."

Manzini's eyes closed as he bit his lower lip. "That's true. But I know how much I miss my wife—and I know how it felt when she died two years ago—-and it still hurts now."

Pools of pain stared back at Manzini. Bobby kicked at the gravel path. "It hurts so much I can't bear it. I can't get away from it," Bobby said almost in a whisper.

"Don't try. It's supposed to hurt. That's what love is."

The intensity of the gaze coming from the eleven year old's piercing blue eyes seared Manzini. He had never felt anything like it.

Finally, Bobby said, "So what are you? A philosopher, a motivational speaker or one of Director Varneys' spooks?"

They began to walk through the gardens, and now Bobby was looking at Manzini and not the ground.

Pulling a leaf from a tree, Manzini twirled it between his fingers. "Well, I'm none of those things. I'm just a guy who grew up in a housing project in Roxbury and studied his butt off so one day I could own a fancy sailboat."

"And do you own one?" Bobby asked, a small grin on his face.

"You'll have to see for yourself. But now it's my turn to ask some questions. What's your favorite music?"

"I don't really listen to music. I don't have the time," Bobby replied.

Manzini shook his head and pursed his lips. "Well, that's going to change in a hurry. And who are your four favorite painters?"

"I don't have any."

Manzini raised his eyebrows in an exaggerated manner. "There's another thing that's going to change real quickly. And in theater—do you prefer comedies or dramas?"

"I've never been to the theater."

"This is getting ridiculous," said Manzini as he stopped walking, put his hands on Bobby's shoulders and said with mock seriousness, "I've got my work cut out for me here. So, tomorrow we start. And by the way, call me, Joe."

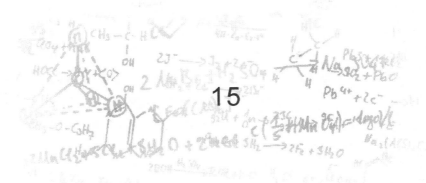

15

THE WIND BLEW THROUGH BOBBY'S sandy brown hair as Joe's vintage fifty-five foot sailboat, *Dreamweaver*, arced its course through the choppy waters of Boston's North Shore coast. Joe guided Bobby in the principles of sailing and Bobby gladly assumed the role of first mate, as Joe's state of the art sound system bathed them in a continuous stream of Joe's favorite music from all genres. They munched on tuna and chicken salad sandwiches as the sun beat down on them and Joe regaled Bobby with funny anecdotes and his philosophic insights. Joe had brought Bobby shopping bags full of his favorite works of literary fiction which Bobby would read curled-up at night in his cozy state room. While Bobby could devour a thick math or science tome in an hour with total mastery of its contents, he would slowly savor the opuses of the literary greats. Sleeping on board the boat and awakening with Joe to greet the dawn was one of Bobby's favorite activities. The smell of eggs and bacon frying and coffee brewing as the boat sailed in the Atlantic with no land in sight freed Bobby's spirit. This, and frequent visits with Joe to art museums, concert halls and the theater were gradually transforming Bobby. They spent every weekend together, and usually saw each other at least once during the week, animatedly discussing philosophy, comparative religion, history and the arts—-everything other than science and math. In short order, Bobby became a veritable art scholar as he quickly absorbed hundreds of volumes of art history and analysis. Joe purchased an Ipod for Bobby and subscriptions to the best download and web streaming services, and from then on, Bobby was never without earphones as he explored jazz, world music, classical, R&B, blues, rock, pop, hip-hop, folk and every other genre of music he could find. Bobby had embraced life as never before and was developing, under Joe's tutelage, into a multi-dimensional sophisticated and well-rounded adolescent.

Uhlman, Vanderslice and Verjee were extremely pleased. With Joe's guidance, Bobby had not only recovered but was thriving emotionally, and intellectually his powers were continuing to increase.

One day when they were eating dinner in Joe's favorite Chinatown restaurant, Bobby asked, "So, when you're not showing me the good life, what exactly do you do with your time?"

Joe laughed. "A variety of things. I read a lot. I tinker with my antique cars and I'm quite active in charitable pursuits."

"Oh, like trying to make me into a real person?" said Bobby, as he drummed his chopsticks noisily on the table.

"And other things," replied Joe as he signaled for the drumming to cease. "I try to be philanthropic financially, but I don't think it's enough to just write checks. I'm fortunate to have the time—so I like to spend it trying to do some good."

"Doing what?"

Joe reached for a fortune cookie and broke it open. "Why don't I take you along so you can see for yourself?"

"I'd like that," said Bobby as he lined up the paper strips from six cookies and flipped them over repeatedly, comparing the Chinese writing with the English.

The next Saturday, Joe picked Bobby up at the Institute. He drove them to the Boston Children's Hospital. Opening the trunk of his car, he removed four large plastic shopping bags which were overstuffed with toys and games. Joe handed two of the bags to Bobby.

"Now let's spread a little happiness," said Joe.

The elevator door opened on the fourth floor. The sign read, Oncology. They began their rounds. Bobby wasn't prepared for this. He had never been exposed to the suffering of people afflicted with debilitating diseases, nevertheless children with cancer. As they moved from bed to bed giving out toys, Joe effortlessly kidded around with the patients, but Bobby had trouble holding back his emotions. Joe put his arm around him and took him aside. "Look Bobby. These kids know how sick they are. They don't need to see that in your face. We're here to help them feel better—not make them feel worse. So snap out of it. They want you to be happy so you can make them happy. Can you do that?"

Bobby nodded. "I'm going to borrow a pad and some pencils from the nurses' station." When Bobby re-entered the ward, he announced loudly, "Who likes comics?"

For the next hour, he went from bed to bed quickly drawing the patients' favorite characters, and also throwing in caricatures of himself, Joe and the kids. Up till then, Joe wasn't aware of Bobby's artistic abilities.

These hospital visits became one of Bobby and Joe's frequent activities and gradually, Bobby became comfortable with them.

"I wish I could do more," he said to Joe as they were getting back into the car after a visit.

"Well, you can. You're in a unique position to do more, a lot more. You have an extraordinary gift. I know you said it freaks you out because you don't know where it came from, and you feel it possesses you rather than you possessing it—but the bottom-line is that you have it and no one else does."

"So, what are you saying?" asked Bobby.

"What I'm saying is – it's not important where your intelligence came from—what's important is what you do with it."

Bobby slumped into the passenger seat and stared at the car's ceiling as he frowned. "Joe—I'm going to wake up one day and it'll be gone—or I'll be crazy. I'll go into one of my trances and never come out."

Joe grasped Bobby's forearm and gave it a hard squeeze. Bobby looked at him, his eyes watery. "That's ridiculous, Bobby. But if you really believe that, it's all the more reason why you need to make some important decisions sooner rather than later."

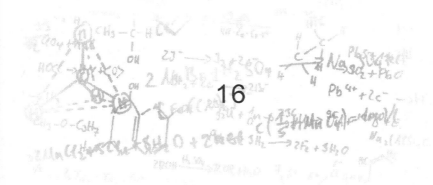

16

BY AGE TWELVE, BOBBY HAD been awarded both bachelor of science and master's degrees, suma cum laude from MIT, through the Institute's special interface with the university. At age fourteen, he received a Ph.D in mathematics from Harvard for his ground breaking doctoral thesis on automorphic forms, and at age sixteen, a Ph.D from MIT in astro-physics with a thesis on cosmic neutrinos that stunned the scientific community and started tongues wagging about it being Nobel prize worthy. The role reversal pattern of Bobby's interaction with his teachers got more pronounced as time went on. His Ph.D oral examinations predictably landed-up with Bobby at the blackboard solving for the examining professors the problems they had been grappling with unsuccessfully for years.

Joe and Bobby's relationship was life altering for them both. Bobby was the son that Joe had always wanted. He poured his time, affection and wisdom into Bobby who absorbed it all gratefully and returned his love. Though Director Varneys was wary of Joe and referred to him disparagingly as "the hippie," Uhlman's selection of Manzini proved to be messianic.

To celebrate Bobby's seventeenth birthday, Joe had a special surprise in store for Bobby—-a three week sail on *Dreamweaver* from Boston to St. John in the U.S. Virgin Islands. It wasn't easy for Joe to get permission. Uhlman broached the subject to Varneys.

"Are you nuts?" Varneys asked. "You think it's okay for the hippie to take Austin in treacherous waters on his dinky little boat for three weeks?"

"He's an expert yachtsman and the water is calm this time of the year."

The veins in Varney's right temple began to pulsate as he glared at Uhlman. "Calm my ass. We have a huge investment in this kid and a lot riding on him. Three weeks alone with the love guru could ruin everything. It doesn't sit right with me."

"Orin, it's a special seventeenth birthday present for Robert. He's done everything you could hope for. He has two Ph.Ds already and he's working on more. He has his heart set on this."

" Manzini already told him before getting permission? Brillant, just brilliant!" exclaimed Varneys.

"Don't worry. We'll get it back in spades. Robert will come home so rejuvenated, he'll be more productive than we can imagine."

Sitting down behind his desk, Varneys leaned forward and thumped the folders in front of him. "Here are the conditions, John. I want the charts for the route, and I'm having a cutter follow that boat just five miles away for the whole trip. Don't tell them that — but that's how it's going down. I'm not having them get hijacked, sink, or let hippie-dip decide to skip and start a new life with the kid in Ghana. Jesus. I can't believe I'm going along with this craziness."

———————————

Joe loaded *Dreamweaver* up with three weeks of food, wine,

volumes of books for them both to read, a hundred DVDs, a satellite-connected sixty- inch TV, and lots of sunblock. Bobby was so excited about the trip and wanting to make sure that there was no last minute problem of unfinished work assignments, that he burned through the quantum physics problems he was analyzing at a speed that was startling even for him.

"Are you ready for the greatest adventure of your life, my able first mate?" Joe asked.

"Yes I am Captain. I'm more than ready," said Bobby, beaming as he stood at attention like a navy sailor.

And so they were off. Within forty minutes, *Dreamweaver* cleared the Back Bay and Boston Harbor and entered the endless expanse of the Atlantic Ocean. Over the last few years, Bobby had become a proficient sailor, and he and Joe worked together instinctively to guide the boat. Joe took off his wristwatch and asked Bobby for his. "We don't need these now," said Joe as he threw them into the water.

"Are you crazy?" said Bobby.

"We can always buy new watches. But these days come only once. Anyway, I put a cheap one on because I knew I was going to do that." Bobby grinned.

One day melded into another and Joe was right. Time became irrelevant. The wind cooled them, the spray from the waves salted their skin and hair, and the sun purified them. Within a week at sea they both looked like deeply tanned beach bums and were proud of it.

There were long periods of contented silence as the ocean's solitude embraced them. But there was plenty of lively discourse and aimless banter. Joe took note of how Bobby had grown. No longer a gawky boy, Bobby had become a handsome young man.

Already six feet tall, he had a lean physique, dark brown hair with a natural auburn tint, strikingly clear light blue eyes, aquiline nose, high cheek bones, full lips and a strong chin. But despite his sculpted features and the eerie iciness which would at times project in his gaze, there was a vulnerability in his personae which was easy to discern.

"So Bobby. What's happening on the girl front?"

"Well, it's been a little slow. I've never had the opportunity to be with girls my age when it counted. By the time I was interested in them, I was out of the Institute and over at the universities. And there I was the freaky little kid from outer space."

"Is that what they called you?"

"Worse than that," Bobby said, shaking his head.

"So what about the university girls now?"

"I've been in grad classes or one-on-ones with professors, so it's hard to meet anyone anywhere near my age. They're so much older than me, they don't take me seriously."

"Sounds to me like you have to double-back. You're a grad student, but you're just about the age of incoming freshmen, so start hanging out where they do."

Bobby smiled and nodded.

After ten days at sea, *Dreamweaver* cruised past Great Thatch Island, Jost Van Dyke, and Tortola, and anchored a quarter mile offshore of St. John, an under-developed and unspoiled oasis in the Caribbean Sea, with U.S. National Park status to preserve its beauty. Joe taught Bobby how to snorkel off the side of the boat. And then into the dinghy they would go, pulling up on the soft beach sands of Trunk Bay, Cinnamon Bay, Cruz Bay, Turtle Bay and Caneel Bay. Each day, Bobby would select which beach to hang out on by how good the girls looked and how small or non-existent their bathing suits were. Joe's criteria was that there also had to be an outdoor bar and preferably a band playing. For dinner on their third night at St. John, they ate at Asolare, a two-story restaurant on Great Cruz Bay beach, featuring freshly caught seafood, a terrific calypso band and the kind of island cocktails that taste like juice but leave you seriously impaired. At the bar waiting for a table to become available, Joe, always a convivial magnetic presence, started to chat up an attractive middle-aged blonde tourist. Her daughter, tanned dark as a local, stood next to her wearing a simple white summer dress that appeared to be transparent. Bobby was mesmerized. After awkwardly shifting on his feet and looking around the room for a few minutes, he got up the nerve to address the girl.

"Excuse me. Were you on Trunk Bay beach yesterday? I think I saw you there," Bobby said. Kate stood five feet six inches tall, long silky dark brown hair that glistened as if coconut oil had just been applied to it, almond shaped light green eyes, pouty full lips, and teeth that looked amazingly white in contrast to her dark skin. Bobby could easily discern a shapely athletic figure under the gauzy dress. He tried not to stare.

"Yes, we were there," she responded.

Bobby's photographic memory instantly started to flash vivid images as his mind sorted through them like a high-speed collater. *It was her—-that girl in the tiny faded blue string bikini,* he recollected.

"I thought you looked familiar. Great beach, huh?" he said.

"Fantastic. Are you staying here on the Island?"

"Sort of. We're on our sailboat anchored just offshore. We sailed here from Boston".

"That's so cool. Must have been awesome."

"Oh yeah, it was beyond belief," he replied.

"Is that man your dad?" she asked as she motioned to Joe.

Bobby paused before he answered, "Yes."

"Is that your mom?"

"That's her. I think she's had like three of those drinks already," she said as she laughed. "By the way, my name's Kate."

"Mine's Bobby."

"How long are you guys down here for?" Bobby asked.

"Another two days."

Joe said to Kim, Kate's mother, "Perhaps you both would like to join us for dinner? I think it's easier to get a table for four here than for two."

As Kim laughed and leaned into him, she said, "That would be fun, Joe, but we're actually meeting a group of friends here for dinner." Bobby's heart sank.

"I have a great idea," countered Joe. How would you ladies like to go sailing with us tomorrow? Kim cast a glance at her daughter whose sheer dress was gently being blown by the island breeze. Kate smiled back at her. "That sounds fantastic," said Kim.

"Great. We'll pick you up in our dinghy at 10:30 in the morning right on this beach. Don't forget to bring a bathing suit," Joe said.

The restaurant hostess came up to Joe to announce that the table was ready. Joe and Bobby bid good night to Kim and Kate.

As soon as Bobby sat down, he said to Joe, "You're a genius. And you're so smooth. Do you know who she is? She's that girl I was looking at yesterday on the boat with my binoculars. The one in that tiny faded bikini. You know, the reason we picked that beach".

"Well, how fortuitous."

"I think she may like me, Joe," Bobby said.

"Why shouldn't she? Just relax and be yourself."

For Bobby, the rest of the evening was a magical blur. The din of the music from the beach band, the smell of the bougainvillea in the humid night as it wafted its way through the open air dining room, the sweet pungent taste of the island food. As Joe and Bobby walked to the dinghy, Bobby looked heavenwards. The stars shined as brightly as those in the Institute's planetarium, but they were real. Bobby sat back in the dinghy as Joe followed the moonlight path on the water that led back to *Dreamweaver*.

Ten thirty the next morning couldn't come quickly enough. As the dinghy neared the shore, Joe waved and Kate and Kim left the shade of the sea grape trees and walked toward the water. Kate was wearing very tight white shorts and a bikini top covered by a thin light pink camisole. Her hair was tied back in a pony tail. It took all of Bobby's mental stamina to keep from gawking at her long tanned legs. Once on board, Joe gave them a tour of *Dreamweaver,* and then with all of the flair of a sommelier in a five star restaurant, he opened a bottle of Dom Perignon that had been chilling in a silver ice bucket, and prepared mimosas for everyone. As he held his champagne flute up to the sun, he said, "I toast—- today. It comes but once."

Joe and Bobby sailed the boat thru the Sir Francis Drake Passage on toward Tortola. The mountainous islands, azure blue water and dazzling sun were breathtaking. Bobby asked Kate to assist him with the sails, which she gladly did. He could feel her body pressing up against his own as she stood close to him and they bent to the task of hauling the sail ropes. After about ninety minutes of sailing, *Dreamweaver* anchored a few hundred feet from a pristine deserted beach on the easterly side of Virgin Gorda. Bobby and Kate went snorkeling for awhile, while Joe and Kim continued to drink Dom as Sarah Vaughn serenaded them.

"Joe—-Kate and I are going to swim to the beach. Do you guys want to come?"

"No, I think we're content to relax here on the boat." Bobby looked at Joe with gratitude. Kate and he swam into the beach and began to walk its soft powdery sand. Toward the far end of the crescent shaped shore, they climbed some giant rock formations and sat down high above the water looking out to the open ocean.

"God, this is magnificent," said Bobby.

"Beyond beautiful," Kate replied.

Bobby's hand found hers. "Are you in school?" he asked.

"First year at the Fashion Institute in San Diego. What about you?" she asked.

"I'm in school in Boston. I'm a science and math major."

"Where?"

"A combined program of MIT and Harvard."

Kate laughed. "Oh, excuse me. A big brain here, I see."

They chatted on as they climbed some more rocks, Bobby doing his best to keep his hand glued to hers. "I'm getting really hot. Let's take a swim," Kate said, wiping her forehead.

They walked down to the edge of the water. "Don't you hate tan lines?" Kate removed her bikini top, threw it on to the sand and glided into the aqua sea, cocking her head to signal Bobby to join her.

Bobby wondered what he owed the gods for letting him play with Venus. He joined her and they swam underwater together among the schools of psychedelically colored reef fish. When they surfaced their tan faces glistened in the sun.

"You look so amazing," Bobby said.

"You think so?"

"I know so. You're gorgeous." Kate laughed and swam some

more and then, turned around and yelled, "Let's race." Bobby was a good swimmer, but not like her.

"Where did you learn to swim like that?" he asked.

"Swim team. I've been racing since I was six."

He treaded water closely to her and looked into her eyes. She felt an intensity in his gaze quite unlike anything she had previously experienced. He put his arms around her waist. The buoyancy of the water supported them as her naked breasts gently pressed against his chest. They kissed, and then flipped over and floated on their backs holding hands as the sea gently rocked them. The sun was low in the sky but its heat still warmed them. The boat's bell clanged three times.

"I think we have to head back Kate. Joe's calling." They swam back to shore to retrieve her bikini top and then swam to *Dreamweaver*. Joe was beginning to prepare dinner and Kim was helping to set the dining table.

"Did you kids have fun?" asked Kim.

"It was great," said Kate.

The sunset on the boat was awe inspiring. Bobby and Kate went to the bow alone to watch it. Bobby stood behind Kate and lightly kissed her on the neck. He pressed against her and she leaned back into him.

Among candle-lit lanterns, they all feasted on local prawns, lobster, and Joe's famous garlic mashed potatoes. A snappy chilled Domaine Fournier Sancerre complemented the main course, and a 1968 Chateau d'Yquem and Vosges chocolates were dessert. At the outset of the meal, Joe announced that since *Dreamweaver* was in international waters, it was the captain of the vessel who set the drinking age. Joe declared that seventeen was the threshold. It didn't take long for everyone to be happily inebriated, and by eleven that evening, all passengers were ready to retire for the night. Bobby and Kate took one last walk around the boat to view the stars.

"This has been a fantastic day for me. I'm so happy we met," he said.

As Kate nuzzled against him, she whispered in his ear, "You're sweet, Bobby. Very sweet."

Kate and Kim shared a stateroom. Joe and Bobby each had their own. At three, when the alcohol wore off, Bobby woke up. He lay in bed thinking about everything that had transpired. He couldn't fall back asleep and after thirty minutes of trying, he went above deck to get some fresh air. Lying on his back on the cushioned recessed lounging deck, he stared up at the stars and remembered how he had loved to do the same thing in Peter and Edith's tiny backyard. But that seemed like five lifetimes ago. Feeling elated and sad at the same time, he drifted off to sleep in the cool sea air. A short time later, Kate stood looking down at him. She knew there was something special about Bobby, she could sense it, but couldn't define it. She slipped out of her sleep camisole, grabbed a deck blanket from the bench locker and slid next to him as she covered them both with the blanket. She pressed her lips to his as she stroked his left temple. His eyes half-opened and he smiled.

"You're overdressed," she said. Without lifting the blanket, he stripped off his tee shirt and underpants. Kate maneuvered herself over him.

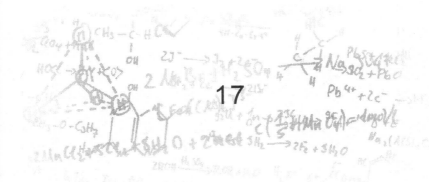

17

THE DAWN AWAKENED BOBBY. KATE'S silky hair was pressed up against his face and he felt the warmth of her naked body against his. He peeked under the blanket and then smiled. *I am the luckiest guy in the world,* he thought. As he stood up, the early morning sea air chilled him. He grabbed another blanket and wrapped it around his shoulders and headed to the galley to make a pot of coffee. After it brewed, he filled two large mugs half way, and then substituted Bailey's Irish Cream for milk and sugar. Returning to the still sleeping Kate, he put her coffee down on the deck and then stood by the side railing of *Dreamweaver* looking out to sea. *Maybe it will all really turn out okay after all,* he thought. *Maybe the nightmares will stop, and maybe I'll stop worrying about losing my mind or disappearing into the ether.* Right now it all seemed good to Bobby. "Thank you God for Joe Manzini," Bobby whispered to the sea.

Bobby sat next to Kate and kissed the side of her head as his right hand slipped under the blanket and caressed her shoulder. "I have some coffee for you. I made it a special way. They call it a 'sticky' in England."

Kate opened her eyes, squinting in the bright sun. "A sticky?" She laughed as she sat up and took the mug. Her face shone in the morning light. "I wish Mom and I didn't have to rush back today to St. John, but it's our last day and we have three islands worth of shopping to do."

"I wish we could stay out here forever," Bobby said.

The sail back to St. John went too quickly for Bobby, but everyone else was in a jubilant mood after Joe's "secret formula" Bloody Mary's and western omelets. Anchoring offshore in St. John by noon, the sadness in Bobby's eyes was obvious as he said goodbye to Kate after exchanging email addresses and phone numbers.

"Stop sulking," Joe said to Bobby.

"Joe, she was so incredible. I can't even put it into words. Isn't she the most beautiful girl you ever saw?"

"Kate is lovely. But the good news is that you're seventeen and trust me, you will rise again. Now there's a soca beach party today on Grand Cruz Bay beach —-I say we need to be there."

"What's soca?"

"It's a kind of dance music that originated in Trinidad and Tobago. The dancing is called "wining" —as in wind the body up. It's the sexiest dancing in the world."

As Bobby discovered, Joe knew what he was talking about. The local dancers were scantily clad and "wined" sensually. Bobby had never seen women move like that. He and Joe, along with a few hundred tourists and locals, found themselves swept along in a people train of happiness between the gyrating beauties. The sheer vivacity of the scene encompassed them as they laughed and hugged, bumping butts and hips with the uninhibited dancers.

"Joe, this trip is the best thing that ever happened to me," said Bobby.

"It's amazing, right?" replied Joe.

"Actually, I said it wrong. Joe—you're the best thing that ever happened to me."

"Bobby, we're a winning team. I love you, kid."

———————————————

Finally, it was time for Joe to point *Dreamweaver* in "the wrong direction" as Bobby put it, back to Boston. "Don't worry—there's more big adventures ahead for both of us, Bobby." Despite a few harrowing thunderstorms on the sail home and Joe's bouts with severe indigestion which he chalked up to too much rich food and alcohol, the sail back north was wonderful and *Dreamweaver* re-entered Boston Harbor on schedule.

Uhlman was at the Institute to welcome Bobby home. "How do you feel, Robert?"

"Like I was re-born," replied Bobby.

"It was that good?"

"It was beyond good. It was my recrudescence. Did I ever thank you Doctor?"

"For what?"

"For finding Joe Manzini for me and knowing that I needed him." Uhlman blushed as he nodded.

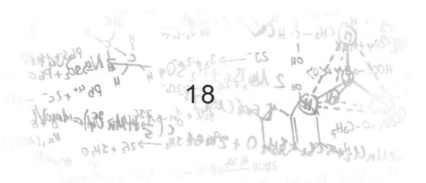

18

JUST AS UHLMAN HAD PREDICTED, Bobby came back stronger than ever. He was newly energized. He completed his doctoral thesis in biochemistry within three months after his eighteenth birthday. Bobby expanded on an idea that he had first described when he was nine years old. In his doctoral thesis, he posited that all biochemical interactions could be expressed mathematically and that if this was done, it would reduce the need for laboratory experiments, as all combinations and permutations of chemicals and elements could be run mathematically at lightning speed, thereby isolating which situations were worthy of the time consuming process of laboratory work. He gave a few examples, but many academics criticized the premise as "intrinsically fanciful and unrealistic." Bobby responded by saying, "What I'm proposing will take a lot of work and won't be easy, but if we want to solve tomorrow's problems, we can't rely on yesterday's tools."

As Bobby approached his nineteenth birthday, he was engrossed in an inter-disciplinary molecular bio-physics program that he had cobbled together at MIT which approached problems at the human cellular level quantitatively, utilizing statistical mechanics. Director Varneys made it clear to Uhlman that he wasn't pleased.

"The Austin kid is going way off track. He was where we wanted him to be—theoretical mathematics, physics and astronomy. Then he veered off with all this biology and chemistry crap. Probably Manzini's fault. You need to straighten Austin out. He's the long-term key to our military and aerospace supremacy. I don't want him wasting his time like this."

Uhlman's face flushed as he responded, "He has time for everything. You have to admit he's been cooperative with all of the questions that NASA and the NSA have thrown at him".

"That's not good enough. I want one hundred percent of his attention. It's time you gave him a reality check."

"I'll talk to him," said Uhlman.

"There's no free lunch for him. We've made a huge investment and we expect to get our return. I don't condone coddling anybody."

Bobby had become increasingly aware that Joe's energy level was waning, and his radiant glow had been dimming. He was looking pallid and thin.

"Joe, what's up with you? Have you been on some weird diet? What happened to the guy who's famous for saying, 'I'll eat anything anytime and wash it down with something that will kill the germs?"

Joe laughed. "I guess my cast iron stomach must be rusting. Ulcers, no doubt. I've been eating less to avoid cramps. I'll tell my doctor when I go for my annual physical next month."

Bobby thought back to Joe's bouts with indigestion on the sail home from St. John. "Get it straightened out pronto Joe. I don't like drinking Jack Daniels by myself," Bobby said, as he playfully punched Joe's shoulder.

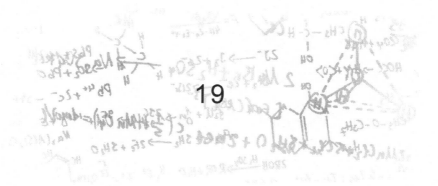

19

JOE HAD ALREADY BEEN TO the doctor many times. He had consulted with four leading specialists in Boston and New York. All of them gave him the same prognosis. Joe would die from pancreatic cancer within the next four months. He hadn't been able to bring himself to talk to Bobby about it. He dreaded telling Bobby about his condition more than he dreaded his own fate. But Joe knew that he couldn't put it off any longer. He was getting his affairs in order while his mental faculties were still free of the mind numbing pain killers that would overtake him in the final weeks of his struggle. Speaking to Bobby and helping him transition through this time period was of paramount importance to Joe. There was a lot of ground to cover and little time to do it in.

"Hey Bobby—want to be my date this weekend and go sailing on *Dreamweaver*— or do you have some hot co-ed lined up?" asked Joe over the phone.

Sitting back from his computer monitors, Bobby's face relaxed and his eyes lit up. "Well—I was planning to direct a porno and teach the actresses some new moves, but I guess I could put that off to the following week."

Joe laughed. "Good. Then we're in business. I'll look forward to it."

As *Dreamweaver* headed out of Boston Harbor, Joe handed over skipper duties to Bobby. Joe found it difficult to haul the sails anymore and he wanted to see what Bobby still needed to learn to sail *Dreamweaver* by himself, as soon the boat would be his.

"Ok my boy—let's see if you can pilot this vessel all by yourself. Take us up the coast past Marblehead, Manchester and Magnolia, and then swing around into Gloucester and let's dock at Rocky Neck and eat lunch at The Studio."

"Aye aye, Captain. Just sit back and leave the driving to me."

Bobby was almost finished with his doctoral thesis in biophysics and was excited by the prospect of completing his university studies, as he didn't intend to pursue any more educational degrees. "Joe, I'm almost done with being a school boy. I'll get my biophysics Ph,D in the next month or two, and then I'm off to the races. Time to get a job and become a taxpayer."

Joe grimaced. "A taxpayer. Anything but that. The government gets us all into a lot of trouble when it has too many tax dollars to spend. But I'm glad you brought that up, as I've been meaning to speak with you. Do you remember what I said to you a long time ago, when you told me that you wished you could do more to help the kids we were visiting in the hospital?"

"You said, 'It doesn't matter where my intelligence came from, what matters is what I do with it'."

Joe's eyes narrowed as he looked at Bobby. "Exactly. Well Bobby, you're about to complete your fourth doctorate, you know more anatomy than a medical school professor, and your intellect and energy are unique. Don't be like some of the others who could have made a big difference but blew it."

"What do you mean?" Bobby glanced at the compass and turned the ship's wheel.

"What I mean is that they wasted their time and talent. Some of them wasted it on abstract theories—they thought they were pure scientists. That's a load of BS. Their theories got adapted into weaponry, or just made big bucks for some fat cats. You know what I'm talking about. What do you think Varneys wants from you?"

Bobby looked askance at Joe. "He's given me a lot of opportunities."

"That's right, but payback doesn't have to be on his terms. The OSSIS didn't give you the gift that you have. If you owe anyone, it's not them. Take control, Bobby, don't let anyone use you or manipulate you."

Bobby smiled, hoping to lighten the conversation. "You're scaring me, Joe. What else can I do wrong?"

"You can get seduced by the limelight. I've known others who did. They wanted publicity, adulation, glamour—they thought they were celebrities—rock stars of the intelligentsia. They wasted their time on the cocktail party circuit. It can be tempting—-pretty girls, free booze and great hors d'ouevres."

Bobby raised his eyebrows and cocked his head.

Joe laughed, "If I had been good enough, that's what I would have done."

"I could believe you would have, Joe," Bobby said, grinning.

Joe stood behind Bobby and put his hands on his shoulders. He leaned to Bobby's side and said softly in his ear, "Son—you have something very special—don't squander it. Listen to your heart. We all have our allotted time. Use yours well."

Dreamweaver docked offshore in the marina at Rocky Neck. Bobby and Joe paddled the dinghy to the floating dock of The Studio restaurant, a rambling shingle structure precariously pinioned on old wooden pilings some thirty foot above the water. Bobby effortlessly bounded up the steep ramp to the dining room, while Joe held on to the ramp's railings and climbed slowly. Joe was visibly out of breath when he reached the top. The fried clams and lobster rolls were succulent and magical. "It's all about the batter the chef conjures up for the clams," Joe said. "Just a hint of sweetness. And never over fry them or let them get limp and greasy."

"And don't skimp on the tartar sauce for the clams, or the mayo on the lobster," said Bobby.

Joe ordered a chilled bottle of the best Meursault he could find on the wine list and proceeded to violate Massachusetts liquor laws by pouring Bobby a full glass also.

"Is it cool—me drinking wine in a public place?" Bobby asked.

"It's for medicinal purposes. It aids the digestion. If we lived in France, you'd start drinking wine at eight. That's why the French are so happy and charming."

As always, the conversation flowed and Joe had a seemingly endless supply of funny stories. His wit was as sharp as ever and his sardonic sense of humor was a joy to Bobby. Bobby had long ago come to the realization that it wasn't that Joe had more funny experiences in his life than anyone else, it was just his unusual perception of common occurrences that allowed him to find the comedic in the mundane. Bobby loved this about Joe and hoped to emulate it.

Back on *Dreamweaver*, Bobby steered the course home. Out in the open ocean, the sun burned low in the sky and the life sustaining orange ball seemed to grow bigger and brighter by the minute as it began to melt into the sea.

"Bobby, there's something I have to tell you that's not pleasant. I need you to be strong."

Bobby laughed. "You've lost all your money playing the stock market so you have to sell *Dreamweaver* and move in with me. It's okay Joe. I'll still love you when you're poor."

"I wish it were that simple," said Joe. His eyes grew watery.

Bobby's face lost its color. "What is it?"

"I'm dying Bobby. Very quickly. Pancreatic cancer. No one can help me. I only have a few months."

Bobby grabbed Joe in a crushing bear hug and buried his face against the side of Joe's head. *No God. Not again. Kill me instead. Not Joe. Don't take Joe away from me.*

Bobby's body shook as he grasped on to Joe. Joe tried as hard as he could for as long as he could but finally he broke down. As darkness set in over the ocean, two figures overwhelmed by grief and their love for each other stood entangled on the deck of *Dreamweaver* as if their physical closeness could leave no room for death to come between them.

Finally, Joe broke the embrace. "Damn. All of this emotion is making me thirsty. We need some cognac." Joe stumbled in the darkness to the galley bar and poured two large snifters of Hennessy, as his hands quivered from the emotional overload to his nervous system. He walked back to Bobby, handed him one and said, "Let's sit down. Pull a few blankets—it's getting cold out here."

Joe and Bobby sat huddled next to each other under two deck blankets as Bobby extended his long legs and steered the boat's wheel with his feet. Silence engulfed them for the remainder of the trip.

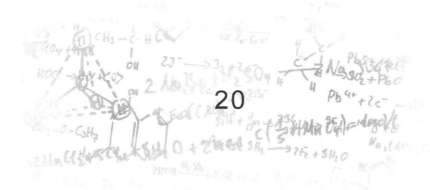

20

THE NEXT FEW MONTHS WERE intense for Bobby. He buried himself in his biophysics doctoral thesis, working at least eighteen hours a day seven days a week, finishing it two months after that last fateful trip on *Dreamweaver*. His thesis was considered so ground-breaking, it was published in its entirety in the *Cambridge Quarterly Review* and became the subject of protracted analsyis, accolades and international academic debate in the scientific community for the next two years. As soon as Bobby finished the document, he left the Institute and moved into Joe's Brookline house full-time to help care for him. By then, physically Joe was a shadow of his former self. He had lost at least thirty pounds and looked twenty years older. His olive complexion had gone pale and pasty, his face was lined and gaunt, his body appeared small and fragile, and his hands boney with bulging veins like those of an old man. Joe's elegant master bedroom had been converted into a veritable hospital room, complete with hospital bed, IV drips, vital-signs monitors, respirator, bed pans, and wheel chair. Because of his wealth, he had the privilege of fading away within the dignified confines of his home rather than in a hospital ward or hospice.

Joe laughed. "You see, Bobby. It always pays to have a few bucks socked away so you can deteriorate in style. There's no pine disinfectant smell here, linoleum floors, swinging doors or surly orderlies. I'm going out with panache."

"I don't know how you can keep your sense of humor, Joe."

"Would I be better off without it?" Joe smiled at Bobby. "I've had a fantastic life, son. It could have been longer, but it could have been a lot shorter too. Particularly when I think about some of the crazy stuff I've done. I have only one regret."

"What's that?"

Joe grasped Bobby's hand. "That I won't live to see what you can do. What I know you will do."

Bobby shook his head and looked down at the floor. "Don't say that, Joe. I'm a shooting star. Here today gone tomorrow. I'll be a burnout like most of the others were."

Joe squeezed Bobby's hand as hard as he could. His face reddened and his voice raised, the effort making it raspy. "Oh no you won't Bobby. You will be what you make yourself be."

Bobby looked up at Joe with glassy eyes filled with love. Joe's voice softened, as did his grip on Bobby's hand. He smiled and continued, "If you let me down kid, I'll come back and haunt the crap out of you and then you'll really know what bad dreams are." They both laughed, but the interchange seemed to have tired Joe. Bobby held a cup of crushed ice up to Joe's lips and helped him put some into his mouth to hydrate him.

The last few weeks of Joe's life were horrific. He was fed intravenously and was on a constant morphine drip. Drifting in and out of consciousness, he slept most of the time. Bobby sat at his side for hours on end, holding Joe's unrecognizable hand. He slept on a roll-away bed only ten feet away from Joe. Bobby missed talking to him so much that on a few occasions, he asked the nurse to stop the morphine drip so that Joe would regain consciousness. Bobby soon abandoned that when he saw that without the constant influx of mind numbing drugs, Joe would be in excruciating pain. It was unbearable for Bobby to watch Joe disappear from his life this way.

"How much longer will this continue?" Bobby asked Joe's attending physician.

"We're very close to the end now, son. His lungs and heart will shut down within twenty-four hours. We've done everything we could for him," responded the doctor.

Bobby's eyes were wild. "No, you didn't. Everybody just let him die. No one helped him."

"We did everything that modern medical science can do."

"Then modern medical science sucks. It stinks. It's a big fucking joke. He shouldn't be dying." Bobby buried his face against the thin remnant of Joe's chest.

"I'll be back in the early morning. You should then be ready to say your goodbyes. I'll try to bring him out of it just for a few minutes then," said the doctor as he packed his bag and made his exit.

That night Bobby went to the bar in Joe's library. It was a hand carved, polished mahogany bar, modeled after those found in English pubs. Bobby took two heavy crystal tumblers off the shelf, filled them with ice and generously poured Joe's favorite single-malt scotch, an eighteen year old Macallan. He took the glasses into Joe's bedroom, placed one on Joe's lap as he slept and wrapped Joe's claw-like hand around it.

"Joe, I thought you might want a drink. God knows, I need one."

Bobby swallowed the smooth Scottish elixir, and then brought Joe's glass up to Joe's lips.

"I know you can smell this Joe and you're thanking me right now." Bobby dipped his index finger into Joe's glass and traced the scotch on to Joe's lips.

"A toast to you, Joe. You'll always be my captain."

The next morning at eight, Joe's doctor arrived back at the house. It was evident that he wanted to get this over with as quickly as possible and get on with his day. Bobby was annoyed by the doctor's perfunctory attitude. *So is this how it ends for all of us?* thought Bobby. *Is this all there is? The denouement to the life of an accomplished and loved man is that he just becomes an inconvenience in someone's busy schedule.*

The doctor disconnected the morphine drip, and then gave Joe an injection. "This will make him lucid but still keep the pain at bay for a few minutes, but then the drip has to go back or he'll go through the roof."

Joe's eyes gradually opened. He looked at the physician and Bobby.

"Joe, you don't have much time," the doctor said.

Hearing these words, Joe's facial muscles tensed and his eyes watered. The sadness of recognition that registered on Joe's face was an image Bobby knew he would never forget. He stood by Joe's bedside and bent over and kissed Joe's forehead as he grasped Joe's left hand.

"Joe, I've been here the whole time. I never left. I've missed you so much." Joe smiled.

"Why do I smell scotch?" Joe asked.

Bobby held up the tumbler so Joe could see it without having to crane his neck.

"Macallan 18. I've taught you some valuable things, Bobby," Joe said, as he chuckled.

"Joe, do you remember the soca dance party on Cruz Beach? Wasn't that amazing?"

"I remember it like it was yesterday, Bobby. Those girls sure knew how to shake what the good Lord gave them."

Joe stiffened and his eyes glared. He bit his lower lip and clutched Bobby's hand. "We have to put him back under," said the doctor as he got ready to stab the needle of the morphine drip back into Joe's IV.

"Wait," said Joe as he grimaced in pain.

Bobby put his face against Joe's as he cradled Joe's head in his hands.

"Joe, thank you for taking me into your life. I'll love you forever."

With difficulty, through clenched teeth and uneasy breathing, Joe's voice came out as only a weak whisper, "Bobby, don't forget what I told you. I love you kid."

Within seconds after the morphine drip began to dispense its salutary poison, Joe's eyes went dead.

21

BOBBY DIDN'T ATTEND JOE'S FUNERAL. Three weeks after Joe's death, OSSIS agents found him in a flop-house on Dudley Street in the Roxbury section of Boston. Bobby was disheveled and alcohol sodden. The agents brought him back to the Institute where Vanderslice had him cleaned-up and Verjee began a de-tox program. Uhlman flew to Boston and made arrangements to stay at the Institute for an indeterminate period of time.

"Robert—what the hell's going on? You had us all scared out of our wits."

Bobby didn't look at Uhlman. "I'm responsible for Joe's death."

"What are you talking about?"

"You gave me Joe and I let him die."

Uhlman shook his head. "Robert, you're not making any sense."

Bobby's eyes were flat and dull as he looked in Uhlman's direction, but continued to avoid eye contact. "Joe told me when I was eleven years old that I could make a difference and use my intellect to help those kids in the oncology ward at the hospital, but I didn't. I just went about my merry way with all the abstract math and science bullshit. That was eight years ago. I could have done a lot in eight years. It might have helped Joe in the end."

"You've been learning all these years. Gaining the tools, the knowledge. It takes time."

Looking down at the floor, Bobby wagged his head. "I could have done something. I waited too long".

"You can honor Joe by moving forward productively, or you can chuck it all and fall apart—and then it's all been for nothing".

"I let him down," said Bobby, barely audible.

Uhlman walked over to Bobby and gently lifted Bobby's chin with his large hand so he could look squarely into Bobby's eyes. "You didn't let him down. But you will if you destroy yourself with this nonsense." As Uhlman spoke and he saw no reaction, his voice hardened with frustration. "Now get a grip and stop this self-pitying self-indulgence."

The harshness of Uhlman's tone snapped Bobby out of his torpor. Glaring at Uhlman with startling intensity, Bobby yelled, "You can tell Director Varneys to go fuck himself. I'm done with anything he's interested in. I'll do what I want, when I want and how I want. NASA, the NSA and all the generals can figure things out for themselves."

Uhlman recoiled and broke eye contact. His shiny shaved head turned crimson and the veins on his right temple throbbed. "If you want to give that message to the director after all he's done for you, then you can deliver it to him personally. I won't be your courier. If it weren't for him and the OSSIS, where the hell do you think you'd be? Do you think you'd have the knowledge you have? The opportunities you have? The facilities you have? Do you think you'd have four Ph.Ds at age 19 from the finest universities in America?

There's something called a 'happy medium' Robert—and you need to find it."

Bobby shot back, "I don't have that luxury. I don't know where this intellect came from and neither do you. It can disappear in a heartbeat for all we know, or I can go insane from my nightmares which get worse every day, or my next trance can last forever, or I can get hit by a car, or drop dead like anyone else can. I'm not going to waste any time while I have what I have. I'm going to find cures for diseases. That's all I'm interested in. And that's what Joe wanted."

———————————————

Later that afternoon, Uhlman called Varneys to report.

His voice low and menacing, Varneys responded, "I knew Manzini would prove to be a problem. I told you so at the outset. He was too liberal. Too much a do-gooder. And he poisoned Austin. He poisoned him, goddammit."

"Let Robert cool down for awhile. He'll mellow out. We should give him some time," Uhlman replied.

Varneys voice was strained. "We had the kid in the palm of our hand and we blew it. Damn that Manzini. Filled his head up with all that crap. The kid was subverted in front of us. Now he wants to be Jonas Salk. John, I'm very disappointed in you. This is serious."

"Well, what do you want to do?"

"Bring Austin to me," ordered Varneys. "The gloves come off now. Either he plays ball and does what we need him to do, or he gets cut-off. I'm not running a chari …." Uhlman didn't wait for Varneys to finish.

"No Orin. Now's not the time. He's not himself. He's overcome by grief. Give him six months. Then we'll see. There's no rush."

There was silence on the other end of the line. Uhlman wiped the perspiration off his forehead.

"Did you say 'no' to me?" asked Varneys.

Uhlman's voice turned honey smooth. "Orin, please. We want this to come out right. Let's think with a clearer head than Austin."

"I'll listen to you one more time. But I'm telling you that your credibility is wearing thin."

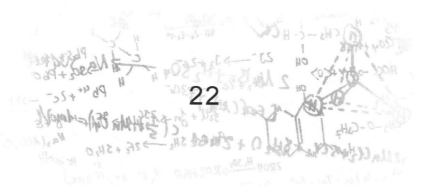

22

OVER THE NEXT FEW MONTHS, Bobby immersed himself in researching various diseases and the progress that had been made in science's efforts to find cures. He was dismayed. Tens of billions of dollars had been spent on research and where were the cures? No major disease had been cured in decades. Research seemed to be fragmented, unfocused and uncoordinated, with much duplication of effort, and researchers going off on their own tangents, distracted by forays into matters of general academic interest. Cure research appeared to be a self-perpetuating industry of its own with no sense of urgency but lots of people making a living from it. And more often than not, the thrust was not to find a cure, but to create a treatment—a product that could be sold. Ongoing treatments with drugs rather than cures seemed to be the focal point. Keep selling those pills day after day rather than eradicate the need for them. Was that cynicism or reality? Bobby didn't know.

He decided that he would first concentrate his efforts on autoimmune diseases. He digested every treatise, article, analysis and laboratory report he could find. He slept little and worked on average, nineteen hours a day. Armed with an uncompromising sense of purpose, his mind was more focused than ever before. There was to be no respite for him.

Bobby was once again living at the Institute, but he spent all his time encamped at MIT's supercomputer labs, the most sophisticated of any university in the world. Five months after Bobby started to research neuromuscular diseases, he sat in his cubicle, head bowed, eyes closed, lost in thought. He had been sitting in the tiny room reading and running analyses on the computer for the past twenty hours straight. Several knocks had come on the cubicle door but Bobby was oblivious to them. Finally, the knocker, an undergrad who was assisting the University administrators as part of his financial aid package, stepped into the tiny office and poked Bobby's shoulder to get his attention. Bobby swung around, startled. The undergrad apologized for the interruption, but asked Bobby to accompany him to the office of the dean of Graduate Studies, Jeffrey Bowles. When Bobby walked into Bowles' office, Bowles wasn't alone.

"Robert, there's someone here I want you to meet. An esteemed visitor, and a very good friend of this University. Meet General Aeurbach," said Bowles.

The bright autumn sunlight coming through Bowles' large office windows reflected off the three brass stars on each of the general's lapels. There were so many multi-colored ribbons on Aeurbach's chest pocket that it looked like he was wearing a color palette from a paint store.

Aeurbach smiled, which allowed his crooked yellow teeth to come into view as his thin lips parted. "You're the one everyone's talking about, you know."

"Who's everyone?" Bobby asked.

The general's light green eyes became animated. "Everyone is just about every scientist and mathematician who helps us out on problems we're working on. They say that you're the one to watch."

"I'm not sure I want to be watched."

The pasty complexion of Bowles' pudgy face took on a pink hue as he said reverently, "General Aeurbach has been instrumental in securing tremendous financial support for MIT over the years which has greatly expanded our resources. In fact, the lab that you've been working in was funded through the general's good auspices."

"That's wonderful. Thank you general," Bobby said.

"And that's why it behooves all of us—students and professors alike—- to help the general in every way we can." Bowles nodded in enthusiastic agreement with himself.

Aeurbach reached down to the floor and put his briefcase on his lap. This minimal amount of exercise caused his face and neck to become engorged. Opening the briefcase, he removed a folder and said, "And that's where you come in, Robert. I have here in this file some questions from our mathematicians who are working on a project for us. They seem to be stumped on a few things and could greatly benefit from your input. And then, there's an equation that our physicists can't seem to get passed the roadblocks on."

Bobby slowly shook his head. "I can't do that, general. I'm spending all my time on one thing. I can't get distracted."

The general's eyebrows rose at the unfathomable prospect of being rebuffed, particularly by a twenty year old who had been on a government funded scholarship since he was five. The general's voice grew louder. "And what the hell might that be? What's more important than helping your country?"

"I'm concentrating all my efforts on finding cures for diseses, sir."

Aeurbach's eyes narrowed into slits as he stared at Bobby. "That doesn't mean you have to be a one trick pony. There's a lot of hours in a day."

Bobby scratched his left temple. "And I'm particularly disinterested in anything that has military applications."

"No one is asking you to build a bomb, boy. We just need your help with some arithmetic."

"Please don't patronize me, general. It's not just arithmetic. It's those answers that make the applications possible."

Aeurbach grimaced and then scrunched up his nose as if there were a bad odor in the room.

Dean Bowles inhaled sharply, all color having drained from his face. "Robert I need you to rethink this. You've been a direct beneficiary of the general's largesse to this University. Your refusal to help is not appropriate and is, frankly, very disturbing."

Bobby felt the time was right to excuse himself and everyone appeared relieved when he did. Staring hard into Bobby's eyes, the general extended his hand as he said, "I'm sure you'll come round our way once you give this some more thought."

23

ON THE ENTIRE FLIGHT FROM Boston to Washington D.C., Bobby noticed that Uhlman was peculiarly quiet.

"The Director is ready to see you now," said Doris, one of Orin Varneys' two secretaries, both of whom were in their fifties and looked like they put up with a lot for their money.

Doris led Uhlman and Bobby from the large reception room with its ornate gilded paneling through a long marbled hallway lined with a seemingly endless number of portraits of humorless looking men. *Probably spooks who died in the line of duty*, thought Bobby. Finally, they came to a set of ten foot tall heavily lacquered mahogany doors. Doris opened them with a purposeful flourish and ushered Uhlman and Bobby inside. Of course, Uhlman had been through this drill countless times, but Bobby was enjoying the pomp and circumstance.

Director Varneys' office was impressive by anyone's standards, but Varneys radiated such imposing authority and gravitas that he overshadowed it. Orin Varneys stood five feet seven inches tall and appeared to be in his mid forties. Although portly now, his build was still so broad and thick that no one would be surprised to learn that he went through college on a wrestling scholarship. His almost square head was far too large for his body and looked suitable for mounting in a hunting lodge. Thinning black hair was oiled and combed straight back, and his small dark eyes were set wide on his head, almost like a fish. His mouth was a long lateral slit with no discernible lips and his ears were large, swollen looking items. While his teeth were peculiarly small, he appeared to have many more than was usual and they were badly stained, probably from too much cigar smoking.

Varneys rose from the chair behind his ebony Louis XVI desk and motioned perfunctorily to Uhlman and Bobby to take the two seats in front of him. They sat down, as he did, and Varneys proceeded to just stare at Bobby. He said nothing to him. He just kept staring intently at him with his shiny dark eyes. He propped his left elbow on the desk, rested his chin in his left hand and then stared some more. When a seemingly inordinate amount of time had passed, Varneys said, "So, finally, I meet Robert James Austin. John, why didn't you let Austin and me get together years ago? Shame on you." Varneys laughed. Uhlman managed a mechanical smile.

"You know, director, on the trip to D.C., I was thinking how strange it is," Bobby said. "You're a person whose had such a major influence on my life, and yet we've never met or even spoken with each other. You came into my life at age five and now I'm twenty. All these years have passed. That's quite extraordinary when you think about it."

"I prefer to be behind the camera. That's where I perform best."

"I see. You're the wizard behind the curtain. The puppet master."

"I don't see myself that way. But I understand the analogy. I have a job to do and I try to do it as effectively as possible."

"I want to thank you, director. You've done a great deal for me and I'm cognizant of that and highly appreciative. I want you to know that I don't take it for granted."

"All of that is well and good Robert, but the bottom line is that there's no free lunch. I'm not running a charity or an altruistic organization. I have a boss. It's the American people. They've made an expensive investment in your education and room and board. They're entitled to a return on that investment. "

"Before we get into that subject director, there's something I have to ask you. I think you know where I come from —what my background is—who my birth parents were. My foster parents told me that they took me in when I was only a few weeks old and that they didn't know anything. I wager to say, director, that you do know. I feel I'm entitled to this information."

"Austin—sometimes ignorance is a good thing. I suggest that you just leave this subject alone. I had your background files delivered to me when your foster parents died and I sealed them for confidentiality reasons. Your background should never become fodder for the media—it's nobody's business."

"But that confidentiality shouldn't extend to me."

"You're barking up the wrong tree. Leave it alone."

"Thanks for the concern, director, but I want the information."

"You're making a mistake digging this up, Austin. But if you're intent on this, I won't fight you. We have bigger problems than your curiosity. I'll let you see the first volume of your files. That's the one that has what you want to know." Varneys pressed the intercom buzzer on his phone. "Doris, bring in volume one of the Austin files."

Within a minute, Doris knocked on the door and then entered

132

the office holding a file that was at least six inches thick and handed it to Varneys who placed it on the desk in front of him.

"When we've finished what we need to discuss, I'll let you take this file into my conference room and you can read it there. But don't pull anything out of it. Now let's get on with what we need to talk about. I heard about the meeting with Bowles and General Aeurbach. What the hell is going on with you Austin?"

"Director, do you know the expression 'all the time in the world'? That's exactly what I don't have. I've been given a gift—which is why you're talking to me now. None of us understands why I have it, where it came from or how ephemeral it may be. And, of course, none of us knows how long any of us will live. Things happen. So, the clock is ticking, and I need to set my priorities on how I'm going to use this resource for as long as I have it. I can't be distracted or waste any time."

"Exactly right Austin. And the right way to use it is by helping your country remain the most scientifically advanced and militarily secure nation on earth."

"But that's where we differ, director. As I told General Aeurbach, I've made the decision to concentrate one hundred percent of my energies on matters related to human health."

As Varneys' eyes narrowed, Bobby continued, "There's been a dearth of progress in the last five decades. If all of the best scientific talent had spent its time and energy to combat disease over that period of time, this world would be unrecognizable. Too much intellect was siphoned away. I'm not going to add to that problem."

Varneys' left hand trembled. Rising from his chair, Varneys rasped, "Who filled your head with this polyanna bullshit? Was it Manzini? You used to be cooperative. You never balked at helping.

Now you're ready to move to Africa and become Albert fucking Schweitzer. Someone's responsible for this."

Bobby glared at Varneys with an intensity that startled the hardened agent. Standing up abruptly and roughly shoving his chair back, Bobby spat out, "I never want to hear anyone disparage Joseph Manzini. Never. Do we understand each other?"

Realizing his mistake, Varneys sat down and said softly, "I apologize. I know how much Professor Manzini meant to you. I approved of his becoming your mentor. I was shocked by his premature passing and I understand what a devastating loss it was to you. No disrespect intended."

Taking his seat, but still looking shaky, Bobby said, "Apology accepted. Thank you."

Varneys forced a smile as he continued. "Robert, maybe I'm not doing a good job explaining my position. In the abstract, I commend your altruistic inclinations. But it is my agency, the OSSIS, that discovered you, nurtured you, virtually raised you, gave you the finest customized education in the world and took care of your every need. We did this, not the CDC, NSF, NIH, or any other health agency. I need some pay-back for the OSSIS agenda. At least give me a portion of your time."

"What I'm trying to do is a 24/7 job. I can't give you time I don't have. I'm sorry."

Varneys sat silently. He propped the elbows of his stubby arms on the desk and then rested his head wearily atop his fists as if in an effort to support the weight of his responsibility.

"Austin —the bottom-line is that we won't continue to support you if you have no intention of helping us. We'll cut you off immediately. The Institute and the two universities will be gone."

Bobby shook his head in denial. "I have supporters there. They'll want to stand behind my research."

Varneys laughed. "Oh you think so? They'll throw you out on your ear. Trust me."

Bobby's face flushed red. "Has it ever occurred to you that one day you might be happy I didn't listen to you?"

Varneys stood and began to gather some folders on his desk. "Austin, stop dancing. I have an agency to run. For forty-five years, the OSSIS has labored to find and develop someone like you. We finally succeed in doing so, and now you cast us aside. This is a dark day. I have a meeting to go to. Goodbye."

"My file, please. You said I could look at it."

Varneys shoved the tome across his desk over to Bobby. "You have thirty minutes. You're a fast reader. Go into the conference room through those doors."

Uhlman, who had been silent throughout the meeting said, "Robert, I'll wait for you in the reception area."

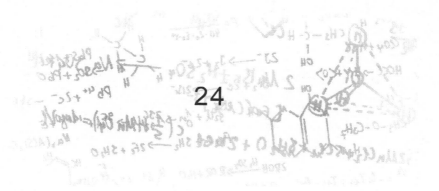

24

BOBBY SAT DOWN AND BEGAN to read. At first, he didn't get it, but then it became clear. It was there in full detail: Photographs of a tiny infant whose picture was stamped #2764 with the official imprint of the Bureau of Child Health and Welfare Services; mug shots of a disheveled looking man named Alan Gottschalk and the full transcripts of his police interrogation; pictures of a shanty house made out of cardboard and tarps; a case analysis by the District Attorney; and images of a black plastic garbage bag and a DNA report on its contents.

Bobby read the newspaper headlines that had sensationalized an American tragedy: "DUMPSTER BABY," " GARBAGE BAG BOY," "LEFT TO DIE," "WHO IS JOHNNY DOE?"

Varneys' file also contained Dr. Drummond's examination report on the physical condition of #2764, Natalie Kimball's own personnel file complete with a photograph of herself (from which Bobby realized why she had approached him at the funeral of his foster parents) and her official explanation for why no one wanted to adopt him:

"Unfortunately, many prospective adoptive parents were scared away by the media vilification of the unknown parents. The popular assumption was that either or both parents were serious substance abusers at the time the child was conceived, or that the mother was drinking heavily, taking drugs or having unprotected sex during the pregnancy. Others thought it likely that either or both parents suffered from mental illness, learning disabilities or retardation. And so, a cloud of uncertainty hung over the infant. People don't want to adopt a problem, and they know that many problems don't show themselves until later in a child's development. Some prospective adoptive parents even voiced their belief that the reason the infant was discarded was because the mother knew that the baby would have serious disabilities of one type or another and she didn't want to have to deal with the problems incident to raising a child who would be so impaired."

As Bobby read, he grew smaller and smaller. His shoulders hunched over until they were almost touching the table. Shock gave way to despair, his eyes grew wet, and he began to quietly sob, his body rocking weakly and his hands trembling. He continued to read the file through his tears, as he was cognizant he only had thirty minutes. No doubt, Doris would appear exactly on time. *Trash. Left to die alone, in the dark among the stench and vermin.*

Doris walked in. Her face blanched when she saw the deterioration in Bobby's appearance. He looked disoriented and disheveled, his eyes bloodshot, and his face stained with tears.

"I have to take this away now. Did the director bully you, young man? He can be so overbearing sometimes." Obviously Doris had never read Bobby's file.

"It's nothing he did, but thank you for asking."

Doris took the file and left the conference room. Bobby sat motionless, staring at the empty table. Straining to stand, his legs felt weak and his entire body ached. Waves of nausea coursed through him. Bobby made his way back to the reception area. Uhlman was waiting there.

"Doctor, did you know?"

"Yes I did Robert."

"Why didn't you ever tell me?"

"You never asked. I was hoping you never would, because then I wouldn't have to decide if I should lie to you or not."

"How long do I have to vacate my dorm at the Institute?"

"The director wants you out within a week."

Bobby and Uhlman said nothing to each other on the flight back to Boston. Bobby was in a daze. When the SUV finally pulled-up to Bobby's dormitory, Uhlman got out of the vehicle with Bobby.

"Robert, I just want you to know that I don't agree with the director. I've tried to fight him when it comes to you, but he's immovable. He's a very stubborn and resolute man. Unfortunately, he calls the shots, not me."

Bobby's eyes were watery as he looked at Uhlman. "I know you've always done everything you could for me. We go back a long ways. I was a little kid when we met. Do you remember? My parents would come pick me up every day at your office at the Mayo. Do you remember our lunches together? You held my hand at my parents' funeral."

"Of course I remember."

"I don't have anybody who has known me as long as you. You're family to me. You even found Joe for me. Please don't cut me out just because of Varneys."

"I won't, Robert. I promise." Uhlman grabbed Bobby's shoulder and pulled him in with a big hug. Bobby wrapped his arms around Uhlman's back and held him tightly.

"Thanks for everything all these years," Bobby whispered in his ear.

As Uhlman climbed into the SUV, he turned and looked at Bobby. Bobby stared intensely at him in the probing way that was so unique to him. Uhlman broke the gaze and motioned to Ray to drive him to the airport. Bobby watched until the vehicle disappeared down the road. He knew he would never see Uhlman again.

Once in his dorm room, Bobby collapsed onto the bed fully clothed. He was exhausted. The weight of everything that had happened in Washington crashed down on him. Bobby felt even more alone and isolated than when Edith and Peter had died, because then at least he still had the support of his Institute family. Like a cracked dam that had finally reached its bursting point, Bobby broke down, burying his face in his pillow because he was embarrassed he would be heard by someone in an adjoining dorm room. *Why did my parents hate me so much? Why wouldn't they give me a chance— just one week, or even one day? Just one fucking day to see if I was worth loving.*

Eventually, Bobby fell asleep. It didn't take long for the nightmares to kick-in with full force and now there was new material with which he could be terrorized. It was as if he were there at his own birth watching it all unfold, his newborn cries echoing eerily through an abandoned factory building in which his mother, a teenage drug addict, lay on a blood stained blanket on the cold concrete floor. His cries seemed so small, so inconsequential, so pitiful as they reverberated through the decrepit cavernous structure. There was no welcome for him. No teary eyed parents, filled with gratitude and wonderment. No doctors and nursing staff officiously performing their duties. No incubator to warm its new occupant. There was only silence punctuated by the urgent cries of a tiny human being thrust into a world that didn't want or need him.

A nursing student, a friend of the mother, he presumed, did her best to clean him with the paper towels and bottled water she pulled out of a bag from a convenience store. With difficulty, she cut his umbilical cord with a cheap scissor. She triple-wrapped him from head to toe in a too-big bed sheet she had taken from the hospital where she studied. Only his doll-like face remained visible. His mother didn't want to hold him or even look at him, and she didn't seem to be in very good shape after the birth. The father—- well who knew who the father was anyway? The bedraggled young man who was standing there, shifting nervously, perspiration pouring out of his pasty face, wasn't acting like the baby was his.

Kissing the mom on the top of her sweaty dirty head, the nursing student said her goodbyes quickly and exited. She left a baby bottle, two cans of formula and a few diapers.

The young man opened one of the cans of formula and poured it into the bottle. He held the infant the way the nursing student had told him to, and he gently tried to get the little mouth to open and accept the bottle's nipple. Eventually, some of the liquid made its way into the baby. He looked at the tiny boy's face trying to discern if he saw any resemblance to himself. He put the infant down on the concrete floor. He removed from the pocket of his rain slicker, a neatly folded 30 gallon triple-mil black plastic garbage bag. He opened the bag, shook it, and rotated his arms inside the bag to open it fully. He dropped the diapers, the half consumed bottle, and the other can of formula into the bottom of the bag. Hands trembling, he then picked the infant up, still wrapped like a mummy in the bed sheets the nursing student had affixed to him, and delicately placed him in the bag. It had only been a few hours since the child had been born.

"I'm going now," he said to the mother, who lay motionless on her side. She didn't reply.

Struggling to breathe in the stifling darkness of the garbage bag, a paralyzing sense of helplessness overwhelmed the infant. As the putrid odor of decay in the dumpster permeated the air, Bobby was jostled by the bloated bodies of scurrying rats slamming against the garbage bag in their frenetic search for an entrance point. He felt the wind and rain pelt and pull at the bag and threaten to dislodge it from its perilous perch, toppling him into the vermin ridden dumpster. Completely alone, he screamed.

Gasping for breath, his chest, face and hair drenched with sweat, his hands trembling, Bobby awakened from his night terror. Feeling like he was burning up with fever, he dragged himself into the bathroom, pulled off his clothing and lay naked on the cold bathroom floor, sweating and shivering simultaneously. Afraid he was going to pass out, he grasped the toilet seat, pulled himself up to a wobbly standing position and guided himself back toward his bedroom vanity where he grabbed a bottle of Vodka and gulped down half of it, searing his throat.

He gave up trying to sleep any more that night. In the darkness, he made his way on the mass transit system to Harvard. His head buried in his hands, he sat on the steps of Massachusetts Hall for four hours waiting for it to open. Finally, when it did, Bobby walked down the long marble corridor feeling an odd combination of despair and optimism. He pumped himself up. *They love me here. I've helped so many of the professors for so long. They won't want me to go. They need me around. They're not going to throw me out. I'm part of the family.*

When Bobby entered Dean Winterthur's office, the dean greeted him warmly.

"Hello Robert. You're looking a bit under the weather. Are you feeling okay?"

Winterthur smiled without parting his lips. "Well, I understand you've had the pleasure of meeting Director Varneys."

"Yes, and how do you know that, sir?" Bobby shifted from one foot to the other.

"He called me and told me, of course. Varneys isn't one to beat around the bush."

"And I assume then that he told you to cut me off?"

Winterthur walked over to his enormous Edwardian desk. Once comfortably ensconced in his high-backed burgundy leather chair, he motioned for Bobby to take a seat on one of the narrow wooden guest chairs which faced the desk. Bobby noticed that Winterthur had gained at least five inches in height relative to him since he sat down, as the desk stood on a platform. Winterthur leaned forward toward Bobby and thumped his forefinger against his desk as he spoke. "Robert, no one tells Harvard University what to do. Absolutely no one. We have the largest endowment of any educational institution in the world. That gives us independence, unlike our brethren at MIT, who are heavily dependent on government funding."

Bobby smiled broadly. "What a relief. I'm so happy I can continue here."

Winterthur's New England patrician face was expressionless. "I didn't say that. I said that Varneys doesn't tell us what to do. We decide. But nevertheless, with great regret, Harvard must withdraw its support."

"But why?"

"Because it's the correct thing to do under the circumstances. Harvard has been associated with the Institute for over thirty years. You came to us via the Institute. It would be disloyal of us and a slap in the face to the Institute if we purloined you. Frankly, it would be dishonorable."

His face flushed, Bobby shook his head. "Do the professors here whom I've worked with agree with you?"

Winterthur leaned back in his chair. "That's irrelevant. I haven't discussed this with them, nor would I. They don't run this institution, I do."

"Dean—putting aside the Byzantine politics —-do you know why Varneys is cutting me off—did he tell you?"

"He said that you refuse to support the Institute's research goals."

"And did he explain that the goals of the Institute are limited to military and aerospace applications, and that I want to devote my energies to disease research?"

"Robert, that's beside the point," Winterthur said, waving his hand dismissively.

Bobby grew rigid. Glaring at Winterthur, he said, "With all due respect, dean, I think that is the point. I would have hoped that this university would put world health above placating the ego of a narrow-minded bureaucrat."

Winterthur's face turned Harvard crimson. "When you're twenty years old, Robert, things are black and white. But that's the illusion of youth. I'm very sorry to disappoint you, but I have no doubt you'll find your way. It's been a privilege to have known you, and for that I'll always be indebted to the Institute. I hope that your memories of your time here at Harvard will be positive."

Bobby remembered how Varneys had laughed at him when he said he had supporters who would stand behind him. Sitting in front of him was a man he had known since he was seven years old. The same man who had broken the news to him that his parents had died and who had held him while he wept on the floor of Jefferson Hall. The same man who had trotted him out and put him on display innumerable times to important alumni, contributors and visiting scholars. The same man who had listened to Harvard's most renowned professors expound on his talents after he had fixed errors in their work so that they could receive accolades on their publications. Bobby sat silently for several minutes, his fists clenched, staring icily at Winterthur. Feeling the intensity of Bobby's gaze, Winterthur shifted uneasily in his oversized chair. *Discarding me is just one more task on his "to do list". No doubt, he'll be on the phone to Varneys within sixty seconds after I walk out the door.*

Bobby rose from his seat. "One day when you, or your wife or one of your kids fall ill with a disease that should have been cured thirty years ago, call your friend Varneys—see if he can help you. That'll be a good time to commiserate with him about the priorities of the Institute and your own judgment. When that happens, remember what took place here today. Goodbye, dean."

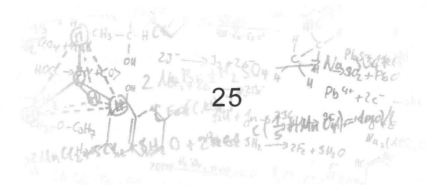

25

NAVIGATING THROUGH HARVARD YARD FOR the first time as an outcast, Bobby was in a daze. He felt dead and invisible. There was life around him but he wasn't part of it. His home and all the people in his support system had been taken away. He could hear Varneys snarling to Uhlman, "I'll bring the Austin kid to his knees. I'll starve him out. He thinks he's such a know-it-all, you'll see. In a few weeks, he'll be begging to come back on my terms. And then we'll have him for good." As despondent as Bobby was, these thoughts strengthened his resolve. "I'll sell hot dogs on the street before I let Varneys win," Bobby muttered to himself.

He walked through Harvard Gate into the bustling streets of Cambridge and was jostled by people who were alive and determined, moving briskly as they chatted animatedly. Wandering aimlessly for several hours, his mind was reeling in despair. Eventually, he realized that he had walked miles and was now in the worst part of Boston. This felt right to him. He was ready to lay his fate at the feet of the gods. He contemplated how good it would be to be mugged. To be killed, quickly and dispassionately. To be released. No more nightmares. No more fears. No more loneliness. *Everyone who ever loved me is dead.*

As he walked down a narrow side street in Dorchester, he passed several ratty bars that advertised their cheap beer prices on hand-written signs taped to their windows. Farther down the street, he saw a large flashing pink neon sign that featured the silhouette of a woman and the words "Pussycat Lounge," alternating with "Nude Dancers." Bobby had never been to a strip club, but now seemed like the right time. Walking up to the shabby windowless clapboard building, he opened its heavy door. "Five bucks to get in, two drink minimum. Keep your hands off the girls," said the bouncer.

Bobby was patted down roughly and directed toward the ticket office, which consisted of a small booth manned by a middle-aged woman with decaying teeth who was shielded from the customers by a pane of glass. After sliding his five dollars through the slit in the bottom of the glass pane, Bobby walked through an old metal turnstile.

The club's walls were painted black and the maroon carpet on the floor looked so filthy that Bobby made a mental note that if anything fell out of his pockets, he wasn't picking it up. The room was dimly lit, which all things considered, was a wise interior design decision. A large central bar was surrounded by a U-shaped counter. Behind the bar, there was a stage that was backed by a mirrored wall which was badly smudged with hand prints. A few spotlights hung precariously from the ceiling and a brass stripper pole was positioned at each end of the stage.

Taking a seat at the U-shaped counter, Bobby ordered a bourbon, which was served in a flimsy plastic cup like the ones next to water coolers. Only five other customers sat at the counter. The nubile dancer worked the pole perfunctorily, performing her routine with

146

disinterest, as she glanced out at the almost empty room. And then, to Bobby's surprise, he came to understand that the counter at which he was sitting was a runway. Taking turns, the strippers who weren't currently performing on stage, would climb onto the runway and walk along it in their spiked heels, their hips rolling in an exaggerated motion, pouting all the awhile, and wearing nothing more than stockings and a thong. They would stop for a few moments in front of each seated patron, throw a few provocative moves, and crouch down to engage in some light banter. Bobby quickly learned that protocol dictated that the customer give each of the ladies a dollar or two tip, depending on the enthusiasm displayed by the dancer. The ladies were casual and uninhibited and accepted the modest tips with gracious acknowledgment. Bobby experienced a new found appreciation for the value of American currency.

"Hey, honey. Come with me to the VIP area and I'll give you a private dance."

"How much does that cost?"

"Fifteen dollars."

"Oh, that's way out of my budget, but thanks anyway. I'm sure it's worth it," Bobby said.

He found it ironic that a club this down and out, matched by a clientele of equal stature, could have anything that deserved to be called a "VIP area." Nevertheless, as Bobby continued to drink bourbon after bourbon, he decided that strip clubs were one of the greatest inventions on the planet. Six bourbons later, he was pondering *who—what incredible genius—had first conceived of the strip club? Did the same person also invent the concept of the VIP room and the 'private dance'? Did this person ever get the public recognition that he or she deserved?* Bobby felt humbled in the shadow of such greatness. "*Now that person was smart—-seriously smart."* The combination of ninety proof liquor and barely clothed exotic dancers on a runway inches away from him was having an ameliorative affect. He was calming down. He could think. And then, as a voluptuous lady, with derriere displayed to maximum advantage, was trying to convince him to explore the pleasures of VIPdom with her, it came to him like an epiphany. "I know what to do," he exclaimed to her. "Tufts. That's it. Tufts."

"I not tough. I be gentle. Do you have a girlfriend? Come to VIP with me, and I be your girlfriend."

"No, no. I didn't say you were tough. I said Tufts. Tufts University. That's what I have to do." Bobby gave the lady two dollars and thanked her for the inspiration.

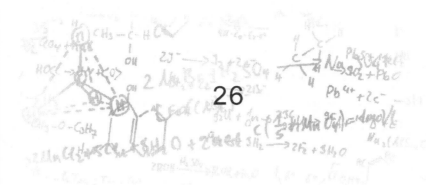

26

THE NEXT MORNING AT TEN, Bobby placed a call to Robert Walterberg, the Dean of Graduate Studies at Tufts University in Boston, the school where Joe Manzini had been Chair of the Biochemistry Department for nine years before he retired to care for his sick wife. Walterberg's secretary answered the phone.

"Hello, Dean Walterberg's office. How may I help you?"

"Is the dean in? My name is Robert Austin. I'd appreciate if I could speak to him."

"And who are you, sir?"

"I'm a graduate student."

"Here at Tufts?"

"No."

"Perhaps someone else can help you and I can direct you to them?"

"Thank you, but I really do need to speak to the dean."

"Alright then, I'll give him the message. Is there a number you'd like to leave?"

"I'd better call back. My cell service is going to be disconnected."

The secretary neglected to give Walterberg the message. Two

days later, when she was reviewing her message pad and going over unreturned calls with the dean, she said, "Oh yes. And there was this call from some grad student named Robert Austin. He didn't say what it was about or leave a number. And then, we haven't yet responded to the invitation you received to attend the University of Pennsylvania Biology Symposium Dinner, or the Mayor's fund raising benefit for the expansion of the zoo."

Dean Walterberg stopped her. "What did you say about a grad student? What was that name?"

"Robert Austin. He sounded very young."

"Did he leave his full name?"

She flicked through the pages of calls. "Oh yes, the second time he called, he said Robert James Austin."

"He called twice and you didn't tell me?" the dean said.

"He sounded very young and seemed very nervous and wouldn't say why he was calling. It seemed unimportant."

"Rebecca. If he calls again, don't let him hang up. Keep him on the line. I don't care who I'm with, what I'm doing or where I am. Find me and get me connected to him. Is that clear?"

Bobby sat under a tree in the most remote part of the Institute's gardens. He had just been told that his cell phone would be turned off in two days. He was embarrassed to call Dean Walterberg again, as it was apparent to him that the dean wasn't interested in speaking to him, but he felt he had no choice but to be a pest. He dialed the number again.

"I'm sorry to disturb you again. It's Robert Austin. Is there any chance the dean is in?"

Rebecca reached Walterberg at a breakfast meeting at the

Yachtsman Club where he was trying to get a pledge from a prospective donor. She conferenced Bobby in.

"This is Dean Walterberg."

"Hello dean. Thank you so much for taking my call. I apologize for interrupting whatever you're doing. My name is Robert James Austin. I'm a graduate student."

The dean interrupted Bobby. "Mr. Austin. If you are who I think you are, you need no introduction and need not make any apologies. Are you the Robert James Austin? The Dr. Robert James Austin who is affiliated with MIT and Harvard?"

"Well, yes and no, sir. I am Robert James Austin, but I'm no longer affiliated with MIT and Harvard as of a few days ago. That's why I'm calling you."

"Well, it's a pleasure to speak with you. How can I help?"

"To put it bluntly dean, I need a new university at which to do my research. I'm not sure if you're aware of it, but I came to MIT and Harvard by way of the Institute for Advanced Intelligence Studies in Newton. I've separated from the Institute and that had the effect of terminating my relationships with MIT and Harvard."

"Dr. Austin. This is far too important a matter to discuss on the phone. May I suggest a personal meeting? Are you available to come to my office—let's see, I'm out tomorrow. How about Thursday morning at eleven?"

———————————

On Thursday morning, Bobby arrived on the Tufts campus by nine. He wasn't taking a chance on being late. No matter how much water he drank, his mouth felt dry. He noticed the tremor in his hands. If this didn't work-out, he didn't know what he'd do. At 10:55 AM, Bobby walked into Ballou Hall, an imposing Federal style brick building with a large white pillared portico. He looked on the building's directory and found his way to Dean Walterberg's office. He stood in the building's corridor staring at the door and took a deep breath. "Well, here we go," Bobby said to himself. He opened the door and entered the reception area. Rebecca greeted him warmly.

"So I was right. You are very young. I thought so from your voice. How old are you anyway?"

"I'm twenty."

"A whiz kid and a hottie too." Rebecca laughed heartily. "Too bad I'm old enough to be your mother."

At the mention of 'mother,' Bobby's face grew pallid as he thought of being hoisted into a dumpster.

"Let me show you in. They're waiting for you."

Rebecca opened the door to Dean Walterberg's office and Bobby walked in. To his surprise, the room was crowded.

Walterberg left the head of the conference table at which he had been sitting and walked over to Bobby. Extending his hand, he said, "Welcome Dr. Austin. On behalf of all of us here in this room, I can truly say that it's a pleasure and honor to meet you."

Bobby blushed and shifted uneasily.

"Thank you sir. I appreciate your taking the time for this meeting. If you can do me one small favor—please call me Robert. The Dr. Austin thing is scaring me."

Nervous laughter came from the men assembled around the conference table.

"Let me introduce you, Robert," said the dean as he presented each of the seven men at the table, the youngest of whom was in his late forties and the oldest of whom appeared ready for life support. Each of them shook Bobby's hand enthusiastically and genuflected in some manner to signify deference to him. The assembled were the chairmen of the Graduate Departments of mathematics, physics, biology, chemistry, astronomy, biochemistry and computer sciences.

Dean Walterberg said, "So Robert, tell us what brings you here and what we can do for you."

"Well, dean. My mentor—a man I love deeply, was a professor here for a number of years. His name was Joseph Manzini. He always spoke highly of Tufts."

"Robert — all of us here knew Joe well and are aware of his relationship with you. Joe kept a close bond with this University after he retired and when we would get together with him, he spoke of you frequently. He was a wonderful man, and a brilliant scientist."

"He was very precious to me," Bobby said softly as he looked down at the table.

"I was surprised that I didn't see you at Joe's funeral," the dean said.

Bobby blushed. "I wasn't well at the time. I couldn't attend."

"I see. So —you were saying."

"Right, well Joe impressed upon me the importance of using my abilities in a socially productive way—particularly for medical research. Since his death, that has been my sole focus and it will continue to be."

"That's admirable."

"Only in certain circles," said Bobby. "The Institute's mission statement is related to military applications and aerospace. When I told them of my intentions, I received an ultimatum which was supported by MIT and Harvard. They threw me out as of last week."

"Surely they'll come to their senses."

"No they won't. So I'm going to be blunt. What I need is a cubicle to work in and around the clock access to your high-speed computers, library and laboratory archives, and when needed, access to the grad and medical schools' research laboratories and assistants. Oh—and just to put all my cards on the table, I also need a dorm room to live in, because I get evicted tomorrow."

As Bobby spoke, Walterberg was busy making notes. He then looked up and said, "Robert, after our call the other day when you told me you were looking for a new home in which to do your research, I met with the president of this University in preparation for today's meeting. He authorized me to make whatever arrangements were necessary to bring you into the Tufts family. We're an institution that takes great pride in our academic independence from outside influences including the government, and while our resources are not as grand as those of Harvard, we're not poor. We can satisfy your needs."

In what appeared to be an involuntary response to Walterberg's comments, the chairman of the mathematics department clapped his hands several times, like a little kid bursting with enthusiasm.

His face flushed, Bobby said, "dean—and chairmen—I can't thank you enough. This is the best news I've had in a long time."

"Robert, here's how we envision this working. Tomorrow, we'll have a studio apartment ready for you in the graduate dormitories so you can move in. It's not fancy, but I think you'll find it adequate. Effective immediately, you'll be awarded a graduate fellowship stipend which will cover your food requirements and put a little spending money in your pocket."

"That's wonderful dean. Extremely generous."

"As for the cubicle, I think we can do a bit better than that. We'll find an office for you in the computer sciences lab, which will afford you enough room and complete privacy so that you can work undisturbed and keep whatever hours you want. Of course, twenty four hour access to our supercomputers and laboratories is not a problem. You'll coordinate all of this through Professor Charles Alan, our chairman of Computer Sciences who is seated here at the conference table."

Professor Alan raised his hand and nodded in Bobby's direction.

"How does that sound, Robert?" asked the dean.

"I only hope I'll be worthy of your faith in me."

"We have no doubt that you will be, Robert. We admire your goals. Welcome to Tufts," said the dean.

The seven professors rose from their chairs and broke into applause. Bobby made his way around the table, grasping each one's hands and thanking them profusely.

As Bobby walked out of the building, he murmured to an invisible listener, "Okay Joe, we're back in business."

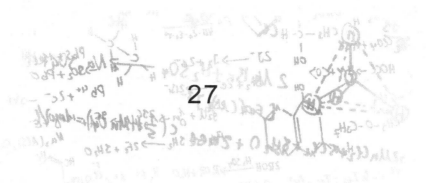

27

WHEN BOBBY RETURNED TO HIS dorm at the Institute, his doorway was blocked by stacks of large disassembled moving cartons, rolls of bubble-wrap, and spools of packing tape. He shook his head. *These guys are all heart.* He kicked the cartons and batted the bubble wrap out of his way. "It's just a school. Who cares? I'm finally free of Varneys," Bobby muttered.

He shoved his key into his door lock, but it wouldn't open. Jiggling it frantically, he pulled hard on the knob as he kicked at the door. "I can't believe it. The assholes changed the lock. They locked me out of my own room," he hissed as he slammed his weight into the door. Suddenly, the door opened. As the heat flash that had coursed through his body began to dissipate, he shook his head, realizing just how upset he was.

Hoping to ward off an impending migraine, Bobby walked over to Copernicus Hall to get some lunch. Was it his imagination or did it get very quiet in the cafeteria when he walked in? Was everyone looking at him? As he filed along the cafeteria line, one of the food servers said to him as she heaped extra gravy on his hot turkey sandwich, "So today's your last day. Don't worry, you're a nice kid, you'll do okay."

Before she finished her words, Bobby's mind raced. *How does she know it's my last day? If she knows, everyone knows. No wonder they're all staring at me.* Bobby walked to the nearest table he could find in a corner away from everybody. Shoveling food into his mouth, he studied the ceiling tiles with apparent interest. He then made an exit as quickly as he could while not looking left or right. On the way out, he saw a group of the Institute's teachers standing around and talking. He could swear they were looking at him and talking about him.

Relieved to get back to the privacy of his dorm room, he began to assemble the moving cartons robotically. Trying to be stoic, he took his possessions down from the crowded shelves, some of which had been there since he was a little kid. It only got worse when he took down the framed photos of Peter and Edith which they had given him when he had first entered the Institute. Sitting down on the edge of his bed, he buried his face in his hands as he massaged his temples with his finger tips.

Go away. Just leave me alone, he thought. But whoever began knocking shortly after he sat down, knocked again, and then a few seconds later, a third series of knocks, harder and louder. *They probably want to know if I'm packed up already. Want to inspect the room. Probably will put my stuff in a shopping cart and point the way to the highway.* Bobby hurriedly wiped his eyes with the back of his hands and opened the door. Extending down the jammed hallway was a large crowd of kids from the Institute, six of Bobby's teachers, Dr. Verjee and a bunch of the teaching assistants.

One of the kids yelled, "Hey Robert—we're here to help—to give you a hand packing."

"Yeah, we heard what they did to you. It's really screwed up, really wrong," said a grad student.

Bobby burst into a huge smile, but from the expressions on a few of the kids' faces, he thought they noticed his bloodshot eyes and tear stained cheeks.

"I was just having an allergy attack," he said, as he rubbed his eyes. "Thank you all so much—I can't believe this."

The crowd piled into his room and one of the grad students appointed himself foreman and directed the packing. "Just leave it to us. We'll be real careful with everything." Another kid bounded into the room toting a huge boom-box. Within a minute, Jay-Z was blasting loudly.

Dr. Verjee put his arm around Bobby's shoulders and led him to a corner of the room. "I want you to know that you're leaving here doesn't mean that I'm not available to help you. If you ever need me, you can always call me." Verjee handed Bobby a card.

At ten the next morning, one of the Institute's vans pulled up in front of Bobby's dorm to collect his belongings and take them over to Tufts. As the van was being loaded, a sparkling white golf cart emblazoned with the Institute's logo in blue and gold lettering pulled up. Impeccably dressed, as usual, Avalon Vanderslice got out of the cart.

"Robert—I just came to say goodbye. I'm sorry to see you go."

"Thanks, dean. I'm sorry too—but you know what happened."

"It didn't take you more than a moment to make a new affiliation. Tufts is a good facility. It's not Harvard or MIT, but it's good. At one time, the Institute was thinking of associating with Tufts, but when Harvard and MIT came into the fold, what was the point?"

"Tufts is an independent facility, Doctor. I've only recently begun to understand the significance of that." A sour expression overtook Vanderslice's face as she got back into the cart.

28

T HE PARADE OF VISITORS BEGAN within the first hour of Bobby's
arrival at his office in the Tufts computer lab. The head of the
lab, Dr. Alan, was in the process of showing him around, when the
first "Sorry to interrupt-I just wanted to say hello" occurred. It was
rapid fire after that. Apparently, every professor and grad student in
the math and science departments wanted to meet Bobby, as did all
of the University's senior administrators. Oblivious to the reputation
he had already garnered in the academic community at only twenty
years of age, Bobby was surprised by all of the interest. "I guess
I'm something of a circus attraction," he said to Dean Walterberg.
Because of their extraordinary content, his doctoral theses had
been widely circulated in the international academic community.
Scores of graduate students in different parts of the world had
earned their own doctoral degrees by analyzing the first two theses
that Bobby had written at ages fourteen and sixteen. It also had
become folklore that starting at age ten, Bobby had made crucial
contributions to highly regarded treatises written by Harvard and
MIT professors. Always polite and accommodating to his visitors,
after a few days he said to Walterberg, "It's great to meet so many

of the folks here, but it's kind of impossible to concentrate with all the interruptions." Realizing that the situation was out of control, Walterberg imposed a moratorium on unscheduled visits.

Bobby's first year at Tufts was spent almost exclusively in the computer laboratory, as Bobby endlessly conducted research and began to build his new mathematical language. He became resolute in his belief that one of the problems causing roadblocks in disease research, was an artificial division among the scientific disciplines. Carrying on from his controversial hypothesis years earlier, he worked tirelessly to expand what he called "the vocabulary of mathematics" so that it could become the unifying integrative language to encompass all scientific phenomena, thereby allowing biochemical and biophysical interactions to be expressed mathematically and to be run and manipulated, in every possible permutation at computer speed. Bobby felt that this was the tool he needed to rapidly accelerate the progress of disease research. The directions in which he was taking mathematics were astoundingly complex and original. Bobby's capacity for the highest levels of innovative theoretical problem solving, first recognized by his examiners during IQ tests when he was four years old, had now come to full fruition.

Dean Walterberg persuaded Bobby to make a presentation to an inter-disciplinary symposium that he was hosting for science and math professors from Tufts, MIT, Harvard and Amherst. Bobby saw this as an opportunity to talk about his new integrative language. Addressing the attendees, he opened by saying:

"All elements are defined by their relationships to all others. Those relationships can be mathematically expressed and the interaction of those elements can be mathematically manipulated.

There is one continuum of all sciences, phenomena and time. There are no divisions. And math is the language of that continuum."

He reviewed for the audience, with the aid of visual projections from his computer files, what he was working on. When the ninety minute presentation was over, he was greeted by silence.

Bobby's heart sank. Looking out at the sea of blank expressions gazing back at him, he asked, hopefully, "Are there any questions?"

After an awkward moment, the chairman of the Mathematics Department at MIT, who knew Bobby well, stood up. "Robert, I say this with all due respect. And maybe it's just me. But what you have been talking about for the last hour and a half is absolutely incomprehensible."

"That goes for me too. I'm not saying you're wrong, but I can't understand one iota of it. I don't even know where to start," said the chairman of the Harvard Physics Department, one of Bobby's former professors.

"It's absolutely fascinating. But I lost you after the first five minutes," said Tufts' Chemistry chair.

"To say you baffled me would certainly be an understatement," added Amherst's Nobel laureate in chemistry.

"I see," said Bobby. "Does anybody get it?"

"No," was the resounding answer delivered in unison by the attendees, their heads wagging from side to side to emphasize the definiteness of the 'no.'

"I'm sorry then. Obviously, I've been too obtuse in my presentation. I'll have to find a way to explain this better. This 'new language,' as I call it, isn't intended to be anything other than a tool to be used to accelerate problem solving. It just takes some time to get your head around it. But I've prepared some materials which may be helpful. I'll email them to you all."

The materials were beyond the mental capacity of the recipients. Some of the individual equations and formulas which Bobby devised ran two hundred pages each.

———— ·•· ————

Alternating between his walls of blackboards, stacks of notebooks and computer console, Bobby's presence in the lab was intense. The mental energy radiating from him was palpable. As had been the case since he was a young child, his level of concentration and focus was extraordinary, and his intellectual stamina was inexhaustible. Seemingly in his own world, he frequently became the object of jokes and sarcastic comments, all made discretely behind his back. But Bobby was aware of them. He had grown used to this ever since his early years at the Institute.

Sitting behind his desk lost in thought, Bobby would fall into one of his trances almost every day. By now, each one usually lasted almost two hours. When he would rejoin the present, he would pick-up where he had left off in his work. Frequently, that would mean discarding the tact he had been on, and embarking on a new direction to tackle the problem. His co-workers, who observed this phenomenon, came to believe that the trances were an extension of Bobby's thinking process, during which he rose to a higher level of cognitive activity that could only be attained by disconnecting with normal human consciousness.

Relentless in pursuit of his singular goal, Bobby had turned Joe Manzini's admonition of "Don't waste your talents, make a difference" into a mantra of self-abnegation. His small office became his de facto apartment as he frequently crashed on its sofa to sleep, rather than taking the time to walk back to his dorm only to return just a few hours later to start again.

"Dr. Austin, do you ever sleep?" asked one of his lab assistants. "You're always here."

"Sleep is my least favorite thing in the world, Mike. I don't do too well with it. It's always been that way for me."

" Beauty sleep never hurts, Doc."

"There's no beauty in my sleep. Believe me."

On one particular Friday night when he was only twenty-two and he sat in the lab pouring over the results of experiments, he realized that he could no longer concentrate. His nightmares had become so extreme over the last few months that it had been impossible for him to get any uninterrupted sleep. He was physically and mentally exhausted. He had to find an escape. He left the lab and went into the city.

29

WALKING THE STREETS OF BOSTON, Bobby was desperately looking for diversion. He came upon a dance club named, "Venu." Paying his admission fee, he entered a warehouse that had been converted into a throbbing strobe lit bacchanalia of blisteringly loud music and swirling partiers. No one knew who he was or cared. Making his way to the crowded bar, he drank endless numbers of blue luminescent alcoholic drinks, and then he moved on to shots of Jaegermeister served on the dance floor by scantily clad hostesses. He opened his shirt and breathed deeply. He lost himself in dance as the alcohol anesthetized his intellect. He felt dissolute and superficial and he loved it. His striking good looks and tall lithe physique didn't escape the attention of the girls. Two of them sandwiched him in between them as they danced and sensually rubbed their bodies against his. High from all the booze, his hands lightly caressed them as his body moved to their rhythm and he pressed his face against their hair.

"Damn, you smell so amazing," he said to one of them, a curvy Latina in tight satin pants.

"It's called perfume, baby."

"It doesn't smell like that in the bottle, that's for sure," replied Bobby.

"You're an expert?" she said, as she laughed and bumped her left hip against his.

"It's chemistry. Trust me, I know," he replied.

The other dancer, a leggy Black girl in a white leather mini-skirt, whispered in his ear, "You move really good, sweetie."

"I'm inspired."

"We already got inspired. We're rolling. Do you want to roll too?"

Bobby raised his eyebrows. "Roll. What do you mean? Are you leaving?"

"No hon. E— you want some?"

As inebriated as he was, Bobby declined, wary of the potential effects of drugs on his psyche. The girls picked up the pace of their movements as they ground against him. He closed his eyes and felt the music wash over him as the drinks kicked in like depth charges. His mind transported him back to the dance party on Cruz Beach in St. John. He was there again with Joe and they were laughing and hugging like drunken sailors as they bumped hips with the socca contestants. Joe's face was tanned and his eyes sparkled in the blinding tropical sun. His smile was broad and radiant. The music grew louder and louder and the percussion more urgent. Bobby shook his head hard, opened his eyes to the glaring strobe lights, and grabbed two more shots off the hostess' tray and downed them in quick succession. He put his arms around the girls and suggested that they continue their party in more intimate surroundings. They were game and took him back to their apartment. As he and his two companions intertwined in varying combinations throughout the night, he finally escaped his demons. When the three had finally exhausted each other, Bobby slept soundly for eleven hours.

He had found his replenishment mechanism. He knew it was superficial, but it would suffice. He felt he had no alternative. Relationships were time consuming luxuries that he believed he wasn't entitled to. Joe's words reverberated in his mind, but they had become distorted: "Don't squander your gifts. We all have our allotted time—use yours well. Don't be like some of the others who could have made a big difference but blew it." Twisting this into a dark commandment requiring unrelenting discipline and self-denial, Bobby rejected any semblance of normal balanced living.

But there was more to it than that. As Dr. Uhlman had explained to Peter and Edith when they were contemplating having Bobby enroll in the Institute, intelligence of the magnitude possessed by Bobby was self-isolating. His intellect would confine him and alienate him from society at large. Bobby's intelligence was a roadblock to social intimacy. It awed and intimidated others to such a degree that he was ostracized by those who were enamored of him. People who knew who he was felt awkward around him. What should they say? Should they make small-talk? They worried they would sound like idiots. They didn't realize that simple normal human interaction was something that Bobby craved, but his inherent shyness and undeveloped social skills inhibited him from taking the initiative. He got a reputation for being distant, detached, "in his own world," and often impatient.

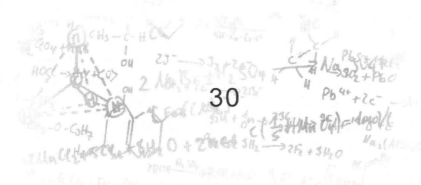

30

EVEN BEFORE LOSING HIS AFFILIATION with MIT and Harvard, Bobby was concentrating his efforts on autoimmune diseases and to do this, he had focused on multiple sclerosis, one of over eighty diseases classified as autoimmune which afflict millions of people. In an autoimmune disease, the body turns its own immune system against itself, utilizing its antibodies to attack healthy cells as if they were hostile foreign agents. In effect, the body begins to destroy itself. Despite years of research and hundreds of millions of dollars spent, science knew little about what actually caused these maladies. Because of this, all that was available were ineffectual treatments, typically immuno-suppressing in nature, which had the undesirable side-effect of reducing the overall efficacy of the body's immune response, thereby making the patient more susceptible to illness.

Eighteen months into his experiments, he was frustrated. Every avenue he explored took him no further than his predecessors. "Damn, this is brutal," Bobby muttered to himself as he decided it was time to call it quits for the night. It was two in the morning, he had a bad cold, and he had been in the lab since nine the previous morning. Walking in the downpour of the unrelenting thunder storm without an umbrella, he was soaking wet in less than a minute. As Bobby trudged across the deserted campus, Tufts looked like the set of a grade-B horror movie as its looming buildings were sporadically illuminated with strobe like intensity by the lightning flashes. Bobby sniffled and sneezed his way into his bathroom and pulled off his wet clothing. He stuffed his feet into his slippers, put on his terry cloth robe and then shuffled his way into the kitchen to get some orange juice. Grabbing the refrigerator door handle, the static shock that Bobby received was so powerful that his hand flew off the door, a spark blinded him, and he was propelled backwards from the force of the electrical discharge.

"Holy crap," he yelled out. Shaking his head, he went into the living room, this time being careful to gingerly lift his feet. Sitting by the window, he watched the violent storm intently and as he did, his mind began to drift. Becoming lost in thought, eyes closed, his cognitive processes gradually accelerated and then began to race. Bobby's mind was now awash with thousands of numbers and scientific symbols flashing by in a blindingly white light as if he were careening along a mathematical autobahn. He clutched the arms of his chair as if to steady himself. And then his flight came to an abrupt stop.

Oh my God. That's it. That's been it all along. Like I had to be hit over the head. Why didn't I realize it? Bobby threw on some dry clothes, grabbed an umbrella and ran out of his apartment to get back to the lab. *Electricity.* His new research and experiments began that night, but within a month, he was sure he was finally on to it.

It took another year and a half, but shortly after Bobby turned twenty three, he was ready to announce his findings. He submitted his scientific conclusions, together with over one thousand pages of formulaic and laboratory proofs to the *New England Journal of Medicine*, the premiere medical research publication in the United States. What Bobby had done was discover the underlying cause of autoimmune disease. The cause was something that no one had ever conceived of. In making this discovery, Bobby marshaled his full panoply of immense abilities in physics, chemistry, biology and mathematics.

He proved that the reason the body's antibodies attacked healthy cells was because those particular cells displayed irregularities in their bioelectrical current. Such irregularities were detected by the antibodies and led them to identify the cells as hostile foreign matter that needed to be attacked and destroyed. Having found the underlying cause of autoimmune diseases, Bobby knew what the cure needed to be. His submission to the *New England Journal of Medicine* included his reports and data on a complex chemical compound which he had formulated, which would travel in the bloodstream, detect bioelectric cellular irregularities and lodge in the affected tissues. The compound would then, through a process of regulating the exchange of potassium and sodium across cellular membranes, balance out any irregularity. Once the irregularity in the bioelectric current was eliminated, the affected cells immediately ceased to appear to be antigens to the body's antibodies, that is, they no longer were earmarked for destruction as foreign matter. The attacks would stop and previous damage that had been done would in many cases be repaired by the body over time. This compound could be ingested in pill form as an ordinary daily medication. Bobby playfully named the compound, "Eversteady" — a take-off on the famous battery trademark, and a reference to the effect the medication had on the body's bioelectricity.

While Bobby had focused primarily on multiple sclerosis, it was clear that this same approach would be equally valid across the full range of autoimmune diseases. The editors of the *New England Journal of Medicine* were flabbergasted. If Bobby was correct, then what he had achieved was one of the greatest scientific breakthroughs in history. They took his entire treatise including the thousand pages of proofs, and published a special edition, which due to its length encompassed five volumes. Over the course of the ensuing year, Bobby's conclusions were tested in over two dozen of the leading universities and research hospitals of the world. The verdict was unanimous. Bobby had done it.

31

THE NEWS OF BOBBY'S DISCOVERY galvanized the worldwide media. But beyond the interest in the medical achievement, the curiosity about Bobby was intense. As one television newscaster asked, "Who is this prodigy who we understand is under 25 years old? Where does he come from? Who are his parents? What's the next disease on his hit list? And just how smart is he anyway?" Reporters from newspapers, wire services and television stations descended on Tufts University in droves. They all wanted statements and interviews with Bobby. Dean Walterberg met with Bobby to discuss how this should be handled.

"Robert, I've consulted with the university's press department, and they would like to set-up an official televised "meet the press" session for you, to then be followed by a series of separate interviews which you'll do with the *New York Times*, the *Washington Post*, the *Los Angeles Times*, and then one major newspaper from each of eight designated international territories. Then, you'll be scheduled for appearances on no more than three of the national talk shows."

"I don't want to do any of that, dean."

"What do you mean Robert? This is a major public relations event for you and the University. It's highly newsworthy. The public wants to know."

"Tufts can have all the publicity it wants. It deserves it. It supported me and gave me the use of its facilities. But I want none." Bobby remembered the admonitions that Joe had delivered to him on *Dreamweaver:* "Don't get seduced by the limelight... Some who could have made a difference went astray because they wanted publicity, adulation, glamour—they thought they were celebrities. They wasted their time."

Walterberg shook his head. "You're the hero here. You've worked like a dog for years to get to this point. The world wants to know you."

"I'm not a celebrity. I'm a scientist. And I can't take credit for a gift I've been given. I'm not interested in making public statements or being photographed. Please dean, leave me out of it. You make the speeches."

"They don't want me. They want you," Walterberg said. "What should I tell them?"

"Tell them that the patents to my 'Eversteady' medication will be held by a non-profit corporation which I'm establishing, to be called 'Uniserve.' I'm going to use that company for all medicines I invent. These belong to everyone. They're not there to profit me or pharmaceutical companies. I want them to be made available as cheaply as possible."

While Bobby shunned publicity and guarded his privacy, Dean Walterberg didn't miss an opportunity for media attention. He took to the media like a mosquito to a picnic. The publicity had the benefit of attracting huge amounts of donations. Checks poured in from around the world. Bobby established a charitable fund for the contributions, The Edith and Peter Austin Foundation For Medical Research. A special bank protocol was set up to allow checks with Bobby's name on them to be deposited into the fund, because despite the instructions that Tufts gave, donors just seemed to want to write the name Robert James Austin on their contributions.

———————————

"Robert, I have some good news for you," Dean Walterberg said. "I've spoken to the Trustees and they agree that some changes should be made. It's no secret that you live in your office, so you're getting a bigger one—and we're customizing it for you so it will have an attached apartment. And let me be the first to call you 'Professor'."

"I feel like the big winner on a TV game show," Bobby replied, smiling.

Walterberg rattled on excitedly. "There's more. We're hiring two additional lab technicians for you, and you're going to have your own secretary."

"Now, you're overdoing it, dean. I'm fully capable of making my own coffee and I never answer my phone anyway, so I really don't need that."

"Yes, you do. More than you know. There's a lot that needs to be taken care of and it will only increase. You have baskets full of unopened mail, the IT guys tell me that your voice-mail has never been listened to, acknowledgments need to be sent for donations, and invitations should be answered, one way or the other."

Walterberg gave Bobby a choice of several candidates. The one selected by Bobby was a woman in her early forties named Susan Corwin. She was five foot three, weighed somewhere in the vicinity of one hundred seventy-five pounds, and had short light blonde hair styled in what was at one time politely referred to as a "gentleman's haircut." She dressed in loose fitting slacks, simple blouses and flat shoes. Her face was round, her facial features small, and her fair complexion was made even lighter by her white face powder which contrasted sharply with her rouge and deep red lipstick. While her job recommendations touted her efficiency and organizational skills, it was her outgoing, bubbly, up-beat personality and sarcastic sense of humor that were the deciding factors for Bobby. Susan was fearless and full of life and Bobby loved that. She was outspoken and didn't hesitate to say what was on her mind, even if that could be impolitic at times. Susan was a very strong woman, but it hadn't always been that way.

Life had not been easy for her. When she was sixteen years of age, she left home against her parents' wishes to move-in with her lover, a man twelve years her senior. He promptly impregnated her, and by age nineteen, Susan had two children by him, a son and a daughter. The beatings began before her twentieth birthday. He terrorized and demeaned her daily. By age twenty-one, no remnants of her self-esteem or confidence remained. When the children were old enough to open the refrigerator, he put a lock and chain on it—and food could be removed only with his permission. It often was hard to obtain permission from someone who had passed out drunk, so it wasn't unusual for the kids to go to bed hungry. It didn't take long for them to realize that their mother was an abuse victim, as he raped and beat her with regularity. They heard her sobs and pleading through the bedding under which they would bury themselves trying to stifle the noise. When her son, Richard, was eleven, he made a stand to defend her, but his father pummeled him about the face and head so severely that Susan was afraid he had suffered brain damage. By the time Susan was twenty-eight, she had become an alcoholic and was beginning to eye drugs to further enhance her mental refuge.

It was in a supermarket, armed with coupons and too few dollars clutched in her hand for groceries, that Susan met the person who would change her life forever. Anna saw her standing in the dairy section, looking glazed over as she tried to compute whether or not she had enough money to buy eggs. Anna saw the young woman's hands trembling, the watery vacant eyes, and sensed the despair of a life being crushed. At the time, Anna was thirty-five years old. She was five feet seven inches tall and weighed over two hundred pounds. Her hair was silverish and styled in an Elvis Presley cut. She wore a black leather jacket, loose fitting dark colored jeans and black Doc Martin boots —the kind that have steel tips and are popular with punk rockers and motorcyclists. She thought Susan was adorable. Wounded but adorable.

After two cups of coffee in the diner with Anna, Susan began to realize that she and her children didn't have to live the way they had been living. There was a better life out there. A life without him —that mistake she had made when she was sixteen. Anna said she would help her. She would take control because Susan was hopelessly incapable of doing that. Back then, Susan didn't know that Anna would eventually become the love of her life. Anna accompanied Susan back to Susan's apartment. She saw the drunken bum sleeping on a decrepit lounge chair in the living room. She pulled him up to his feet and woke him by delivering a beating that was so punishing that he had to be hospitalized for two weeks. Anna broke four pieces of living room furniture over his head. She said to Susan, "Don't worry. It was lousy stuff anyway. That's why it broke so easily when I hit the fuck with it. He was lucky. If it had been good stuff, he'd be dead."

Susan and the kids moved in with Anna and they lived together as a happy family unit in the rent-controlled apartment that Anna had grown up in. When Bobby hired Susan, her kids were already young adults. Richard was a young man—succeeding in the Army, and Susan's daughter, Grace, was a vivacious young woman, about to graduate from secretarial school. Susan and Anna's love affair was fifteen years deep and counting. As Bobby got to know them, he was inspired by the devotion they had to each other. Their love was as vibrant as it had ever been. When Bobby asked Susan about how she had switched from loving a man to loving a woman, Susan said, "Ever since I was eleven I knew I was attracted to women but it terrified me. I felt ashamed. Like something was wrong with me. If I went that way, I thought my parents would never forgive me. And I wanted kids- how was I going to do that and be with a woman? So I had to bury it—very deep. I ran away with the first man who seemed interested. I didn't know he would turn out to be the world's biggest asshole. But every time he beat me, I felt like I deserved it. I had betrayed myself."

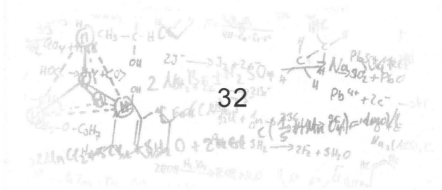

32

IT HAD BEEN FIVE DAYS and no one had seen or heard from him. Finally, Bobby showed up unshaven and looking like he hadn't changed his clothes in a week. Fast on his heels, Susan followed him into his office and closed the door.

"Bobby, where the hell have you been?"

"Relax Mom. I just needed some time off."

Susan's face was flushed and she spoke quickly. "You're so irresponsible sometimes. It wouldn't kill you to call and let me know you're still alive. For such an intelligent guy, I don't know what's wrong with you. You're going to get yourself in some real trouble one of these days."

"Oh yeah?" said Bobby as he kicked off his shoes.

Susan wasn't about to let up. "You hang out God knows where. With some bimbos I'm sure. Where were you sleeping? What kind of clubs did you go to? Those places can be dangerous. You're not exactly a tough guy, you know."

"I can handle myself."

"I could kick your ass down the block, and Anna— forget it."

Bobby laughed as he sat down on the sofa and pulled off his

socks. "Well that's not fair. Anna could win the world heavyweight championship."

"Watch it, sonny."

Bobby smiled as he looked up at Susan who was standing over him. "Calm down, Susan. I know what I'm doing. And the young ladies whose company I enjoy are hardly bimbos—they're libidinous creatures with impeccable powers of discernment."

Susan threw her hands up. "Good choice of words—creatures. Bimbos, like I said."

Bobby grinned. "Are you implying that only promiscuous floozies are interested in me?"

Susan shook her head and sat down next to Bobby. "If you'd give nice girls a chance –girls of the caliber you should be going out with, of course they'd be interested. But you have this craziness in your head about 'no relationships,' so you limit yourself to these harpies of the underworld. Maybe one day, you'll stop with the BS and accept that you're worthy of being loved."

"Now you're kicking below the belt. You're such a ball buster, Susan. I'm your boss—remember?"

"And I'm quaking with fear. Now go into the apartment and clean yourself up. When was the last time you ate?"

"I don't remember."

"I thought so. I'll make you some bacon, eggs and coffee. Jesus. You boys are all the same. Doesn't matter how smart you are. You still got no sense. How much have you been drinking?"

"More than you could ever comprehend," he said.

Picking up Bobby's shoes, she waved him into the apartment. "Into the shower—and then put on some nice clothes. Remember, you have a staff that looks up to you. You're not supposed to look like a bum."

When Bobby reappeared, clean shaven, hair shampooed and brushed, Susan was once again struck by how good looking he was. This was particularly apparent when he came back rejuvenated after one of his "mini-vacations," as he called his descents into dissipation.

"Now look how handsome you are when you're all clean and shiny. Sometimes I almost wish I wasn't gay," she said.

"I still got some left," he teased.

Susan laughed. "Oh, shut up. You're so crude."

"My best personality trait," Bobby said, playfully planting a kiss on top of Susan's head.

Bobby dove into breakfast and Susan watched him like a doting mother. Clearing the dishes away, she paused to pour herself a cup of coffee and sat down at the table. "You were gone five days. What's up with that?"

Bobby glanced away and then rested his chin in his left hand as he leaned into the table. Looking into Susan's eyes, he said softly, "The nightmares. They're really bad. I had to turn them off. This is the only way I can."

"Can't you wake yourself up when they happen?"

"I do—all the time. And then I'm afraid to go back to sleep because they're waiting for me."

Bobby looked down at his cup as he sipped his coffee. "Susan— if I show you something, I don't want you to think I'm crazy."

"I'll never judge you, Bobby. Except when it comes to your choice of women, your drinking and your being a slob," she said.

Bobby didn't smile. "I can't have you thinking I'm nuts. I have a lot of work to do in the future and I need you to be at my side."

He went into his bedroom and came back with several sketch pads, one of which he handed to Susan. "Sometimes when I get up in the middle of a nightmare, I try to sketch what I've seen in my dreams while it's fresh in my mind. Take a look."

Susan put the pad on the kitchen table and cautiously opened it. She slowly examined the first two pages of his detailed drawings.

"Oh, my God," she said. She sat down and pulled the pad toward her face as she continued to look at the sketches carefully, page by page. The images were gruesome, bizarre and other-worldly, and the context of it all was death, physical decay and mayhem. Interspersed among the images of misery was Bobby's face— apparently at different stages of his life.

"These are horrific. I don't know what to say."

"And imagine it with sound and action like in my dreams," he muttered.

"Has it always been this bad?" she asked.

"It's always been terrible— ever since I can remember. But it gets worse. It constantly gets worse."

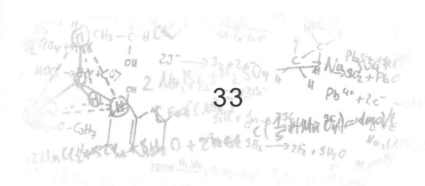

33

TOWARD THE END OF THEIR second year together, Bobby called Susan into his office and closed the door. "Susan, I need you to do something and I can't go into details right now as to why. You have to be at your discreet best on this —it's private and I need it to stay that way."

"Of course, just tell me what it is," Susan said, as she took a seat in front of his desk.

"I need you to hire a private detective. Use your own name," he said, pulling on his chin. "Actually, don't use your name, make one up and pay him in cash. You'll ask him to find a certain person and report back with a detailed dossier as to this person's whereabouts —assuming he's alive—- health, job, finances, marital status, family, the works."

"Wow, that's weird. Who is the guy?"

Bobby walked to his desk and picked up a sealed envelope which he handed to Susan. "His name and the details that will help the PI find him are in here. The contents are for his eyes only. I appreciate your respecting my privacy on this."

Susan stared at him. "Bobby, are you in some kind of trouble?"

Combing the advertisements in the Boston telephone directory, Susan picked the Bay Colony Detective Agency because it offered "national services and had assisted clients across the country." At the company's headquarters, she was escorted to the office of one of their investigators, Rollie Carter. About thirty five years old, he was tall and wiry and had a blonde crew-cut that was stiff and shiny from too much styling wax. His compact GI Joe facial features, restless blue eyes and an ever present smirk completed the picture of someone who had been the perennial wise-guy in high school.

"You've come to the right place, Miss Jones. We can find anyone, anywhere. It's just a question of cost and time. I defy anyone to elude us. We are the best."

"And how much does the best charge?"

"Do you want us to just locate him—an address, or do you want more?"

"Mr. Carter—I want the works. Address, phone number, photographs, background info, financial info, what he's been doing since he was born. To be blunt, I want to know how often he has a bowel movement and how firm or loose it is."

Rollie half-smiled. "So you want what we call the 'deluxe package.' That can mean travel expenses. But, to minimize that, once we locate him—if he's out of state, we can get a local agent to do the footwork."

"So how much are we talking about here?"

"Eighty-five dollars an hour, plus out-of-pocket expenses. A deposit of three grand up-front. You bring the account up to date when we find him, and the balance is due simultaneously when we hand over the report and photos. No checks—unless they're certified. We take all major credit cards."

"Is cash okay?"

"That'll work."

"How long will it take?"

"To get you the level of detail you want—three weeks or less if he's in the tri-state area, five weeks if he's elsewhere in the U.S. If he's overseas, it all depends. Why do you want to find this guy anyway? Does he owe child support, or you need him as a witness in a lawsuit?"

Susan's eyes narrowed. "Mr. Carter, your ad says that your company offers a discreet service."

"Sorry, Miss Jones. Point taken."

"I'll be back tomorrow with the deposit."

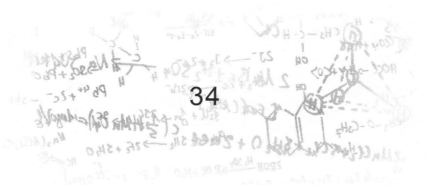

34

CRUISING DOWN NEW YORK CITY's elegant Park Avenue, a midnight blue Bentley limousine stopped in front of # 550, a sleek glass and steel palace of capitalism which was home to the corporate offices of several Fortune 500 companies.

The imposing looking bodyguard sitting next to the driver exited the vehicle. An observant passerby could have caught a glimpse of the shoulder holster under his left arm. Speaking into his earpiece, he alerted the waiting security guard in the building's lobby that he and Mr. McAlister would soon be entering. As they approached the building's entrance, they were joined by building security and then were ushered into an awaiting elevator which had been taken out of service and placed "on standby." The guard checked the elevator's control panel to ensure that the elevator would make only one stop, the sixty-eighth floor, penthouse level.

Floor sixty-eight was one of twenty-three floors at 550 Park Avenue that were fully occupied by Bushings Pharmaceuticals, a New York Stock Exchange listed corporation and one of the largest drug companies in the world. The entire sixty-eighth floor, comprised of over twenty thousand square feet, was used solely for the offices of Bushing's eight top executives.

Looking like finalists from the Miss Universe pageant, McAlister's two secretaries sat at matching zebra wood desks in McAlister's opulent private reception area. "Good morning, Mr. McAlister," they said in unison.

Without acknowledging their presence, McAlister commanded, "Coffee. And have Turnbull come in right away."

No more than three minutes after McAlister barked his orders, the CFO, Martin Turnbull, entered McAlister's office holding a thick folder. Turnbull pulled a crumpled wad of tissues from his pocket and patted the perspiration from his nose and forehead as he glanced at the re-circulating waterfall which comprised an entire wall of the immense office with its soaring fourteen foot ceilings. One of McAlister's secretaries hurried in behind Turnbull with a large sterling silver serving tray.

Colum McAlister was the CEO of Bushings. Standing six feet tall and at one hundred seventy pounds, he was trim and in good shape for a man of sixty-three. Working-out every day under the supervision of his personal trainer in the private gym of his office suite helped in that respect. He had a perennial tan and his sparse silver hair was perfectly groomed, as were his manicured highly polished finger nails. His complexion had the toned radiance usually reserved to movie stars and only obtained through a regimen of weekly facial treatments. He dressed in "bespoke" shirts, suits and neckties from Saville Row and his shoes were custom made in Italy. His gold and sapphire Cartier cuff-links and tie-pin perfectly complemented his gray suit and pale blue monogrammed shirt. The only items that he was wearing which weren't personally created for him were his argyle socks, underwear and Hermes belt. Even his pink gold Patek Philippe wristwatch was custom designed at a cost of almost two hundred thousand dollars, a sixtieth birthday gift from his wife. While McAlister's appearance had been painstakingly tooled, there was an inherent roughness to the man which was discernible in his eyes and the way he carried himself. The street fighting kid who grew up in one of Brooklyn's worst neighborhoods wasn't far beneath the polished veneer.

"How bad does it look, Marty?"

"The Board's going to be all over our ass again at the meeting."

"What the hell do they want us to do? Our product line is being eroded. How much are we losing because of the discontinued meds?"

"We've seen seventeen of our drugs go into the shitter because they're obsolete. Nobody needs them anymore, and on six of them we didn't even recover our research and development costs so we took a huge hit to the P&L. Bottom line, our sales are down 21% this year alone. We've lost some of our real 'cash cows.' But it's not just us. Everyone's suffering."

McAlister slammed his desk as he leaned forward toward Turnbull. "Exactly. And that's what we have to stress to the Board. It's that guy. He's killing us all."

"You're absolutely right. Look," said Turnbull, as he placed a list in front of McAlister. "Here are drugs that you can't even give away now."

McAlister held the piece of paper and shook his head. "Has Collins been reaching out to him? Can't we make a deal?"

"He's reached out, several times. But Austin's not playing ball. You can't even get to him. He has this gatekeeper bitch. No one gets past her."

"Did we try to buy her?" asked McAlister.

"We got nowhere. She's another goody two shoes."

"If we could make a deal with him, and get a license on his patents, we'd be fine even if we took a haircut on our margins."

"It's not going to happen. He has his damn Uniserve company, and he's having it do non-exclusive deals with generic drug manufacturers to make his meds available as cheap as possible."

McAlister's eyes narrowed and he chewed on one of his lips. "The guy's crazy. He's giving his stuff away. Who the hell does that?"

"I just read an article in Forbes that said that if Austin operated Uniserve for profit, he'd be one of the richest guys in the world inside of ten years."

McAlister's jaw pushed forward and a vein on his right temple began to throb visibly. Seeing these familiar signs, Turnbull stepped back, as McAlister's temper was legendary. He always tried to deflect the brunt of McAlister's anger to someone else in the organization which was one of the reasons he had survived so long at Bushings. McAlister's eyes took on a wild look.

Glaring at Turnbull, he said, "Enough of this crap. You're not helping me. Something better get figured out soon. Austin's young. Who knows what else he'll do. The damage could be limitless."

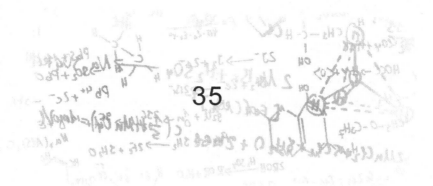

35

A DUSTY OLD SILVER HYUNDAI PULLED up to a parking spot at "The Conch Shack." When Bill Owens finally managed to maneuver himself out of the driver's seat, the car rose two inches from the ground and you could almost hear it hissing air in relief. Owens was wearing black wrap-around sunglasses and a Hawaiian shirt that featured dice, martini glasses and hula dancers in an assortment of jarring colors. The shirt had to be a XXL, but it was barely able to stretch around his protruding belly. A camera hung low from his negligible neck and rested soundly on his gut. His face looked like a sunburned jack-o-latern. Owens was hungry. Sizing up the little roadside take-out joint, he tried to determine how likely it was that he'd get food poisoning if he ordered any of the fish specialties. He read the handwritten menu which was posted at each of the three take-out windows that were equipped with slide-up screens to keep the flies out. The word "fresh" appeared next to almost every item on the menu—even the hamburgers and hot dogs. *What does that mean?* he wondered. *A fresh hot dog?*

Finally, he said, "I'll have a bowl of the conch chowder, and the fish and chips. How fresh is that?"

The old-timer behind the take-out window wore a white apron that looked like it had been new ten years ago. "Caught this morning. That's what we're famous for."

"This place is famous?"

"Everybody knows you come to The Conch Shack for the freshest. We've been here before most, and we'll be here when the others pack it in."

"Is this your place?"

"Yup. Built it myself from scratch. Over twenty years ago. Of course, it wasn't always this big." Turning his head from side to side, Owens estimated it was under nine hundred square feet.

"So you're the owner?"

"I'm the owner, the chef and sometimes the fisherman too." Let me get movin' and cook your food. Listen for your number."

Walking back toward his car, Owens snapped a few photos of the front of the Conch Shack and then walked around the side and back, taking a few more. The Shack was located in Islamorada on the Overseas Highway, a 127 mile section of Route U.S. 1 which runs the length of the Florida Keys and connects them to the U.S. mainland.

After eating his meal, Owens walked back to the take-out window.

"That was delicious. You're right. It was incredibly fresh. I'm Bill Owens, by the way."

"Pleased to meet you. I'm Alan Gottschalk."

"You live around here?"

"Just two miles down the road," Alan said. "Used to be my only neighbors were gators. Now everyone lives here".

"Do you have a menu I can take back home? I'll spread the gospel."

"I can even sell you a T-shirt." Alan laughed as he handed Owens a copy of the menu, which was stained with tartar sauce. "Just kidding about the T-shirt. Maybe we'll get to that next year."

Before pulling out of the parking lot, Owens surreptitiously took a few close-up shots of Alan in the take-out window as he wrote down orders from some more customers. Owens had driven in from Miami two days ago at Rollie Carter's request when Bay Colony's research over the prior four weeks indicated that Alan might live in Islamorada.

He had already photographed Alan's house on Madiera Road, including shots of Alan coming and going. Owens' search of the town's property records showed that twenty five years ago, Alan had purchased a run-down two room cottage on an over-grown acre of water-front land. In those days, Islamorada was just a sparsely inhabited pit-stop on the road to Key West. Alan had paid fifty-five thousand dollars cash for the house, which at that time, was considered a lot of money. Owens couldn't find out where Alan had obtained the purchase money, but Rollie had determined that already.

Over the years Alan had hacked through the tropical vegetation surrounding his cottage, planted a garden and fixed the place up and expanded it to two bedrooms and one and a half baths. It was his little slice of paradise that he owned, free and clear so no one could ever take it away from him. And now, two decades after his purchase, Islamorada had become known as "The Sport Fishing Capital of the World" and resorts, marinas and real estate developments had sprung up throughout the area. His small house was in the midst of an upscale luxury development that had grown up around him and although his home was not much bigger than the garages of some of his neighbors, his full acre of waterfront property was the envy of the community.

A year after he had purchased his cottage, Alan bought the quarter acre fronting the highway on which he, with the help of itinerant workers, built The Conch Shack. He paid twenty thousand dollars for the land, and built the Shack for six thousand. Running the Shack himself over the years and acting as cook, waiter, busboy, dish washer and food procurer, Alan was able to eek out enough of a living from the Shack to support his modest lifestyle. And in recent years, with Islamorada on the radar of tourists, business had picked up. Life was slow on Islamorada and the climate was tropical. The Keys were the only place in Florida that never get a frost. Alan had had enough of cold weather and big cities.

Owens emailed his report to Rollie Carter including photographs of Alan, his house and The Conch Shack, copies of the official Islamorada property records, Alan's driver's license, his home phone number, the phone number for the Shack, copies of three years of Alan's telephone bills, a copy of the Shack's menu, and his description of Alan which was as follows:

"The subject is six feet two inches tall. His driver's license indicates his age to be 69. He's clean shaven, has mid-length thinning grey hair, brown eyes, displays erect posture and is lean in build. He wears tortoise-shell eye glasses. He appears to be vigorous and is alert, talkative, and displays what might be described as a wry sense of humor. There was nothing in his superficial physical appearance or observed behavior to indicate substance abuse. My further investigation over a three day period in the community of Islamorada indicated that he's a well-known personality in the town, prone to being outspoken on matters that interest him and is regarded by some as cantankerous. However, his reputation is good, particularly as a result of his involvement for many years in relief efforts for the needy. I wasn't able to find any evidence of current romantic or familial relationships. An examination of the decorative contents of his home (conducted from the outside) did evidence in his bedroom, framed old looking photographs of two children, approximately three years and five years of age. My examination of three years of his telephone bills showed no calls to or from outside the local area code. He has no criminal record in the State of Florida. No unusual items were found in the contents of his garbage. There are no liens on any of his real or personal property, and no judgments against him."

Rollie read Owens' report and combined it with his own findings and those of several local agents from other locales whom he had engaged in the process of locating Alan. The research showed that Alan had tried a succession of southern cities, staying in each for a period of months, doing the odd part-time job and living in short-term rental accommodations. Though it had been two decades prior, Rollie and his agents were able to retrace Alan's nomadic journey through Atlanta, Charlestown, Little Rock, Pensacola, Miami and then the Keys.

When Susan picked up the report, Rollie said, "Well, Miss Jones. I've written a lot of missing person reports, but this one's a doozey. What a freaky story. And wow—-so much press on this guy. That's why the report is so thick—-I stuck in a lot of the press clippings. It provides 'flavor' if you know what I mean."

"Mr. Carter, that's very interesting but I don't want to hear anymore. Please put it in a sealed envelope for me."

When Susan gave Bobby the package, he locked his office door, cut the tape and removed the black folder. He placed it in front of him on his desk and stared at it for awhile. Then he began to read.

Two hours later, he buzzed Susan on the intercom and asked her to come in.

"I read the report. I think you made a good choice on the detectives you hired."

"Well, they cost enough. Did you find what you were looking for?"

"Yes I did. It's actually better than what I was expecting." Bobby looked into Susan's kind brown eyes. There wasn't a person on Earth that he felt closer to or trusted more. He had confided everything else, and the openness of their relationship entitled her to know. But he just couldn't bear to tell her. "I'll tell you soon, Susan. I promise. Now's just not the right time. Thanks for helping me."

That night Bobby brought the Bay Colony report with him to the living quarters which were attached to his office at the laboratory. He opened the folder to the page which had Alan's contact details. Sitting down at his computer, he began to type a letter to him. It wasn't an easy letter to write but finally Bobby was satisfied. He folded the single page into the stamped envelope. He then removed stacks of books from atop an old trunk that he had stashed in a far corner, and placed the report inside of it. The trunk already contained hundreds of press items he had researched on the internet and printed out, or sent away to publishers for, which dealt with the "Dumpster Baby" story. Bobby closed the trunk and began to stack the books back on top of it. But then he stopped. He sat down on the floor and just stared at the envelope that held his letter to Alan. He opened the trunk and threw it in.

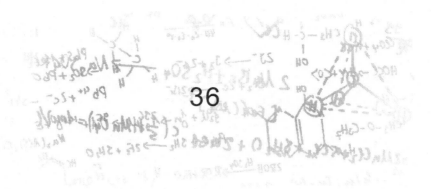

36

IT WAS A WARM TUESDAY in early October six years later. The leaves were beginning to turn their autumnal colors. Bobby lounged on a day bed drinking a large Bloody Mary. It was one in the afternoon and he had awakened only an hour ago. He squinted from the sun shining into the room and cupped his left hand against his forehead to block the rays. He had been on one of his binges and his last night's companion was still asleep in the bedroom. Bobby looked around the room. It was a typical scene for this apartment. Wine and liquor glasses, their contents in various states of consumption, were all over the place. Overflowing ashtrays were on the coffee table and floor. The sofa looked like it had been attacked. Its cushions were everywhere. Various items of female attire were strewn about. The apartment's air was stale with the mixed odor of booze, incense, pot and sex. This was one of the rare times when Bobby was actually in his own loft apartment on Front Street.

As Bobby sipped his drink, he reflected that this apartment was really no more than his den of iniquity. He was only there when he needed a private place for one of his crash landings. Otherwise, he lived in the small quarters adjacent to his Tufts office. To put an end to Susan's badgering, Bobby had rented this place so that as she put it, "You can make believe you have a life." That was eight years ago. The one bedroom apartment wasn't luxurious, but it was the nicest place of his own that he had ever had. Susan had found it for him and the lease was in her name to preserve Bobby's anonymity, of which he had become increasingly protective after the media circus that his autoimmune disease breakthrough had inspired. Bobby had taken an immediate liking to the apartment because most of the living space consisted of a large open area with oak floors and expansive floor to ceiling windows—"very un-claustrophobic" was how Bobby described it. The apartment was cluttered with the hundreds of books that Joe had given him, large sketch pads which stood against the walls, an electric piano, two blackboards on wheels, boxes full of CDs, and endless stacks of scientific periodicals.

Bobby glanced in the mirror. He pondered which looked worse, him or his old abused sofa. The two day bender that he had just been on was the pressure valve release which had followed three months of intensive work. Switching on the TV, Bobby flicked the remote from channel to channel, settling on a twenty-four hour news network. Looking at the screen blankly, he was about to change the channel when the reporter excitedly jumped on a new story:

"This breaking news just in. The Nobel Prize Committee in Stockholm announced minutes ago that it has awarded this year's Nobel Prizes in both medicine and chemistry to Dr. Robert James Austin for his revolutionary discoveries in gene augmentation therapy that have resulted in a cure for Muscular Dystrophy. The Committee's announcement went on to say— and I quote, "These tools are of such extraordinary significance that they have established a new paradigm for the entire scientific community in battling other human maladies." Bobby settled back into his chair and sighed. He knew what this would mean. She continued, "We now go direct to our reporter in Stockholm, Richard Shaffer, who is at the headquarters of the Nobel Foundation where the announcement was just made".

"Thank you, Sally. There's a lot of excitement here. The awards announced today will be Austin's fifth and sixth Nobel Prizes. He received his first two, chemistry and medicine, when he was twenty-five years old for his multiple sclerosis cure, which established the scientific blueprint and methodology that led directly to the cures for over eighty other autoimmune diseases. Two years later, he stunned the world when he won a Nobel Prize in biochemistry for his cure of ALS, commonly known as Lou Gehrigs disease, and then three years after that, a Nobel in biophysics for his selective electromagnetic cellular regeneration methodology." There's speculation as to whether this time Austin will personally attend the awards ceremony. He never has done so in the past and has directed the Committee to pay the cash award directly to his research foundation. If he does the same this year, that will bring the total to over eight million dollars."

"Thank you, Richard. Truly amazing. But so little is known about this reclusive thirty- three year old genius who shuns publicity and all celebrity. We don't even have photographs of him and there appear to be no records of his life prior to his years at MIT and Harvard. Tune in tomorrow evening at eleven for a special report— "Miracle Man In Our Midst."

Bobby downed the rest of his drink. Every time he received an award or made a discovery, it became an impetus to the press to dredge him up as the subject of a story or special report. The snooping began anew. He hated to admit it, but in retrospect, he was grateful to Orin Varneys for having taken possession of all records relating to his childhood and sealing them under the protection of the OSSIS. Bobby shuddered to think about the field day the media would have if they had been able to discover his past. The mere thought caused him to grab the half empty bottle of Macallan 18 that was perched on the coffee table, fill a glass that was lying on the floor and take a long gulp. He glanced uneasily at the old trunk that was tucked into a corner of the living room, piled high with books. As he stared at the amber liquid that had been Joe's favorite scotch, he became lost in thought. Later that night, he opened the trunk and retrieved the letter he had written to Alan Gottshalk some six years earlier. This time he would mail it.

Over the course of the ensuing year, the name used by that one news network to describe Bobby in the title of their special report gained increasing traction. Much to his embarrassment, Bobby began to be routinely referred to in the worldwide media as "Miracle Man."

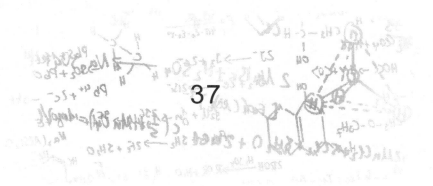

37

ALAN GOTTSCHALK SMILED AS THE screen door of his house banged shut behind him and he breathed deeply of the cool fragrant air coming in off the surf. Holding a mug of steaming black coffee that he had just poured, he walked to his mailbox. His dog, Jackson, a large brown mutt that he had rescued from the dog pound two years earlier, followed him dutifully. The tall sea grass in Alan's garden swayed rhythmically in the salty breeze. The few clouds looked like torn white ribbons in the azure sky. Alan's favorite sound, that of sea gulls, was overhead and as he looked up to see them, the sun shone so brightly that his eyes squinted shut. He never tired of the climate and beauty of the Keys. He was thankful every day that he had been given a reprieve from the darkness of his former life. Opening his mailbox, he took his few pieces of mail and brought them back to the kitchen and threw them on the kitchen table as his two pieces of toast popped up. He gingerly grabbed them out of the toaster, buttered them and then cracked two eggs into the frying pan with the casual expertise of a short-order cook. When his sandwich was ready, he placed it on a plate and sat down at the table. As he sipped his coffee and ate his breakfast, he perused the mail. Phone bill, electric bill, advert flyer from the local supermarket, and a plain white envelope with no return address. Opening the envelope, Alan unfolded the piece of paper in it and read:

Dear Mr. Gottschalk,

I am so happy that I was able to find you and I apologize for any intrusion that I may have caused in doing so. Many years ago, you were very kind to me. You showed great courage and moral character and in the process, you saved my life and gave me my first home. I am indebted to you beyond words and will always be. I hope to meet you one day, but for now I have work to complete. My accomplishments are your accomplishments.

Sincerely,
Robert James Austin a/k/a 'Little Fella'

P.S.—I would greatly appreciate if you would keep our communications confidential as privacy is very important to me.

He read the letter again. He then stared at the piece of paper incredulously. *Is this some kind of sick joke? Who the hell would do this to me?* Alan sat at his kitchen table gazing blankly out the window. Like he was watching a movie, his mind began to replay with uncanny clarity and detail, events that had taken place over thirty years ago—-events that had changed his life forever. How he had brought the infant back to his shanty in a rambling homeless community that the media cynically had dubbed "Riverview

Estates." How he had roughly fashioned a baby bottle out of a hypodermic syringe that he had sanitized with crazy Mary's cheap vodka, how his neighbors had embraced the child and stolen every supply needed for his sustenance from strollers in the city's parks that were left unattended by distracted nannies, and how after two weeks of taking care of the baby, the police had found them. Slumped in the chair with his eyes closed, vivid memories asserted their supremacy over him as if it had all happened yesterday.

The squad cars screeched up to the station house. Two social workers from the Bureau of Child Health and Welfare Services were already there and waiting. Alan was escorted out of the car, still holding the infant and surrounded by four police officers. The social workers' eyes widened as they looked at a man in full homeless regalia tenderly holding a baby who appeared to be happily accustomed to being in his arms. The more senior social worker, Natalie Kimball, reached out to take the child from Alan. He lowered the baby from his cradled position and held him out vertically, directly in front of his face. Looking deeply into the child's clear light blue eyes, he said, "Look how handsome you are 'little fella' and look how much you've already grown."

Alan pressed the baby against his chest and planted a kiss on top of his head. Putting his scraggly whiskered face against the baby's right ear, he whispered, "You're a very special little boy. Never forget that. I love you 'little fella'."

As he gave possession of the infant over to Kimball, she looked intently at Alan as if she were trying to understand what he was all about. His eyes were swollen and tear-filled. He looked defeated and worn.

"It appears you took good care of him. I hope the law takes that into account." Kimball then began walking to the precinct door as she held the infant.

Running up to her, Officer Jackson, the cop who had arrested Alan, said, "Look, it's important that you have the infant examined thoroughly. We'll need to know anything that would help us find his parents or what hospital he was born in. We don't know from where that crazy bum stole this baby, but we'll find out."

Kimball replied, "There's nothing worse than kidnapping. And a newborn yet. It's so horrible. The parents must be suffering so."

"Would you believe that degenerate told us he found the kid in a dumpster?"

"In a dumpster?"

"Yeah, in a garbage bag inside a dumpster."

Shaking her head wearily and looking down, Kimball murmured, "If that's true, then God have mercy on all of us."

As Kimball left the station house, 'little fella' was crying fiercely and struggling in her arms with all the strength that could be mustered by a two week old baby.

Jackson and one of the other cops pushed Alan over to the booking desk. The lieutenant behind the desk asked Jackson what the charges were.

Jackson responded, "Kidnapping and grand larceny."

Alan was then led through the station house on the way to an interrogation room. *Look how they're looking at me. They think I'm barely human.*

One of Alan's interrogators was detective Joe Parsoni. He was 51 years old, 5' 8" and 195 pounds with a bloated face and bulbous nose permanently reddened by a severe rosacea condition caused by chronic high blood pressure and excessive alcohol consumption.

Parsoni had four more years to go before retiring at full pension. He hated every day at his job. After over two decades on the force, he had come to the conclusion that he had wasted his life surrounding himself with the "scum buckets of the universe", as he described those suspected of committing crimes.

The other interrogator was detective Jack Warden, who had majored in psychology at John Jay Criminal College and had only recently received his detective's badge. Tall and trim, with slicked down dark hair sharply parted on the left in the manner popular among movie stars in the 1940s, Warden's almost classic good looks were marred by a badly pocked complexion. He was the fashion-plate of the office with his designer wire glasses, starched oxford shirts and three-piece suits. Warden had wanted to become a lawyer, but the financial pressures of having to care for two babies and a young wife who was more fertile than the Euphrates Delta, had led him to put his dreams on hold and join the police force so he could sign up to the city's health insurance.

Detective Parsoni tried to goad Alan by putting his fat oily face two inches from Alan's as he screamed at him, sputtering in his face and shaking Alan's chair with both hands as he loomed over him like a grizzly bear.

"Look, you bum. Don't bullshit me. You stole the kid so you could sell him. Admit it." Parsoni stood back and rubbed his large hairy fists as he glared at Alan. "We'll get it out of you sooner or later. You think you're smart. You're not. You're a loser. Don't waste my time. I got a family to go home to. You are nothing."

After two hours of relentless grilling, Alan was done. He put it bluntly to Parsoni and Warden.

"I don't have to answer any more questions. I told you—and I'll tell you one final time. So type it up in your report. I found 'little

202

fella' in a large black plastic garbage bag in a dumpster on 3rd and Avenue A about two weeks ago." He then reached into his pocket.

Lunging on to Alan, Parsoni yelled, "He's got a weapon," and delivered three hard punches to Alan's face in rapid succession with fists as large as catcher's mits.

Warden bear-hugged Parsoni. "Stop it. You know he was frisked and run through the detector. Get a grip." Warden pulled Parsoni off of Alan and backed him away.

Parsoni fumed, "Warden, get your head out of your ass."

Alan's eyes were closed as he turned his head from left to right a few times trying to ascertain if his neck still worked after the assault. He opened his eyes and spat some blood on to the floor. His lip was bleeding and so was his nose. Seeing this, Parsoni's face lit up as he said, "Now we're going to get somewhere with this lowlife." Warden handed Alan a bunch of paper napkins and put a metal waste basket by his feet.

Alan looked straight at Warden. "As I was saying before I was interrupted by Cro Magnon over there—- I found 'little fella' in a dumpster on 3rd and Avenue A." He then cautiously began to again reach into his pocket as he stared at Warden. Warden nodded permission. Alan pulled out a crumpled black plastic bag.

"This is the bag that the baby was in."

Warden looked shocked as he took the bag from Alan. "This is it?"

"Yes that's it. 'Little fella' was in that bag."

Warden spread the bag out on the interrogation table, patting and smoothing it to its full size. He gazed at it as if he had never before seen a garbage bag. He then lifted it up, delicately opened it and looked inside. Then he neatly folded the bag and put it in a clear evidence bag which bore a label, "Exhibit A."

"You're not going to believe this crap?" Parsoni said to Warden. "A few more love taps and he'd being telling the truth instead of this fairy tale. Why don't you go get a Coke and come back in five minutes while I make some progress here."

Alan continued, "I could have left 'little fella' where I found him and then I wouldn't be here now. But I wasn't going to let him die. To me, he wasn't a piece of trash like he was to whoever threw him out. And as for the stroller and the other baby stuff—- do you have any witnesses who saw anything stolen? I don't think you do. So leave me alone and go write some parking tickets. And while you're at it, get me one of those free lawyers."

The veins on Parsoni's temples were bulging. He spat into the wastebasket next to Alan's feet and largely missed the basket so that most of his spit spattered on to Alan's pants. He kicked the basket with so much force that it flew past the door and half way across the room, spilling its contents. Alan was removed and taken to a holding cell.

A few more days went by. Weeks went by. *What the hell was going on?* officer Jackson wondered. *There gotta be some heartbroken parents out there who just haven't reported this yet because they're still searching for themselves. Damn, this is a white baby. A perfect white baby. They'll call. We'll find 'em. Just a few more days.*

Jackson kept telling the head of his precinct, Captain Palmer, to let the case sit for awhile longer. "Give it time to breathe," he said. "Meanwhile, I'll tell that two-bit lawyer the court appointed for the bum to go screw himself."

Jackson was sure that the aggrieved parents would come forward, claim #2764 and press charges against Alan Gottschalk for kidnapping. Jackson would then be the hero cop who rescued the adorable caucasian infant from a deranged hobo kidnapper, and reunited him with his loving parents. This would be the career watershed moment that he had been waiting for. It was all just around the corner. *The only thing I need is for these goddamn parents to show themselves and claim the kid, and then I'm set. I'm set,* he mused.

Dr. Drummond's conclusion that the infant wasn't born in a hospital or with the assistance of an experienced nurse or mid-wife, coupled with the absence of anyone claiming a lost or stolen infant, was making it look like the police officers had rushed to judgment. Alan's court appointed lawyer was making noises about contacting the American Civil Liberties Union with false imprisonment, malicious prosecution, and civil rights claims.

Five weeks after Alan's arrest, no one had claimed that their infant had been kidnapped or was missing. The coffin which contained the remnants of Officer Jackson's dreams was hammered shut when DNA tests taken from hair and saliva samples that were found inside the garbage bag matched that of the infant. Captain Palmer called Officer Jackson into his office.

"Jackson, this case is a total fiasco and one of the worst embarrassments that this department has had in the last ten years. The commissioner called me today and he was fuming. The mayor is all over his ass."

"Who would know? Who the hell would know that hobo was telling the truth? " sputtered Jackson.

Palmer was not placated. "It's your job to find the truth. And you blew it."

His face and neck the color of a boiled lobster, Jackson looked like his blood pressure would blow the top of his head right off. He began to leave Palmer's office.

"Wait, Jackson, I didn't dismiss you. There's more," Palmer said. "As part of the settlement, which your Mr. Gottschalk, now represented by the American Civil Liberties Union, has made—- the mayor and the police commissioner will both issue a public apology to him to be delivered in person at Riverview Estates, and he'll receive a six-figure settlement payment so he doesn't sue the city."

It was an election year and a litigation by the ACLU on behalf of a homeless person that would attract national attention was not the kind of publicity that the mayor and city council wanted. And anyway, this was no ordinary homeless person. Alan Gottschalk was a hero. A full-blown American hero.

The media outlets had a story they could exploit relentlessly. It dominated the local newspapers, TV and radio stations for almost a week, and spread to national coverage. It was the subject of talk shows, special reports, blogging and editorials, all speculating as to what had led to #2764's fate. Gottschalk was dubbed "HOBO HERO," "THE GOLDEN TRAMP," and "HOMELESS KNIGHT." His photo, taken from old employee records at the now shuttered manufacturing plant where he had worked before the jobs were sent overseas, was plastered everywhere within twenty-four hours of the story's breaking.

The apology ceremony which was to take place at Riverview Estates as part of the ACLU litigation settlement was re-jiggered by the mayor's office into a political photo-op event for the Mayor, all members of the city council and the police commissioner. In preparation for the event, the city's sanitation department showed up with an advance-crew to "spruce up" Riverview Estates so it wouldn't look quite as shocking on television. The mayor had his speech writer prepare a long dissertation about the plight of the homeless and jobless and what his administration, after his re-election, would be doing to help the members of Riverview Estates and "all the other good people of this city who find themselves in need."

————————◆•◆•◆————————

Alan shuddered as he shook off the past. Bringing his cup to his lips, his trembling hand caused some coffee to spill on Bobby's letter. He wiped it as carefully as if it were an ancient document and then gently blew it dry. Getting up slowly, Alan placed the letter back in its envelope and put it in his jacket pocket. He headed off to work in a daze.

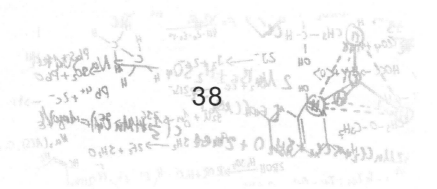

38

As Bobby pushed the door open and walked out of the deli, the small brass bells hanging from the string over the door jingled loudly. He took a sip from his twenty-four ounce cup of coffee, the first of five he had every day. Bobby squinted from the brightness of the sun, which was intensified as it reflected off the remains of the prior week's substantial snowfall. There was no wind and the temperature was just slightly below freezing, which made it a warm day for February in Boston. Bobby inhaled the crisp air deeply and smiled. He loved this kind of winter's morning.

Walking toward Tufts, he saw a large crowd of people gathered in front of the main gates. This was a sight that had become all too familiar to him over the last few months. He put on his sunglasses and pulled down hard on the visor of his baseball cap.

Their overhead lights flashing, five police cars were askew in front of the main entrance to Tufts, and at least fifteen officers and a dozen campus security guards were trying to contain fifty or more demonstrators who were intent on blocking the campus entrance. A remote broadcasting truck from one of the local television stations was also on the scene. Some of the demonstrators were picketing with placards that said "Stop Austin Now" and "Let God Decide." Others were waving signs and chanting, "Austin Will Bring His Wrath." As Bobby weaved through the crowd, he looked like any other student trying to make his way to class. Having eschewed the media and avoided being photographed for years, no one outside of a small circle knew what he looked like. As a leaflet was thrust into his hand that was titled, "God Has A Plan," Bobby noticed that someone had splattered the ornate wrought iron gates with red paint.

Other than their disdain for Bobby, the demonstrators had little in common. But Bobby's accomplishments had managed to unite Christian Scientists, Jehovah's Witnesses, Muslim Fundamentalists, Scientologists and Pentecostalists. But the largest contingent was comprised of an angry looking group, dressed in pseudo-military garb, who were rhythmically shouting, "The Anti-Christ Works Here." They were members of a radical organization called RASI which was an acronym for Retribution Against Scientific Interference. RASI advocated violent opposition to modern medicine which it believed to be contrary to the ordained natural order of life and God's divine plan. Over the years, RASI had picketed and defaced research laboratories and pharmaceutical companies.

It was Bobby's recent double Nobel Prize win that seemed to have changed everything. Prior to that he had been able to maintain a low-key presence at the university and the privacy of his research had not been a problem. There had been some forays from reporters and curiosity seekers but these were sporadic and usually petered out within a few days after the announcement of a discovery or an award. But the weight of the most recent Nobels, on top of the four prior ones, coupled with the worldwide impact of Bobby's discoveries, had escalated media and public interest to a new level. The limited resources of Tufts' campus security staff were being overwhelmed. Tufts was now highlighted on all of the Boston tourist maps and was a regular drive-by attraction on the tour-bus schedule, where Tufts was called, "Home of the Miracle Man."

Dean Walterberg summoned Bobby to his office. As the dean looked outside the windows of his office, he pointed toward the main entrance gates. "Robert, the Trustees and I are very concerned about what's been going on out there with these demonstrators. Yesterday, ten of those characters scaled the side-entrance fence, placards and all, and were scouring the campus, questioning students, trying to find you and your lab. They staged a bizarre ceremony in the middle of the commons and blew up a model of the science building with M-80s. The blast shook the windows on half the campus."

"That's crazy. I'm really sorry," said Bobby, his face ashen.

Walterberg gazed out his windows onto the campus below. "We're worried about the safety of the students and the facilities— and quite frankly, we're worried about you." Walterberg turned to face Bobby and he looked pained. "These RASI people are potentially very dangerous—they're on the FBI watch-list. Our security people aren't equipped to handle this. We're going to double our guard staff and we're thinking of barb-wiring the perimeters of the campus. Entirely new security procedures need to be put into effect."

Bobby shook his head. "This campus shouldn't have to be a fortress."

"The paparazzi are also out of control," Walterberg said. "It seems they're being offered substantial bounties for photographs of you."

Bobby plopped down into one of the guest chairs and leaned into its sidearm. " I never wanted to be disruptive or cause a problem. It's probably going to get worse as time goes on."

Walterberg pulled over a chair and sat next to him. "Robert, make no mistake. You're the best thing that has ever happened to this University. We're so proud to have you here, and quite frankly, your presence has raised our profile and reputation incredibly. We're now attracting the absolute top rank of students and professors—no school has it over us anymore. And alumni contributions have more than tripled. We'll do anything and everything to support you."

"That's very generous and I appreciate it. But the spotlight isn't a light that I can work in. And sooner or later, someone's going to get hurt. I can't live with knowing that my presence here might do that or get one of your buildings blown up. I hate to say it dean, but the time has come for me to start making arrangements to move to a more private location."

Bobby and Walterberg crafted the details of the plan going forward. Bobby would continue to be listed as a professor (this was important to Tufts for prestige reasons and would give Bobby a personal income since he took no salary from his research foundation), but he would be newly denominated as a non-resident professor emeritus. It would be publicly announced that Bobby would no longer work on campus. Bobby would have unlimited access to Tufts' supercomputers via a remote interface from his new location, and he and his staff would continue to utilize the laboratories in the physical sciences departments and the medical school on an 'as needed' basis. Tufts would not object to Bobby's taking with him whatever Tufts' lab assistants or other staff he wished, but these people would then be on the foundation's payroll.

While Bobby knew that he had made the right decision, he was concerned about the logistics of setting up his own research facility. As usual, he turned to Susan.

"I have a little job for you that should provide a nice distraction from your everyday routine. I've noticed you're getting bored," Bobby said, smiling.

"There's hardly anything to do around here," Susan replied, rolling her eyes.

Bobby gestured toward the window. "With all the craziness that's been going on out there, we have to leave Tufts as soon as possible and set-up our own facility. We need to find a place that's private, remote and secluded—but not far from Boston. And we need to get it up and running pronto."

Susan's eyes narrowed as she looked at Bobby. "I'm concerned by the way you're using the word 'we.' Why are you telling me this? It's just information, right?"

Bobby smiled. "No, my dear— you're in charge. You're going to make it happen."

Susan's voice rose as her words came tumbling out. "Are you kidding me? I don't recall 'lab relocator' in my job description. What makes you think I can do it? It's a huge job."

Bobby walked over to her and put his hand on her shoulder. "And that's the beautiful thing about your job. It's constantly evolving because I have unlimited faith in your abilities. Our time frame is ninety days to find the space and get in there. You can do it, Susan. You're like that stubborn little train in the children's story that gets to the top of the mountain by saying, 'I think I can, I think I can.'"

"Thanks for that. I'm like a fat locomotive."

Bobby laughed, "I didn't say fat."

Susan groaned. "Why is your belief in me always so convenient for you?"

As he sat down at his desk and turned his attention to his computer, Bobby smiled and said, "I love you Susan. Thank you."

———— ••• ————

Susan combed the Multiple Listing Service on the internet for real estate offerings in communities within a thirty mile radius of Tufts. After much investigation, she came to the conclusion that Bobby's marching orders—- a secluded, private and remote location—- meant that a residential property was needed, as commercial properties were invariably situated on main roads that are easily accessible and visible to the public. After searching for two weeks, she came across the following listing:

Beverly, Mass—prestigious Prides Crossing area—"fixer upper" with great potential; 8 acres fenced and gated, large single story house. Priced for quick sale by estate.

Susan called the broker and made an appointment to see the property. As Susan drove around with her, she was encouraged by the difficulty the broker had finding the house. Once off the main road, they got lost in a labyrinth of twisting private roads that were inadequately marked, lanes going nowhere, dead ends and cul de sacs. The vehicle's GPS was of no help. Finally, after two calls to the broker's office for directions, they pulled the black BMW up to a nameless dirt road, wide enough for one vehicle to pass at a time. The only sign was one that said "No Trespassing Violators Will Be Prosecuted." The broker ignored the sign and turned into the road which rambled in a seemingly aimless fashion. After driving a quarter mile, the road led them to a set of very tall metal electronic gates that were distinctly non-residential in appearance.

There was no address number, mail box or other identification. Two signs were posted. One said, "Private Property" and the other said, "Guard Dogs On Patrol." Security cameras were mounted on tall posts next to the gates, and there was a "call box" for visitors to request admission.

"The person who built this place was a security freak," said the broker. "The entire property is fenced in with a twelve foot high commercial grade chain link fence."

"What was the owner afraid of?" Susan asked.

"The executor of his estate told us he was a Russian gentleman in the import/export business. He wanted to keep out any wildlife that might eat his vegetable and flower gardens."

"A naturalist," said Susan as she rolled her eyes.

The broker pressed a remote control device which opened the gates. "Don't worry, the patrol dogs are gone now."

After two minutes of driving, the forest gave way to the cleared land, and it started to become evident why the house was called a 'fixer-upper.' The expansive lawns were near dead and the shrubbery around the house was so overgrown that it looked like nature was reclaiming the building.

"As you can see, the lawn's irrigation system hasn't been working for some time, and a good garden clean-up and trim is necessary," the broker said.

"You think?" Susan raised her eyebrows.

The house was a very large single-story stucco structure that was built in a 1980s architectural style that can only be described as "early bomb shelter." The building looked remarkably like a military bunker. All of the corners of the building, and the entrance façade, were broadly rounded in much the same way as the concrete "pill-box" fortifications overlooking the beaches of Normandy.

As Susan looked at the building's peeling paint and other signs of neglect, she smiled. "Exactly how large is this monstrosity?"

The broker's brow furrowed. "Actually, there's more demand than you might think for this particular architectural style. Some people seek this out."

"Do they bring their orderlies from the sanitarium or are they allowed to come alone?"

The broker ignored the crack and said, "The house is approximately 7000 square feet, not counting the guest house which is 1500 square feet." She motioned toward another section of the property, and Susan could see that quite a distance from the main house, there was a much smaller bunker that stood guard over what appeared to be disheveled rose gardens.

Opening the front door, the broker said, "You'll see that the house has good bones. All it needs is a little TLC."

"Did you say DDT?"

The interior looked as if it hadn't been painted in twenty-five years. The hard wood floors were badly damaged and there were large water stains on at least ten different areas of the ceiling.

It was obvious to Susan that the house could easily be converted into a satisfactory research facility. There also was a huge basement that could be utilized and the guest house too held promise. Susan said to the broker, "As God awful ugly as this place is, it just might work for my boss. So what's the price?"

"It's listed for $1.8 million," the broker replied.

"What's the real price?"

"The land alone is worth that."

Susan's belly laugh was convincing. "Not in this neighborhood—with its four acre zoning and wetland habitat restrictions. And if someone just wants this place for the land, they'll have to pay plenty just to ball and chain this architectural abortion and cart away the debris."

"If you're not interested, we can just move on. There are other properties I can show you that may be more to your liking."

"How long has it been on the market?"

"Nine months. Originally it was listed for $2.1 million."

"I think I can get authorization for $1.1 million. It would be an all-cash deal."

"That's ridiculous. The estate will never accept that."

"Ask them. You and I both know this place can easily sit on the shelf for another two years, and by then it will look even worse. Sell it before the termites carry it away."

After another two weeks of haggling, a deal was struck at $1.375 million, with a closing to take place in fifteen days. Conversion and repair work was set to begin within two weeks after the closing. Bobby was elated.

Within four months after Bobby's foundation purchased the property, he and his staff of eight assistants were ready to move in. The interior of the house had been converted into a computer research lab. Between the equipment there and the remote interface to the Tufts computer lab, Bobby had an extraordinary amount of computing power at his disposal. Installing science or medical labs would have been far too costly, so he'd continue to use those at Tufts. For security reasons, the Prides Crossing property had no exterior identification, signs, address or mail delivery, and none of the construction contractors or crew knew who the occupants would be.

Late in the evening of the first day on which the lab became operational, only Susan and Bobby remained on the premises. Bobby sat in front of a bank of three computer key-boards running equipment tests. Susan interrupted him and asked for help with something in the reception area.

After repeated prodding, she prevailed upon him to go with her. "An adjustment is needed," she said, as she pulled over a tall ladder that was standing in the room and climbed it. "Now hold the ladder steady and don't look up my dress."

"You're wearing pants," Bobby said.

"I know, but I always wanted to say that."

Standing atop the ladder, Susan tugged hard on a tarp that Bobby thought was covering a light fixture in the process of being installed. When the tarp fell to the floor, a sign was revealed — The Joseph Manzini Research Laboratory. Bobby beamed. He lifted Susan down from the ladder and hugged her as he twirled her around.

Laughing she said, "Tarzan, put me down before you rupture yourself. Now be honest. Was I being presumptuous with the name? I wanted it to be a surprise gift for you."

"It's fantastic. It makes me feel like Joe will be here with us. And it's a lot better than the name I was thinking of."

"And what was that?"

"The Alamo."

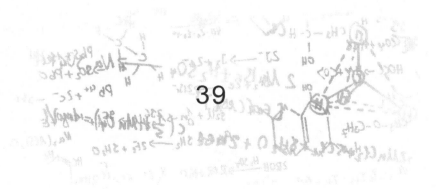

39

THE PREVIOUS WORK BOBBY HAD done was in the autoimmune, neuro-muscular and genetic areas. Now Bobby was turning his attention to bacterial, viral and parasitic diseases, a completely different scenario in which, rather than the body itself malfunctioning, the body comes under attack from an external force. The disease that Bobby initially set his sites on—malaria—afflicts five hundred million people annually and kills three million a year, the majority of whom are young children, one of whom dies every thirty seconds. Malaria is caused by a protozoan parasite which is injected into its victims by female Anopheles mosquitoes. What Bobby learned is that this protozoa has an extraordinary ability to evade the immune system of the human body. Because of this, vaccines to prevent malaria have been unsuccessful, and while there are some anti-malarial drugs, the protozoa is also expert at evolving to be resistant to them.

Immersing himself in his research, Bobby began to ask himself questions that never had occurred to him in his prior work where no external force was attacking the human body. *How strange it is,* thought Bobby, *that a one cell organism, among the most primitive of all living things, has the capability to defeat the most complex and sophisticated life-form.* An organism as simple as protozoa has killed more than half a billion people in the twentieth century alone, and defied two hundred years of active human endeavor to outwit it. *How could an inconsequential microbe be so adaptive and resilient that the human body becomes nothing more than a vessel to be exploited and pillaged? What powers this protozoa? What gives it the ability to endlessly change, evolve and mutate so that it can defeat its human hosts?*

Bobby knew that wars aren't won by foot soldiers alone. It takes commanders, generals —the strategists and tacticians that direct the rank and file. *So—who is the commander of this parasite?* Bobby wondered. *What force empowers this to happen?* The more Bobby thought about this, the worse his nightmares became. He continued to research tirelessly and run endless numbers of experiments. But they were going nowhere. As the months went by, he was certain that he felt the force of resistance at every turn. He believed he was being opposed, actively blocked. He was being check-mated by day and night-mared at night. He became increasingly convinced that he was in a battle with an active opponent. Susan noticed a change in his behavior. He was becoming moody, withdrawn, more reclusive and depressed. He began to disappear during the day for long stretches of time.

She confronted him. "Bobby, where have you been?"

"The beach," he replied.

"At this time of year?"

"It's the best time. The beach is empty. It's beautiful and solitary."

"You've been taking quite a few breaks from working."

"I work on the beach."

"With no computers?"

Bobby waved his hand. "Thinking. I've just been thinking. Sometimes you have to get a distance away from something to really see it clearly. I've been too myopic and it hasn't been working. I'm just not getting to the core of the problem. I've been losing, Susan. Getting my ass kicked, to be frank."

"What do you mean?"

"I have to break through a barrier that's been erected or I'll never cure this disease. Everything I'm trying isn't working. I'm up against a very powerful force."

Susan's eyebrows rose as she looked at him. "What are you talking about Bobby?"

"Forget it. You'll think I'm crazy."

"Well, don't let that stop you at this late date."

Bobby's demeanor didn't lighten with Susan's crack. "I've come to some conclusions. Certain things have become very clear to me now."

"Like?"

"Like this is a dangerous universe. Like there are forces of real evil out there—and I'm not talking about people or governments. Like diseases aren't accidents and everything isn't explainable by natural scientific phenomena."

"What are you talking about Bobby?"

"The universe isn't benign or neutral. It's not just about science and rationality. Everything has its reciprocal, it's opposite. There are forces that define our reality and they're in opposition. There's a reason why a one-cell parasite can't be stopped from killing a child every thirty seconds. There's a reason why the immune system of the most complex, advanced and highly evolved organism on earth—a human being's body—can't successfully fight-off a protozoa. There's a reason why that one-celled organism can mutate endlessly like a magician to defeat drugs as quickly as they're invented."

"And that reason is?"

Bobby's voice rose with his increasing agitation. "Because there's a powerful force of negativity and destruction out there —-a supreme evil—it's empowering all of this to happen, Susan. It's no accident and it's not just science. I think I've been feeling this force in my nightmares my whole life. One day, it will destroy me. It will take me out. I know it."

Susan exhaled loudly and shook her head. "I have to tell you, Bobby —-that sounds really bizarre and paranoid."

Bobby avoided eye contact. "Well, I'm sorry but that's what I think. I began to feel this—to get a glint of it—about five years ago. And as I've continued to work on this new research, it's become clear to me. Maybe I'm wrong, but I don't think so."

Susan couldn't recall ever seeing him so unnerved. "Bobby, do you believe in God?"

After a moment of silence Bobby replied, "I don't know why —but I do. What about you?"

"Off and on. When I was a little kid I did because that's what I was taught. Then when I got older and I would go to church with my parents, I would see girls there that I was attracted to. I would try to keep from blushing when I said hello to them. I blamed God for that, for making me different. And then, when I was being abused by that loser I was living with and he almost killed my son, I hated God for not protecting us. I decided he didn't exist at all. It was just one big lie as far as I was concerned. But I believe in God now, very much so."

"And why's that?" asked Bobby.

"Because after I met Anna, I knew God sent her to me. I'm sure of that. He delivered us. She was his angel."

Bobby rubbed his right temple. "Well, unfortunately, God has some serious adversaries. In this universe, everything has its polar opposite. If you believe in good, you can't deny the existence of evil, and evil is not passive."

Susan placed her hands firmly on Bobby's shoulders and looked directly into his eyes as she said softly, "Bobby, I don't know. Maybe you're right or maybe you're just plain nuts. But either way, you're the best shot we have. So please — give the beach a rest and get back to the lab. Whatever it is that you think is out there—beat it."

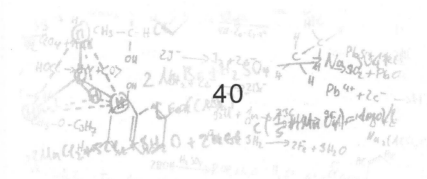

40

STARING AT THE MULTIPLE VIDEO monitors in front of him, Colum McAlister sat on the edge of his chair in the private den that was accessible only through hidden panels in the wall of his library. He played the video again and smiled. The deputy commissioner of the Food and Drug Administration had surprising stamina for a man of his age, but in all fairness, a good deal of the credit had to go to the two young latex clad women that McAlister had provided for that particular evening's entertainment at "Lands End," his remote Adirondack estate. Carefully removing the disc from the security surveillance recorder that was connected to cameras hidden throughout the house, McAlister placed it in his safe with the other discs in his alphabetical file. Here, in the wilderness of northern New York State on a private peninsula that jutted into Saranac Lake, McAlister had the perfect setting to ply his trade of influence peddling and corporate blackmail. Once the luxury "camp" retreat of a late nineteenth century robber baron, "Lands End" now served McAlister well as the playing stage for what he liked to call, "situations of delicacy." And tomorrow, the estate would host the CEOs of the five other leading pharmaceutical companies whom

McAlister had invited to discuss matters of common interest. Each would arrive at their appointed times in their corporate helicopters. The invitation itself and all other communications related to the event were oral and innocuous. McAlister was meticulous in avoiding paper trails and telephone discussions which could be used for evidentiary purposes.

By 12:30 the next afternoon, all the CEOs had arrived at the estate and were walking its grounds marveling at the vistas. Far above them, McAlister stood unseen in the circular celestial observatory which was located in the main house's watchtower. This striking architectural feature provided him with a 360-degree panorama of the entire property and its surroundings. McAlister peered down at his guests. Martin Turnbull was at his side.

"Should we have an idiot roll-call, Marty? Look at them. A bunch of pompous dopes. If Milken hadn't been busted and we could have kept the reins tight on the Justice Department, I could've bought half those companies."

"Keep it cordial, Colum. No recriminations. They're here for a purpose. They came a long way at your personal invitation. That says a lot."

McAlister glared at Turnbull. "No need to lecture me, Marty."

A butler whose jacket bore a gold embroidered "Lands End" monogram, directed the CEOs into one of the more intimate dining rooms of the colossal log house. After they had been served their beverage of choice and had been kept waiting for what McAlister deemed to be an appropriate period of time, he seemed to materialize out of nowhere, greeting each of the executives by their first names. Holding up a tumbler filled with his favorite single batch bourbon, he looked at his guests and made a mental note as to which of them was drinking Chardonnay, which he felt was for women and sissies. In his most affable voice, McAlister said, "Thank you all for making time in your busy schedules to attend today. I toast to our unity of purpose and the future prosperity we will have if we work together toward a common goal."

Lunch consisted of an elaborate buffet, but after barely thirty minutes, McAlister gave the nod that signaled the staff to clear the dining table. Most of the guests still had half their food on their plates. They were shepherded into the library, a two story masterpiece of "twig-and-branch" craftwork, with a soaring native stone fireplace. Once they all were seated around the conference table, McAlister started the meeting.

"There are several subjects which I'd like to discuss today and, of course, the floor is open to all of you to bring up anything you wish, but frankly the matter that I think is of the greatest concern is Robert Austin."

"What do you mean by that?" Jessup Halsey asked, the seventy-four year old CEO of Veranicus Pharmaceuticals.

"Austin is single handedly ruining our business and we all need to get pro-active to do something about it."

Halsey shook his head, his sparse but still graceful silver hair curling down to his right eye like a septuagenarian superman. "I don't see what we can do. The man's a genius. He's making discoveries. What's there to say?"

McAlister smiled condescendingly. "Jessup, that's a passive attitude to take about a guy who's making your stock options worthless. Does anyone else here have any opinions?"

"Colum, I completely agree with you," said Lincoln Raynor, a fifty year old Philadelphia patrician whose grandfather founded Tyer Drun. As tan and polished as a middle-aged GQ model in his impeccable Paul Stuart pin stripe suit, he said, "We can't sit by idly and let this character destroy our companies. I've already spoken to our outside counsel about the feasibility of filing an anti-trust complaint against him."

"Anti-trust. For what?" asked Anthony Bello with a throaty laugh. He was the youngest executive present. His lack of understanding of the pharmaceuticals business wasn't a concern to the venture capital company he worked for who appointed him CEO when it seized control of venerable Meyer Bessel Laboratories in a leveraged buyout. Once a profitable and stable company with large cash reserves that had helped fund its research into new drugs, Meyer Bessel now struggled to survive under a mountain of junk bond debt. Bello's greased black hair was combed straight back from his forehead, which only served to draw attention to his rodent like eyes and the prominent mole on his unusually pointy nose.

Lincoln Raynor's diamond and gold Asprey cufflinks sparkled in the light of the chandeliers as he raised his arms for emphasis. "Austin's discriminatory. He won't do business with any of us. He'll only deal with the generic guys, and he's controlling the retail prices of his drugs—keeping them artificially low. We can build a case around that."

"Sounds like a bullshit claim," Bello said smiling. "It will never fly."

"It doesn't have to go the distance," Raynor said. "All we need to do is hassle Austin, distract him, cost his foundation a fortune in legal fees, slow him down. We'll make him pay attention to us and he'll understand he has to play ball. It's time he got a dose of reality."

Several of the assembled began to shift uneasily in their chairs. Charles Farner, CEO of Kenderson Cooper, slowly navigated his obese body to the liquor cart. Dropping two ice cubes into a tall water glass and filling it almost to the top with scotch, a hoarse voice emanated from his blowfish like head, "We can't count on the Justice Department. Austin's pretty damn popular. But more importantly, we have to be careful about giving Justice an excuse to nose around our business."

Raynor grimaced. "Come on Charley, don't be afraid of your own shadow. We're the ones who've lined pockets in D.C. for years. Washington needs us and they know they'll never get a dime from Austin."

McAlister interrupted, "Let's not get bogged down, gentlemen. Antitrust is one idea and it's certainly worth pursuing. Who else has a suggestion?"

Bello spoke up. "I'll have my company use its FDA connections to object to the speed at which they approve Austin's new meds. They fast-track everything for him. We'll slow that down. The longer we can keep his stuff off the market, the more time we have to sell ours before he makes it obsolete."

Jessup Halsey stood up abruptly and cocked his head as if he had just had an epiphany. Enlightened after having had more time to reflect on the decreasing value of his stock options, he declared enthusiastically, "Good point. Every month of delay, can mean hundreds of millions for us."

McAlister interjected, "Ultimately, public perception is crucial. So I've met with one of our strategic ad agencies about starting a 'dis-information' campaign to plant doubts in the public's mind about Austin's discoveries. We'll make them realize they need to be cautious about embracing his stuff and abandoning our 'tried and true.' The thrust will be that progress takes time. Short cuts are dangerous. If it's too good to be true, then it's not true. We'll focus on horror photos of Thalidomide babies and other nightmares caused by 'miracle drugs.' And to bolster it, we'll create 'adverse reaction' reports to arouse suspicions about his meds and the quality of their manufacture. The script is being written by our best guys. Our internet team will go viral with this and get massive coverage. You can bet the news outlets will jump on it—they're always looking for something controversial to talk about. We can do some real damage. Our PR people know the drill. It will be like taking candy from a baby, because Austin won't interact with the media to defend himself."

"Brillant," Raynor said. "That's what we need to do. Undermine his credibility. Destroy his sainthood. One of us should get an investigation going into his personal life. There has to be some dirt somewhere."

Fritz Obermeir, the seventy-three year old CEO of Teifling Pharmaceuticals, stood up with difficulty using his cane for support, his tall thin body bent by severe arthritis. With his crooked finger pointing accusingly at those seated, he shook his leathery head, "Are you all crazy? This is disgraceful. Austin is a godsend. He's changing the world. He's doing what nobody else can do. Is our greed so great that we sink to this level?"

McAlister smacked the table loudly. He stood up and walked slowly to his massive desk, the same one that had once belonged to the robber baron who built "Lands End." He opened the lower left drawer and removed a large wooden box that was decorated with elaborate marquetry. Reverently carrying the box over to the conference table at which the CEOs were seated, he placed it on the table next to his chair and opened the Davidoff humidor with a flourish. "Who would like a Cuban? These are rather special. Not just Cohibas, but Cohibas produced by Habanor S.A. at the El

Laguito factory itself. The same place where Fidel's personal cigars have been made for decades."

The faces around the table lit up. One by one, they filed over to McAlister. Eventually, even Obermeir came by. McAlister delicately removed the cigars from the humidor, and presented them individually to each executive. As the cigar cutter was passed from one CEO to the next, the end of each esteemed stogy was cut with appropriate deliberation. McAlister summoned the butler to light the cigars and distribute ashtrays to each of the assembled. The butler poured each man a snifter full of 1949 Hugo Armagnac, which McAlister advised was the perfect accompaniment to the Cohibas. By the time they all finished expounding upon the quality of the cigars and liquor, the better part of an hour had passed. Now comfortably ensconced on the library's well worn leather club chairs and sofa, no one remembered what Fritz Obermeir had said.

Framed by the library's imposing fireplace, McAlister spoke as if Obermeir had never uttered a word. "Gentlemen, I love our industry and I know you do too. I've given my life to it. I started out as a stock boy at a warehouse loading dock when I was seventeen. And now, Austin is destroying our business. Nobody knows who this guy is or where he came from. Some say he's a mutant. For all we know, he's an alien. But who cares? He's going to cost a million people their jobs and destroy the nest-eggs of tens of millions of our shareholders. If he keeps going on like he has—the only thing left for us to manufacture will be tampons and laxatives. So we have to confront realities. We've been entrusted to run our companies and to do what's best for our shareholders. That's our job and we're paid well to do it. Austin's our competitor and we have to beat him. It's really no more complicated than that. I hope I have your support."

With the exception of Obermeir, all of the CEOs present agreed that Robert James Austin was the enemy and the enemy had to be stopped.

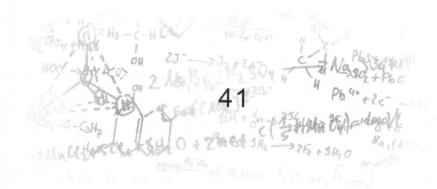

41

AFTER HIS DISCUSSION WITH SUSAN, Bobby settled back into his lab research with a new resolve that was born out of acceptance. He now understood that he was in an active conflict with a powerful force of indeterminate origins that sought to oppose him. He accepted that his death or insanity might be the outcome of this struggle. Rather than weaken him, these realizations imbued him with a heightened sense of defiance. For Bobby, now more than ever, it was all about keeping his wits and level of concentration for as long as he could, and accomplishing his goals.

In a constant state of intellectual preoccupation, he was operating on a cognitive plane that was largely removed from normal consciousness. His trances became more frequent and prolonged. He often didn't seem present. He would hold staff meetings with his lab assistants at which he would perfunctorily outline their assignments, and it was as if only a portion of him was actually in the room interacting with them.

One afternoon, Susan brought Bobby's favorite lunch into his office. As she sprinkled grated parmesan cheese on his spaghetti

Bolognese, just the way he liked it, she said, "So where's the real Bobby Austin? Will he ever come back?"

Bobby smiled. "I've just been working really hard. I'm going to crack this thing. I think I found an angle."

"I hope so. Because sometimes I feel like I'm watching 'Invasion of the Body Snatchers.' I'm thinking about bringing in a bunch of bimbos to gauge how you react. You know— to see if you are really you."

"And if I don't pass the test, because maybe I'm not in the mood to play with the ladies at that particular moment?"

"That would be unfortunate, Bobby, because I'd have to pour gasoline all over you and light you up. The test gets administered only once," she said, smiling.

He nodded. "That's sweet. I'll try not to screw up."

Bobby decided that the problem with prior attempts at formulating a malaria vaccine was that the battle wasn't being initiated soon enough—the parasite wasn't being engaged at the outset of its intrusion into the human body. The human antibodies needed to attack the parasite before it had time to propagate in the red blood cells and liver — because once that occurred it was too late.

To accomplish his goal, Bobby concluded that the body's defensive action must start as soon as the protozoa are inserted into the body as part of the mosquito's saliva. The way to do this, he hypothesized, was to create a vaccine that consisted of a genetically programmed virus that would immediately detect the presence of two things: mosquito saliva and the nucleic acids of the protozoan parasite. If that were done, and if the virus was also engineered to strengthen the antibodies' already existing ability to destroy the parasite, then the human body would be protected no matter how often the patient was bitten by infected mosquitoes. Bobby's virus would reproduce continually in the human body so that it was always present and ready.

When his computer analysis confirmed the feasibility of his hypothesis, Bobby designed the lab experiments that would be necessary. This began a marathon effort at the Tufts biology, chemistry and medical labs. So many experiments had to be run that Bobby quadrupled his lab staff to thirty-two.

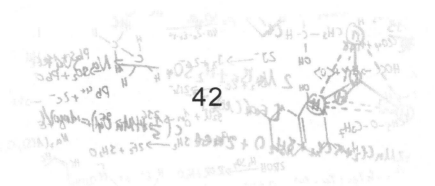

42

ARRIVING AT THE PRIDES CROSSING facility late one morning, Bobby made his way through reception and the busy "bull-pen" area filled with the work stations of staff members with whom he exchanged quick 'hellos.' He unlocked his private office and closed the door behind him. Silently stepping forward from a dark corner of the office, a large Black man pointed his Beretta M9 at Bobby, aimed directly at his head and pulled the trigger twice.

In an instant, Bobby felt all the blood in his head drain as the bottom fell out of his stomach and his bladder started to give way.

"Bang, bang, you're dead," the assailant said.

"What the fuck?" Bobby shouted, realizing that he still was in one piece.

"I just saved your life. Isn't 'thank you' in your vocabulary?"

"Who the hell are you? How did you get in here?"

The man reached into his right chest pocket and pulled out a worn leather billfold. He flipped it open. The photo matched his face and identified him as Calvin Perrone, Central Intelligence Agency.

"It's a pleasure to meet you, Doctor Austin."

Still shaken, Bobby replied, "How did you find me? This location is top secret and this place is totally wired."

"Yeah, I can see. Very impressive. Let's take a walk." Perrone grasped Bobby's forearm firmly with one hand as he opened the door with the other. Walking briskly he ushered Bobby past his staff and out the front door.

"I didn't feel any security guards tackle me. Did I miss something?" He led Bobby to Bobby's car. "Get in and start it up."

Bobby's brow furrowed as his eyes narrowed, but he did what he was told. Perrone gave one hard clap of his hands next to Bobby's left ear as he shouted, "BOOM."

Bobby's face contorted in pain. "Why the hell did you do that?"

"I saved your life again. Get out and look under the car near the exhaust."

Bobby got on his hands and knees and peered at the underside of the car. He looked up at Perrone blankly. "You don't see it, Doctor, do you? Here," Perrone said as he detached the magnetized bomb that had been affixed to the car. "Let's see if you can find the bomb that's been planted outside your office—it would take out half the building." Bobby couldn't find it but Perrone did, of course.

"Can you offer me a cup of coffee now that I've saved your life three times in fifteen minutes?"

"There's a coffee machine in the kitchen," Bobby said sheepishly.

Bobby led Perrone to the kitchen. Perrone poured himself a cup of coffee and opened the refrigerator to get the milk. "Whose sandwich is that?" asked Perrone, as he pointed to the one which was wrapped up in white deli paper, with the initials 'RA' scrawled on it in thick black marker ink.

"Mine."

Perrone laughed. "Lots of secrets in this joint, that's for sure.

Now let's see if your lunch is going to be nice and fresh." Perrone took the sandwich out of the refrigerator and unwrapped it. He removed the bread and several slices of the turkey from each half of the sandwich. He then lifted the swiss cheese slice on each side of the sandwich to reveal a small slip of paper on which the words, "You've been poisioned" were neatly printed.

Bobby just shook his head in disbelief. Perrone motioned toward Bobby's office and Bobby followed him there.

Now behind closed doors, Bobby asked, "So what's this all about?"

"Everybody loves you, Dr. Austin, but not everybody loves you."

"What do you mean by that?" Bobby asked.

"Do you know that you're always in the Top Ten?"

"Top Ten of what?"

Perrone grinned. "The Top Ten of Americans that crazies want to assassinate. After your double Nobel trick a few years ago, you made the Top Five for a few weeks. Are you planning to cure any more diseases?"

"I'm trying," replied Bobby.

"Good. Then you'll have a shot at the top spot. That'll take the pressure off the president."

"You're crazy. I think this is just a bunch of spook mumbo jumbo."

Perrone stepped aggressively forward, his face just inches from Bobby's. "What did you call me?"

"I didn't mean it that way," said Bobby. "I meant 'spook' —like in CIA guys being called spooks—any CIA guys."

Perrone continued to glare at Bobby, his body tense as if ready to pounce. He then broke into a broad smile. "I know that—I was just busting your balls." He gave Bobby a playful punch in the shoulder that Bobby thought was a lot harder than necessary.

Perrone asked, "You think I'm making this stuff up?" He pulled out a laptop from his attaché case which he had stowed in Bobby's office while he was waiting to "kill him." "Here, I can access this stuff easily since my computer is pre-loaded for the sites. Enjoy reading. If you need a translation on any of the chatter, just press this button and it will put it in English for you."

Bobby's mouth went dry as he read.

Perrone's tone turned serious. "So Doctor, you need real security, because you obviously don't have any currently. And if you think nobody else can find this facility, you're wrong. Obviously, my agents had no difficulty in planting the fake bombs and poison, just as I had no difficulty in gaining access to your office so I could shoot you."

Shaking his head, Bobby replied, "Well, you're the CIA so you have the expertise to do all that, but the crazies on the internet don't."

"If I were you, I wouldn't count on that. These fanatics can have sophisticated resources."

Bobby's eyebrows raised as he stared at Perrone. "And why is the CIA wanting to help me?"

"You're a hot topic in Washington, Doctor. You're a national asset."

"I see," said Bobby. "So it's bad for business if I get snuffed out on the current administration's watch."

"Don't sell yourself short, Doctor. It would be bad for any administration. You're one of the few that cross party lines."

Bobby wanted to keep government meddling to a minimum, so the arrangement he made with Perrone was that the CIA technicians would design a state of the art security system for the lab, but it would be installed and monitored by a private security firm that

Bobby would select from a list of recommendations. Additionally, the lab would engage a security service to patrol the premises with bomb sniffing dogs.

"So with this system, I'll have nothing to worry about, right?" Bobby asked Perrone.

"I didn't say that, Doctor. This system will protect you against the ninety-five percent. There's no protection that this facility could realistically have that would protect against the other five percent."

"And who is the 'other five percent?'"

Perrone smiled. "Well, my boys, of course. And the other really good government operatives—ours or overseas. But we're all on your side. As far as the private sector goes—there are very few outfits that have the necessary expertise. But there are some for hire that can be formidable. Unless you want us on the premises at all times, there's nothing you can do about that."

"Thanks for the offer, Calvin. I'll take my chances with the five percent."

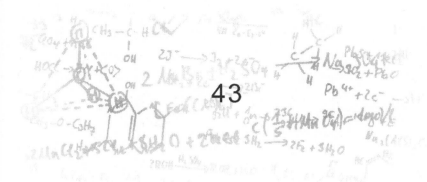

43

SEVERAL WEEKS LATER WHEN BOBBY failed to show up at Tufts or the Manzini lab, Susan was relieved. He was overdue to go incommunicado. She knew he was close to a breakdown from the combined stress of working continuously on the malaria project and his lack of sleep due to the escalation of the nightmares. Every day she'd check his apartment to see if he had crash-landed. Finally, after six days, when she walked through the door, she saw from the disarray that he was back. But there were two things different this time that caught her eye in the apartment. First, there were a large number of sketch pad pages that had been torn out and were strewn haphazardly around the living room. When she examined them she saw that they all bore horrific images that Bobby had drawn. Many of the pages were intact, but others had been crinkled up, and the pictures on those were exceptionally disturbing. Secondly, in the middle of the living room, there was a trunk that was turned over on its side. Susan recognized this trunk as the one that usually sat in a corner of the room, piled high with books. Scattered around the trunk in a large perimeter were piles of magazines, newspapers and clippings.

Bobby was asleep in his bedroom. An empty bottle of vodka was on his nightstand. Happy to see him getting some sleep, she went back into the living room intent on not disturbing him. She stood in the midst of the fallout from the trunk. Unable to resist, she decided she wasn't snooping because the items had been left out in full view. She sat down among all the materials and read for over an hour. Rollie Carter's report wasn't in the pile. She then cleaned-up the living room, loaded the dishwasher, emptied the ashtrays, placed the sketches in a neat stack, arranged the sofa cushions in place, and then righted the trunk and placed its contents back inside.

When Bobby finally stumbled into the living room, she said, "The prodigal son emerges. You look awful. I'll make a pot of coffee."

As hung-over as he was, Bobby instantly scanned the living room and realized that not only had Susan tidied up, but the contents of the trunk had been touched.

"Susan, thanks for cleaning up the place," he said, trying to sound matter of fact. "You really shouldn't have. I guess you just threw those papers into the trunk?"

Susan looked at Bobby. She could read him so well. He was uptight. "Yeah, I just threw the papers into the trunk after I read them."

Bobby inhaled quickly. "You read them? Why would you do that? They were my private papers."

"If they were so private, you shouldn't have left them strewn all over the room for all to see."

"All to see? This is my apartment. Nobody was supposed to see anything here. Damn it, Susan. That was my private business. Just because you have a key doesn't mean that everything is open to inspection."

"Bobby, I'm sorry. But I was curious. I couldn't help it. Anything that's important to you is important to me. And I'm always worried that something or someone is going to hurt you and I want to know what's going on. Blame it on my maternal instincts."

"This is just not how I wanted you to find out. I'm really pissed."

"I'm sorry, Bobby."

"Well, it's done. You read it. So what did you think? Were you surprised?"

"The story was pretty terrible and shocking, but these things do happen," said Susan.

"That's all you have to say?"

"About what?" she asked.

"About me."

"What do you have to do with it, Bobby?"

"What are you talking about, Susan?"

"I don't know. I've lost the plot. What's going on?" she asked.

"What's going on? I can't believe you read all that stuff and missed the whole point. Susan—I'm #2764. I'm Dumpster Baby."

Susan's face drained completely of color as she collapsed into one of the living room chairs. She stared at Bobby. "What did you just say?"

"I'm the baby in the garbage bag. I'm the kid you were reading about. Alan Gottschalk saved my life. He was the guy you hired the PI to find."

"I never knew his name. I never looked at the stuff you gave me for the investigators, or their report, because you asked me not to."

"Well now you know. That's who I am."

"Why didn't you ever tell me?" she asked.

"I've never told anyone."

There was silence as Susan and Bobby looked at each other

forlornly. Susan put her arms around him. She hugged him tightly and sensed the tension in his body. As she pressed her head against his chest, he could feel the wetness of her tears penetrating his thin undershirt. "I wish I could take away all the hurt from you Bobby. I wanted to be your Anna. I wanted to protect you like she protected me."

"I just can't understand why they did it to me. To leave me alone to die like that. What was wrong with me?" Bobby said.

Releasing her grip on Bobby, Susan stood straighter, took a few steps back and commanded, "Sit down."

Bobby sank into the couch obediently. He looked like a lost teenager. Sitting close to him, her knees touching his, she said, "Bobby, people do terrible desperate things for all sorts of reasons, and if they are fueled by drugs or alcohol or have mental problems, horrible things happen. But one thing's for sure— a baby who's a few hours old, didn't do anything wrong. You have nothing to feel ashamed or guilty or embarrassed about. They were defective —not you."

Bobby got up and began to walk around the room aimlessly. Shaking his head, he said, "But there's too much that's unexplained, Susan. Look at what I am. How did that happen? What are the odds that a newborn who's thrown into a dumpster is going to turn out like this? It's too weird. Sometimes I think that what's been said behind my back all these years is true."

Susan put her hands on Bobby's shoulders, giving them a squeeze for emphasis.

"The only way you'll find the answers you're searching for is to look to your faith. I believe you were given your abilities for a reason. I believe you were saved for a reason. Everything that has happened in your life has happened for a reason. You are not alone.

And you're worthy of being loved, and you have been loved. Edith and Peter loved you, Joe loved you, and I love you."

Bobby interrupted, "And I worry about that every day when I see you. Everyone who's ever loved me is dead. So what does that say about your prospects? When people get too close to me, they die."

"That's crazy," Susan said, smiling, as she brushed a strand of hair away from Bobby's eyes. "To get rid of me, you'll have to tie me up and put me on a boat to Shanghai. Otherwise, I'll be around to badger you until you find a special woman to build a life with. And I don't mean a bimbo. I mean someone I approve of."

"Fat chance on that."

"And believe me—when you find her, she'll love you back. But first you have to let go of these demons from your past. You have to put them in that trunk and close the lid tight. You can't keep looking over your shoulder. You have to move on Bobby."

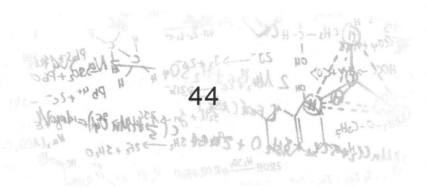

44

CALVIN PERRONE SAT IN HIS small office at CIA headquarters in Langley, Virginia and gazed out his narrow window at a vast parking lot, which was now beginning to accumulate snow as the flurries escalated. He answered the phone and was informed by an officious female voice that the director wanted to see him immediately. He couldn't believe it. The director of the CIA was summoning him, a plain talking guy from a blue collar background, with a Puerto Rican mother and Black father, who grew up in the Bronx and graduated with a B average from St. John's College in Queens. Hired at a time when the agency had fallen into such disfavor that it had no choice but to expand its recruiting practices to include 'types' like him that it had previously shunned, Calvin Perrone was now being invited into the director's inner sanctum. The director knew he existed. Calvin had made the big time. In the ten year period during which Calvin had been a CIA agent, there had been three directors of the CIA, none of whom Calvin had ever met or been permitted to communicate with. The individual who currently held that position was new to the Office, having been confirmed by the Senate only six months previously.

Calvin pulled out the mirror he kept in his desk drawer. He spread his lips into a broad clown's smile so that he could examine his teeth to be sure that no remnants from his lunch were discernible. From his waste basket, he fished out the napkin he had discarded with his food, and wiped his face so it didn't look oily. Holding the mirror up, he straightened his necktie and then maneuvered the mirror so that he could see how his suit looked, or at least how segments of it looked. Walking out of his office, he headed to the far left elevator bank, over which a sign indicated, "Restricted Access."

"I presume you are Agent Calvin Perrone?" The woman in the director's private reception area who asked the question spoke in a voice that was simultaneously authoritative and condescending. "The director will see you now."

As Perrone entered the director's office, the director was standing with his back to him, gazing out his wall of windows onto the CIA campus below. Perrone quickly estimated the size of the director's office as being at least ten times the size of his. The director wasn't a tall man, but he was extremely broad shouldered. *Good guy to have on your side in a bar room brawl*, thought Perrone. "You can sit down, Agent Perrone. Make yourself comfortable," he said without turning around.

Perrone took a seat as the director slowly paced alongside his wall of windows. "So tell me about your meeting with Austin."

Perrone's mind raced. *So that's what this is all about? The lousy little cat and mouse game I played with that crazy scientist.*

"What would you like to know, sir?"

"I want to know everything. Spare no details."

Perrone told the director the minutiae of the fake shooting, bombings and food poisoning, and how that ultimately resulted in an agreement for the design and implementation of a security system for the Prides Crossing premises. The director was silent throughout Perrone's recitation.

"And how did he look? Did he seem healthy?"

Perrone responded with agent learned exactitude. "Since I had never met him previously, I have no prior to compare his current appearance to, but he looked okay. Perhaps a little tired around the eyes, but he's trim and his overall appearance is healthy, although I can tell you that he's not a particularly strong man."

"Oh really—and how can you tell that?"

"He's too thin, and when I grabbed his forearm, he had no real muscle mass or tone there."

"And how was his frame of mind?"

"He's cut from a different piece of cloth, sir. He's very intense, but at the same time, there's something detached about him, like not all of him is present. Sometimes when he'd look at me, it was as if his eyes were searing right through me. I never had anyone look at me the same way. It was definitely odd."

"So why aren't we installing the security system. How did you let that slip by?"

Perrone felt the jab of criticism as if it had been a hard right to his jaw. *So this wasn't a congratulatory, 'job well done' kind of meeting. My first and probably only contact with the director and he's going to tell me I fucked up.* Perrone shifted uneasily on his feet and his posture became rigid. "It wasn't an option, sir. Austin was emphatic about there being no government involvement in his operation. It took a huge effort on my part to get him to agree that the Agency could design the security system and that he'd use a firm on our recommended list to install it and patrol his grounds. Believe me, he has a deep felt suspicion about government. He's very negative on the subject."

Orin Varneys stared at Perrone with his shark eyes for what seemed like an eternity to Perrone. Finally, he nodded in acknowledgment that it could be possible for Austin to hold such a view. "It is what it is. We'll put our people into whatever firm he selects. We need to have control of the situation."

"Understood, director. Any way I can help, please consider me. I think I have a relationship of sorts with Austin at this point."

When Perrone got back to his office, he loosened his tie, took off his jacket and Googled "CIA director's Senate Confirmation Hearings." He then read the transcripts and learned that Orin Varneys, then director of the OSSIS, had garnered appointment and confirmation as CIA director six months earlier, predominantly on the strength of his connection to Robert James Austin. As Varneys said in the course of his testimony before the Senate, "I can say, without hesitation or qualification, that by virtue of the programs and procedures that I established and executed at the OSSIS, Robert James Austin was discovered, recruited, nurtured, developed and educated, and that without this, Dr. Austin would simply not exist as we know him today."

In the history of the CIA, no prior director candidate had ever been able to associate himself with anything even beginning to approach the appeal and visceral impact of claiming personal responsibility for giving the world an asset like Bobby. The fact that Varneys was responsible for cutting-off Bobby from the Institute's resources because Varneys opposed medical research, was an irony that didn't come to light in the confirmation proceedings. The Senate quickly and unanimously approved him as CIA director, and praised him in the Congressional Record for his "extraordinary service to a grateful nation during his tenure as director of the OSSIS."

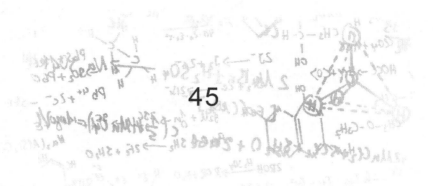

45

SEVERAL MONTHS BEFORE THE RESULTS were published in the medical journals, rumors were already sweeping through the academic community. Bobby's "Sentry Virus," as he had named it because it was always 'on guard and ready to act,' was said to do exactly what it was designed to. The scourge of malaria would soon come to an end. But when Bobby's analysis and lab reports were published, the reality was much bigger than vanquishing this age-old killer. The methodology behind the "Sentry Virus" was also applicable to any "vector" transmitted disease—meaning any disease that is spread to humans by mosquitoes, ticks, lice, fleas or other insects. Bobby's formulas and solutions were there in detail, just awaiting application to diseases such as encephalitis, typhus, sleeping sickness, plague, dengue and leishmaniosis. Additionally, the "Sentry Virus" could be engineered to combat other diseases, such as amoebic dysentery that infect the human body by way of protozoa and other one-celled parasitic organisms. The implications were staggering in scope. As had been the case with Bobby's other breakthroughs, his findings were tested and verified in scores of hospitals worldwide and then in the field.

These discoveries, more than any of his prior achievements, embedded the name Robert James Austin into the vocabulary of tens of millions of people throughout the most populous and economically underprivileged places in the world.

For Bobby, however, the struggle to reach this breakthrough had taken its toll on both his physical and mental health. He was in a severe state of exhaustion that he couldn't pull himself out from under. He looked haggard and beat-up, he was alarmingly thin, and his facile wit had dimmed.

The world media was apoplectic in their determination to find him. They descended on Tufts, but were not satisfied with what they got so they fanned out, frantically looking for the Manzini lab. Susan holed up Bobby, moving him around like a fugitive between the Prides Crossing guest house and his city apartment. But she realized that he was burned-out and needed a complete change of environment, so when Calvin Perrone showed up on the doorstep of the Prides Crossing lab and offered a secure and private "safe house" vacation escape for Bobby to any destination desired, she made the decision that this was an offer that needed to be accepted.

"Just tell me where the good doctor wants to go, and we can provide a perfect absolutely private setting," Perrone said.

"Bobby told me about you, Calvin, and you know his feelings. We're not looking for any freebies from the government. The foundation is perfectly capable of paying for this. Dr. Austin hasn't had a holiday in years and I don't think anyone would begrudge him that."

"Completely understood. We'll work that out later. But no one can give you the privacy and security that we can. Just tell me where."

"You understand that he can't be disturbed or intruded upon in any way by anyone —including you guys?" said Susan.

"That's the whole point, isn't it?"

"And why is your organization doing this?"

"It comes from the very top—it's bigger than my firm. People are concerned about the doctor."

———————————•·•———————————

Susan went to Bobby's apartment and began to pack his suitcase. "Where are your bathing suits, shorts and casual clothing for the summer?"

"All I have is what's in the closet and drawers."

"Forget it. We'll do some shopping in St. Thomas. "

"St. Thomas?" asked Bobby.

"Yes, We're leaving tomorrow morning. It's all arranged. It'll be totally private. You'll love it. I'm bringing Anna. She's the best security you'll ever have."

"How private can it be when the check-in people see my ticket and passport, and we go through customs in St. Thomas?"

"We're not flying that way. We're hitching a ride. Trust me. Just relax."

The next morning a taxi swung by to pick up Bobby. Susan and Anna were already inside.

"What time's our flight?" Bobby asked.

Susan ignored his question and instructed the driver to take them to Hanscom Field in Bedford.

"That's an odd place to leave from," said Bobby. "What time's our flight?"

"Whenever we get there," responded Susan.

Bobby looked at her. "What's the airline?"

Susan raised her eyebrows as she glared at him. "Bobby, please just sit back and relax and stop with the questions. Leave it to me. Take a nap or something."

When the taxi pulled into the small airport, Susan called the cell phone number she had been given by Perrone and got further instructions. She told the taxi driver that he could drive on to the tarmac directly in front of runway seven. The taxi pulled up to the side of a gleaming white Learjet 45XR. It had no airline name or any other markings on it, other than a registration number. Two tall well-built men in dark blue suits and sunglasses were standing outside the plane, together with a uniformed crew member.

"Now that's what I call traveling in style," the taxi driver said.

Bobby's eyes narrowed. "Susan, what's going on? The Foundation can't afford private planes, and those two guys standing there don't look like flight attendants."

"Bobby, please. For once, just relax. I've made these arrangements and I've covered all the bases, and it's fine. Don't micromanage. You're not in the lab. Your vacation starts now."

The plane landed on a military airstrip in St. Thomas. It taxied right up to a black SUV that was waiting. After a thirty minute bumpy ride that seemed to traverse the entire island, the SUV approached the gatehouse of what was obviously a large estate. Credentials cleared, the vehicle drove along a winding drive majestically lined with Royal Palms on both sides that led to a circular driveway fronting a palatial coral stone mansion in the Mediterranean style. As they disembarked, they were cheerily greeted by a staff member of the property who was casually dressed in white slacks and a red and white flower print shirt.

"Welcome to Villa Azur Reve. I'm George Harkens and I'm in charge of this wonderful home. I hope your journey was pleasant. Don't worry about your bags, they will be attended to. Please come with me."

It was only when they walked up the carved coral staircase and entered the columned open-air reception atrium, that they realized the house was beachfront. The only thing standing between their weary Boston bones and the sun baked sands, was a series of beautiful terraced gardens which led passed the mosaic tiled swimming pool to the healing waters of the aqua blue Caribbean Sea.

"This is drop dead gorgeous," Susan said.

"I'm never going home," proclaimed Anna.

"I'll show you around Azur Reve later. You'll see that we have every amenity you could desire including a chef, of course. But first, you must be thirsty."

Seemingly out of nowhere, a very attractive young lady appeared holding a tray with three festive looking cocktails.

Smiling broadly, Bobby said, "I'm beginning to feel relaxed already."

Azur Reve proved to be exactly what Bobby needed. He spent hours a day on the beach, staring out at the ocean and walking for miles. When he got hot, he plunged in to the purifying froth and body surfed. Susan and Anna were great companions, but he enjoyed just zoning out and falling asleep on a bed sheet he'd place on the hot sand, his head hard pressed against it, hearing the surf as he drifted off while his body replenished its supply of vitamin D. In the late afternoon, he went to the pool and did scores of laps. Throughout the day, he ate well and refreshed himself with a steady stream of island cocktails. In the evening, he enjoyed walking in the illuminated gardens of the estate, listening to the sounds, and breathing deeply of the scents, gifted by the Caribbean night. His nightmares ceased and he didn't think about work. He began to grow stronger physically and restore himself mentally. His appearance improved markedly as his rejuvenation proceeded. "You're beginning to look like some kind of tanned Greek god," said Susan.

"I have to admit that you're looking pretty good," Anna said.

"I feel so free here. I haven't felt this way in so many years. I wish I could always feel like this," he said.

"You can. You've earned it. You owe nothing to anyone. You've made a contribution worthy of twenty lifetimes. Let it go, Bobby. Live. You've done enough," said Susan.

"I don't know how much longer I can go on with what I've been doing. But I can't give up yet. It's not right."

"It is right. Let it go. It's time for you to live a normal life. The world owes you, you owe nothing."

"Not yet, Susan. There'll be a time."

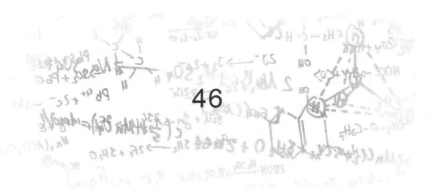

46

A YOUNG WOMAN, PROBABLY NOT MORE than 27, stood perusing beach bags in the store aisle of "Traders Paradise," one of the numerous tourist shops in Charlotte Amalie, St. Thomas' capital city.

For one so slender and athletic looking, she was remarkably shapely. Standing five feet nine, she had the legs of a Broadway dancer —technically too long relative to her torso, but no man would ever complain. Her silky dark hair hung mid-way down her back and was held in place by a light green paisley headband that accentuated emerald eyes. A transparent orange print sarong was wrapped around her hips, low-slung and extending down to leather sandals, whose straps were decorated with beadwork. Underneath the sarong, one could discern a pale yellow bikini bottom. There were so many bangle bracelets on her tanned arms that it looked like she was selling them, and sets of simple silver rings adorned five of her graceful fingers. On her, the entire bohemian outfit was beguiling and natural.

On a mission to supplement his island attire, Bobby entered the store and began making his way past the souvenirs to the clothing.

He turned into her aisle and noticed her immediately, as she stood on her toes stretching to pull down some beach bags from a high shelf. When she reached upward, her back arced gracefully and her toned thighs flexed. She grabbed the edge of one of the bags, and a huge pile of them came tumbling down on her head.

"Let me help you with that," Bobby said as he hurried over to her.

Blushing as she bent down to pick up the bags, she said, "I'm such a klutz sometimes."

Bobby crouched down to help, his mind registering the heady scent of her perfume combined with the remnants of coconut oil from her sun-tan lotion.

As she continued to examine the beach bags which they had stacked on a more accessible shelf, Bobby began sorting through the men's clothing, quickly picking out items. "Could I impose on you for just a moment?" he asked.

She turned her head and looked directly at him for the first time. He felt a jolt of energy, almost like an electric current. He had never felt anything like that before. "This store was recommended to me for shirts and shorts, but I don't have a clue what will look good on me. Can you give me a hand so I don't embarrass myself?" he asked.

Her laugh was followed by a smile that allowed her flawless teeth to gleam as her full lips parted playfully. "I'll give you my opinion, but I warn you — my taste can be quirky."

"Well— here are the ones I picked. What do you think?" Bobby asked.

"You're kidding, right?"

Bobby feigned a hurt expression.

"Unless you want to be refused a table in any good restaurant, put those down and step back from the shelves immediately."

She pressed past him in the narrow aisle as she focused her attention on the clothing displays and began to pull items off the shelf.

Bobby said, "I didn't mean to put you to so much trouble."

She turned to face him. Those emeralds, perfectly framed by elegantly determined eyebrows and long heavy lashes, looked right through him. "This will be my good deed for the day. The entire St. Thomas community will be spared the debilitating effects of severe color clash. And besides, you were very kind to help me with those bags."

A few minutes later, she said, "Now let's see how these look." She began to hold up each garment against him while she evaluated. "Very good— if I say so myself. You're all set. You won't scare small children."

"You've been so incredibly nice— let me buy you a cold drink. I just passed this big open-air bar in Hibiscus Alley right around the corner." Bobby was jabbering like an excited school boy. "It's just this huge crazy free-standing bar in between all these stores." He extended his hand. "I'm Bobby."

Smiling as she touched his hand lightly, she replied, "Christina Moore."

Bobby paused and mumbled quickly, "Bobby Nitsua."

"I'd love to—but I really need to finish my shopping and get back to my hotel," she said.

Bobby was crestfallen. *What would Joe do now? He was the king of smooth.* "Please, I insist. You've done a service for all of St. Thomas—even the wildlife—by keeping me from making a sartorial fool of myself. Just one quick drink."

Christina looked at Bobby. She was wondering if this whole clothing selection process had just been a pick-up scheme. But she had to admit— he was very good looking—and his eyes were mesmerizing. She had never seen clarity and depth like that before.

"Sartorial. Now there's a word you don't hear too often. You must play a lot of scrabble," she said.

Bobby laughed. "I guess I do have to get out more."

"OK, one quick drink," she said.

One of the things Bobby loved about St. Thomas is that unlike most mainland U.S. cities, in St. Thomas alcohol is permitted everywhere. People walk up and down Main Street at all hours sucking on twenty-four ounce drinks which are 4 parts local rum and 1 part fruit juice. Bobby and Christina sat down on the chrome stools of the Hibiscus Alley bar, a thirty foot long mirrored wonder that looked like it had been swept in by the sea from a distressed cruise ship.

"And what can I get you folks to drink?" asked the bartender, who seemed like he already had sampled a few.

"Any special drink you're famous for?" Bobby asked.

"Well, my favorite is my own recipe developed over years of experimentation. I call it 'The Billy Punch.' If you're not satisfied, the drink's on me."

"Can't refuse that deal," replied Bobby.

"Make it two," Christina said.

Bobby watched the bartender prepare the concoction with one hand, as he sipped from his own tall glass which he held in the other. 'Billy Punch' featured five different flavored rums, topped off by a 151 proof variety. Composed entirely of alcohol, the drink tasted like harmless fruit juice.

"How long are you here for?" Bobby asked Christina.

"I only arrived a few days ago. I'm here for another week or so. What about you?"

"I've been here for a week, but I'm staying for another two. I haven't had a vacation in ages and I got pretty burned out. But I'm on the mend now."

They clinked glasses. "Where are you staying?" he asked.

"Over at Bolongo Beach Resort. It's nice and I got a great deal. What about you?"

"I'm staying at a friend's. He has a fantastic beach house on the other side of the Island."

"Sounds swanky," she said.

"It is actually. In my next life, I'm going to be a drug lord so I can buy one just like it."

"Is that what your friend does?" she asked.

"No, he's in the government. An even more lucrative racket," replied Bobby smiling.

"What do you do back in the real world, Bobby?"

"I'm a research scientist. Sounds pretty dull, huh?"

Christina laughed. "It's refreshing. Every guy I meet says he's in banking."

"Right. That's just one move on the monopoly board before you get to drug lord."

Christina laughed again. Her eyes sparkled and her face radiated a warmth that Bobby could feel. "Now don't be bitter about career choices. Where do you live?" she asked.

"Boston. You?"

"I grew up in New York City, but I moved to California for grad school. I just moved to Rhode Island for a post-grad fellowhip at Brown."

"What did you study?" Bobby asked.

"In college—Sarah Lawrence—I was kind of a hippie. Dual major—performance arts and math. At Stanford, I was in a math and chem grad program, but my doctorate is in math."

Bobby whistled silently. *This goddess has a Ph.D in math. Yikes!* "That's amazing. I never heard of a dual major like that." Bobby was half through his drink and feeling it.

"My mom was a dance teacher at the Music and Art High School in New York, which I attended. She's incredibly artistic. My dad was a mathematician. A real prodigy, but he died when I was very young. So I guess I got a little bit of each of them in me. Anyway—that's enough about me." Christina stared at her drink.

Bobby took a long swig of the mind numbing potion in his glass and then got up the courage to say, "I hope you won't be offended, but I have to tell you that you are without doubt the most beautiful mathematician I've ever seen—and I've seen quite a few, trust me."

Christina blushed. "That's sweet of you. But in academic circles, a nice appearance isn't always an asset for a female." She sipped at her drink looking pensive. She then glanced at her wristwatch and said, "Oh my God. Look at what time it is. I'm sorry, but I really have to run. Thank you for the drink." She dismounted the barstool.

Bobby scrambled to do damage control. "Perhaps we can hang out on the beach or have lunch one of these days? Could I have your number?"

"My cell's gone bust. Just call the hotel. Nice to meet you, Bobby."

As she left, he caught a last whiff of her perfume as it wafted toward him in the gentle breeze.

47

WHEN BOBBY GOT BACK TO the mansion, he was excited but also disappointed. He sought Susan's counsel. "I met an incredible girl in town."

"I can just imagine," replied Susan.

"Artistic, brilliant, gorgeous and a heart of gold."

"And you determined all that out in how long?"

"We helped each other in the store and had a drink. Even you would be impressed. She has a Ph.D in math from Stanford."

Susan looked shocked. "Where's George? I have to ask him for some gasoline so I can set you on fire. You are not Bobby Austin. Bobby Austin never went out with a girl who even had a college degree."

Bobby smiled. "Susan, I'm telling you. When she looked at me I felt something I never felt before. It freaked me out. She's incredible."

"When do I get to meet her?"

"That's the problem. She blew me off after our drink. Gave me the brush."

"You're telling me that the greatest scientist in the history of the planet, who just happens to be a really good looking guy—got kissed off without getting a first date?"

"She didn't know who I am. I told her my name was Bobby Nitsua. I never tell girls who I am."

"Nitsua? You pulled that one out of the air?"

Bobby waved away the question.

"Bobby—that's fine when you're hanging out with strippers, hookers and club kids and you need to be anonymous—but if it's a woman you think might be right for a relationship—what are you—crazy?" Bobby looked forlorn. "Oh that's right," she continued. "All the intelligence in the world, but no common sense. I forgot."

"I'm going to call her in the morning," he said.

"Fine, or you can even text her later today."

"I don't have her phone number. She said her cell was broken. I can try to reach her at the hotel."

"Terrific, Romeo. Just terrific."

Next morning at nine sharp, Bobby called the Bolongo Beach Resort and asked for Christina Moore. He held his breath, hoping that they didn't say they had no guest by that name. The receptionist put him through. After six unanswered rings, the voice-mail came on and Bobby left a message with his number. Bobby was on edge the entire day and didn't go swimming to be sure he didn't miss her call. There was no call. He called again at 5 pm and it was the same situation. At dinner that night, Bobby was quiet. Disappointment was written all over his face. Finally, he said to Susan and Anna, "I guess she has no interest. I wish she had given me a chance."

Anna put down her fork and said, "Bobby, I know a thing or two about chasing women. When you want a woman, you don't hold back. You can't be afraid to go out and pursue her—show her you're really interested. You have nothing to lose."

Bobby nodded and slapped the table. "You're right, Anna. Sometimes it takes a lesbian to set a guy straight," he said chuckling.

At eight in the morning the next day, Bobby called George. "Can someone drive me to the Bolongo Beach Resort now? I have some business over there."

"No problem. I'll have Steven do it."

At 8:40, Bobby walked into the Bolongo Beach Resort's lobby. He asked where the breakfast room was. He got a table and figured he'd wait for Christina to show up. He waited until 10:30. He then called her room—no answer. He walked down to the beach and began to cruise among the lounge chairs and sun umbrellas, trying to look casual. Finally, at the far end of the crescent shaped beach, he spotted her lying on a lounge in a pale pink bikini, eating a banana and sipping water from a large bottle. He felt his heartbeat immediately accelerate and the pulse in his head began to pound. He was happy and excited, but also nervous. *I've got to get a grip. I'm like a high school kid. What's wrong with me?* Summoning his gumption and steeling himself for rejection, he walked toward her, trying to look as confident and matter of fact as possible.

"Hello there," he said to her. "I thought I'd check this place out for some friends who are coming down from back East, since you said it was so good." As soon as the words left his mouth, he knew how lame it sounded. Christina just looked at him and said nothing. After an awkward moment had passed, he said, "Actually, I had left you a few voice-mails and thought that maybe you didn't get them, so I wanted to stop by and say hello."

"And why's that— Bobby Nitsua?" She was clearly busting his chops and it made it all the worse because she looked so stunning in her little bikini—her tanned oiled skin glistening in the sun.

"You're not making this easy on me are you?" he said.

"No one ever said I was easy."

"I really enjoyed our meeting the other day and I wanted to see you again. I was hoping you felt the same. Evidently I was wrong."

"Do you reach conclusions that precipitously in the lab also, doctor?"

Bobby smiled. "Well, I do owe you an apology. My name isn't Nitsua."

"You're not Japanese?"

"I'm so used to protecting my anonymity—it comes as second nature to me."

"And anagrams are your chosen method?" Bobby blushed. Christina laughed and broke into a broad smile. Bobby couldn't get over how naturally beautiful she looked.

"It's a pleasure to meet you, Dr. Austin." She laughed again. "You're different from what people expect. Everyone thinks you're some fat bald nerdy myopic ogre who lives in a laboratory cave and eats small children."

"I hope I didn't disappoint you," he said.

Christina smiled again. "You look flushed—have a drink of water." She handed him her bottle, which he interpreted as an initial gesture of intimacy. "I hope that's a swimsuit you're wearing", she said.

"It just became one."

"Good, let's go in."

Christina sprang up from her lounge chair with the grace and energy of a professional dancer. Pulling up on her bikini top, she said, "Damn, the sand's hot," and began to run to the water. Bobby took the cue and started to run beside her. The two dove into the crystal clear aqua elixir at the same time.

"You can swim right? I don't want to drown you and become the most hated woman on the planet."

She began heading out to the deeper cooler water and Bobby did his best to keep up. Now alone, well past any other swimmers, they both flipped over on their backs and floated effortlessly in the buoyant water. They just floated and said nothing. The sun warmed their faces and the top sides of their bodies, while they were kept cool from below. Finally, Bobby said, "It's so incredibly beautiful out here I almost can't bear it."

"Afraid it will end?"

"I'm always afraid good things in my life will end. They always do."

"You have to believe in the future or there is no future," she replied.

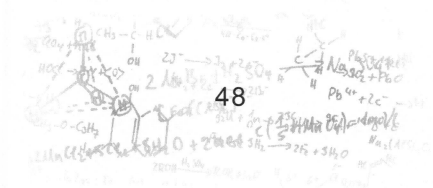

48

BOBBY PREPPED SUSAN AND ANNA for Christina's visit to Azur Reve. "Ladies, I need you to promise me you'll be on good behavior with Christina."

"What does that mean?" asked Susan.

"It mainly means that you shouldn't say or even intimate anything negative about me that might turn her off."

"Like what?" asked Susan, who was enjoying every moment of Bobby's nervousness.

"Like no comments about me being an obsessive workaholic, having nightmares, falling into trances, not having any social life, only going out with bimbos, drinking too much, being a slob or a recluse."

"So we shouldn't give her any insight into what you're really like?" Susan grinned.

"Let me clarify it for you honey," Anna said to Susan, "Bobby wants us to help perpetuate the illusion he's trying to create."

Bobby shook his head. "I knew I could count on your support. But seriously, I don't want to scare Christina away."

Susan smiled at Bobby. She realized that he was bringing this woman to meet the only family that he had. "Bobby, don't worry—we'll be perfectly charming. Your secrets are safe with us." Anna let out a hearty belly laugh.

Bobby picked Christina up at Bolongo Beach. Radiant in white shorts and a tight aqua T-shirt that made her eyes almost look blue, she wore no make-up other than pink lip gloss and some light mascara. Her hair was pulled back into a pony tail that gave her the appearance of a college freshman. Her simple outfit highlighted her lithe but voluptuous figure. Bobby was enthralled.

"You look amazing," he said.

"I'm just dressed for a day at the beach. My bathing suit is under these clothes."

"Really— I don't see any lines—that must be one small bathing suit."

"You have a problem with that, Doctor?"

Bobby had asked George to have some rum punches served as soon as he and Christina arrived at the house, but George did one better. He and a server were waiting at the bottom of the stairs when Bobby's car pulled up. Extending his hand to Christina, George said, "Welcome to Villa Azur Reve."

Susan and Anna were discretely absent as Bobby showed Christina around the estate, and then they headed down to the beach where two lounges, a sun umbrella and an assortment of beach towels were awaiting them. Already wearing a swim suit, Bobby took off his shirt. Christina began to remove her shorts and T-shirt while Bobby tried to act like he wasn't watching her undress. "I'll put some sun screen on your back, if you'll do me," she said. Bobby's face lit up as she handed him the bottle. Placing his lotion drenched hands on her lean toned back, her skin was satiny smooth and supple. As he ran his fingers down the full length of the arced indentation of her spine, and around to her sides, and over the two perfectly placed dimples right above her bathing suit line, he marveled at just how sexy a woman's back can be.

"You alright there?" she asked, laughing. "You didn't get lost, did you?"

"I think I zoned out for a moment."

"Thinking about an equation?"

"Sort of." He laughed.

As they walked along the beach, she said, "So you said you came down here with your assistant and her girlfriend?"

"Susan, my assistant, and Anna. Susan's much more than my assistant. She's really my surrogate mother at this point, for better or worse."

"And your real mother?"

"I don't know who my birth mother was. I was raised by foster parents from the time I was a few weeks old. They died in a car crash when I was 11. I've been on my own since then."

"Oh my God. I'm so sorry. I had no idea."

Bobby stopped walking and turned toward Christina and gently took hold of each of her hands. "Christina, I need to know that everything I tell you will remain absolutely confidential between us. That's the only way I can be open with you." Christina looked into Bobby's eyes and nodded.

The remainder of the day was spent swimming, body surfing and sunbathing, followed by a late lunch and drinks served to them on the beach by the Azur Reve staff who set-up a white linen covered dining table and chairs not far from the water's edge. Gazpacho, lobster salad, assorted cheeses and berries, and an ice-cold Pinot Grigio made for the perfect repast. Afterwards, Bobby said to

Christina, "That was spectacular, but I think the sun is getting to me. I'm going to get some rest in the shade. Care to join me?"

Christina blushed. "Sounds like a good idea."

They retired into the estate's beach side cabana, which was a simple but elegant looking structure comprised of rustic beams supporting a thatched roof, and enclosed on all sides by sheer white flowing drapes. As Bobby and Christina lay facing each other on the large sectional sofa, he said, "Do you know that you have very unusual eyes?"

"And why's that?"

"Well, they have the color and clarity of emeralds, and they're large and almond shaped, but they curve upwards at their outer ends. Very exotic."

"So you studied this in some detail, I see," said Christina.

"I try to be observant." Bobby's arm reached around Christina's waist as he moved his head toward hers. The smell of sea salt on her warm skin intoxicated him. Her eyes closed and her lips parted. As they kissed, she placed the palm of one of her hands gently against the side of Bobby's face and pressed her bikini clad body against him. As excited as Bobby was, he realized he felt something else also. He felt comfortable. He felt like he was where he should be.

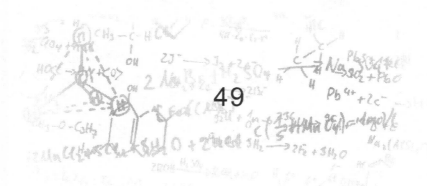

49

THE NEXT MORNING, BOBBY CALLED Christina at her hotel to say he couldn't get together that day because he had some personal business to take care of. He asked Steven to give him a ride to the docks of Red Hook where he boarded the ferry from St. Thomas to St. John, a distance of eight miles. As Bobby sat on the ferry staring at the island of St. John as it came closer into view, his mind took him back to that magical seventeenth birthday trip with Joe on *Dreamweaver*. Stepping onto the weathered wooden boards of St. John pier, he was lost in memories, alive and vivid, his powers of recall being photographic to the extreme. The Asolare restaurant was still there. He went into the bar and sat down. How much had happened in Bobby's life since he last was here. It seemed like an eternity ago.

"Do you have McCallan 18 scotch," he asked the bartender. "I need two doubles. Please put each in a separate glass, with rocks."

As Bobby sipped the scotch, he looked around. The décor hadn't changed. *Kate's mom and Joe were standing there. Kate right over here. Me, next to her.* He remembered it all—even every word of his conversation with Kate—a conversation that as far as he was concerned, had changed his life. Bobby finished his drink and then told the bartender he was taking the other glass down to the beach. "No problem—just bring it back when you're finished."

Bobby walked down to the water's edge and looked out at the bay. *Dreamweaver was anchored right there. We pulled our dinghy up over here when Joe and I had dinner that night and met them.* Bobby remembered how excited he had been that night, barely able to sleep in anticipation of the next day, and how his heart literally was skipping beats as the dinghy approached the beach with Kate and Kim standing in the shadow of the sea grape trees, waiting for them. Bobby sat down on the sand and closed his eyes. He let the memories completely overtake him, his inner eyelids becoming the movie screen on which they played in cinematic detail. After awhile, he became self conscious as he felt he was being watched, so he got up and walked toward the deserted end of the crescent beach.

Standing by the water's edge, he held the glass of scotch up high. The sun's golden threads refracted on its edge, making a rainbow. "I hope you can hear me. It's been a long time since we were here together. Do you remember, Joe?" Bobby sipped the drink and looked up to the sky, his eyes squinting from the brightness, but he struggled to keep them open. He wanted to keep them open and feel the strength and purity of the light. The tiny waves of the incoming tide lapped at Bobby's feet as the most delicate of undertows undermined his steadfastness, pulling the smooth lava sand through his toes in an oddly comforting way. After a time, Bobby felt a different kind of wave. It was a wave of overwhelming contentment washing through him. "You're here," he murmured. "My Captain is here." Bobby's face instantly looked years younger as his smile became that of a seventeen year old on the best adventure of his life. "I'm trying to make you proud, Joe. I really am. It's not easy, but I'm doing the best I can. I miss you every day. Every single day, I miss you." Bobby stood there for a few more minutes with his eyes shut tight. He felt so peaceful. So protected. So loved. When the warmth of the sun became obscured by a dark cloud that had moved across the sky, Bobby opened his eyes. He took another sip of the drink, and then crouched down low to the ground. He slowly poured the rest of it into the ocean water, right where the sea breaks on the shoreline.

———————————

At breakfast the next morning with Susan and Anna, Bobby seemed unusually serene.

"Are you okay, Bobby?—you seem almost zen -like today," said Susan.

"I just was thinking about yesterday when I went to St. John."

"Fond memories?"

"More than that," replied Bobby. His cell phone rang.

Christina's voice surged through him like an electric current instantly reminding him of their closeness in the beach cabana. "Good morning, doctor. It's time for me to reciprocate so I'm inviting you to the official Bolongo Bay Resort beach party tonight. Care to be my date?"

"Now that's a rhetorical question," said Bobby.

"Good. Be here at seven and don't tell me you don't know how to dance. I'll meet you in the lobby."

When Bobby hung up the phone, he saw Anna nodding at Susan knowingly, with a smile on her face. "I've never seen you blush when you're on the phone," said Anna to Bobby.

"Well, you two haven't met Christina yet," he replied.

When Bobby walked into the Bolongo Bay Resort a bit before seven in the evening, the calypso band was already playing on the beach and people were milling about in the dimly lit lobby, happily cradling large flammable drinks. Bobby didn't see Christina. He walked through the portico on to the beach. The only illumination came from the dazzling astral display in the Caribbean sky and the tiki torches burning in the breeze, their long plumes of fragrant smoke evocative of ancient tribal rituals. The moist tropical air was heavy with the sensual scent of bougainvillea and hibiscus which mixed with the smell of the sea to create an intoxicating perfume that went straight to Bobby's head. Finally, he spotted her on the beach, near the band, her body gently swaying to the melodious rhythms. He didn't go to meet her. He just wanted to look. And he noticed that he wasn't the only one looking. Many of the men present, whether they were alone or with their wives or girlfriends, were looking at Christina. Some were more discreet than others, but they were definitely looking. And it was no wonder. Wearing white leather sandals that laced to just below her knees, a striking contrast against her darkly tanned and oiled skin, Christina was attired in a white silk mini skirt and matching backless halter top that tied around her neck. Her luxuriant shining dark hair was swept up and held in place by two white chop sticks—adding an exotic Asian touch, which also highlighted her slender neck. Her eyes were made up more than usual, looking like those portrayed in Egyptian artwork. Her bare midsection, adorned with a small diamond belly ring, was as flat and toned as that of a gymnast. As she moved to the music, the gracefulness of her figure evidenced itself from all angles.

Bobby made his way over to her from behind and placed his hands on her waist as he leaned into her and whispered, "So how does it feel to be the most beautiful woman on this entire island?"

Christina turned and gazed into his eyes. As gorgeous as she had looked at fifty feet, to be this close to her took his breath away.

Laughing, she said, "Well, you're not so shabby looking yourself. Now— are you going to get me a drink or do I have to ask that guy over there?" She nodded discreetly in the direction of a hotel guest who was loitering nearby.

By one in the morning the crowd was thinning out as inebriated guests headed back to their rooms. Giddy from more than their fair share of rum cocktails, Bobby and Christina began to walk along the beach. Christina let go of his hand, kicked off her sandals and began to run along the shore. "Come on slow poke—try to catch me," she yelled over her shoulder.

Bobby soon caught her up to her, and then they ran together, holding hands, ankle deep in the warm ocean water which splashed up against them. The band kept playing, but as Bobby and Christina got farther and farther away, the music became a faint backdrop to the sounds of the nighttime sea. With the tiki lights now far in the distance and both of them wet from their run, Bobby stopped to catch his breath. He gently pulled her close to him. "I'm so happy we met. I've never known a woman I could really talk to and feel comfortable with like this." Bobby began to kiss her, lightly and playfully at first, but it didn't take long for the heat of their attraction to ignite. Christina's body melted into his as she buried her hands in his hair. His hand moved down her back.

Tiny waves gently lapping at their feet, their bodies were pressed together so closely that from a distance their silhouette appeared to be that of a single person. Face flushed with excitement and lipstick smudged, Christina suddenly pulled her head back from his.

"What's wrong?" Bobby asked.

"I just want to look into your eyes. I love your eyes, Bobby."

———————————————

As Bobby and Christina exited their taxi, the only sound they heard was the relentless drone of the pounding surf at Azur Reve. By the time the humid breeze blowing in from the sea reached the swimming pool area where they encamped, it had been scented with the heady fragrance of the estate's gardens, imparting to the night air an eroticism peculiar to the Caribbean. The pool glowed like a huge sapphire, as steam rose seductively from the surface of its warm waters and dissipated in the palm fronds towering above.

"My God, this is beautiful," said Christina.

"Certainly is," said Bobby, looking at her. "Let's go to the kitchen, but be quiet so we don't wake Susan and Anna." Stealthily, the pair made their way into the villa and removed a bottle of champagne, cheese, and pate from the well stocked refrigerator. They lay their bounty on a lounge chair next to the pool.

"Oh damn—I've got to get my swimsuit."

"That's not fair—I don't have one," said Christina.

Bobby smiled. "We'll have to improvise." Without wasting any time, he began to remove his clothes and motioned for her to do likewise.

"Hey buddy. There's no free show here," she said.

"Oh come on."

Christina waited for Bobby to get completely nude and enjoyed his self-consciousness as she walked over to him fully clothed.

Sauntering around him in mock inspection, she said, "Not quite a Chippendale- but not bad for a 6-time Nobel winner."

Bobby blushed. "Now it's your turn," he said, as he waved his hand signaling that she should get on with it.

"No," she replied. "I think I'll just jump into the pool with all my clothes on like they do in those old movies."

Seeing the disappointment instantly register on Bobby's face, Christina laughed, "Look at you. You're like a little kid who arrived at the candy store just as the 'closed' sign got hung on the door." Unbuttoning her skirt, she let it fall to the tile floor. She removed her halter top in one seamless movement. Walking over to the deep end of the pool, she dipped her foot into the water to test its temperature. Then, looking at Bobby, she teasingly stripped off her panties. Bobby watched mesmerized.

"I've seen a lot of good looking women in my time, but you're in a whole different league. You're a freaking goddess."

"Bobby, stop trying to butter me up and let's go swimming." She dove in, her svelte form cleaving the water without a splash. Gliding effortlessly underneath its glimmering surface for the entire length of the pool, she looked luminescent in the underwater lights. When she surfaced, her emerald eyes glowed, and her long dark hair hung straight back, close to her head like the helmet of an ancient female warrior.

Standing up in shallow water, only a few feet away from Bobby, her strong back was arced, her breasts projected forward, and her dancer's thighs flexed gracefully, as the droplets of water on her skin reflected the Caribbean moonlight. Bobby waded in next to her.

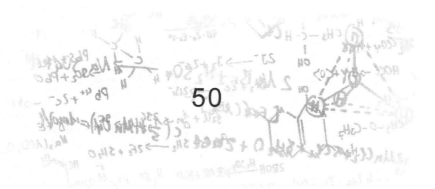

50

SLEEPING POOLSIDE ON A DOUBLE chaise-lounge, Bobby and Christina didn't awaken until almost noon. When they walked back up to the mansion, they were greeted by Susan and Anna who were sitting on the patio. Bobby made the introductions.

"Susan, Anna—I'd like you to meet Dr. Christina Moore. Christina—this is Susan, my right arm and very close friend, —and Anna, her wife, and also my good friend." Christina looked mortified, standing there barefooted, hair unkempt, no make-up, wearing a rumpled terry robe. This was not how she wanted to meet Bobby's surrogate family for the first time.

"It's such a pleasure to meet you both," said Christina. "I've heard so much about you. But I really have to apologize for my appearance. It's been a crazy twelve hours."

"Sweetie—when you look like you do, you never have to apologize for your appearance. Bobby said you were gorgeous and you are," said Anna smiling broadly.

"Don't be silly," Susan said. "You're dressed for the beach. I've been wondering when we'd get to meet you. Why don't we all have lunch together a little later."

"I really should go back to the hotel to get some clean clothes."

"Don't worry about that," said Susan. "Your outfit from last night has already been dry cleaned and put into one of the guest rooms by the Villa staff. Believe it or not, they have their own dry cleaning machine here."

"That's amazing," said Christina.

"This place is like a six star hotel," said Anna.

As Susan escorted Christina to her room, she said, "You'll have to tell me all about yourself later. Did you have a good time last night?"

"We had an amazing time," Christina said, beaming.

"That's terrific. I haven't seen Bobby this happy—ever."

"He's so different from anything I ever imagined," said Christina.

"Bobby has many facets. He's a complex person. You're bringing out something wonderful in him that's been buried. But you'll find everything out in your own time. Bobby doesn't like me talking about him."

The guest room that the Villa staff had put Christina's things in was a huge corner bedroom with views out to the ocean. Christina let her robe drop to the floor and stood in front of the full length mirror looking at herself. "He called me a goddess. No one ever called me a goddess," she said softly to herself. She smiled as she traced her body with her fingers.

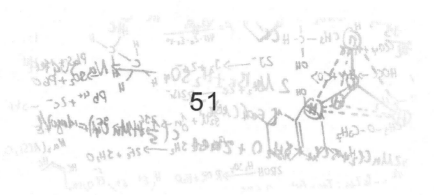

51

SITTING IN HIS OFFICE, CALVIN Perrone examined the large stack of eight by ten photographs on his desk one more time. There were at least fifty of them, taken at all times of the night and day at various locations, but all were of uniformly good quality. He sealed them in a manila envelope. He then walked out of his office, went over to the far left elevator, and went through the procedure that he now was familiar with to see the director. He handed Varneys the envelope, who removed the photographs and methodically studied each one while Perrone sat in silence for almost twenty minutes. "This is all of them?" Varneys asked.

"Yes, sir."

"Do you have audio tapes?"

Perrone nodded. "All conversations in the house, its vehicles, phones, the pool area, the beach cabana and when they were sitting on the beach chairs."

"Did you bring me complete transcripts of the tapes?"

Perrone pursed his lips as he handed a second envelope to Varneys.

Varneys drummed his fingers on his desk. "Did you listen to the tapes?"

"Yes."

Varneys eyebrows raised. "And your opinion?"

"A worthwhile read for you, sir."

"The surveillance will continue for the duration of the trip?"

"Of course."

A miniscule smile appeared on Varneys' face as he said, "Well, it looks like our boy is getting the rest and relaxation he needed. And how do things stand overall?"

Perrone's brow furrowed. "We're picking up an escalated danger level. His malaria cure is the final straw for some of the fanatics. And there's other information we're coming across which is disturbing."

Varneys resumed his finger drumming. "Like what?"

"The pharmaceutical industry."

"Anything concrete?"

"No."

Varneys pointed his right forefinger at Perrone like it was a gun. "Watch that one. There's been trouble with them before. Are you satisfied with his safety in St. Thomas?"

"He hasn't been out of our sight for a moment."

"And you implemented our discussions?"

Perrone nodded emphatically. "With him and the Corwin lady out of the way, we were able to get the Prides Crossing facility and his Boston apartment totally covered."

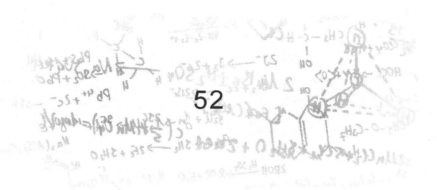

52

"SO, CHRISTINA, I UNDERSTAND YOU had an unusual dual major in college," Susan said, as she, Bobby, Christina and Anna enjoyed lunch on the mansion's veranda overlooking the ocean.

"I love dancing and playing piano, so I had an opportunity to really develop those skills, but at the end of the day, I'm more talented at math and science so that's what I pursued in grad school."

Bobby said, "I've seen Christina dance. So if she's better in the sciences —it's time for me to hang it up."

"Yeah right," said Christina.

"I bet she's poetry in motion," said Anna smiling as she looked at Christina.

"Why did you do your Ph.D in math and not—was it chem—that you also studied at Stanford?" asked Susan.

"Math is my favorite. It's always given me a sense of order. It grounds me. I actually find it calming."

"What was your thesis about?" asked Susan.

Bobby interrupted. "Christina—please excuse the interrogation.

Susan's been reading, 'Gestapo for Dummies' and it's having an effect on her."

Christina laughed. "My NSA fellowship assigned me to Professor Wilem Berkenthal. I worked with him at Stanford on his negative sequential gravitation theory, which was a major breakthrough and my thesis dealt with aspects of that."

"His theory doesn't work," said Bobby.

"What? What do you mean?" said Christina.

"His theory breaks down. If he'd extrapolated it the way he should have, he'd see this."

"Why didn't you tell him? He's devoted his life to this."

"That's not what I do."

Christina glared at Bobby, her mouth pressed into a straight line. Seeing this, Susan came to his rescue.

"You have to understand how Bobby spends his time. He doesn't do any work in the pure or theoretical sciences. Everything has to be directly applicable to disease research. He never digresses."

"That's right," said Bobby, eager to add to the damage control. "So even if I happen to come across something that someone is doing in the theoretical area which I realize is wrong, I can't get engaged. One distraction leads to another. I made my choices long ago on what I do."

"And the results speak for themselves," Susan said.

Christina smiled as she put her hand on Bobby's. "I get it. That makes sense. I was just surprised about Dr. Berkenthal, that's all. I killed myself working for him. I was putting in fourteen hour days."

"Are you close with your mom?" asked Anna, changing the subject.

"We're very close now. You'd love her. She's this wonderfully warm and artsy lady. She's so full of life. She's like a gypsy."

"Did she every remarry?" Susan asked. "Bobby mentioned that your father died when you were very young. I'm sorry—am I getting too personal?"

Christina looked away and then stared down at her plate. "She did remarry—when I was nine. But she finally left him when I was fourteen and then things got a lot better between us."

"Not a good choice she made in number two, I gather?" asked Susan.

Christina was silent as she pushed her food around on the plate.

The remaining few days of Christina's stay in St. Thomas were dreamily relaxing, with she and Bobby exploring the Island and sampling its many beaches. On her last night, before dinner, she and Bobby joined Susan and Anna for cocktails at Azur Reve. As Bobby and Christina walked into the outdoor living room, both of them dressed for the evening, they were a stunningly attractive couple. Bobby held Christina lightly around the waist. He was beaming and Christina glowed. It was obvious that there was a magic between them.

"My my," Anna said. "You two look like movie stars."

"You certainly are a beautiful couple," said Susan.

As they all sipped on cocktails and nibbled on the delicious canapés that the staff had put out, Susan asked Christina, "So what are you working on in Rhode Island?"

"I have a grant to work at Brown on topology and number theory with Dieter Dierks. He's a visiting professor from the University of Bonn."

"Are you excited about it?"

Christina nodded as she reached for a stuffed mushroom. "It should be interesting."

Susan inhaled the rest of her rum cocktail through the small straw. "I have a better idea. Why don't you move to Boston and come work at the lab?"

The color drained out of Christina's face. "You mean Bobby's lab?"

"Exactly," said Susan, grinning. Bobby looked panicked. Christina saw his uneasiness. Bobby glared at Susan and nodded in the direction of the kitchen.

"Would you excuse us for a moment please?" said Bobby.

Once inside the kitchen, Bobby pounced on Susan. "Are you crazy? Why did you do that?"

Susan stepped close to him, whispering so she wouldn't be overheard. "Because, I know you. Once you get back to Boston, you'll fall into your old routine. She lives in Rhode Island. You live in the lab. You'll land up never seeing her, and it will all just slip away."

"I don't think that's true," replied Bobby. But one thing that will really kill it, is if she comes to work at the lab and sees me in that environment. She doesn't know that side of me."

Susan shook her head. "Bobby—you are who you are. You can't hide it. But I'm telling you—if she's not physically present, you'll blow this. I know what I'm doing."

As soon as Bobby and Susan sat down again, Christina said, "Susan—that was an extremely generous idea you had, but I don't think it would work."

Bobby said nothing.

As midnight approached, Bobby and Christina sat together under a blanket on a large catamaran that sped through Magens Bay. Only five other passengers were onboard, and the boat was large enough so that everyone had their own private space. Bobby and Christina were unabashedly making out like teenagers. "This has been so wonderful. I wish I didn't have to go back tomorrow," she said.

Bobby held her close. "Would you like to work in my lab?"

"Who wouldn't want to? Professionally I mean," she replied.

"Forgetting the 'professional' thing?"

Christina didn't answer, but she didn't have to. She snuggled closer to Bobby, her head cradled under his chin. "Would you want to have me around that much?" she asked.

Bobby squeezed her shoulder. "Are you kidding? I'd love it, but it worries me. The guy you've spent the last week with isn't the person I really am. You've seen the best of me. I'm not really like this."

Christina laughed. "You mean you are the child eating nerdy ogre that lives in a cave, like the legends say?"

Bobby lowered his voice. "Well—almost. I'm obsessive. I work constantly. I'm reclusive, in my own world, absent, prone to trances, plagued by nightmares, I drink too much, I'm short tempered —and the list goes on."

"You haven't accomplished what you have by being a laid-back bon vivant. I know that."

Bobby stood up and leaned against the boat's railing as he gazed at the moonlight reflecting on the water. After awhile, he faced her, his eyes watery. "I don't want to lose you, Christina. I'm afraid that if you're around me too much, that's what will happen."

"So by keeping me at a distance—you can maintain a façade, and we can have a superficial relationship? Is that what you want?"

Bobby slowly shook his head. "I want you, Christina. That's all I know. "

She walked over to him and stood just inches away, her eyes probing his. "What makes you think that the woman you've been with this week—is the way I am all the time? Have you thought about that? I'm a damn hard worker too. And I care about what I do, just like you. But we're on holiday—so, of course, we're relaxed. And by the way—don't think I look like this all the time, because I don't, so don't get used to it." A faint smile crossed Bobby's face. "Now, I'm pretty perceptive when it comes to men. I'm not afraid of who you are. I think I know. And I think I'll just get to love you more."

Bobby's face brightened. "Did you say 'more'?" Christina smiled and cut him off as she brought her lips to his. "That's right, silly."

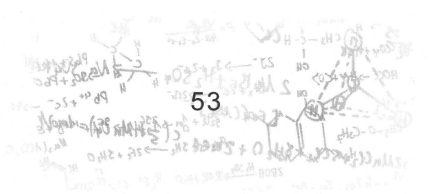

53

COLUM MCALISTER WAS IN A foul mood when he called Turnbull into his office. Standing in front of his wall of windows almost ninety stories above the streets of New York City, McAlister looked lost in thought as he stared out at what usually was an awesome view. But today, all he saw were sheets of rain slamming against the panes, as storm force winds relentlessly pummeled the skyscraper.

Turnbull entered the room and then stood patiently waiting for McAlister to acknowledge his presence. The other two executives already there, the Heads of Bushings' Information Technology and Public Relations departments, were still reeling from McAlister's tirade against them. They now sat quietly, waiting for the next salvo, and hoping they would escape the room without losing their jobs. McAlister turned around and faced them again, "So let me be sure I understand this. You're telling me that you can't get any traction in disseminating our viral internet campaign against Austin because it's being blocked?"

"Someone's detecting it and sabotaging the proliferation. They're worming it into oblivion."

"Who could do that?" asked McAlister.

"Only someone with extremely sophisticated monitoring capability and programming resources."

"Who would have that? Someone in Austin's office?"

"No way."

"And it doesn't matter who sends it off? You tried using our outside people?"

"Of course. It's the content that's detected. The interception is content based."

With a wave of his hand, McAlister motioned them to leave, which they did as quickly as possible without appearing to run out of the room.

Turnbull stayed. "The Austin problem's only getting worse, Marty. Nothing's working to derail him. So far, none of the authorities will cooperate with us, and you just heard that he's being shielded on the smear campaign—which is troubling for a variety of reasons."

Turnbull's florid complexion was indicative of his blood pressure problem, which had grown worse in recent months. He mopped his oily forehead with a crumpled tissue that he pulled out of his pants pocket. "It's not good, Colum. His malaria cure is vetting out perfectly in field tests, and now every scientist is glomming on to the methodology he laid out for them. All vector transmitted diseases will be a thing of the past within three years. He made it so easy for them it's like shooting ducks in a barrel. Our share price is diving and the formal announcements haven't even been made yet."

McAlister nodded. "It's only going to get worse. Austin's been on a tear since returning from his little Caribbean holiday a few months ago. He's working on tuberculosis now. That's a big ticket item for us."

"TB's currently worth two billion in revenue. And that's just to us. To the industry, we're talking at least six. A third of the world's infected, two million deaths a year," said Turnbull.

McAlister looked out at the rain pelting his windows. "It's much bigger than that. If new strains of drug resistant TB become the pandemic that the CDC and WHO are predicting, that'll be the jackpot we've been waiting for. It'll be a license to print money. It'll be worth more than AIDS."

Turnbull wagged his head. "Unless Austin ruins it."

McAlister glared at Turnbull. "You mean until Austin ruins it. With that guy, it's not a question of 'if,' it's a question of when."

Turnbull shook his head. "I can't believe we haven't been able to get anything of value from him. We've been hacking his computers for how long?"

McAlister waved his hand as if shooing away a fly. "All his data is incomprehensible to our guys. No one can figure out what the hell he's doing."

Turnbull said, "He probably realized he was being hacked ages ago and he's just playing with us." The scowl on McAlister's face was reprimand enough for the crack. "So—what's next Colum?" "Do we just lay down and die?"

"You know me better than that," replied McAlister.

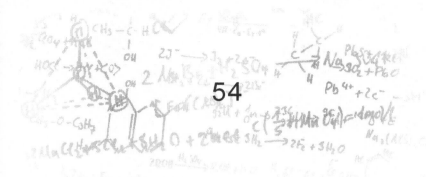

54

T HE INTERCOM BELL RANG IN Bobby's Boston apartment and he buzzed up the delivery guy from the local diner. Taking the paper bag from him, he noticed the bottom was alarmingly soggy. Bobby rushed to his kitchen just as the bag fell apart and his dinner tumbled on to the stainless steel countertop. The styrofoam cup holding the thick brown gravy for his meatloaf hit the counter with a thud, dumping its contents, which combined with gobs of Italian salad dressing from another tumbling container.

"What a mess," Bobby groaned.

It had been another intense week at the lab as Bobby grappled with his research into tuberculosis. Grabbing his martini shaker, he filled it with ice, poured in at least six ounces of gin, a capful of dry vermouth, and shook vigorously with one hand, as he reached for a glass with the other. The top of the shaker flew-off and half of his drink hit the counter, co-mingling with the greasy mess already there. "Perfect. Just perfect," he grumbled. He poured the remnants from the shaker into his glass, grabbed his dry meatloaf and mashed potatoes, and walked out of the kitchen disgusted. The phone rang.

"Hi, hon. I just had Armageddon in the kitchen. I'm dead tired. I'm going to wolf down what remains of my dinner, have a drink, and try to get some sleep."

"Don't forget about this weekend," Christina said. "We're going to the Impressionist exhibit and the Debussy recital."

"I think I might have to cancel. I'm in the middle of things at the lab."

"Bobby—you're not cancelling on me. It's called 'having a life.' You need to try that."

At eight in the morning, Bobby stumbled into the kitchen to make a cup of coffee. He wasn't looking forward to cleaning up the mess from the night before. To his amazement, there was little evidence of the mayhem on the stainless steel counter. His martini had acted as a solvent, emulsifying the grease.

As the day wore on, Bobby thought more and more about the kitchen incident. Standing by his bank of computers as he looked over print-outs, he mentioned it to Susan and Christina. "You see I told you. Alcohol is healthy. If that martini can clean my sink—think what it does for my insides."

Susan rolled her eyes. "That's why alcoholics are in such good shape."

Bobby laughed. "Right. But if gin can dissolve grease, there must be some substance that can clean people's pipes —don't you think?"

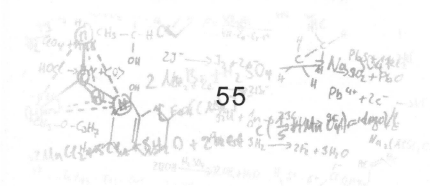

55

A SOLITARY FIGURE SAT IN THE dimly lit den of the austere looking limestone townhouse on East 72nd Street. He wasn't used to typing his own letters, but the message was short:

Dr. Robert James Austin:

Laboratory Address— 17 Grapevine Road, Prides Crossing, Beverly MA.

Home Addresss— c/o Susan Corwin, 5 Adams Way, Apt # 4W, Boston MA.

He printed nine copies of the letter and the address labels for his intended recipients, and then affixed a stamp to each plain white envelope. He was confident that the recipients would know what to do with the information. He then placed the laptop and mini-printer he had purchased that same day in a small black duffel bag.

Taking the letters and the bag with him, he left the house, hailed a cab and went down to Battery Park, at the southern tip of

Manhattan. He dropped the letters in a mailbox and then walked to Whitehall Street where he boarded a ferry to Staten Island. Halfway across the massive harbor, he went up on deck. It was freezing outside so he was alone. He threw the duffel bag into the deep turgid water, and caught the next ferry back to Manhattan. Colum McAlister was back in his townhouse enjoying a cognac and cigar within an hour.

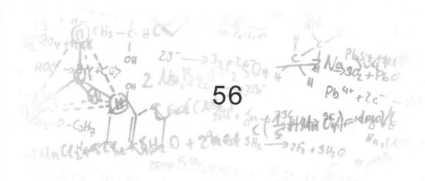

56

BY THE END OF HER first year working at Prides Crossing, Christina had become a veteran of Bobby's intensity. He was juggling research simultaneously on both TB and arteriosclerosis and would bounce from one to the other, in much the same way that he had stood in Peter and Edith's living room at three years of age encircled by scientific treatises on different subjects, absorbing them all. Immersed in his research, he was neglecting his personal well being more and more. It was as if his physical self was being subsumed to the mental. He slept little, minimized interpersonal communications, ate poorly and drank too much alcohol. He seemed increasingly detached from the present and was in and out of trances for hours a day. Although Christina was the first to arrive for work at the lab, and the last to leave other than Bobby, he saw her infrequently there, as he had asked Susan to assign her an office far from his. His mind was elsewhere and he wanted no distractions.

After stopping at a bakery to pick-up blueberry muffins and cappuccino as a surprise, Christina knocked on Bobby's office door one morning and then peeked in. Having spent the night in the lab,

Bobby was lying on his sofa, still sleeping under a thin blanket. His hair was damp with perspiration, as was his face. He looked sallow and feverish. Suddenly, he jerked up as if he had been given an electric shock, and sat bent over the edge of the sofa gasping for air and holding his chest. He looked dazed, as if he was in a terror induced stupor. She quickly put down her bakery bags.

"It's okay, Bobby. I'm here." He pulled the blanket around him as he shook from a wave of chills that surged through him.

"Leave me alone," he said hoarsely.

"Just breathe in deeply and let it out very slowly."

"I don't want you to see me like this. Go away."

"Breathe. Deeply in—as deep as you can go. Then hold it. And then let it out slowly. Just keep doing that. You'll be fine."

His eyes were vacant as he stared at the floor. "The nightmares. They're getting worse. It's trying to stop me. It wants to kill me."

Christina stroked his forehead. "Nobody's going to hurt you. Keep breathing the way I told you."

After several minutes of following her instructions, she led him to the bathroom which was adjoined to his office. She helped him out of his sweaty clothing and ran a hot shower for him. The water cascaded down on him as the shower stall grew thick with steam. After awhile, she leaned in and said, "Now I'm going to make it cooler." With Bobby standing under the shower head, she gradually lowered the water's temperature until it was bracing. The water continued to rain over him, and finally Bobby began to calm down and relax. She got some clean clothes from his office closet and brought them into the bathroom. "When you're dressed, I have some fresh blueberry muffins and cappuccino for us. I'll go heat them up."

Sitting down for breakfast, Bobby said, "You really brought me out of that. How did you know how?"

Christina spoke softly as she reached for the butter. "I've had a little too much experience with nightmares and panic attacks."

"What do you mean?" Bobby asked.

"We'll talk about it sometime," she said.

Bobby took her hand in his and squeezed it. "No, tell me now."

"Things aren't always as simple as they appear."

"That's not an answer".

"Another time, Bobby."

As they cleared the table, her hands trembled. "You're pushing yourself way too hard. You're putting yourself under tremendous pressure. It's not healthy. You can't go on like this."

There was no leeway in Bobby's response. "I have no choice, Christina. People are dying every day. I have to move as quickly as I can."

Late that afternoon, Susan saw Christina sitting at her desk looking glum. "What's wrong, sweetie? Why the long-face?"

"I'm worried about Bobby. You know how he's been lately. And he's increasingly paranoid. He was saying that 'it' wants to kill him. Who the hell is 'it'? Do you know?"

Susan nodded. "Yes, I know. But he'll have to tell you himself. He will eventually. He just doesn't want you to think he's crazy, that's all."

Christina's face paled. "Is he crazy?" she asked, her voice soft.

Taking a seat across from Christina, Susan leaned in toward her. "Bobby has more demons than a fright house. His personal history is very dark. He's been left alone many times."

"What should I do?"

Susan put one of her hands on hers. "Build the trust. You two shouldn't have secrets from each other. Get him to open up and do the same with him."

"He said he has a trunk to show me."

Susan cocked her head. "He said he'd show you the contents of his trunk?"

"Yes, the one in his apartment."

"That's a major step. Bobby has never shown that to anyone. I once saw the contents by accident and he freaked out."

Christina nervously picked at one of her fingernails as she looked down. "I have secrets too. Things I'm ashamed of."

Susan leaned in close. "Don't we all? But one thing I've learned in life is that love is more powerful than secrets. Sometimes it doesn't seem that way. But it is."

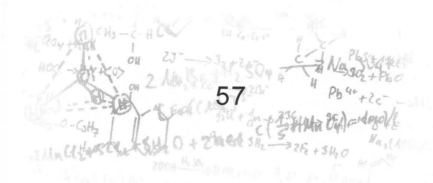

57

A S CALVIN PERRONE HELD A glass of champagne in one hand and a shrimp canapé in the other, he marveled how his career had taken such a huge turn for the better. Here he was, not a guard—but an invited guest—at the director's Christmas cocktail party for Washington insiders.

He thought back to when it had all begun to fall into place for him—-that night, just under two years ago, when he had navigated so well in the dark using only his pocket flashlight. He had made his way through the small office of the gynecologist, quickly located the file room, and in a matter of seconds picked the flimsy lock on the cabinet. Finding the patient file he was looking for, he had photographed each page, and was out in under ten minutes. Just like all of his other intrusions, that one went undetected too. And then, the next morning, he had carefully incorporated the pertinent information into his analysis. That was the final piece of data he needed to complete the research for Project WS, to which he had been designated as lead agent by the director himself. It had taken him and a staff of four agents over three months to narrow the field down to ten candidates for the director's review. He had placed the ten individual files in a large black binder and hurried to the director's office. It was so fresh in his mind it was as if it had happened yesterday.

--------•••••--------

"What do you have for me?" Varneys asked.

"Based on the previously agreed screening criteria, I've narrowed it down to ten people for you to consider, sir," replied Perrone.

"Re-cap the criteria for me".

"We employed seven basic filters to initially identify potential candidates:

Age: 25—31

IQ: minimum of 145

Education: minimum of one doctorate in physical sciences or math

Social Status: heterosexual, single, never married, no serious current relationships, no children

Physical Health: excellent, with no record of hereditary disease in the last three generations

Psychological Profile: No mental health impairment or history of same in the last three generations

Physical Appearance: Above average

"Let me see the files," said Varneys. Perrone placed the binder containing the ten files on Varney's desk. "This will take me awhile. Let's re-convene at 8:30 AM tomorrow."

As the elevator descended to his office, Perrone smiled. If

Project WS were successful, he knew that his relationship with Varneys would be made.

The next morning Perrone was directed into Varneys' private conference room. All ten files were already laid out on the large oval table. On top of each file was a photograph of the candidate whose personal information was contained in the file. Entering the room, Varneys said, "There are some credible candidates here. Well done, agent."

Perrone stood at ease. "Thank you, director. It's taken a great deal of effort. We started with data in the computer banks on all doctoral and post-doctoral government sponsored fellowship recipients in the last three years, and worked on from there. These are the ten females who made the final cut out of almost nine hundred we identified. They've been vetted fully."

"And who do you think is the number one candidate out of the ten?"

Perrone knew that this was his moment to impress. "I think it's that one," he replied, pointing to one of the photographs on the table. "She has among the highest IQs of all the prospects we screened—155. She has knock-out looks and she's not a nerd like most of the others. I think she's the best match."

Varneys laughed. It was a low guttural sound that came from a place deep within him from which few laughs emanated. "I'm inclined to agree with you, but I'm concerned about her background—she could be unstable."

"You're referring to the abortion?" Perrone asked.

Varneys shook his head. "It's more than an abortion don't you think? She was only 14. It was her step-father. She'd been raped by him for years."

"Her gynecological reports indicate that the abortion didn't affect her fertility or her ability to carry to full term," replied Perrone.

"I read the reports, agent. What I'm referring to is the breakdown she had after the abortion."

"But she bounced back strong. Her psychiatric records are clear on that."

Varneys began to pace the room. "She became a wild kid in high school, didn't she?"

"Wild yes, but brilliant. And she buckled down in college. Her professors still rave about her."

Staring out the window, Varneys stood in silence, looking pensive. Perrone waited patiently. Finally, Varneys said, "I just hope she's not a nut case."

"I think Christina Moore is exactly what we're looking for," replied Perrone confidently.

"But will she do it?" asked Varneys.

Perrone wagged his head. "That's the tough question."

"It's down to you Agent Perrone. Make it happen."

Ten days later, Christina picked up her mail at the graduate student housing facility at Stanford. As usual, there wasn't much to look at —a few catalogs, a credit card bill and a cell phone bill. But what caught her attention was a letter whose envelope bore the name and address of the NSA. Once inside her small studio apartment, she opened the envelope. The letter on NSA stationary read:

> Dear Ms. Moore:
> Regarding certain important matters in connection with your current NSA fellowship award, it is important that you meet with the undersigned as soon as possible. The meeting

will be arranged to take place on the Stanford campus so as not to inconvenience you. Please contact the undersigned upon your receipt of this letter.

Very truly yours,
Calvin Perrone (819-549-8121)

Concerned that there could be a problem with her fellowship, she dialed the contact number. Perrone picked up after three rings.

"Is this Mr. Perrone of the NSA?" Christina asked.

"Who's speaking please?"

"This is Christina Moore. I received your letter asking me to contact you about my NSA fellowship."

Perrone smiled. He could tell from her voice that she was nervous, afraid her fellowship was being terminated or reduced. He thought of the beautiful young woman on the other end of the phone line holding his letter. She had so easily fallen in line with his plan. He mused about the power of a piece of stationary. "Oh yes, Ms. Moore. I'll be on the Stanford campus tomorrow taking care of a few matters. Is it possible for us to meet then?"

"Is there some problem with my fellowship? I was quite alarmed by your letter."

"I'll explain everything when we meet, Ms. Moore. Shall we say tomorrow at three in the afternoon in room 129 of Berringer Hall?"

When Christina walked into room 129, Perrone and two other agents were already there. Her eyebrows rose when she saw three people and immediately noticed that the size of the men and their dress and demeanor didn't look like that of NSA fellowship admin personnel. Perrone smiled broadly as he stepped forward extending his hand, "Hello Ms. Moore. I'm Calvin Perrone. And these are my two associates," said Perrone, without introducing them. "Why don't we make ourselves comfortable and sit around the conference table." As they all sat down, Christina placed the NSA letter on the table in front of her.

"So, Mr. Perrone. Please tell me what this letter is all about."

Perrone blushed as he folded his hands on the table and leaned toward Christina. "Ms. Moore, there's no problem with your fellowship."

"So then—what's the issue? Why did I get this letter?"

Perrone shifted uneasily in his chair. "Let me be frank with you, Ms. Moore. The letter was a discreet device to get you here for a meeting without alarming you. We need to speak to you about a matter of significant national security."

"Are you with the NSA or not?"

"No."

"Then the letter was a lie." Christina was red faced as she began to get up from the table.

"I am Calvin Perrone, but I'm with the CIA not the NSA." Calvin pulled out his ID and showed it to Christina. He motioned to the two other men at the table who pulled out their IDs.

Christina settled back into her chair. "So what's going on?"

Perrone tried to sound matter of fact. "Ms. Moore—we're here to talk about Dr. Robert James Austin. We trust you know the name."

"Who doesn't know that name? What about him?"

"As best we can guess, Austin's intellect is the result of some kind of genetic mutation. We don't know that for sure, but it's all we can surmise. The bottom-line is that his intelligence is a perishable resource, the likes of which may never be seen again."

"And your point?"

"Like any of us—he can die at any moment," replied Perrone somberly.

A small smile parted Christina's lips. "Was that an epiphany you had recently?"

Perrone frowned. "My point is that when he dies, this extraordinary resource—a resource that has drastically changed the world for the better—will be extinguished. The resource is irreplaceable. And I'll tell you— there are a bunch of nut cases out there who want to kill him— so his life expectancy is anyone's guess."

"All of this is fascinating, Mr. Perrone, but how does it concern me?"

Perrone inched his chair closer to hers. "Austin is a very peculiar guy. He's single. He doesn't date in any normal sense. He's so obsessed with his work that he swears off any possibility of a real relationship with a woman. In short—he's not likely to have any children. We don't know if his intelligence might be capable of being passed down or not. But the possibility exists. We need this guy to have kids."

"Who's we?"

Perrone leaned back in his chair and spread his arms out expansively. "The world, Ms. Moore. The world needs him to have kids."

"So why don't you get some sperm samples from him and impregnate some female volunteers. I'm sure there wouldn't be a shortage of them."

Perrone shook his head dramatically as if he were beyond the point of exasperation. "That would make sense if Austin would cooperate. But he won't. He has a pathological aversion to the government." He leaned in close to Christina. "He's very suspicious."

Christina raised her eyebrows. "Really? I wonder why?"

Perrone stood up and began to walk slowly around the room as he continued to speak. "So—the only way it's going to happen is the 'old fashioned way.' The Agency's view is that the quality of Austin's genetic material will be diluted by any female—because obviously, there's no one in his league. However, the dilution will be minimized to the extent that the female is as intellectually potent as possible."

"And your point?" said Christina, her words clipped.

Perrone was now standing next to her chair, looking down at her. "We've gone to great pains to identify potential candidates and you're our #1 choice," he said smiling broadly, as if he were telling Christina she had just won a lottery.

Christina's face flushed scarlet and her voice rose as she looked up at him. "You're kidding right? This is all some crazy practical joke?" Shaking her head vigorously, she said, "You're good, Perrone. Real good. But I actually have some lab experiments I have to get done." She began to stand up. Towering over her, he gently motioned her down and then sat next to her.

His voice was stern. "This project of ours can change the course of human history for the better."

Her eyes wide, she said, "Project? You guys have a name for this?"

Perrone leaned in so his face was only inches from hers. "Yes. It's classified, but I'll divulge it to you. It's Project WS."

Christina laughed. "Does that stand for "we're sickos?""

Perrone frowned. "It stands for "World Save.""

Christina rested her face against her palm and closed her eyes. "Does Austin know you're out here trying to run a stud service?"

Perrone shook his head emphatically. "He has no idea—and can't know. He would flip out."

"Well, at least he's sane. Goodbye Mr. Perrone." Christina stood up, crumpled the NSA letter, threw it on the table and began to leave.

"You're a selfish person, Ms. Moore. A very selfish person," said Perrone as he trailed after her.

Just a few steps from the door, Christina whirled around, her eyes burning with anger. "You have a hell of a nerve, Perrone. You get me in here under false pretenses and outline a hair-brained scheme that only an outfit as crazy as yours could conjure up—and then when I don't agree, all of a sudden I'm a selfish person. Do you think I went to school all these years, earned honors, a Ph.D and fellowship, just so I could be bred like a bitch at a kennel? What do you think I am?"

Perrone inhaled quickly. "That's not it—calm down—that's not it at all."

"Like hell it's not," Christina said, reaching for the door knob.

Perrone pleaded. "Please—wait a minute. Look- I've screwed this up. I shouldn't have handled it this way. But please—just sit down—give me ten more minutes—just ten minutes—that's all I ask. Please."

Christina shook her head but then sat back down at the conference table as she tried to regain her composure. Perrone turned off the lights in the room, lowered a projection screen from the ceiling and began to run a dramatic compilation video that the Agency had put together highlighting Bobby's accomplishments and the impact that he already had on the lives of hundreds of millions of people throughout the world. The video showed the extent of human suffering that existed before his discoveries and the difference he had made. The screen was filled with the faces of the grateful from all walks of life, all ages and many nations, who expressed, often with tears of gratitude in their eyes, the respect, admiration and love that they felt for him. The contribution which he had already made, at not even 40 years of age, was overwhelming in its magnitude, and the spirit of hope and renewal that he had engendered was heartwarming and uplifting. Renowned scientists expounded on Austin's brilliance and selfless devotion, and echoed the same thought −"Robert Austin is much more than a genius—we don't have a word for what he is—but thank God for it."

At the video's end, Christina Moore, Calvin Perrone and the other two CIA agents sat in silence in the dark, a heavy residue of human emotion in the air. Even one of the hardened agents flicked his eyes. Nothing was said. Perrone turned the lights on. Christina stood up, straightened the impeccable black suit that she wore only for interviews, and headed for the door. Perrone stared down at the table and looked defeated. When Christina reached the door, she turned around. Her eyes swollen and wet, she said, "OK. Here are the ground rules. I'll meet him. That's all—nothing else. I'll consent to meet him once."

Perrone bounded over to her. "That's great. That's all we ask. No strings. Just check him out. You'll see—he's even a pretty good looking guy."

"Where's the meeting going to take place?" she asked.

"Leave that to us."

———◆◆◆———

Perrone's walk down memory lane was interrupted by the director's heavy hand on his shoulder. "I see you have a glass of champagne. That's a good start. Are you enjoying yourself, Agent Perrone?"

"Very much, sir. Thanks for inviting me."

"You deserve it. You proved yourself on Project WS. It was a delicate assignment and you executed it with precision."

"May I ask you a question about it?"

"I may not answer it—but ask."

"Where did the directive come from for the project? Was it the White House?"

The flush that came over the director's cheeks signaled his annoyance at the question. "The directive came from me."

Just as Perrone was about to say something to mollify Varneys, a tall elegantly dressed older man who looked like Washington had been good to him for a long time, stepped forward and said, "Director —Merry Christmas and congratulations."

"Congratulations?" asked Varneys.

"You haven't heard? It's going to be announced tomorrow. Your boy just won two more Nobels. For the malaria cure and the other parasite disease work he did. And he got an Abel Award for math also."

Varneys did his best to conceal his embarrassment that the Chairman of the Senate Committee on Homeland Security had information he didn't have. "An Abel Award," repeated Varneys matter of factly.

The senator swirled the ice cubes in his gin and tonic, and moved closer to Varneys as if he were about to impart a personal confidence. "The story goes that Alfred Nobel's wife was having an affair with a mathematician—so Al's revenge was to exclude math from the awards. That's why there's no Nobel Prize for math. The Abel was established to fill the gap."

"Yes, of course. I knew that," said Varneys, flicking his hand.

"The best part," said the Senator, laughing, "is the statement from the Abel Committee."

How the hell has he seen the statement already? wondered Varneys. In a town where information is the most valuable currency, the look on the senator's face signaled his sense of superiority. He continued, "Orin—you have to read it when it's released. It's hilarious. They say they're giving him the award because they know he deserves it for his new math language, even though no one understands it, but they hope they will one day."

"That's rich," said Varneys, clasping the senator's arm.

Looking at Varney's wide-spaced eyes and the innumerable small teeth that were exposed by his forced smile, Perrone wondered if he was the only one who thought Varneys resembled a piranha.

As the Senator walked away, he turned toward Varneys and raised his glass as if to make a toast. "Don't think any of us have forgotten who we have to thank."

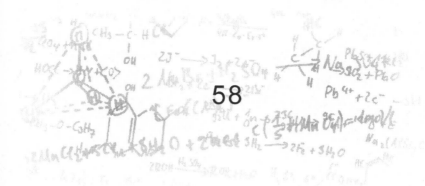

58

PATIENCE AND PLANNING WERE VIRTUES that Colum McAlister long ago learned to value. Sitting in front of the video monitors in his Lands End office, his safe open, he flipped through his alphabetical file of video discs and prepared to make copies of the small screen debuts of:

Neil Foster, the Undersecretary of the Department of Health and Human Services

Randall Lindsay, the Deputy Commissioner of the Food and Drug Administration

Graham Waters, the Chairman of the Senate Judiciary Committee

Michael Petersen, the Chairman of the House Committee on Ways and Means

He smiled. *Politicians have so little will power. They want it all.* Whatever their proclivities, penchants and weaknesses, McAlister

had catered to them over the years —sometimes at Lands End—
but more often at entrapments that McAlister had orchestrated
in Washington D.C., New York, Aspen, Los Angeles—wherever the
opportunity best presented itself. The incriminating antics of his
hapless stars —all venerable and vulnerable public servants —would
be preserved on video and land-up in McAlister's alphabetical file.
He had been building what he called his "insurance portfolio" for
a long time. Often his coverage spanned years, and began early in
the careers of upwardly mobile subjects that he had identified as
potentially useful. When things went as they should, the videos
would remain McAlister's secret—secure and hidden away. Most
of the time, he could rely on the more subtle tools of influence
peddling, which he plied with great acumen. But over the years,
his videos had proven invaluable and had given Bushings the edge
it needed in many regulatory and legislative contexts. Now, at this
point in time, McAlister felt that he had to pull out the stops.

The deputy commissioner of the FDA had a preference for
young dominant women attired in fetish gear who would gag and
bind him, subject him to humiliating violations, and then lead him
around on a leash like a disobedient puppy. The chairman of the
Senate Judiciary Committee enjoyed infantilism. McAlister smiled
as he thought how shocked the American public would be to see
the "lion of the senate" attired in nothing more than a diaper and a
baby bonnet, sucking on a pacifier, his eyes wide with anticipation.
The Ways and Means Chairman, a conservative Republican with
a picture-postcard American family, was partial to boyish looking
males, the younger and skinnier the better, particularly in pairs.
And then, there was McAlister's personal viewing favorite, the
Undersecretary of the HHS Department and his beautiful wife,
twenty years his junior, who enjoyed cuckold scenes in which she

would have sex with young well endowed men, while her husband watched and pleasured himself as he was taunted by them for his inadequacies. As McAlister reviewed the videos he had selected for duplication, he was pleased. "Each one a career killer," he muttered.

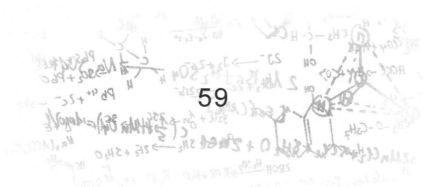

59

I T WAS WELL AFTER ELEVEN at night when Bobby stepped out of the elevator, walked down the narrow non-descript hallway, opened the door to apartment 4W and flicked the lights on. This was the first time in five days that he had come home to his apartment instead of staying at Prides Crossing. He pulled the living room curtains closed, poured himself a drink and kicked off his shoes, all within what seemed like a single movement. Collapsing on the sofa, he was exhausted. *What's that foul odor?* he wondered. Tracking it to the kitchen, he realized he hadn't emptied the garbage in almost two weeks. He grabbed the overflowing trash bag, stepped into the building's hallway and walked over to the disposal chute, only to find that it was taped shut, with a sign posted, "Out of Order. Put Trash in Basement Bin."

The force was so astounding when it blew out the windows of the entire fourth floor, that a fireball was propelled across the street, scorching the face of a building fifty feet away. Within a few minutes, the police cordoned off a three block area, and the roads became clogged with fire engines and emergency vehicles. The media reported that a gas leak emanating from the kitchen of Apartment 4W at 5 Adam's Way, leased to a Susan Corwin, had caused the explosion and that anyone in the apartment would have been killed instantly.

"What the hell happened?" Varneys yelled at Perrone.

"From our surveillance tapes, we know that a cable TV repair crew entered the building last week. While we can't be sure, we think they might have opened the manifold on the roof and somehow delivered explosives into the air- conditioning ducts of Austin's apartment, probably by way of a radio controlled trolley that was operated remotely using video guidance. They must have been watching the apartment waiting to see Austin enter, at which point they detonated the bomb. It was a highly sophisticated operation."

Varneys' head wagged. "But how would they know what Austin looks like? There aren't any photos of him out there."

Perrone's words were cadenced as precisely as he could manage under Varneys' gaze. "They didn't necessarily know. But they saw the lights go on in 4W. Somehow they knew it was really Austin's apartment and not Corwin's."

Varney's voice was a cold monotone. "And your team picked up nothing."

"We picked up the cable truck arriving."

Varneys began to pace. After a few back and forths, he stopped in front of Perrone. "But the guys who entered the building weren't with the cable company were they?" he asked rhetorically. And your agents didn't check their IDs when they entered the building?"

"That wasn't the protocol, sir. This was a covert operation, not a lock-down. The apartment and the fourth floor hallway were under twenty-four hour surveillance. The intrusion escaped detection only because of the use of the ducts."

Varneys smacked the corner of his desk with his open hand and the loud slap caused Perrone to wince. Varney's voice was a harsh rasp with a rapid staccato delivery. "The surveillance was a total failure, a complete waste of time. If Austin wasn't in the basement dumping his crap because of a busted compactor, he'd be dead. We don't get paid to be lucky."

Perrone shifted uneasily. "No, sir, we don't."

Varneys glared at Perrone. "Now—who's responsible for the blast?"

"From what we can tell so far—it's RASI," Perrone replied. "They have a contingent of ex-military operatives and they also have the funding to contract privately."

Varneys began to pace again. "How the hell did they ever find out Austin lived there?" "Don't know yet, sir."

Plunking down in his desk chair, Varneys exhaled loudly, swiveled around so he was facing the windows, and stared into the gloomy overcast sky. Perrone stood stiffly, waiting in silence, hoping the inquisition was almost over. Finally, Varneys turned to face him. "It's amazing how much you don't know isn't it?" Perrone studied the floor as he waited for the next salvo. "So, how did Austin take it?" asked Varneys resignedly.

Perrone's face brightened. "The good news is that he doesn't blame us because he doesn't know we had his apartment under surveillance. But he's hard to read. He acted pretty stoic. Made some weird comments. "

"Like what?"

"He said he'd always had a special relationship with garbage. I don't know what the hell that's supposed to mean." Varneys emitted a grunt in recognition of Bobby's sarcasm. Perrone continued, "And then, when I told him I thought it was RASI that did it— he said, 'That should be my biggest problem.'"

"Did you ask him what he meant?"

"He just smiled at me —and thanked me for stopping by—you know, dismissively."

"Did you see anyone else we know?"

"The Corwin lady and Christina Moore. They were both worked up over the blast." Perrone grinned. "When Corwin introduced me to Moore, I thought Moore was going to melt into the floor."

Varneys stood up so Perrone knew the meeting was over. "Two things, agent. When the perps don't see any announcement of Austin's demise, they may slip and say something somewhere that implicates them because they know who really lived in that apartment. So, we need maximum penetration on RASI. Secondly, starting immediately, I want every male working at Prides Crossing to wear a baseball cap and sunglasses just like Austin does. No exceptions."

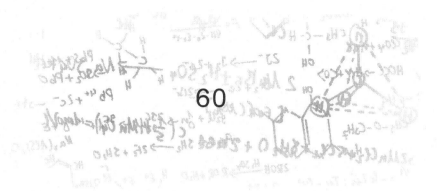

60

AT THE CONCLUSION OF BUSHINGS weekly meeting of its most senior executives, after everyone else had filed out of the conference room, Turnbull closed the door and excitedly asked McAlister, "Did you see the news report about the explosion at that Corwin lady's apartment?"

McAlister appeared to be almost oblivious to the question. "What are you talking about?"

"The explosion at Susan Corwin's place."

"Who cares? Who's she?"

"Who's she?" replied Turnbull. "She's Austin's right hand. She's the gatekeeper I've talked about. It was her place. The apartment was obliterated. Too bad she wasn't having Austin over for dinner. He would have been vaporized. Would have solved a lot of problems for us."

McAlister smiled patronizingly. "Let's not get draconian. We still have arrows in our quiver. I'm going to Washington for a few days to make the rounds. Shake some hands. We need to shore-up our good will with the people who make the rules."

Turnbull's face lit up. "Damn, I hope it works. We need a break."

McAlister walked over to the antique chinoiserie mirror hanging at one end of the conference room and carefully adjusted his tie and studied his hair from a few different angles. "I'm going to sit down with some old friends and see if I can enlist their support. I want to get some quality time with Neil Foster, Michael Petersen and Randall Lindsay. And hopefully, Graham Waters can fit me in."

Turnbull nodded. "You're really going for the heavies."

McAlister flashed his newly whitened veneers. "That's why I get paid the big bucks, Marty."

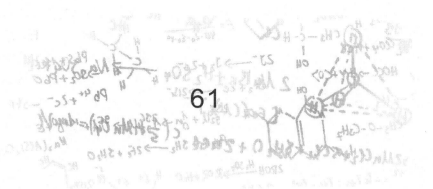

61

T HE EXPLOSION TOOK ITS TOLL. Having come so close to death, Bobby's paranoia increased markedly, as did his sense of urgency and reclusiveness. While previously, he had believed that the greatest threat to his physical and mental well being was posed by intangible forces, the blast in his apartment caused him to realize that he had lost the protective cloak of anonymity against more prosaic foes that he had taken for granted. It was now evident that he was an identifiable and achievable target. He was alive only because of happenstance. Every day counted —now, more than ever. He became increasingly obsessive in his work. All he thought about was how much he needed to accomplish before someone or something succeeded in taking him out.

While the blast disoriented Christina for several weeks, the anxiety that descended on her wouldn't dispel. She had always thought Perrone was just being dramatic when he said that Bobby's life was at risk, but now she realized how vulnerable he was. She had come very close to losing him.

Christina knocked on Bobby's office door and went in. He was sitting on the edge of his chair, his back to the door, staring at the computer screen, chin resting against his open hand. He was so pre-occupied that he didn't hear her come in or even sense her presence as she moved to his side.

"Bobby, it's Friday afternoon."

He jumped—startled by the intrusion.

"Don't sneak up on me like that. Damn."

Christina laughed. "A little high strung are we?" She tenderly raked her fingers through his hair. "So here's the deal. Let's both leave the lab by seven. I'm going to make us Steak Frites for dinner and we'll open that bottle of Chateau Latour we've been saving."

Bobby smiled and the stress began to drain from his face. "Is that the steak with the garlic butter melting on top, the way I love it?"

"Yeah, that's the one," she replied, as she bent over to look at his computer screen. "Have you tried inserting those variables I ran this morning?" she asked.

"Later. But they look interesting."

Standing behind him, she began to massage his neck. Eyes closed, he let his head relax forward as she continued to knead his muscles. After a while, she could feel the tension in his body ebbing and she kept it up for several more minutes until Bobby stood up and faced her, his eyes looking into hers. As their lips met, Bobby pulled her against him, one hand underneath her sweater pressing against the small of her back. Her perfume mixed with the scent of her warming skin and sent heat surging through him as her heart beat began to accelerate against his chest. Without separating, he managed to pull off her sweater and push her jeans to the floor, while at the same time, she fumbled to unbutton his shirt while unzipping his pants with her other hand. As Bobby lifted her, she wrapped her legs around his waist giving him easy entry. A few minutes later they lay entangled on the floor exhausted.

―――――――・‥・――――――

Christina had a dry Bombay Gin martini waiting in a shaker, with three olives skewered on a silver pick resting in the over-sized cocktail glass. Bobby had moved into the sparsely furnished Prides Crossing guest house after his apartment had been destroyed. The lights in the dining room were dimmed to almost nothing, and the table was set with a crisp off-white linen table cloth, candles burning in a wrought iron candelabra. She handed him his drink as he settled into the sofa. Bleary eyed from hours of reading the computer screen, Bobby sighed. "Thank God for you, and thank God for gin."

Christina laughed. "Rough day at the ranch, huh?"

Bobby smiled. "Not without its pleasant surprises, however."

Christina blushed and sat down close to him, resting her head against his shoulder. Snuggling into him, she planted a soft kiss on his cheek. "What a combination," he said. "Your lips, a martini, and steak frites cooking. I could smell it across the lawn as I walked here."

"The gin, the steak or me?"

"All three," replied Bobby.

"And your favorite is?" she asked.

Bobby smiled. "Now you know you don't have to ask."

"That's right. Because it's the gin. I'm no fool."

Bobby put his arm around her waist, drew her even closer to him and whispered in her ear, "I've known Bombay longer than you. You'll move up. Just give it time."

As the evening progressed and the Chateau Latour was almost

gone, Bobby seemed more relaxed than she had seen him in weeks, so she decided it was time.

Hesitantly, she said, "There's something I have to talk to you about. I've been meaning to for a long time." Christina could see Bobby gearing up to make a sarcastic comment—but she cut him off with a shake of her head.

"I'll behave. Now what is it?"

Christina spoke haltingly, her voice soft. The expression on her face had turned dour. "You remember when we met?"

"How can I forget?"

She looked at him and then broke eye contact. "Well—it wasn't really a coincidence."

Bobby wrinkled his brow and looked at her.

Christina agonized over each word as her voice grew unsteady. "I knew you were coming to that store. So I got there ahead of you."

Bobby's voice lost its playfulness. "What do you mean?"

Christina answered his question with her own. "Well—how did you find out about the store?"

Recalling perfectly, Bobby replied, "From George—at Azur Reve. I told him I needed to buy some clothes—and he recommended it. He had Steve, the driver, take me there."

"Right. And when you left the house—George must have called and told them."

"Who's them?" Bobby asked.

Christina's eyes watered and her face lost its color. "The CIA guys."

Bobby's face reddened.

"Calvin Perrone's crew."

A bewildered look came over Bobby and his voice grew louder. "Perrone. What the hell does he have to do with you?"

Christina was having trouble speaking coherently, and she avoided Bobby's searing eyes. "It's not him really –it's his boss. Perrone's just doing what Varneys—the head of the CIA told him."

Bobby's nostril's flared and his eyes took on a wild look. "Varneys—Orin Varneys? When did he become head of the CIA? That son of a bitch tried to destroy me when I was a kid." Bobby stood up and began walking around the room aimlessly. "Christina—what's going on?"

Christina began to cry as she recounted to Bobby the phony NSA letter she had received from Perrone, the nature of Project WS, the video they showed her and what she had agreed to do, and that they had set her up at Bolongo Beach so that she could meet him while he was in St. Thomas. Bobby crouched down on the floor in a corner of the room with his face hidden in his hands. When he finally looked up several minutes later, his eyes were swollen. "Why would you do that to me, Christina? Why would you betray me?"

"I never betrayed you, Bobby. Never." Christina was having trouble catching her breath.

"How can you say that? You betrayed me from the first moment we met. It was calculated. It was a lie from the beginning. You and Varneys. Why would you do that to me? Why would you want to hurt me like that?"

Christina was shaking. "Nothing was a lie. Everything was real. All I agreed to do was meet you once. Nothing else. The deal with them was finished in that store. Everything after that was me—just me—not them."

Bobby looked at her as if she were a stranger. "I trusted you."

As Christina walked toward Bobby, her arms outstretched, she looked frail. "And you were right to trust me."

Bobby turned away. "They have photos of us don't they? Recordings of everything we said. Probably have videos."

Christina stood alone in the middle of the room, her head bowed. "Bobby stop it. I love you."

Bobby had now retreated into the coldness of his intellect. His words came quickly and cut with precision. "When is the mission over, Christina? Is it when we have one baby or three babies? What does it take to end it?"

"Bobby—stop it. Please."

"And when did they transfer your fellowship from Stanford to Brown? I bet that didn't happen until after you agreed to work with them—they wanted you real close to Boston didn't they?"

Christina's eyes had become wells of despair. She pleaded, "Bobby please. Stop. I love you so much. Don't do this."

Bobby waved his hand dismissively. "Love. How can there be love without trust?"

"I never lied to you," she said.

"My whole life I've trusted almost no one. But I trusted you, Christina."

She looked at Bobby, but saw only his narrowed eyes glaring back at her. The door slammed behind her as she ran out.

That Monday morning when Susan arrived at the lab, Bobby wasn't there and Christina's office had been emptied. Susan knocked on the door of the guest house and when no one answered, she went in. The remains of Friday's dinner were still on the plates. She called Bobby's cell number repeatedly over the next hour, but there was no answer. Finally, several hours later, he picked up her call. "Where are you Bobby?"

"I'm at a motel in Concord." His voice sounded hoarse and tired.

"Why?"

"I had to get away."

Susan paused for a moment, digesting his answer. "Do you know what's going on with Christina? Her office is empty."

Bobby shot back, "Did you know about her? Were you in on it too, Susan?"

"What?"

"She's been a CIA plant from day one. My meeting her was no accident—it was a pre-arranged plot."

"What are you talking about?" replied Susan.

"She admitted it. Perrone set up the whole thing. You fell for it and so did I."

Susan's voice rose. "Bobby—your paranoia is out of control. Where did you come up with this crazy stuff?"

Bobby's voice was loud and strident. "She confessed it all on Friday night. She's a CIA operative who agreed to get pregnant with my kid to fulfill Varneys' sick vision of the future."

"Varneys?" Susan sounded bewildered. "You mean that guy you told me about that you knew years ago?"

"Yes. Now they made him the head of the CIA. Can you believe that?"

Susan sat down, stupefied. Her mind was reeling. *So that's why Perrone made the holiday offer that was too good to refuse. I never should have had anything to do with him. I was duped.* She buried her head in her hands and massaged her forehead as a throbbing headache pounded into her. "Bobby, I have to come see you. Where's this motel? I'll be there in thirty minutes."

Susan's car pulled up to the nondescript roadside building and she found room 327. When she entered, the air was stale and heavy with the stench of old pizza and liquor. Bobby was sitting at a little work desk which was littered with pizza boxes, plastic cups from the bathroom and an assortment of liquor bottles. Looking despondent, it was obvious he hadn't shaved or showered in several days. "You look terrible. This place is a real dump."

"Who gives a crap?"

Susan pulled over a chair and sat down opposite Bobby. "Look. The CIA is what they are and I won't argue with you about them. But I've gotten to know Christina really well and I don't buy what you're saying. Tell me her side of the story."

Bobby picked up one of the plastic cups and downed whatever was in it. "She told me on Friday night. We were sharing a nice bottle of wine and then she got very serious and told me she had to unburden herself and she did."

"And she said what?" Susan asked.

"That she agreed to meet me at Perrone's request because the CIA wanted her to have kids with me to propagate my intellect."

Susan raised her eyebrows.

"She said they showed her some tear-jerk video that convinced her. She says she only agreed to meet me once, nothing more."

"And you don't believe her?"

Bobby shook his head and picked up another plastic cup that was half full.

Susan's face turned crimson. "So what was the last thing you said to her? Tell me the exact words."

"I can't remember."

"Bullshit Bobby. You can remember the serial number on your parents' computer from when you were three years old. Tell me what you said to her."

Bobby downed whatever was in the plastic cup and stared at the half-empty pizza box in front of him. "I think I called her a lying scheming whore who betrayed me and ruined my life."

Susan got up from the chair and slammed it against the desk. "You sanctimonious son of a bitch. God help me to keep from slapping your face." She walked to the other side of the small room and just stood there, glaring at him. Then she bounded back and stood over him, looking down at him with disgust. "You need to get over yourself, mister. You're so damn self-righteous and judgmental. Stop thinking you're the only good person in the whole world."

Bobby looked up at her. "What are you getting so huffy about? So she's right and I'm wrong—it's that simple for you? Somehow she's the victim."

"Bobby—did Christina ever talk to you about her childhood? Did you ever wonder why she was so knowledgeable about night terrors and could bring you out of them so well?"

"We never talked about that."

"Well—she talked a lot to me. Maybe it's easier for women to talk to women about some things. Or maybe you just never cared enough to really engage her in a discussion. Christina's step-father started raping her at age nine. It went on for five years. He got her pregnant. That's when her mother finally threw him out. After the abortion, Christina had a breakdown. She tried to kill herself twice when she was fourteen. It took years for her to rebuild the self-esteem that bastard destroyed. That's the girl you accused of being a lying whore and chased away. You know Bobby—you're not the only person in the world who's had hardship and suffered. You need to get off your high horse."

Bobby closed his eyes. "Oh my God. I had no idea."

Susan didn't relent. "If Christina told you something—she told you the truth. That lady was so in love with you that she glowed every time you walked into a room. More than you deserved. You're a damn fool."

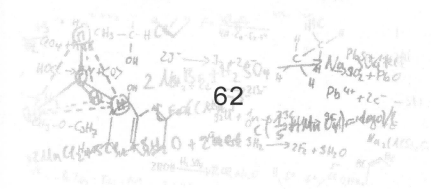

62

THE HEAT OF BOBBY'S ANGER was burning through him. The more he thought about what had happened, the more livid he became. He dialed the phone number for CIA Headquarters in Langley. The operator's voice that answered was as bland as if she worked at a clothing store. "Central Intelligence Agency, how may I help you?"

"Connect me to the director's office, please."

There was a minute's delay and then a different voice said, "How may I help you?"

"Is this the director's office?"

"This is the office in charge of general inquiries. How can I help you?"

"I'm not interested in general inquiries. My name is Doctor Robert James Austin and I need to be put through to the director's office."

"Did you say, Robert James Austin?"

"Yes."

"*The* Robert James Austin?"

"Yes."

"Hold on, please."

After a brief pause, another voice said, "Director Varneys' office. How may I help you?"

"This is Robert Austin. I need to make an appointment to see the director right away."

"Hold on please." Another delay. The voice returned. "I'm sorry—-your name was?"

"Austin. Doctor Robert James Austin."

"Thank you, sir. Hold on please." Another several minutes went by and then a different voice said, "The director will see you, Doctor. When would you like to meet with him?"

"Tomorrow."

"The director suggested that we make transportation arrangements for you, for security reasons."

"That won't be necessary. I'll make my own arrangements. Is two o'clock okay?" After several more minutes, the voice came back on the line.

"The director is busy at two but will see you at three. He insists that we take care of your travel arrangements."

"I don't care what the director insists on. I'll be there at 3 PM. Thank you." Bobby hung up the phone.

The next day, when Bobby walked into CIA headquarters at 2:45, he was escorted to the reception area of the director's office. Varneys' assistants asked him for his autograph, which he declined to give them. At precisely, 3 PM, he was shown into Varneys' office, which was so large that, unlike Varneys' previous office at the OSSIS, this one made the man look small. Varneys was seated behind his mammoth desk and stood when Bobby walked in.

"Well, well. Robert Austin. It's been a long time. I was twenty years younger and much better looking the last time you saw me," Varneys said as he smiled and stretched out his hand to Bobby.

Bobby's body was stiff and tense, his face gaunt and deadpan, but his eyes were raging. He let the director's hand languish in the air. He waited for the assistant to close the door and then, his voice hoarse with anger, said. "I want you out of my life forever, Varneys. What do I have to do to make that clear enough for you? What you did to me with Christina Moore was unconscionable. It was the cruelest thing that ever happened to me."

Varneys smiled. "Oh, I don't think that's true at all. As I recall, there was a small incident with a newborn in a garbage bag."

Bobby glared at Varneys with an intensity the likes of which Varneys hadn't seen since his last confrontation with Bobby two decades earlier. "I see you've done pretty damn well for yourself off my back," said Bobby as he looked around the palatial office. "I read the transcripts on your Senate confirmation hearings. Without me, you'd still be checking IQ tests at the OSSIS."

Varneys' eyes narrowed and a vein on his right temple bulged as he leaned forward. "So what of it. You did pretty damn well off of me. If it weren't for me, you'd never have cured any of those diseases, gotten those Nobels or raised all that money for charity. At best, you'd be some geek working in the back room of a software company."

"Drop dead," Bobby snarled back. "You've re-written history so much for the Senate that you've forgotten what really happened. You drove me out and left me for dead. Remember that?"

Varneys took a moment to regain his composure. When he spoke again, his voice was softer. "You're right Robert. I did. But when I cut you off from the Institute, I expected you to come back and do it my way. I was surprised when you didn't. You achieved what you said you would. I was wrong. I've been proud of you for a long time."

"You knew how vulnerable I was. I had no one. You took everyone away from me."

Varneys shook his head. "Robert—did you just come here to vent and tell me what an asshole I am? If so, then you've already done that and this meeting's over. But if you calm down, we can have a real discussion. I'm trying to understand what my latest crime is."

Bobby's face was flushed and his voice had grown strained. "You're that twisted! I can't believe it. You planted a woman to seduce me so she could get pregnant and you think that's okay. All in the course of a day's work for Orin Varneys, the puppet master."

Varneys came out from behind his desk and sat down at one of the guest chairs, and motioned Bobby to do likewise. He didn't begin to speak until Bobby had taken a seat. "You may think that —but it's not true. All I did was find the perfect woman for you, a woman who was worthy of you. Obviously, I chose right. Now I'm to blame because you fell in love with her—and she fell in love with you. I'm to blame for bringing two people together who both needed someone."

"Who asked you to?" Bobby asked.

"Get real, Robert. You had nothing. All you did was screw strippers, hookers and coked-up bimbos."

"And a relationship based on a lie is better? She made a deal with you."

Varneys eyes widened. "A deal?"

"A deal to get pregnant."

Varneys shook his head. "Wrong again. All she agreed to do was to allow us to put her in a situation where you two might meet—

once. Just once. Nothing more. And to get her to do even that—we had to reduce her to tears by making her feel selfish if she didn't. If you remember—she didn't come up to you at that store in St. Thomas—you approached her—you came on to her. She didn't chase you. You chased after her. She wasn't even calling you back. You pursued her night and day. Have you forgotten all of that? Some deal she made with us!"

Bobby scowled. "You knew what you were doing."

"You're damn right I did. You have a gift. Maybe—just maybe—it can be passed to another generation. But you've been oblivious to that. You're as pig-headed and stubborn as you were when I first met you twenty years ago. When the WHO and NHO asked you for sperm samples for artificial insemination—you refused—didn't you?"

"I don't believe in that," Bobby replied.

"Exactly. So I decided you needed a match-maker. You sure as hell weren't going to meet a girl like Christina on your own. And yes, on the off chance that you could ever pull your head out of your self-righteous ass long enough to have a kid—it was important to have a woman as intellectually potent as possible. Christina has a 160 IQ."

Bobby was silent. He sat there looking down at the floor. Varneys continued to pummel him. "So now you've succeeded in driving away a fantastic woman who was crazy enough to fall in love with you and put up with your bullshit. You know, Robert—you need to stop thinking you're the only good person in the world."

Bobby's eyes had lost their angry intensity. Shaking his head from side to side, he finally said softly, "The only two people who talk to me this way are Susan and you." He then muttered to himself, "Mom and Dad—what an unholy combination."

Varneys looked exhausted. Highly charged emotional interchanges were not his thing. Walking slowly to his wall of built-in cabinets, he slapped the door on one of them and it opened to reveal a bar. He poured himself a large Scotch. Bobby saw what he was doing and said, "Is that Scotch?"

"Yes—would you like one?" asked Varneys.

"Please."

Varneys poured Bobby a tall one and then added more to his. The two of them sat down on the guest chairs and sipped their amber elixir slowly, neither of them speaking. After awhile, Varneys said, "You know, it's ironic. I give you advice and criticism. But I've been an unsuccessful father. I have two kids and they both hate me."

Bobby nodded knowingly, like he could see why that would be the case. "How old are they?"

"My son is thirty-three. He's a musician with a drug problem. Left home at seventeen and hasn't spoken to me in twelve years. My daughter's thirty-seven. She's a lawyer with a big L.A. firm. I get a Christmas card and a birthday card. That's it."

"You know, you're a pretty controlling guy. That can be hard to take."

Varneys took another sip of his drink. The two of them were silent, sitting there—each lost in his own thoughts.

Finally, Varneys seemed to snap out of it and said, "So here's where we are. You've broken her heart. You've thrown away the love of your life. We don't even know where she's run off to. And there are people out there who want to kill you. So now what are you going to do?"

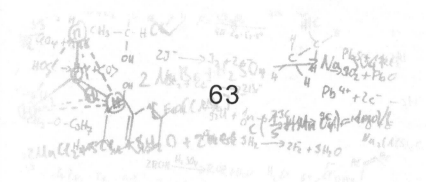

63

WHEN SUSAN TRIED TO REACH Christina on her cell phone, the automated message indicated that the number had been disconnected. Susan drove to Christina's apartment in Marblehead, but she wasn't there. The landlord said that she had seen Christina load suitcases into her car and drive off that past weekend.

Susan scrolled down the directory on her phone and clicked on another number. When her call was answered, she said, "It's Susan Corwin. I'm too angry right now to tell you what I think of you, so I'll just tell you what I need you to do. And it's the least you can do after the train wreck you caused." Susan listened to the voice on the other end of the line. Cutting the person off abruptly, she continued, "I'm not interested in talking about it. Just find Christina Moore for me. Her cell's disconnected and she's left her apartment. But I'm sure you have your ways."

Perrone replied, "Don't hang up. I know how upset you are and Varneys told me about his meeting with Austin, but I thought I was doing something really good. Everybody was supposed to win on this. When I discovered Moore, I knew she would be perfect for Austin. And from her records, I thought she deserved someone special after all she'd been through. I was doing a solid for them and at the same time, satisfying Varneys. And if they had a kid, maybe it would be a genius —so then the world gets Austin #2. I've done a lot of shit in this job—but this was supposed to be something I could be proud of. It was never supposed to backfire like this."

"That's your take on it, Perrone, and in the twisted world you live in, maybe that makes sense to you. But right now, it's not important. Just find her for me."

Perrone and his crew took four days to find Christina since she wasn't using any credit cards that could be traced and she didn't have a cell phone registered to her name that could pinpoint her location. What gave the clue to where she was, were cash withdrawals on her debit card. It took only one phone call for Perrone to get her bank to alter the program on her accounts so that no more than one withdrawal of only $20 could be made from any particular ATM. He figured this would ensure that she would need to make multiple withdrawals from a succession of ATMs, thereby leaving a geographically traceable trail. That led them to Ogunquit, a small coastal town in Maine, halfway between Portsmouth and Kennebunkport. Perrone dispatched four agents to scour the seaside village and find out where she was staying. They located her at a motel called "Peg Leg."

Susan made the drive to Ogunquit in under two hours, arriving at nine in the evening. After scoping out Peg Leg, she checked into a roadside motel about a quarter mile away. By eight the next morning, Susan was in her car parked across the street from Peg Leg, sipping coffee and eating donuts. She waited and watched as she listened to an oldies radio station. Finally, just after 11 AM, she saw Christina exit a room on the second floor and walk down the stairs to her car. She followed Christina at a distance, along Route

1, an old road that hugged the dramatic coastline, until she pulled off and entered the parking lot for the Ogunquit Museum of Art. Susan waited for Christina to go into the museum, and followed a few minutes later.

Susan stood back and observed Christina in one of the galleries. She looked so different. The confident vivacious beauty who radiated energy and spirit wasn't there anymore. In her place, was a pale young woman whose hair was pulled back severely and pinned down in as unbecoming a manner as possible. She looked gaunt and tired and wore no makeup. Formless clothes hung loosely on her thin frame and successfully obscured her figure. As Christina sat on a gallery bench staring vacantly at a painting on the wall, Susan came up behind her. "I never really got Rothko. I can look at his work, but I feel nothing coming back to me."

Christina didn't turn around. She kept staring at the painting. "He was a very troubled artist. Even after becoming famous, he killed himself."

Susan sat down next to Christina and put her hand on top of hers. "Hello, sweetie. I tried to call you. I had to see you."

Christina didn't say anything or even look at Susan. She didn't ask how Susan had found her. She bowed her head. Finally, she turned toward Susan and her green eyes were awash in tears. "I'm so ashamed. I feel so terrible. I wish I was dead." As she burst into sobs that shook her entire body, Susan pulled her close, gently cradling her head against the crook of her neck and patting her.

"You have nothing to be ashamed of, honey. You're a good person. And you've done nothing wrong. Nothing at all." Susan held her and stroked her head and then, after a few minutes said, "Let's get some air. I think there's a beautiful view of the water from the back of this place."

They climbed out over the glacial boulders that protected the museum from the pounding surf and sat down on one of the huge rocks facing the sea.

Her voice still shaky, Christina said, "I would never do what Bobby thinks I did."

Susan put her arm around Christina's shoulders. "Honey, there's a lot that you don't know about Bobby and a lot that he doesn't know about you. Those things make a real difference. When I spoke to Bobby, I told him about your past because he needed to know that."

Christina broke the embrace and sat up straight. "What did he say?"

"He was shocked. He felt horrible. But you also need to know things about Bobby so you can understand him better, and understand his reactions. You remember you told me that he was going to show you the secret storage trunk he had in his apartment? Did you ever get to see it?"

"No."

"Unfortunately it got destroyed like everything else when that blast went off. But I spent the last few days doing research and I printed-out a bunch of stuff that was in that trunk. I want you to look at it now." Susan handed Christina a thick packet.

Christina frowned as she felt the weight of the envelope. "Do I have to look at all this stuff now?"

"It's important. Take your time and read it."

A half hour later, Christina finished reading and said, "This is horrible, but what's it got to do with what we're talking about?"

"The baby in the garbage bag was Bobby," Susan said softly.

Christina's face went white.

"And no one would adopt him because everyone thought there'd be something wrong with him. So eventually, he was put into foster care. Then from age four, he was in a special boarding school— ostracized from society at large, a misanthrope, a freak. His parents died at eleven, then Joe Manzini died when he was nineteen. Then Varneys threw him out of the Institute because Bobby wanted to devote himself to medical research. Again, he was all alone. He denied himself everything over the years, working like a slave. Do you get the picture?"

Christina stared at Susan, as Susan continued, "You were his entire world. His connection with life and some semblance of normalcy and happiness was you. When he thought that none of that was real because you were playing a role, it devastated him. That's why he acted as badly as he did. Because that's how much you mean to him."

Christina looked down at the frothing sea. "Why didn't he tell me?"

"He's told no one. He didn't even tell me. I found out by accident. The fact that he said he was going to tell you—-that says an incredible amount right there. But you're no better. Why didn't you tell him about yourself?"

"I was going to. But —I know this sounds terrible. I was ashamed. After all these years, I still was ashamed."

Susan's head wagged disapprovingly. "Just like Bobby. As crazy as that is for both of you—there you have it."

Both women were silent and in their own thoughts.

Then Susan said, "Bobby went to see Varneys."

Christina's eyes widened. "I can't believe he'd do that. He hates him so much."

"That shows you, honey. The fact that after all these years, he would go see Varneys to confront him shows you how much you mean to him. Varneys will confirm what you told Bobby—right?"

Christina nodded, her voice now soft. "Unless he lies. But what difference does it make? It's all ruined. It will never be the same again."

Susan took Christina's hands in hers and squeezed them as she looked directly into her eyes. "That's not true. I told you a long time ago—love is stronger than secrets. Everything happens for a reason. I believe that and I've always told Bobby that. The two of you were destined to be together. The circumstances that brought you together are immaterial—that was just the vehicle. The only thing that matters is that you found each other."

Christina looked down. "He hurt me so badly."

"Do you love him?"

The emeralds looked up at Susan. "I'll always love Bobby."

"Then promise me this. When he comes to you. And he will come to you…"

Christina cut Susan off and nodded.

"I'll keep my heart open. But I need time, Susan."

"So does he, honey."

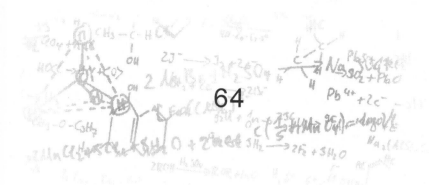

64

B ACK FROM WASHINGTON, BOBBY WAS emotionally exhausted and overwhelmed by remorse. He desperately wanted to see Christina or at least speak to her, but Susan told him she wasn't ready. So, Bobby did what he had done so often in the past. He retreated from the emotional turmoil in his life by immersing himself in a punishing and unrelenting regime of work.

Bobby estimated that tuberculosis was only six years away from becoming a worldwide pandemic that would dwarf cancer and AIDS in its destructive power. He called it "the sleeping giant of diseases." While it wasn't too long ago that the scientific community thought they were close to eradicating the disease, the landscape was dramatically altered by two things: new mutant "smart strains" of the Tubercle Bacillus that are multi-drug resistant, and the weakened immune systems of tens of millions of people infected with HIV that makes them particularly susceptible to TB and transforms them into fertile breeding grounds for the highly contagious disease. Sitting in his lab, Bobby knew that there were now more cases of TB in the world than at any other time in history, with one-third of the world's population already infected and a person dying from it every second.

Perhaps it was Bobby's sleep deprivation, fueled by his nightmares, and the absence of Christina to help him cope, but as the months of grueling work progressed, he felt increasingly detached from the present. As Bobby watched through his microscope as the *Mycobacterium Tuberculosis* mutated to become more and more resistant to the newest and most powerful antibiotics, he found himself experiencing an emotion that he never felt in his research.

He became angry. "Look at you. You think you're so damn smart. You think you're going to destroy the whole human race, don't you?" he muttered contemptuously to the microscopic creatures occupying the drop of water on the slide. As Bobby stared intensely at the small piece of glass on the microscope stand, he began to feel increasingly uneasy. It was three in the morning but he sensed he wasn't alone. Silently and invisibly, a force of destruction was performing its dark miracles in a drop of water right in front of his eyes. The intellect behind this energy of mayhem astonished Bobby with its efficiency and perverse elegance. Nothing was wasted. There were no mis-steps. It all took place with effortless precision. Was the lab getting colder? He whipped around to look behind him. He dropped to his knees to look under the desks and consoles. There was nothing there that he could see, but he felt a presence bearing down on him, like someone or something was standing very close. A wave of nausea surged through him and he began to shiver even though his body was wet with perspiration. He was scared. But the fact is, he had been scared for a long time. The more he learned and the more he struggled against this omniscient force of negativity, the more scared he became.

Bobby knew that formulating a new antibiotic was a waste of

time. At best, it would work for a few years, after which the bacteria would have built up its immunity so it would be even stronger to take on the next drug. A vaccine was needed—one that could be taken orally and would work on all age groups. Bobby wanted it to be something fitting for this killer with grandiose aspirations. He wanted it to be nasty and punishing. He turned to the neglected science of bacteriophage, which was gaining ground in the 1920s and 1930s, until it was abandoned in the Western hemisphere with the advent of antibiotics. What appealed to Bobby was how it worked. The phage, a type of virus, hijacks the metabolic machinery of the bacterium, forcing it to produce hundreds of new phages that take up so much room inside the bacteria that they cause the bacterial cell walls to literally explode.

While the science of bacteriophage is aimed at finding a virus that already exists in nature to fight a particular bacteria, Bobby wasn't interested in this haphazard process—instead, he would modify, through genetic engineering, a series of readily available phages so that they would target the full array of bacteria that cause TB. To ensure that the bacteria couldn't escape detection by the phage, Bobby would seek to identify numerous unique characteristics of the TB bacteria, each of which would be capable of triggering the phage's appetite. This was his plan for the vaccine against the plague about to come.

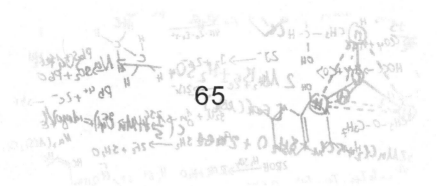

65

THREE MONTHS HAD PASSED SINCE Bobby and Christina had broken up. When Susan got to the lab, she found Bobby pacing nervously in her office waiting for her. His voice strained, he pleaded. "I can't live like this. I can't go backwards. I've got to see her. You know where she is. Tell me."

Christina's absence, coupled with the pressures of his work had taken its toll on Bobby. Susan looked at him pitifully as she wagged her head. "I shouldn't do this," she said, writing down an address and handing it to him. As he rushed out of her office, she yelled after him, "Take a shower, shave and change your clothes first. You look terrible."

Bobby made the drive to Providence, Rhode Island in less than an hour and a half. He pulled up to a nondescript three story building in a run-down part of town. A cheaply made sign affixed to the structure bore the name, Harmony House. Bobby walked through the institutional glass and aluminum door into a small reception area.

"How may I help you, sir?" asked a chubby, angelic girl who couldn't be more than sixteen.

"I'm here to see, Christina Moore."

The girl smiled as she looked him over.

"And you are?"

"Doctor Austin."

"You're here on business?"

"Yes."

"Sign here," she said, pointing to the visitor log. Pulling out a schedule and running her finger down and across several columns, she said, "Doctor Moore should be in the auditorium now. Just go through those doors, make your first left, and then go to the end of the hall and make a right." Before heading off, Bobby noticed a plastic receptacle containing some printed materials hanging from a nail in the wall and he took one. The cover page of the pamphlet described Harmony House's mission as follows:

'To provide a safe and caring environment for runaway
girls in which their mental and physical health can
be nurtured, their self-esteem reaffirmed, and their
dignity as human beings re-established.'

Bobby walked to the auditorium, opened the door and slipped inside. He took a seat in a corner of the back row. There were about twenty girls on the stage whose ages seemed to range from twelve to seventeen. They appeared to be concentrating hard as they looked at the young woman who stood in front of them. Christina was dressed in a black leotard with leggings. Her hair was pulled back in a pony tail and glistened in the stage lights. She called out instructions in a clear authoritative voice. The girls watched her execute dance routines as they tried to emulate her.

At the end of the class, Christina reminded them to attend the math tutorials that she was giving in the afternoon. After the last girl had left the auditorium, while Christina was facing the other way, Bobby walked toward the stage.

Though he wanted to seem relaxed, the tenseness in his voice betrayed him. "So how does it feel to be the most beautiful woman on this entire island?" He regretted the words as soon as they left his mouth.

Christina stiffened. She stopped what she was doing, but didn't turn around.

Bobby kept walking toward the stage as he spoke. "Christina, I was wrong. I said some terrible things. I'm so sorry." Now she stood facing him, only fifteen feet away, glaring down at him from the stage. Her skin- tight leotard accentuated the grace and strength of her figure and her face glowed with the aura that was peculiar to her.

Her almond eyes showed no softness and her voice was hard and detached. "I'm not ready to see you. You shouldn't have come here."

Bobby stopped walking. "I'm dying without you. I miss you so much."

"What do you miss? This?" she said, as she roughly ran her hands down her body. "You hurt me, Bobby. Very badly."

"I had no idea what happened to you when you were a kid. When Susan told me, I was shocked."

"It doesn't matter. What you did triggered something inside me that made me realize I had unfinished business with myself. That's why I'm here."

"I'm not sure I follow," he said.

"I needed to stop being ashamed for what was done to me. To

344

really stop. Not just intellectually, but deep down. Being here—I'm learning by helping these kids understand the same thing."

Bobby hoisted himself up on the stage and stood inches away from her. He took her hands in his and gripped them tightly. "Christina. I love you so much. Don't shut me out." As he looked intensely into her eyes, an energy passed between them.

Christina broke his gaze by looking down. He gently lifted her chin with one hand and kissed her lightly on her lips. He cupped her face in his hands as if he were cradling a jewel and kissed her forehead. "I love you," he whispered. "No one could ever love you more than I do." She leaned into him slightly, but enough for him to feel the heat of her body.

"I've never stopped loving you Bobby, but I'm not ready to come back," she said softly. "I need more time to get my head straight and I want to see these girls through the next few months."

"Are you sure?" he asked.

Christina nodded.

There was no way he could mask his disappointment. He held her tightly against him as he buried his face in her hair, his eyes closed. Her scent shot through his nervous system like an electric jolt and instantly made his memories of their intimacies come alive.

She looked up at his sad face and smiled, her eyes wet. Tapping his lips playfully with her finger, she said, "But you know— that doesn't mean you can't come visit and take me out for dinner."

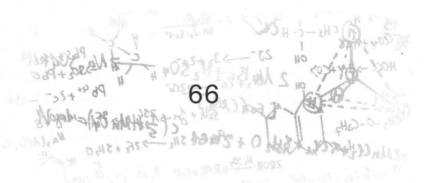

66

AT THE SAME TIME BOBBY was working on TB, he was also researching arteriosclerosis and atherosclerosis—what he called "AA". This diversion helped clear his mind, particularly because it was a different type of exercise for him. Similar to his earliest work in the autoimmune area, with "AA" — there was no bacteria, virus, parasite or other "invader" that was causing the problem. It was purely the internal operations of the human body that he had to grapple with. Just like his spilled martini had emulsified the grease on his stove, Bobby was looking to synthesize a safe ingestible substance that could dissolve away the plaque, cholesterol, calcium, and other deposits that clog the cardiovascular system causing heart attacks and stroke resulting in over fourteen million deaths annually.

Using his integrative math language to design formulas and computer programs to run a seemingly endless process of analysis, he broke down the congesting materials into their chemical components and then structured equations to identify the chemicals which had the capability to dissolve each of them. Further formulas would isolate the beneficial components of the solvents and eliminate the harmful ones. Everything was expressed mathematically and it was this process which held the key not only to finding the solution, but in doing so in a small fraction of the time that traditional methods would take.

Immersing himself in his work, more intensely than ever before, he bounced back and forth between TB and AA, relentlessly, hoping to make the most of every day. But as the weeks went by, Susan began to notice a difference in him. He was becoming increasingly detached from present reality. Even when he wasn't in one of his frequent trances, he didn't seem present. Reclusive and paranoid, he sequestered himself in his office with the door locked—or worked from the guest house for days on end. He began to look disheveled, shaving rarely, wearing the same clothing for days, his hair uncombed and greasy. In only a few weeks, he lost over fifteen pounds as he ate erratically, subsisting on micro-waved chili, pasta and pretzels, washed down with energy drinks or liquor. His desk was cluttered with toppling stacks of computer print-outs and notebooks whose pages were crammed with hastily penciled scrawl. He skipped staff meetings and minimized and eventually eliminated his interactions with everyone. Frequently, he didn't seem to even hear Susan or anyone else who attempted to speak with him. He was in his own world, and that world was fast becoming very separate from the one that others inhabit.

Alarmed, Susan called Christina. Susan's voice was flat, devoid of its usual animated quality. "When's the last time you spoke to Bobby?"

"About three weeks ago. He called me, but since then he hasn't returned my calls. He's buried in work I guess. You know how he gets."

Standing in her office slowly walking in a circle, Susan was holding the phone so tightly that her knuckles were white. "He's in a very bad way, Christina. We're losing him. You have to come back before it's too late."

"What are you talking about?" Christina asked, as she began to nervously run the fingers of her right hand through her hair.

Susan's voice was shaky. "Bobby's losing his connection. He's almost completely detached from reality. I called Varneys."

"You called Varneys?" asked Christina incredulously.

"He sent a big expert down here—some doctor named Uhlman, who knew Bobby when he was growing up and ..." Susan stopped talking in mid-sentence as she gulped in air and became silent.

"Susan, tell me what this Uhlman guy said."

No longer able to maintain her composure, Susan began to sob. "He said this was always something that could happen to Bobby. He can slip into his own world, into schizophrenia or dementia, and never come back. Uhlman couldn't even communicate with Bobby. He said he's surprised it didn't happen years ago. We're losing him, Christina. We're losing Bobby. I don't think he even knows who I am most of the time."

Colum McAlister didn't like what he was hearing about Austin's behavior. To him, Austin's increasing reclusiveness and alienation from his staff meant that something big was going to happen soon. He could feel it. A TB breakthrough. "Two billion a year in revenue down the drain, and our best meal ticket for the future shot to hell. That's what this will mean Goddammit," he scowled as he looked at Bushings latest numbers.

"But you told me you got a good reception in Washington—

you said we're going to get some help from the FDA and Justice Department," Turnbull said.

"That will only plug the dam for awhile." McAlister picked at his manicured finger nails.

"Don't jump to conclusions, Colum. It may take Austin a lot longer. We've got time to plan."

"Plan? I'll tell you the plan I'm interested in. I need you to come up with a liquidation plan on my stock shares. I want to get out as quickly as I can— but smart. "

"Me, too. I've got to get out, also," Turnbull said.

McAlister's face turned crimson and the veins on his forehead swelled. "No way. I don't want this looking like a rush to the exit door. The SEC will be all over us. Your shares stay put until I say otherwise. Do you understand me?"

"My life savings are in the stock—you got to let me get out."

"When I say so. Not before. It's my call or you can leave right now. Don't forget who got those shares for you in the first place."

67

CHRISTINA ARRIVED AT PRIDES CROSSING the morning after her call with Susan. She was shocked when she saw Bobby. His appearance had changed radically since she had seen him in Rhode Island for dinner six weeks prior. Looking like a crazed rock musician, he stood in front of three keyboards, each clued into a separate main-frame computer. He was typing at lightning speed, alternating from one to the other, as if he were possessed. His level of concentration on the equations he was typing was so intense that she could feel the energy radiating from him, something she had never experienced before. Although she stood next to him, his gaze didn't stray from the keyboards and he didn't say anything.

Christina maneuvered in front of him and grabbed his hands away from the keyboards. She looked into his eyes and said, "Bobby. It's me. Christina."

When he looked back at her blankly, her eyes filled with tears. She kissed him on his lips and leaned into him, pressing her body against his as she hugged him, her head cradled under his chin against his chest.

Maybe it was the soft warmth of her body against his. Or the wetness of her tears as they seeped into his shirt. More likely, it was the scent of her hair, only inches from his face. But after a few minutes, she felt his hands stroke her head as he whispered into her ear, "Hey honey. You're here."

Over the next several days, she worked on him slowly. She fed him nutritious food and hot green tea. Every morning, she took him into the shower with her and shaved his face, shampooed his hair and scrubbed him down. He would drift in and out of present consciousness, but physical closeness to her and the sound of her voice seemed to be the key to bringing him out of his nether world. Each day a little more progress was made. At night, she held him closely and that seemed to give him the comfort he needed to close his eyes and sleep. She was alert to any overt signs of night terrors so she could wake him before they became too destructive. Gradually, he began to clock some real sleep time. By the time twelve days had past, he seemed to have crossed the line. Another two weeks after that, and the Bobby she knew was back. Almost. There was a new edge to him, an underlying anxiety. She could even feel it in the way he made love to her.

With a hand on each side of his face, she said, "Bobby—I'm never going to lose you again."

He placed his hands on top of hers and kissed her on the forehead. "I know I scared you and Susan. But you have no idea what I'm up against. I have to go to a whole different place to fight this battle. An alternate state of mind. It's the only chance I have to win. What I'm fighting is too powerful."

Christina pressed her head against Bobby's chest. She didn't want to think he was crazy. "You do what you have to do. I'll be right next to you."

For the next fifteen months, every day was a struggle for Bobby as he worked on TB and AA simultaneously. Christina stayed close at hand—her presence being his anchor, the life-line that would pull him back when he drifted too far for too long. It was a daily challenge for her to keep him mentally present and physically healthy. Nights were a terrible ordeal, as Christina tried to navigate him through his frequent night terrors so he could get some sleep. She was grateful that she was able to divert him a few times a week away from the lab, but even then she found him distracted as his mind was constantly working, like a computer that was always processing information. Susan had increased Bobby's lab staff to over eighty people, most of them working in the Tufts laboratories, as that many hands were needed to keep up with Bobby's genetic programming of the anti-TB phages.

A little less than eighteen months after Christina had first returned, she saw a look of contentment come across his face as he sat in front of a large computer monitor. Smiling broadly, his eyes gleamed.

"Bobby—are you watching porn? Why do you look so happy?" She came over to him and looked over his shoulder. On the monitor were highly magnified pictures of cells in the midst of innumerable tiny particles.

He pointed to the minute dust-like grains. "That's all that's left of the TB bacteria. It's done, Christina. It works."

Calvin Perrone told Susan that things had changed in Washington. He didn't know why —but they had changed. There was now a contingent of powerful bureaucrats and congressmen who felt that Washington needed to pull-back on its unwavering endorsement of Austin. Perrone's sources indicated that the Justice Department was about to launch an anti-trust investigation on Bobby's drug company, Uniserve, and the FDA was going to be more rigid in its approval process on Austin's discoveries. When Susan relayed this to Bobby, he was crestfallen. After the intensity of his work, he couldn't allow the TB vaccine to become bogged down in political maneuverings, not when a person dies from TB every second and the disease was just a few years away from becoming the new bubonic plague.

68

I<small>T WAS A SPARKLING SPRING</small> day in Boston. One of those early May days that's so unseasonably warm that everyone sheds clothes as they linger outdoors aimlessly. The Tufts campus was ablaze with the raucous blossoms of cherry, pear and magnolia trees. Students were sprawled all over the lawns—eating, playing acoustic guitar, sunning themselves and making out unabashedly. As a gleaming black Suburban SUV with dark tinted windows drove slowly through the pedestrian mall, students begrudgingly got out of its way, wondering why the vehicle was being permitted to invade their space. When its doors opened in front of one of the university buildings, seven people piled out—-the first five were CIA agents, the last two were Christina and Bobby, who were encircled by the agents.

Bobby knew that to counter the political machinations brewing in Washington he had to get word out about the TB vaccine so that there would be a groundswell of public awareness and excitement. He had decided to do something he had avoided his whole life. Susan made the arrangements, working closely with Dean Walterberg. The presentation would take place in the largest lecture hall of the

Tufts Medical School. The chief science correspondents from the New York Times, the Washington Post, the London Times, Reuters, and Associated Press, were invited, with the caveat that no cameras were permitted. Also invited were the heads of the most important world health organizations and the directors of every nation's leading research hospitals. None of the invited knew who would be in attendance or what the purpose of the meeting was, but they were promised that it would be an event of major significance that warranted their presence. Having reconciled with Perrone, Susan called upon him to arrange security for the event.

Once all of the invitees passed the security protocols and checked their cell phones and PDAs, the doors to the hall were closed. Always smooth and charming, Dean Walterberg thanked everyone for attending on such short notice and then, almost matter of factly said, "It is my great pleasure to introduce to you a person I've been honored to know for over twenty years, Dr. Robert James Austin."

A gasp arose from the stunned audience. This was beyond unexpected. It wasn't even plausible. A public appearance by Bobby, with the media present no less, was unprecedented. None of them had ever even seen a photograph of him. A nervous energy careened through the hall. At first, people craned their necks in anticipation. Then they began to stand. Many left their seats and stood in the aisles. Others crammed forward toward the stage. The hall grew loud. Bobby let go of Christina's hand. As he left the comfortable anonymity of the back-stage area and walked into the glare of the stage lights, anyone who wasn't yet standing stood up immediately. An odd silence fell over the room as the esteemed audience stared at the greatest scientist who had ever lived.

When Bobby reached the podium, he looked out at the standing, silent audience. He shifted nervously from foot to foot. Opening his notes, he cleared his throat and said, "Thank you for coming."

Someone yelled out loudly, "Bravo Maestro."

That was all that was needed for decorum to break-down and pandemonium to break out. The audience erupted into frenetic applause and shout-outs. The attendees' faces beamed like those of young children at Disneyland first encountering life-size Mickeys and Donalds. Bobby blushed and shifted uneasily, looking anxiously to the off-side of the stage where Christina stood. Several times, he tried to quiet the audience down and begin his presentation, but the audience wasn't having it. It took a full ten minutes for them to wear themselves out and sit down.

When a large projection screen was lowered and time-lapse videos were shown of the phages Bobby had created, the presentation reached its dramatic climax. The audience saw the entire process of destruction unfold. First Bobby's phages identified the TB cells, ignoring human cells. Then they injected their DNA into them. Next, the TB cells began to swell, looking increasingly distorted and grotesque, until they finally burst into countless tiny fragments, thereby releasing thousands of new predatory phages, each of which went on to continue the assault on the disease. The videos showed the process repeatedly, and the faces of the audience registered their amazement.

A powerfully built figure reached out from the recesses of the back stage area and grasped Christina's arm from behind. Startled, she swung around.

"Ms. Moore, I want to thank you."

"Who are you?" Christina asked as she looked into the coal black eyes bearing down on her.

"Orin Varneys."

Christina caught her breath as she realized that the architect of so many things stood inches from her. "What are you thanking me for, Mr. Varneys?" she asked uneasily.

He pointed to the stage. "For rescuing our boy. For making today possible."

As they both looked outward to the stage as Bobby proceeded with a question and answer session, Christina noticed the subtle smile on Varneys face.

"He is so spectacular," she said, unconsciously emphasizing each word as she gazed at Bobby.

"He always was. Right from the beginning," replied Varneys.

They watched Bobby dazzle the audience. After a few minutes, Varneys said, "It's important to me that you know I never intended to hurt either of you."

"I'm over all of that. What matters is that we found each other. Without you, that never would have happened." Christina turned to face Varneys.

He was already gone.

The presentation had exactly the effect that Bobby hoped for. The world press was effusive and the heads of the disease control centers and the hospital directors pledged that getting the vaccine approved and into the field would be their top priority. The Washington politicians that McAlister had muscled were in an untenable position. Bobby had checkmated them. McAlister was livid. Bushings stock plunged fourteen percent on the news of the TB vaccine.

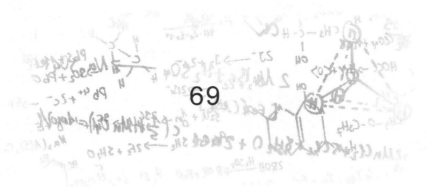

69

"I CAN'T BELIEVE THAT FREAK CAME out from hiding. Those reporters wrote about him like they were teeny boppers gushing over a pop star," said McAlister, breathing hard as he rode the exercise bicycle in his office gym, sweat pouring down his face.

"Look at the bright side," Turnbull replied. "Over the last year and a half, you've been able to dump a third of your stock so you beat the hit that the share price took from the TB announcement."

"But now the Board told me I can't sell anymore—I'm locked in."

"Colum, you got lucky. If the TB discovery had come as early as you originally thought, it would have been harder to get out."

McAlister's irritation was evident in his voice. "That's not how I look at it, Marty. What I keep thinking about is what the stock was worth before Austin started destroying our business. Do you remember? And what about all those options we had that became worthless? He's already cost me over a hundred million dollars. And I'm not even out of the woods yet on most of my shares. He's killing us. Absolutely killing us."

Turnbull shook his head, frowning. "At least you got some money out."

McAlister waved his hand. "What I'm thinking about is what happens next. What the hell happens next?"

----●--●●--●----

Six months later, rumors began to circulate in the scientific community that Bobby had completed synthesizing an organic solvent, which in the course of a ninety day treatment period could dissolve even severe cases of arterial plaque, with no adverse side-effects. The same treatment, taken daily, would prevent further build-up from occurring.

Unlike statins, which suppress the liver's natural production of cholesterol, Bobby's solvent didn't obstruct normal body chemistry, and while statins couldn't destroy arterial plaque already present, Bobby's organic solvent could. It could do everything statins could do and more, with none of statins' side-effects and at minimal cost to the public. The use of Bobby's formula would also drastically reduce the need for coronary bypass surgery and angioplasty.

In the year in which Bobby invented his solvent, over seventy-five million people took statins every day, and annual revenues from them were over fifty billion dollars. Statins were the number one worldwide revenue generating product for the major pharmaceutical companies. And as McAlister loved to point out at the annual Bushings shareholder meeting— once a person was prescribed statins, the regimen dictated that the patient remain on them for life. "Is there anything more beautiful in the entire universe than a customer for life?" This comment, delivered by McAlister as he dramatically held his arms up to the sky in gratitude, was guaranteed to bring the house down.

The expanding use of statins, even as a preventative to be prescribed for healthy people, was being promoted by the industry.

Supported by 'independent researchers,' whom the drug companies funded, and pliable government regulators —the growing use of statins was a seemingly unstoppable juggernaut.

But when Bobby's full report, with all supporting data, was published in a special edition of the *New England Journal of Medicine* all hell broke loose on Wall Street. Bushings stock fell thirty- one percent in one day before the New York Stock Exchange suspended trading in its shares. The stock of the other five major pharmaceutical companies fell in similar amounts on the exchanges on which they were traded.

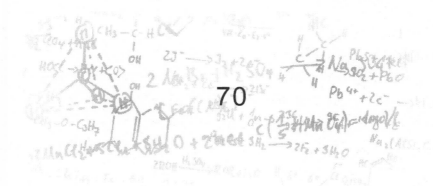

70

THE SUNLIGHT STREAMED THROUGH THE windows of the Prides Crossing guest house and illuminated the bedroom as brightly as if it were being lit for a photo shoot. It was a radiant Saturday morning in late June and Christina and Bobby sipped from their coffee mugs as they lay in bed. She was reading the *Bulletin of the American Mathematical Society* and he was reading, *The Astrophysical Journal*. "Hon, I think we should take a little vacation. Are you up for it?" Bobby asked.

Christina put down her magazine and cozied up against him. "Up for it—I'd love it. Are you kidding me?"

"Let's get dressed I want to show you something."

They drove south in the direction of Boston, but veered east to North Quincy. Navigating the narrow streets, they drove through a wide entranceway in a chain link fence and pulled up to a one-story building covered in white aluminum siding.

Christina hadn't taken note of any signs. "What are we doing here?"

"Come with me. You'll see." Entering, Bobby stepped up to the reception counter. "I'm here to see Mike Allen. He's expecting me—Bob Austin."

Two minutes later, Mike Allen, a portly man with a short beard, bounded into the room, hand outstretched. "Mr. Austin. Finally, we meet—after all the phone calls." He shook hands with Bobby and Christina and then led them out of the building on what seemed like an endless walk through the huge outdoor facility.

As they approached the water, Christina gazed out at the biggest marina she had ever seen. Pointing directly in front of him, Allen said, "There she is. Isn't she beautiful?"

It had been over twenty years since Bobby had laid eyes on *Dreamweaver*. He almost gasped.

Christina asked, "What's that?" Bobby ignored her question as Allen led them on to the vessel. The mahogany deck was gleaming, as were the nickel fixtures. It was as if time had stood still.

"Mike, you guys did a beautiful job. She looks perfect."

"Sails perfect, too. We took her out for a few trips to get the kinks out. Made some adjustments. She's fantastic. You'd never know she was in storage for two decades. We had her wrapped up like a baby. The way we had her, she could have lasted a thousand years." Bobby made his way to the steering wheel. He ran his hands over it admiringly.

"You did great. Just fabulous."

"Bobby—what's this all about?" asked Christina.

"This is my boat. *Dreamweaver*."

"You never told me you had a boat. When did you get it?"

"Joe Manzini left it to me in his will. His estate paid for the storage and upkeep all these years."

Christina walked along the deck and looked up at the huge masts. "It's gorgeous. It looks classic."

"It is classic. Just like you," said Bobby as he kissed her.

"He must have been a wealthy guy."

Bobby laughed. "He was. He left everything else to charity. I think he was afraid I'd become one of the idle rich if he left me a bundle."

"So how come you've had this gorgeous thing in mothballs for all these years?"

"I wasn't ready to use it. And I had no one to use it with. I needed a first-mate."

"So when do we take it out for a spin?"

"Real soon. This is going to be our vacation."

When Bobby told Susan that he and Christina would be sailing off for a few weeks, her face reddened. "Bobby—I don't think that's safe. Someone out there wants you dead. They tried once, and there's no reason to think you've gotten more popular since then. You know what Perrone said."

Bobby waved Susan off. "No one even knows that *Dreamweaver* exists. Christina and I will just disappear for awhile."

"I have to tell Perrone."

Bobby glared at her. "I'm sick of living in a bubble."

"I'm sorry, Bobby, but it is what it is. You can't make it different just by wishing it."

As Bobby left Susan's office, he turned at the door. "I'm going. It's that simple. Tell Perrone what you want, but I'm going and I don't want to see some aircraft carrier trailing me."

Over the next two weeks, Christina stocked *Dreamweaver* with all of the provisions needed for the trip. She'd never seen Bobby this excited. When she asked him where they were going, he told her it didn't really matter because sailing was a destination in itself.

"If we can't take care of number one, we mean nothing. We shouldn't even exist." This entry on a RASI blog attracted Perrone's attention. The CIA analysts agreed that it was a mandate for Bobby's assassination. Internet chatter had grown progressively more vehement after the TB vaccine, but the arteriosclerosis and atherosclerosis cures had escalated the outrage of the fringe groups to another level.

Having requested a meeting, Perrone sat in front of Varneys' imposing desk and said, "I think we need to get Austin out of town for awhile. There are too many outfits that hate this guy. And some of them have the wherewithal to do something about it."

"And where would you have him go?" Varneys asked as he looked up from the papers he had been reading.

Perrone pulled on his chin. "Maybe a military base."

Varneys laughed. "He'll never do it. I hear he's already working on his next project. He won't leave his lab. It just won't happen."

Perrone said, "He's been at that location too long. It's given the crazies time to find him."

Varneys continued to read his papers as if Perrone weren't there. After a few minutes he looked up and seemed surprised Perrone hadn't left. "Agent Perrone —you haven't told me anything I don't know. We have to deal with reality. Just protect the man."

Standing in the living room of his palatial suite at the St. Regis Hotel in Washington D.C., McAlister looked out the window across to the Capital building. *This used to be my town. I could call the shots. That fucking SOB has ruined everything.* The people he wanted to meet told him they preferred a location other than their offices. So one by one, the star performers in McAlister's video collection came to the hotel to placate and plead with the man who had the power to ruin them. They all said the same thing. "We tried, but we can't help you. We want to —but we can't. The momentum is too huge. Austin is unstoppable. You can destroy us but that won't accomplish anything. It's not our fault."

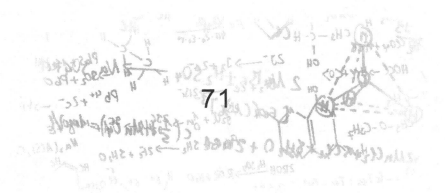

71

BOBBY'S SKILLS WERE RUSTY, BUT within two days on the open water, he felt he had them back. As *Dreamweaver* cut its way through the choppy surf, so many wonderful memories flooded through him. He concentrated on those, rather than on the last trip when Joe had told him of his illness.

Just the two of them, with no work or pressures, amid the solitary beauty of the ocean and the luxury of *Dreamweaver*, was exactly what Christina and Bobby needed. Their days were languorous, and in the evening Bobby pointed out every celestial site as they lay on deck staring at the canopy of stars, drinking wine and listening to Gato Barbieri. They made love whenever the feeling came over them, which was frequent— often out in the open, basking in the radiant sunshine as the sea breeze cooled them and the salt spray misted their skin, or under the night sky, bundled in blankets, the sea's movement augmenting their own rhythm. Never before were they so focused on each other.

The weather got progressively warmer as the days passed and Christina noticed that the compass showed they were traveling due south.

"OK mystery man. So where are we headed?"

"I thought we'd cruise down toward Florida."

"Any particular place?"

"The Keys. I've never been there. Have you?" Bobby asked.

"No. But Hemingway liked them," she said, laughing, her arms wrapped around his chest as she stood behind Bobby while he manned the wheel.

Their first stop was Key West. They anchored off shore and checked into the Reach Resort under Christina's name. During the day, they did nothing but eat, drink rum punch, snorkel, jet ski and luxuriate in the pristine surf. At night, they went bar hopping in Old Town, joining in the non-stop party that Key West is famous for and staying up to watch the dawn. After three days, Bobby said, "This is amazing, but I'm burning out. Time to slow the roll."

Back on the boat, they sailed for two days. As they entered a pristine crescent shaped harbor, Bobby began to lower the sails and drop anchor.

"Where are we now?" asked Christina. "This is gorgeous."

"Islamorada," replied Bobby.

The next morning, Bobby was up early. While Christina was still sleeping, he brewed a pot of strong coffee in the boat's galley, filled a mug halfway and then topped it up with Jameson's and heavy sweet cream. Leaning against the railing, he looked out at the diamond refractions of the sun on the surface of the harbor's protected waters. He squinted his eyes into narrow slits, not because the sun was too bright, but because it exaggerated the shimmering of the light on the water and he loved that. After taking a long slug of the liquor drenched coffee, his gaze became focused on the big brass bell that Joe used to ring to announce that it was meal time. "Doesn't *Dreamweaver* look great Joe? After all these years—we sail again! You and me and that amazing lady of mine. What do you think of her —isn't she incredible?" Two decades of cold storage had done nothing to chill the warmth of Joe's presence on the boat. Bobby could feel him all around.

———————•··•———————

One hundred ten nautical miles away from *Dreamweaver*, a forty foot long mahogany speed boat cut its engines almost to a halt as it got within two hundred feet of *My Time*, Colum McAlister's immaculate white motor yacht that was anchored in international waters off Palm Beach, Florida. Even as it crawled toward *My Time* to minimize its wake, the speed boat's engines growled loudly with their power. One of *My Time's* crew lowered a ladder and a short wiry man dressed in a white linen suit left the passenger seat of the speed boat and climbed aboard. He was escorted to the back of the yacht where McAlister sat on a large blue and white striped sofa under a peak-roofed awning.

"You're looking well, Gunther. Prosperity continues to agree with you I see," said McAlister.

The man's military nod was his hello. "I can't complain. Business is too good to retire. The world only gets more complicated."

Gunther Ramirez was now in his mid sixties. But neither age nor wealth had softened his demeanor. He still looked more dangerous than most men half his age and twice his weight. A transplant to Panama from Buenos Aires when he was a teenager, Ramirez had risen through the ranks of Miguel Noriega's private guard to become his right-hand man and confidante, instrumental in the planning and implementation of Noriega's narcotics and money-laundering rackets. After the fall of that regime, Ramirez took his small fortune and his best men and launched an elite service for hire, specializing in what he referred to as "matters of sensitivity." As the years went by and word of his prowess spread, he attracted a substantial international clientele which included McAlister.

"Gunther, I have a transaction for you but it won't be easy."

"When are they ever easy?" replied Ramirez, smiling.

"First, I'll need you to scope the situation out and see if it's even possible."

"Everything is possible," said Ramirez, as he removed a cigar from a monogrammed gold case in his jacket pocket.

"The person I have in mind is well protected. For sure, by private security forces, but I have reason to believe by the government, also."

"They did a good job protecting the Kennedys," said Ramirez.

"You've heard of Dr. Robert James Austin?"

"I'm alive, aren't I?" Ramirez lit the cigar with his gold lighter.

"It's time for him to go away," McAlister said.

"You don't get nicer as you get older, do you, Colum?" replied Ramirez with a laugh. He blew smoke in McAlister's direction.

"How much will it cost?" McAlister asked.

His chin resting in his right hand and his eyes glazing over, Ramirez appeared to be lost in thought. Finally, he looked up and said, "This is a tough one. Doing the job is one thing. But the afterwards is what worries me. The whole world is going to try to track down Austin's assassin. It's as risky as taking out the leader of a major country—maybe riskier. I have to think about it. I've come this far. I don't want to spend my final years in a cage."

McAlister walked toward the gleaming deck railing. "If the job can be done clean, it's worth a lot of money to me."

"Is this on your tab or Bushings'?"

His fist clenched, McAlister snapped back, "That doesn't concern you. You'll get paid. You've never had an issue with me, right?"

Ramirez smiled. "You're always dependable Colum. Top of my Christmas card list."

"Well—how much?"

"Ten Million Euros. Paid the usual way."

The color drained from McAlister's face as the magnitude of the cost sunk in. He turned toward the ocean's expanse. Ramirez slid back into the pillowed sofa enjoying his cigar.

After a few minutes, McAlister took a seat next to him. "We don't want a spectacle, Gunther. It should look like an accident or a natural occurrence."

Ramirez smiled. "You're telling an artist how to paint."

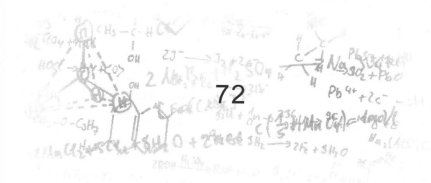

72

AT BUD N' MARY'S MARINA, Bobby and Christina rented a car and cruised Islamorada and did some souvenir shopping. Christina made Bobby buy a white captain's hat complete with anchor insignia and gold braiding, and she bought a white caftan. When they were hungry, Bobby drove for awhile and then they pulled into a gravel parking lot.

"Do you think this place is okay?" Christina asked, as she looked at the tiny roadside eatery.

"I heard it's really good," Bobby replied, knowing exactly where they were.

They walked over to the take-out window to check out the menu.

"So how's the conch chowder today?" Bobby asked as he looked squarely into the eyes of the old timer.

"Fantastic —as usual."

"Is it really fresh, or do you use frozen?"

Alan Gottshalk's eyes narrowed at the insinuation and his annoyance wasn't well hidden. "The Conch Shack is famous for fresh. We never use frozen."

"Famous— really?" replied Bobby, as he stared back at Alan, enjoying how easy it was to wind him up. "And how's the crab roll today?"

Alan looked back into the stunningly clear light blue eyes that were probing him. "Delicious as always."

"Really? I heard all the places around here have their crab shipped in from the mainland," Bobby said.

"I catch the crabs myself. If you want fresher, put on a bathing suit."

The two men's eyes locked for what was a peculiar amount of time. Christina shifted uneasily. There was a weird energy in the air.

"Make it two conch chowders and two crab rolls," Bobby said.

As they walked away she said, "Bobby—why were you giving that old man such a hard time? It's just lunch. It's no big deal."

The order seemed to take awfully long for a take-out place. Finally, Bobby heard his ticket number get called. He went to the pick-up window.

Alan opened the sliding screen and pushed the items out toward Bobby. "Ok, fella. Here it is." The sound of Alan's voice when he said the word, "fella" seared through Bobby. *The voice. That's the voice.* He felt his brain spin inside his head. His memory shot back four decades in a split second. He saw himself cradled in Alan's arms, being fed a bottle as he listened to *that voice.*

When the take-out window banged shut in front of him, Bobby was jarred back to the present. The next thing he heard was a screen door slam loudly, and then, there in front of him in a stained white apron stood Alan, almost as tall as Bobby, but not standing that straight anymore.

"You've grown some, but I know who you are," Alan said. "I'd recognize those eyes of yours anywhere. Geez, you sure took long enough to come visit me!" Without warning and much to his own surprise, Bobby's eyes flooded with tears. The two men grasped each other in a bear hug that was so tight, they were white knuckled. That's when Alan's emotions overcame him too.

"Oh my God," Bobby said, as he picked Alan off the ground and swung him around. Christina stood there flabbergasted, having no idea what was going on.

Finally, Bobby broke the embrace. He and Alan had huge smiles on their tear stained faces. "Honey—do you remember the name, Alan Gottshalk from those newspaper articles Susan showed you? This is him."

Christina gasped. "You knew he was here?" she asked. Bobby smiled.

Turning to Alan, he said, "Alan—-this is Christina Moore, she's my other angel. She saved my life, too."

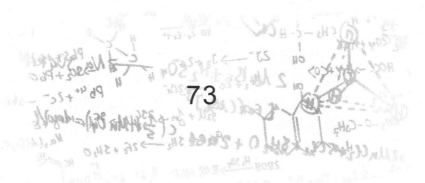

73

GUNTHER RAMIREZ WORE OLD POORLY fitting jeans, a faded red T-shirt, dirt covered sneakers and a Red Sox baseball cap that looked too big for his head. Like the other four similarly dressed Hispanics who sat with him in the back of the crowded van, he was hot and perspiring. They all worked for Green Thumb Garden Services in Beverly, Massachusetts and this was the busy season—late July. Ramirez had replaced Juan Torres who had fallen gravely ill shortly after eating lunch a few days prior. The owner of Green Thumb felt fortunate that Ramirez (using the name and phony ID of one Marcel Santiago), had come in to apply for a job the morning after Torres was hospitalized. He had hired Ramirez on the spot, seeing that his specialty, like that of Torres, was working on perennial gardens and roses.

Ramirez knew that he'd have all the time he needed. The virus causing the debilitating tropical disease which he had injected into Torres while standing behind him on line in a local convenience store would baffle local doctors for months, assuming, of course, that Torres didn't die sooner than that.

As was done every week, the Green Thumb van was buzzed

through the security gates at the Prides Crossing facility. Ramirez smiled as he saw the place for the first time. The van unloaded the workers and the garden equipment, and the foreman pointed out the various places on the property that would need Ramirez' special skills. Ramirez was pleased to see that the perennial and rose garden beds were located on three sides of the main building and also around the guest house.

"How fortunate for me," he muttered to himself.

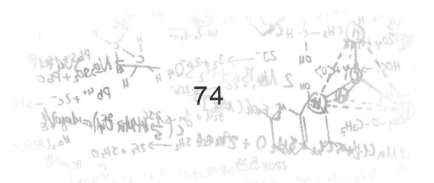

74

WEARING SHORTS AND NO SHOES, Alan and Bobby sat on the thin strip of powdery sand that separated the back of Alan's house from the Atlantic Ocean. As they sipped from beer bottles, Bobby dug his toes into the hot sand and looked out to the horizon. Alan held his leathery face up to the sun, his appreciation of its glistening warmth undiminished even after years of living in the Keys. Over the last few days, they had covered a lot of ground in their conversations, talking about everything that had transpired since Alan handed Bobby over to Natalie Kimball four decades earlier. Bobby mainly spoke about his feelings, which was something that had never come easily for him. But with Alan, Bobby opened up more freely than he ever had.

"Come on—let's take a walk and get some exercise," Bobby said, extending his hand to help Alan stand up.

Strolling along the shore line, the wavelets lapping at their feet, Alan said, "You still haven't told me why you picked now to visit. Why not earlier?"

Bobby looked down at the sand. "I was buried in work. I wanted to get a few more things done."

"In all the years since you wrote me, there was no time for a quick trip?"

"You have no idea how busy I've been," replied Bobby.

Alan wagged his head. "You think you can BS an old street guy? Come on. What's the real reason you're here now?"

Bobby stopped walking and picked up a few small rocks that had been fashioned into perfectly smooth discs by millions of years of tidal tumbling. Throwing them one at a time, they skimmed the water's surface, sending out ripples each time they landed. "Alan—have you ever thought how incredible it is –you and me? If you hadn't walked down that street on that day at that particular time, or if you hadn't noticed that bag—or if you had been afraid, or didn't want to get involved and had turned away—I would have been dead for sure. And if I had died, none of the work I've done would have happened."

Alan nodded. "After you wrote me that letter, that's all I thought about. If you had died, who could have done what you did? No one."

Bobby shook his head slowly. "So why did it happen Alan? Why do I have these abilities? Why were you there? What are the odds on any of this? It's just so weird."

Alan stretched his arm across Bobby's shoulders as they walked along the beach. "Things happen Bobby. They just do. Usually, it's weird bad things that happen. But sometimes, weird good things happen. That's life."

The two men walked on in silence, the only sound being that of pebbles scrambling on the shoreline as the tide came in. After awhile, Bobby stopped and looked out to the sea. "I'm not a big believer in coincidence." He turned to Alan as he asked, "What are your family origins, Alan? Where do your people come from?"

Alan waved his hand. "Who cares? What difference does that make?"

"Just tell me," said Bobby.

"My parents and I were born in the U.S. but my grandparents came from Germany."

"From Germany." Bobby paused as he processed the information. "Do you know what Gottschalk means in German?"

"Should I look it up?"

"I'll save you the trouble. It means 'God's servant'."

As they walked on in silence, Alan sensed that Bobby's mood had darkened. "Okay Bobby —so what's bothering you? I've seen it in your eyes since you got here."

For a moment Bobby hesitated, but then he realized there was no point in keeping it to himself. His voice strained, he said, "I feel like things are closing in on me. Really quickly. And I'm scared. I barely made it back last time. I was gone. Christina was the only one who was able to drag me back. She may not be able to again. If I'm going to have any chance of succeeding on my next project, I'll have to let my mind go very far out there. I can't control it like I used to. This may be it for me."

Alan didn't fully understand what Bobby was saying, but his advice was unequivocal. "Then get out now. Quit. Don't take the risk."

Bobby kicked the sand. "Too many people are counting on me. It wouldn't be right."

Alan grasped Bobby's forearm and looked him in the eyes. "Listen to me. Move down here where nobody will bother you, and live your life with that fantastic woman of yours. Don't push your luck, Bobby."

Bobby pulled away. "I wasn't given this gift so I could lay out in the sun."

"There's a time for everything, son," replied Alan.

Bobby stared out to the water. "And everything has its time," he replied, with a tone of resignation. "Maybe mine has come."

"So that's why you came here now," said Alan.

Bobby nodded. "I wanted to finally meet you. And I wanted to be on *Dreamweaver* one more time."

"Anything else on your list?"

"Yeah, two things."

75

BOBBY'S UNUSUAL ABSENCE WAS HIGHLY opportunistic for Gunther Ramirez, who confirmed to McAlister that he had formulated a plan for Bobby's disposal. A deposit of five million Euros arrived in the bank account of one of Ramirez' corporations in Mauritius through a series of off-shore account transfers arranged by McAlister.

Only days after receiving the payment, while Ramirez was dutifully tending to the perennials at the rear of the Prides Crossing lab, the back door was unlocked at a pre-arranged time and Ramirez slipped in. He had already de-activated the surveillance system. Knowing exactly where he was going, he entered Bobby's office and removed three flat discs from his pocket, each of which looked like a clear wristwatch battery. He disconnected the web cameras in the computer monitors on Bobby's desk and inserted the discs in their place. They fit perfectly and he knew the cameras wouldn't be missed. Ramirez then hid a tiny remote transmitting camera among the dusty clutter on the bookshelves facing Bobby's desk. Within ten minutes, he had re-activated the surveillance system, and was back in the garden meticulously "dead-heading" the hybrid tea roses in the perennial bed.

For their last day on Islamorada, Bobby and Christina invited Alan out for a day's sail on *Dreamweaver*. Alan brought his best friend, Lester Sill, a seemingly quiet thoughtful man who Alan had met years before in his charity work. Catching a strong north easterly wind, Bobby put the boat through its paces to give his guests some high speed thrills.

During a lull in the sailing, he came up behind Christina as she was preparing hors d'oeuvres in the galley. Putting his tan arms around her and taking her hands in his, he whispered into her ear, "Do you know how much I love you?"

Christina melted backwards into him. "I think I have some idea."

"I don't think you do," he said, his breath warm against her face.

He brushed the side of her head with his lips, as his arms enveloped her and pressed her body into his. She nuzzled her face against his chest and breathed in contentedly. A familiar feeling washed through her like a hot wave that wouldn't subside and she wished there weren't any guests on board so she could do something about it. While she had always been attracted to Bobby, on this vacation their connection had increased to such a degree that she found herself physically drawn to him all the time like she was a freshman co-ed in the throes of a first adult romance. Zoning out in the comfort of his embrace, her eyes closed, she barely felt it happening until he had just about finished slipping the diamond and emerald ring on her finger.

"Will you marry me, Christina?"

Stunned into silence but beaming, she alternated her gaze between her ring finger and Bobby's eyes. "Oh my God. Yes I'll marry you," she said, as she kissed him repeatedly like a giddy teenager.

"What date should we set?" she whispered into his ear as she wrapped herself around him.

"Today. At sunset. Here on *Dreamweaver*. Lester's a minister. Alan will be best man."

"Lester's a minister?" she asked incredulously. Bobby's response was his smile. "So his coming today was no coincidence, Dr. Austin?"

"You know I don't believe in coincidence," said Bobby. "And Joe's here too so it'll be perfect."

Christina's brow furrowed. "Joe?"

"He's all around us. Can't you feel him?" Bobby asked, his eyes sparkling.

"But what about Susan and my mom?"

"They'll forgive us. We'll have a reception back in Boston."

Frowning in mock concern, Christina said, "I have nothing to wear."

Bobby put his hands on Christina's waist and pulled her against him. "You and me under God's sky. That's all we need."

"I'll wear the white caftan I bought in town," she said with a chuckle.

With the sun setting spectacularly over the ocean, Bobby and Christina stood at the back of *Dreamweaver* and exchanged their timeless vows. Alan handed the minister identical platinum wedding bands, each of which Bobby had engraved with the mathematical symbol for infinity.

As she gazed deeply into the eyes that she had once described as 'windows to another world,' Christina was radiant. "I do," she said.

Peering into the emeralds that had smitten him on first sight, Bobby seemed almost ethereal in his equanimity as he responded to the ancient question.

76

MARTIN TURNBULL SAT AT HIS kitchen table, busy with the task at hand. It was Sunday, a little after eleven in the morning, and he was doing what he always did at that time on a Sunday while his wife was out running with her trainer. He spread scallion cream cheese on a darkly toasted sesame bagel and then added several thin slices of smoked salmon which he methodically trimmed to fit the bagel exactly. He placed one slice of tomato over the salmon, added a few capers, a slice of onion and then squeezed a generous amount of lemon juice before pressing the two halves of the sandwich together. His doctor had made him promise that he would cut down on bread and fatty milk products, but no medical concerns could impinge upon his greatest weekend pleasure.

The doorbell rang several times and finally his fifteen year old daughter, Samantha, stopped watching TV in the family room long enough to peer through the glass side panels in the entrance foyer.

"Dad, two men in suits are at the door," she bellowed, using all her lung capacity.

Turnbull yelled back from the kitchen, "Don't open it. Just

tell them we're not interested in buying anything or making any contributions."

Samantha did as she was told. One of the men loudly responded through the glass that she should have her mother or father come to the door.

Cream cheese smudged on his lips and a mug of coffee in his hand, Turnbull approached the door but didn't open it. "What do you want?" he asked with obvious annoyance.

"Are you Martin Turnbull?"

"Yes I am."

"Please look through the glass panels, Mr. Turnbull."

He did—and saw that the two men were each holding out badges that were hard to read, but appeared to say Treasury Department on them.

Turnbull opened the door. "What's this about?"

"We're Agents Thompson and McKenna. Securities and Exchange Commission. We need to speak with you and thought you would prefer to talk outside of your office."

In less than two seconds all of the color in Turnbull's face drained. The hand holding the coffee mug drooped involuntarily, spilling much of the coffee on the ornate Persian rug. Turnbull seemed immobilized as he stared at the agents.

"What's going on?" Turnbull asked, sounding short of breath.

"Can we come in Mr. Turnbull? It's not appropriate for us to have this discussion on your doorstep."

Turnbull motioned them into the house.

"Dad—is everything all right?" yelled Samantha from the family room.

"Yes honey," he shouted back as he led them into his study.

The two agents sat on the sofa and Turnbull pulled up a chair.

One of the agents then withdrew a small laminated card from the black leather badge holder and proceeded to perfunctorily read Turnbull his Miranda rights.

When he finished reading the card he said, "Do you understand that you don't have to speak with us in the absence of your attorney?"

"Yes."

"Do you want to proceed?"

"I reserve the right to stop at any point."

"Understood, Mr. Turnbull."

Agent Thompson opened his briefcase and removed a file from which he pulled a piece of paper and handed it to Turnbull. "Do you know what this is?"

Turnbull forced a quizzical expression on his face and made like he was studying the paper, but the look of panic in his eyes answered Thompson's question.

"I think so."

"It's a record of all of the sale transactions of shares in Bushings Pharmaceuticals in which you or members of your family had a beneficial interest. Is that correct?"

"I'd have to check it thoroughly."

"You'll note that you liquidated all of the shares precipitously, approximately six months before public reports began to appear that Dr. Robert Austin had made a breakthrough in medications for arteriosclerosis and atherosclerosis, which ultimately had a highly negative impact on the value of Bushings shares. That's what we want to discuss."

"I don't wish to comment on that." Turnbull glanced away.

"We have time. We're not here to talk about that in isolation. We think you may be in a position to educate us as to the activities of others at Bushings —or perhaps even other pharmaceutical companies."

Turnbull became indignant, his voice rising. "You mean become an informant? A snitch?"

"Your cooperation can make things go very differently for you."

"You're assuming I did something wrong."

"For purposes of this conversation, let's make that assumption. In that case, your cooperation could make a difference, the magnitude of which depends on the value of what you have to say. But it could potentially be life altering for you."

Turnbull was perspiring even more heavily than usual. "Let's be clear," he said. "I'm admitting nothing."

As the agents got up from the sofa, they each handed Turnbull their cards. "We'll be in touch. Enjoy the rest of your bagel," McKenna said.

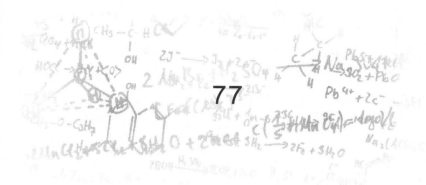

77

THE CRUISE TO FLORIDA SEEMED like a dream from the distant past, even though only six months had gone by since Bobby and Christina's return. Immersing himself in AIDS research, Bobby felt as if he were under attack. All of the difficulties he had encountered in the past were magnified, and now even his lab seemed to be under siege. Frequent computer crashes disrupted his work, hard drives would wipe clean for no apparent reason, back-up memory was inexplicably destroyed, printers wouldn't print, and his notebooks often went missing. His IT technicians had no explanations. His sense of foreboding increased.

Christina had had enough. Bobby was living in the lab virtually full time now. As she busied herself in the kitchen making dinner, she was so annoyed that she avoided eye contact with him. He trailed after her, offering to help.

Amid the clanging of the pots and pans she was impatiently pulling out of the cupboard, she said, "Look mister. You're going to have to make a choice very soon because I'm not going to live like this. If you want to kill yourself, I'm not going to be the cheerleader."

Bobby did look terrible. Increasingly disheveled and unkempt, his eyes bloodshot and bleary, he was exhausted all the time. Obsessed with his AIDS research, the regimen he was following was punishing him brutally. "I'm sorry. I feel I'm getting close to something. I promise you —after this — I'm going to cut way back and we'll lead a normal life. Maybe we'll even move."

Christina brushed her hand against his cheek. "It's crazy Bobby. We agreed to start a family, but what's the point? You can't keep your eyes open you're so tired and you're constantly spaced out."

Bobby tried to use his charm to get over on Christina, but this time it wasn't working. And he couldn't blame her. This was no easier on her than it was on him. The relentless night terrors from which she had to salvage him and her struggle to pull him back to present reality when he got too far out there, were grueling for her. He was endangered and she knew it, and that destroyed any sense of stability for her in their relationship.

"I just can't turn my back on this disease, Christina. It's already killed twenty five million. It's killing almost three million more every year. Thirty five million are infected and another three million get it every year. How can I slow down?"

The situation wasn't helped when Calvin Perrone paid a visit and advised that Bobby's TB cure and arteriosclerosis treatment had lifted him into the number one position on the crazies' hit list, beating out the president. Perrone insisted that the security presence at Prides Crossing be increased.

McAlister and Ramirez agreed an overall time-frame for the completion of Ramirez' assignment. Ramirez wouldn't give an exact date nor would he tell McAlister what method he'd use. "It's in place," was all that he would say. Years of experience had taught Ramirez that the less clients know, the safer he was. "So how will I know when it's going down?" asked McAlister.

"Watch CNN," Ramirez replied.

———————•••••———————

Kurt Osmond, the operations head for RASI, stared intently at the enlarged map of Prides Crossing which was taped to the wall of the command room. Standing next to him was Ashfaq Bashir, a veteran officer of the Pakastani armed forces who had entered the United States on a visitor's visa six years earlier and stayed on illegally. Technically skilled and rabidly anti-Western, his fundamentalist zeal had propelled him to a position of power in RASI in only two years. Osmond and Bashir reviewed every aspect of the meticulously planned assault. They examined the sleek bomb that had enough explosive power to easily obliterate the Prides Crossing laboratory. A single engine Cessna Corvalis stood ready at Woburn Airport. It could reach the lab in under twelve minutes. Prides Crossing had no defense against an aerial attack.

———————•••••———————

Standing in his office at 550 Park Avenue, Martin Turnbull gazed blankly out the window. He realized he had no choice but to cooperate with the SEC investigation. And he decided that maybe he could turn a negative into a positive. His career was in the toilet. He had already been advised by the Bushings board of directors that while they weren't renewing his employment contract "at the present time," they were willing to keep him on as an "at will employee" under the same terms until "they had clarity as to their long-term plans." He knew, of course, that they were already looking for his replacement, and once it became known that he was being investigated by the SEC, he would be a pariah. He would be terminated immediately and would become unemployable. So Marty

Turnbull made his decision. He needed to not only cooperate—but to make himself so invaluable that he could enter the government's witness protection program—- a new identity, a new job, a new life and the retention of all of his assets. That's what he needed.

Turnbull pulled Agent Thompson's wrinkled card from his pants pocket and dialed the number on his cell phone. They agreed to meet at three that afternoon in Bryant Park at 42nd Street on Avenue of the Americas.

Shifting uneasily on a wooden bench, Turnbull's eyes darted around as he surveyed the small park to be sure that no one from Bushings was there. Remembering something he had seen in a spy movie, he held a newspaper in front of him as he spoke to Thompson who was sitting by his side. "Let me be perfectly clear. I'm not admitting anything. I'm here to discuss possibilities that are so far reaching that a deal would have to be cut."

"We already said that things could go easier on you if you cooperated."

Turnbull turned scarlet and his voice rose along with his blood pressure. "No. What I'm talking about is much bigger than that. You don't know what I have. I want full immunity plus first-class treatment for me and my family in the witness protection program."

"That's out of the question," Thompson replied.

"Then we have nothing to talk about." Turnbull clumsily scrunched up his newspaper as he got up from the bench.

"Wait a minute," Thompson said. "That kind of thing is beyond the jurisdiction of our Agency."

"I thought it might be. So what you need to do is to involve the Justice Department—and I mean at a high level. I'll only talk to someone with authority to cut the whole deal."

"Do you really think you have enough value to warrant a deal like that?"

"I know I do."

78

Sitting motionless in front of four computer monitors at 4:30 in the morning alone in the lab, Bobby was in a trance -like state that had already lasted over three hours. Then he snapped out of it. Without a moment's pause, he began to scribble notes in his journal at a feverish pace, breaking only to type on the keyboard at maniacal speed. Page after page, equation after equation, his mental energy was blazing.

A smile crossed his face. "I got you now, you son of a bitch."

The words were barely out of his mouth when he felt a crushing pressure on each side of his head. The chair that he was sitting on was propelled into the air like it was an ejector seat in a jet fighter. His head slammed into what remained of the ceiling. The second blast catapulted him thirty feet across the room. He bounced off a wall and crumpled on the debris ridden floor like a broken doll. Barely conscious, he felt a freezing cold wind blow through what remained of the structure as an unearthly howling sound echoed in the ruins. His head felt as if it were clamped in a vice and being slowly crushed. He expected to hear the sound of his skull cracking at any moment. A few computer monitors still flickered as they lay on the floor not far from him. The distorted image he thought he saw on the screens was a face—the same elongated amorphous face that had terrorized him in his most recent nightmares. "You're finally doing it, you bastard," Bobby mumbled. "Finally, after all these years." When the third blast hit, it sent out a shock wave that was so powerful that it ripped the mainframe computers off their mounts and sent them and anything else in their path hurling through the air. One piece of a huge computer landed inches from Bobby's head. When a large filing cabinet and a jagged piece of the conference tabled slammed into him with crushing force his luck ran out. The last remnants of the ceiling caved in as electrical fires burned. Bobby's limp, cut and twisted body lay buried and bloody under a mountain of rubble.

Christina ran toward the lab screaming. The shockwaves from the blasts had blown out all the windows in the guest house where she had been sleeping and the only reason she wasn't severely lacerated was because the shades in the bedroom had been pulled down and the heavy curtains drawn. By the time she got to the lab, a dozen security guards, brandishing automatic weapons and fire extinguishers were already there. Calls had gone out to the Beverly and Prides Crossing police, fire departments and EMS, all of whom were alerted that they were dealing with a catastrophe at the Austin lab.

The head of the lab's security detail, an undercover CIA agent, had already called Perrone, who in turn called Varneys. Varneys immediately called the president. Standing rigidly by the phone in his bedroom, his voice was uncharacteristically shaky and his face was drained of all color. "This is Orin Varneys, sir. I apologize for calling you at this hour, but you need to know that a few minutes ago, Dr. Robert Austin's laboratory was destroyed. We have every reason to believe he was in the building." Varneys paused as he listened. He then responded, "No, sir. We don't know his condition yet. No, Mr. President, we don't know who's responsible." Varneys paused again. He held the phone farther from his ear as the voice he was listening to grew louder. Varneys replied, "We don't know how it was done. Yes, sir—the facility was under our protection. You're right, sir. There is no excuse. I take full responsibility. Yes Mr. President, I'll call you the moment I have more information."

As soon as Varneys heard the president click off, he slammed the phone down so hard it cracked its cradle. He called Perrone. "How the fuck did this happen? This is the second time we failed to protect him. The president will have my ass." Varneys ordered an immediate media lock-down. Perrone and eight agents sped to Reagan Airport and took one of the CIA jets to Boston.

Three members of the lab's security force were dispatched on motorcycles to await the emergency vehicles and guide them through the labyrinth of private roads that led to the Manzini lab. Within twenty minutes from the first explosion, the facility was jammed with ten police cars, four fire engines, two ambulances and a medevac.

Over thirty police and firemen piled into what remained of the lab. Some of them concentrated on extinguishing the electrical fires while others began to sift through the wreckage looking for Bobby. Christina ran into what used to be Bobby's office. Nothing. She then ran into the section of the main lab where he often worked.

Combing through the refuse, she yelled to some firemen, "Help me move this stuff." Frantically, she pulled and clawed at the piles of debris and twisted fragments of equipment, furniture, walls and ceiling, but there was so much of it that it was overwhelming.

The firemen used their crowbars to move the heavy remnants

as quickly as possible, but all they found under rubble was more rubble. Christina wandered around in a panic stricken daze calling out Bobby's name in the hope that he would answer. Another contingent of firemen entered the ruins with search dogs trained to sniff out people buried in collapsed buildings. One of the dogs began to bark as it stood atop a huge heap of mess. Six firemen hurried over and began to dig. After several minutes of frantic effort, they saw one foot, and then the other. They radioed and the EMS crew came rushing in. Christina joined them, pulling at the rubble with her bare hands. Bobby's limp body was uncovered. His clothes looked like torn rags. He was twisted, his limbs in unnatural positions. His skin and hair were thickly caked with a mix of blood and white sheet rock dust which gave him a gruesome zombie appearance.

When Christina saw him, she became hysterical and lay down in the rubble next to him sobbing, her head on his chest. "No God. Please don't do this to Bobby. He's been so good to you. Please no."

The head of the EMS team yelled out, "Don't move him. Don't let her touch him. His spinal cord may be severed."

One of the firemen lifted Christina away. The EMS chief administered 10 ml of adrenalin for cardiovascular resuscitation, and began to give a very mild form of CPR to Bobby because his injuries looked too extensive to risk a more forceful procedure. Detecting a weak pulse, he put an oxygen mask over Bobby's face. He called for a thin carbonite plank that could be slid under Bobby. To immobilize the spine, a restraining device was attached to his head, and his body was fastened tightly with six wide leather straps that would keep him still. He was then given a steroid drip to reduce inflammation and prevent further damage to the cellular membranes that can cause nerve death. Once this was done, four members of the EMS team gently lifted the plank onto a gurney and rushed him to the awaiting helicopter for the trip to Massachusetts General Hospital.

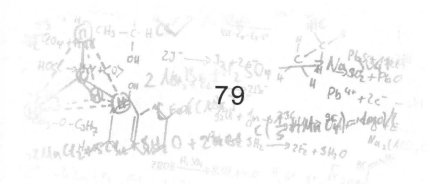

79

PEDALING VIGOROUSLY ON HIS EXERCISE bike later that same day, McAlister had the sixty inch plasma television in his office gym tuned to the Financial News Network. It was 1 PM when the reporter announced that all television and radio broadcasts in the United States were being interrupted for a special announcement by the president. "More bull crap from that jerk," muttered McAlister. The president spoke from the Oval Office, his voice somber:

"My fellow Americans, it saddens me beyond measure to report that approximately eight hours ago, the laboratory of Dr. Robert James Austin was attacked. The laboratory was completely destroyed while Dr. Austin was inside conducting research on AIDS. While he has survived over six hours of surgery to address multiple life-threatening injuries that he suffered during the attack, he remains in critical condition and continues to be in a coma. It is too early to formulate any prognosis as to his chances for survival or recovery. I have asked that he be brought to Washington D.C. so that I can personally oversee his care at a neighboring hospital. An attending team of our leading physicians from all relevant disciplines has been assembled. By presidential proclamation, I am declaring that this week be a week of prayer for his well being. Dr. Austin deserves no less. Nobody has worked harder or with more resolve and efficacy than he, or made greater personal sacrifices to further medical science. He has selflessly dedicated his unique genius to the betterment of the human condition. Dr. Austin's discoveries have already saved tens of millions of lives and will continue to do so. I dare say that there isn't a person on this planet who in some way has not been the beneficiary of his tireless efforts. Dr. Austin is not just a national treasure, he is a world treasure. His presence has been an extraordinary gift to us all, and to the future generations that follow us. We can only ponder what further contributions he would be capable of making if the good Lord graces him and us with that opportunity. I ask that you join my family and me in praying for Dr. Austin's speedy and full recovery. Rest assured that the perpetrators of this heinous crime will be swiftly brought to justice. Thank you, and may God bless the United States of America."

His jaw clenched, McAlister hurried from his office, still in his work-out suit. Rushing across Park Avenue, he found a phone booth in the Hyatt hotel and frantically dialed the number Ramirez had given him for emergencies. When it rang, all McAlister said was "212-549-8121," the call back number of the pay phone. McAlister waited in the booth, rapidly tapping his fingers against the wall. Twelve minutes later, the phone rang. McAlister knew that Ramirez was calling from his scrambler.

"What the hell's going on?" sputtered McAlister hoarsely, the veins in his forehead throbbing. "We agreed it wouldn't be dramatic."

"It wasn't me. It must have been those freaks who hate him."

"Bullshit. You got sloppy, Gunther. You wanted to make an easy buck."

"If that were the case, I'd be asking for the rest of my money right now—which I'm not."

There was silence as McAlister took that in.

"Well, you wouldn't be getting it because the son of a bitch is still alive," McAlister said.

"My plan was perfect. At the right time, by cellular activation, I was going to release toxic gas in his face from discs I planted in the cam portals of his monitors. It induces massive heart failure and leaves no residue. It's undetectable. I've used it before. It's so fucking good, insurance companies pay off on life coverage."

"You waited too long, goddammit," McAlister shouted.

"We agreed the time frame, Colum," replied Ramirez.

"I want my money back," said McAlister, his voice thick and sullen.

"That's not going to happen. I was a migrant worker for two months setting it up. It's not my fault that someone beat us to the punch."

"They'll find us now."

"Impossible."

"What about our little friend?"

"He doesn't know me," Ramirez said

"Well he fucking knows me and I don't live in Panama."

"No one can connect the dots."

"I want it taken care of just to be sure."

"I'll deal with it. But get a grip. Nervous people make mistakes."

The world media ignited with the news of the tragedy. Virtually every newspaper in every country bore a similar headline. Television, radio and the internet were awash in tributes and speculation as to who was behind the crime. The United Nations General Assembly unanimously passed a special resolution in tribute to Bobby, and most countries followed the lead of the United States in designating days or weeks, and in some countries, even months —as official periods devoted to prayer for his recovery.

When the helicopter carrying Bobby landed at Edwards Air Force Base, a caravan of military vehicles led the way to George Washington University Hospital, where he was to be installed in a private room at the end of a hallway reserved for VIPS who required special security. Waiting in the room for his arrival were the president, the attorney general and the secretary of the Department of Homeland Security.

Varneys stood outside Bobby's room in front of a platoon of his agents and delivered his orders in unequivocal terms. "Whoever did this to him won't be happy he's still alive. They may try again and we have to assume that they're very resourceful. I want a six agent rotation—24/7, two at the entrance to this corridor, two outside his room and two inside. I want two additional agents stationed at the elevator and two more at each stairwell. Nobody gets on this floor without being checked and no one comes down this corridor without our say so. Every doctor, nurse and orderly who goes into that room or who has anything to do with Austin must first pass top-priority security protocols. Every medication given to him has to be double-checked by a physician who has been cleared by us—and I want it administered by a physician. He is never to be alone—-do you understand that? Never. His food will come directly from our supplier."

As it turned out, food would not be an issue, as Bobby would be incapable of receiving any nourishment other than that which was administered intravenously.

Varneys installed Christina in a safe house in Washington so that she could be close at hand. "I want a security detail on her at all times. We don't know what we're dealing with yet. No slip-ups, Perrone."

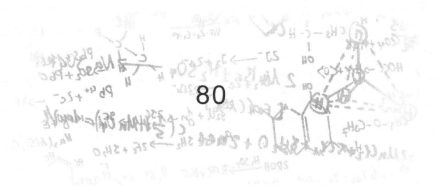

80

MARTIN TURNBULL'S ATTEMPT TO CUT a witness protection deal was languishing. The Justice Department didn't seem interested and the SEC was annoyed that Turnbull was seeking to circumvent them. Finally, Agent McKenna arranged for an initial discussion between Turnbull and a representative of Justice. When Turnbull saw the twenty-something diminutive female assistant U.S. Attorney enter the room, his heart sank. "How long have you worked for the Department," he asked.

"Nine months," she replied in a chirpy voice.

Turnbull shook his head. "This won't work. I don't mean to be disparaging, but I'm only interested in speaking with someone who has the authority to deliver the deal I'm looking for. I made that clear to the SEC agents."

The young attorney looked at Turnbull as if he were a petty criminal trying to bootstrap himself into getting privileges reserved for serious felons. Straightening herself to the full measure of her five feet, she smiled at him patronizingly. "Mr. Turnbull—before anyone at that level is going to even consider investing their time, you have to whet our appetite. We don't get involved in garden variety insider trading violations like yours. They're a dime a dozen. What do you got for us?"

Turnbull glared at her. "The information I have concerns Dr. Robert James Austin."

In an instant, her face turned burgundy and her bravado vaporized.

He continued, "You know—the one the president was talking about on TV the other day."

"Excuse me for a moment," she said as she left the room.

She called her boss, who had only been at the Justice Department for three years. He immediately called his, and so it went on up the chain of command until thirty minutes later, the chief U.S. Attorney for the Southern District of New York, Jonathan Bick, called the attorney general of the U.S. in Washington D.C. He, in turn, called the president who referred him to Varneys. Varneys' assistant reached him on the intercom in his office's private bathroom, and transferred the attorney general's call to him while he was seated there, attending to personal business.

"We have a situation, Orin. The CFO of Bushings Pharmaceuticals was caught by the SEC on insider trading. He's been looking to cut a deal with witness protection, saying he has valuable information. We thought it wasn't big enough. Earlier today, he said it involves Dr. Austin."

The color drained from Varneys' face. "I'll leave for New York now."

Turnbull had been kept waiting in a small room in New York's Federal Building for four hours and he was in a foul mood by the time Varneys walked into the room with Bick. When the two men introduced themselves, Turnbull repeatedly flexed his fingers, alternating from one hand to the other. Bick said, "Mr. Turnbull—I've been apprised of the deal you want, and if you have information that's as highly significant as you've indicated —then you have my word on behalf of the Justice Department that you'll get your deal."

Turnbull responded, "And how can I be sure you won't play games with me as to the definition of what constitutes 'highly significant information'?"

Bick shot back, "You just have to trust us on that. I'm not going to jerk you around. That's not how we work."

Varneys shook his head. "Look, Turnbull. The Justice Department has better things to do than screw you on your little deal, so shake hands with the man and let's get going. We have work to do."

Vigorously picking at a hang-nail on his index finger, Turnbull asked Bick, "Did you bring an agreement for us to sign? I understand there's a standard form for this kind of thing."

Bick opened his briefcase, took out a folder and tossed it on the table next to Turnbull. Turnbull put on his reading glasses and began to read the document carefully. He was sweating profusely and his deodorant had worn off. Varneys walked over to the thermostat and lowered the temperature.

"I'm ready," said Turnbull. As he signed, his hand was trembling. He kept scratching the back of his head as he watched Bick counter-sign the document. Flakes of skin from his psoriasis plagued scalp landed on the shoulders of his frumpy dark blue suit. "I guess my new life begins now," Turnbull said sadly. "I never thought this is how it would end up for me. They should have taken care of me. McAlister and those scumbags on the Board. They put me in this position."

Sitting across from Turnbull with his list of questions in front of him, Bick's face registered neither sympathy nor judgment. "Let's get down to business," he said, as he nodded to an agent to start the video camera and tape recorder.

"Tell us why you sold all your stock in Bushings six months before Dr. Austin's breakthrough on arteriosclerosis became public knowledge?"

"I found out he was working on it and I assumed he'd find a cure so I sold everything."

"How did you find out?"

"Our CEO, Colum McAlister, told me that his mole in Austin's lab told him."

"He had a mole?" Turnbull nodded.

"Is this the first time that happened with company shares?"

"No. Long before that, the mole told him about Austin's TB research and that's when Colum sold as many shares as he could until the Board stopped him from selling more."

"Why didn't you sell your stock then also?"

Turnbull's chin jutted forward and his voice rose. "I wanted to, but he wouldn't let me."

"Was the mole the only source of info?"

"Bushings was hacking Austin's computers for years hoping to steal something. Trouble is —our scientists couldn't understand what the heck he was doing."

"What's the mole's name?"

"I don't know."

"Can you find out by checking financial records in your office?"

Turnbull's breathing had become labored. He thrust his hand in his pants pocket and fished out crumpled tissues and ran them over his face and neck, mopping up some sweat. "I can try—but without knowing the amount or frequency of payments to him or the entity he uses to receive payments, it could be impossible. And he might be paid in cash altogether."

"What does McAlister think of Austin?"

Turnbull laughed. "He hates him. Blames him for everything bad in the pharmaceutical business. He says Austin cost him over a hundred million dollars. That's why he called that meeting of all the other CEOs at his house in the Adirondacks. It was quite awhile ago. The purpose was to see how to deal with Austin."

"What was discussed there?"

Turnbull shook his head. "I wasn't allowed in the actual meeting. It was just for the CEOs."

"So you have no specifics?" Bick rested his pen on the yellow pad in front of him.

"Just from talking to McAlister, I know that Bushings designed an internet defamation campaign that it couldn't successfully launch. It was a bunch of bullshit that was supposed to spook the public. Someone intercepted it and stopped it cold." Varneys blanched and turned away momentarily. "And there was something about trying to use influence to get the Justice Department to go after Austin for anti-trust, and get the FDA to give him a hard time, and I know that McAlister had meetings with a bunch of heavy-weights in the government."

Bick wagged his head. "Can you give us those names?"

"Yes."

Bick stood up and surveyed the room as he tapped his pen on the table. He walked over to Turnbull and stared down at him. "Did McAlister know where Austin lived or the location of his lab?"

"The mole obviously could have told him the lab's location. I don't know about the residence, but I doubt it would be too tough for the mole to follow him home or something."

Varneys and Bick adjourned into a nearby room. "We have to find that mole," said Bick excitedly.

"If he's still alive," replied Varneys, as he called Perrone from his cell. "I need a complete report on all personnel at the Prides Crossing lab—names, addresses, number of years of employment, salary, position, bank records, tax returns, phone records, prior employment—-the works. The Corwin lady should be able to help you. Get it to me by tomorrow—I don't care how many people you have to put on it. "

Varneys and Bick returned to Turnbull's room. "We need you to find out the identity of the mole," said Bick. "Go back to your office and figure out how you can identify payments to him. I want a list of any regular periodic payments to any person, or any company, that's not a full-time Bushings' employee. I'm sure you can devise a screen that will eliminate vendors you know are legitimate. You also need to scrutinize cash disbursements."

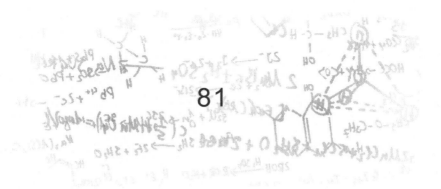

81

Martin Turnbull was the CFO of Bushings, and no one had better access or familiarity with Bushings' financial records. For two days, he scoured Bushings' computer files looking for anything that could provide a trail to the mole, but there was nothing. He wasn't surprised. *Colum McAlister doesn't leave bread crumbs for people to follow home.*

Varneys had already established a command center in Boston. He studied the reports Perrone had given him on the Prides Crossing employees. Of the eleven people who had been working at the lab during the entire time period that Turnbull believed the mole had been active, there was one that stood out. Vincent Amaratto had gross pay of $89,000 at the lab. An examination of his banking statements over a period of years indicated no deposits other than his net after- tax salary of $58,740. The checks he wrote each month to cover his credit card bills, undergrad and graduate school loans, car loan and a monthly payment he gave to his mother, used up this entire amount but still didn't account for his apartment rent or utility bills. But Amaratto had no savings accounts, investments or loans that were being used to fund the monthly shortfall of over three thousand dollars. "Bring him in," Varneys said to Perrone.

As he came out of a Starbucks, Amaratto was intercepted by Perrone and two agents who swept him into an awaiting van that was trailing behind them. Amaratto wiped sweat from his forehead. "I'm not worth kidnapping. I don't have any money. I'm just a lab technician."

Perrone and the other agents ignored him and looked out the darkly tinted windows. The van traveled to the back of Boston's Federal Building and Amaratto was shepherded through a side door marked "Deliveries." Agents on both sides of him grasped his arms and roughly deposited him into a bare room which contained nothing other than two metal tables and some heavy oak chairs. They locked the door and left him there alone for thirty minutes. Finally, a door on the other side of the room opened and an austere figure walked in. Amaratto stood.

"Mr. Amaratto— I'm Orin Varneys, director of the CIA."

When Amaratto heard that, a wave of nausea swept through him. He quickly scanned the room for the nearest waste basket.

"Do you mean the director of the entire CIA? The Head of it?" he asked. Varneys nodded.

"What do you want from me?"

"I think you know, Mr. Amaratto."

His voice breaking, Amaratto responded, "I have no idea why I was brought here and I object to it."

Varneys frowned as he realized that he wouldn't be spared having to give a performance. Varneys motioned for Amaratto to sit down. He stood in front of him and just stared at him. Amaratto shifted uneasily in the chair. After a few minutes, Varneys bent over and glared at him, his piranha face just inches from Amaratto's.

"Why don't I start by telling you what I know. I know six things, Mr. Amaratto –six." Varneys began to pace again, his hands clasped behind him. "First, I know that Bushings Pharmaceuticals had a mole in Dr. Austin's lab for years—the lab where you work. I know that the mole has been feeding information, directly or indirectly, to Bushings. These activities by the mole make him criminally liable for industrial espionage."

"Second, I know that Bushings was hacking Austin's computers, and that in the last year, Austin's computers were being sabotaged and his notebooks stolen, and that the mole may well be complicit in these criminal activities also."

"Third, I know that the information supplied by the mole was used, among other things, for certain executives at Bushings to violate Federal Securities laws. This make the mole an accessory to those Securities crimes."

"Fourth, I know that someone tried to kill Dr. Austin and that it is not outside the realm of possibility that the mole's paymaster might be involved—which would mean that the mole may be a participant in a conspiracy to commit murder or an accessory to that crime."

"Fifth, I know that if there is any connection between the attempt on Dr. Austin's life and whoever was paying the mole, then the mole is in immediate physical danger as he could provide a link to prosecution."

"And lastly, I am intimate with your finances, Mr.Amaratto, and know that you are living well beyond your means. I know that the only income which you have declared to the IRS for years—has been your lab salary. Filing false tax returns and failure to report income is criminal tax evasion." Varneys paused. "Do I need to continue Mr.Amaratto— or is it time for you to tell me what you know?"

Amaratto looked at Varneys sheepishly. His face was wet with perspiration and his greasy black hair looked as if it hadn't been washed for a week. "If I did anything—which I'm not saying I did—how do I know I won't be prosecuted if I cooperate?"

"Because I'm telling you that you won't be," Varneys responded.

"And what if I don't want to rely on that?" asked Amaratto, his knee rapidly jerking up and down under the desk.

Varneys leaned ominously over Amaratto. "In that case, I'll do one of two things. Either I'll throw you back on the street and I wager to say, you'll be dead in forty-eight hours, or I'll get on with my investigation of you and alert the SEC, the IRS and the attorney general to join the party."

Amaratto began to massage the sides of his neck with both hands. "So what do you want from me?"

"I want the truth. You'll be required to swear to it, and to testify in court—if you won't do that, you're of no use."

"Do I get protection?"

"Effective immediately. I don't want anything to happen to you."

Amaratto stroked his left temple. "I'm trusting you, Mr. Varneys."

Varneys face was an expressionless mask. "You could do a lot worse. Now, I'm going to question you while you're hooked up to a polygraph. Do you have a problem with that?"

"No."

Varneys called in Perrone, who hurried in with another agent who set up the video and sound recorders and the polygraph.

"How long were you in the employ of Dr. Austin?"

"For nine years, but before that I was employed by Tufts Medical School as a chemistry researcher. Tufts had me working on Dr. Austin's projects. Then Dr. Austin hired me from there—actually he didn't—it was his assistant, Susan Corwin who did."

"When did you first have contact with Bushings Pharmaceuticals?"

"At a chemistry conference for pharmaceutical research that Bushings sponsored in Boston about eight years ago, but I didn't speak to anybody from Bushings—I just attended the conference."

"How did you start spying for them?"

"About a week after the conference, I received a call at home. A man said he represented Bushings and asked me to meet him for coffee at a diner off of exit 39 on I-95. He said I would be glad if I did."

Varneys showed Amaratto a photo of Colum McAlister. Was this the man you met with?"

Amaratto studied the photo. "It's hard to tell. He was wearing a baseball cap and sunglasses."

"How tall was he and how was he built?"

"About six feet and looked fit—but still he looked about sixty or so. You can always tell from the hands. I remember he was suntanned even though it was winter, and except for the baseball cap, he was very well dressed. He had one hell of a wristwatch. I'm a bit of a buff—not that I can afford any. He had a pink gold Patek Phillipe, real unusual—not like any I had seen. Very classy. It might have been custom made. You know that company will do that for a price."

"What did he ask you to do?"

"Just to keep him abreast of what Dr. Austin was working on. He said he'd pay $3000 a month. I bargained him up to $4000."

"You thought this was ethical?"

Amaratto's face flushed red. "It's ethical to keep my mother living like a human being, and besides—Dr. Austin wasn't in competition with Bushings—he wasn't interested in making money—so what difference did it make?"

Varneys glared at Amaratto. "How were you paid?"

"It was always the same. On the last day of every month, an envelope with forty one hundred dollar bills was shoved under my apartment door."

"How did you communicate?"

"I was given a phone number and told to call it from a pay phone booth on the fifth and twentieth days of every month at 11 PM."

"Did he ask you questions?"

"He'd ask me to try to find out certain things."

"Was he the same person you met in the diner?"

"Yes."

"What was he like on the phone?"

"He seemed to get angrier over the years. Sometimes he would comment about how much money Austin was costing Bushings, but usually he said very little."

"Would you recognize his voice if you heard it now?"

"Absolutely."

"Why did you sabotage the computers in the Prides Crossing lab?"

Amaratto straightened up in his chair. "I swear I never did that."

"Did you facilitate the hacking of the lab computers?"

Amaratto shook his head emphatically. "I'd never do that because it might make me expendable."

"Did you steal Dr. Austin's notebooks?"

"I stole three of them."

"Why?"

"I was asked to. I was paid ten grand for each one. Austin didn't need them. He had a photographic memory."

"Did you give the address of the lab to him."

"Yes."

"What about his residence?"

Amaratto squirmed in his chair and looked up at the ceiling. Varneys repeated the question.

"Austin lives in the guesthouse on the lab premises," Amaratto said.

"I mean before that."

"I don't know. I may have given the address of an apartment."

Varneys moved closer to Amaratto. "What role did you play in the lab explosion."

Amaratto wiped his forehead with his left hand and then pulled on his nose. "I swear on my mother's life that I never knew that was going to happen. I would never do anything to hurt Dr. Austin or destroy that lab."

Varneys asked "What exactly did you do?"

Amaratto looked around the room and shifted uneasily in his chair. "During one of my regular calls, I was given a number and told to call it from a pay phone. I wasn't given a name, just the number. I was told to do whatever the man who answered the call would ask me to do, and I'd be paid twenty-five thousand after I did what was requested."

"What were you asked to do by this man?"

Amaratto buried his face in his hands momentarily and then appeared to be massaging his eyebrows. Looking up at the ceiling again, he said, "When I spoke to him the first time, he asked me to draw a detailed floor plan of the lab. He also asked me to write down the model numbers of the monitors that Austin used at his desk and he wanted to know if Austin used his webcam."

"Were there any more calls?"

"A few more."

Varneys glared. "And then what? Don't sugar coat it, because if you do, you'll be on the street in five minutes."

Amaratto slumped in his chair and looked down. After pausing for a minute and then taking a deep breath, he mumbled, "In the last call, we agreed a day and time when I would leave the back door to the lab unlocked for twenty minutes."

Perrrone shot up from his chair. "You son of a bitch."

Varneys motioned Perrone to sit down. "And why did you think that the man you were speaking to wanted this information and wanted the door left open?"

"He told me he was going to plant some surveillance equipment in Austin's office."

"You don't know his name?"

"No."

"What did he sound like?"

"He had a heavy Latino accent."

"Would you remember the voice?"

"It was pretty distinctive."

"Did you ever see him? Did you see him come through that door."

Amaratto shook his head. "No. He told me that if I tried to, he'd know and I wouldn't get paid my money—and I'd lose my monthly gig, too."

In Washington, D.C., the U.S. attorney general had finished questioning the notables whose names had been supplied by Turnbull: Neil Foster, Randall Lindsay, Graham Waters and Michael Petersen. While these heavy-weight politicos declined to indicate the precise nature of the videos with which McAlister was blackmailing them, they confirmed that they contained 'material of a personal nature.' On the understanding that the recordings wouldn't see the light of day, they agreed to cooperate. The attorney general obtained warrants to search Lands End, McAlister's other residences and the *My Time* yacht.

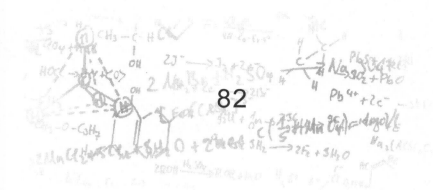

82

T HREE WEEKS AFTER BOBBY WAS admitted into the hospital, the surgeon general briefed the Cabinet:

"Severity of coma is measured on the Glasgow Coma Scale, the worst being 3 and the best 15. Dr. Austin's score hasn't improved beyond the 4 he had on admission. There still is no way to determine when and if he'll ever come out of the coma, or what cognitive or physical impairments will remain from the neurological trauma he suffered. His intravenous feeding will continue, as will a vigorous regimen of physical and electrical pulse therapies to keep his muscles from atrophying and to avoid the onset of pneumonia, which often causes death in long-term comatose patients."

There was no shortage of visitors. Bobby's hospitalization deprived him of the anonymity and privacy that he had so carefully cultivated. His incapacity became the vehicle for luminaries to finally have the opportunity to "meet him." In addition to visits from major U.S. politicians and religious leaders, Bobby's hospital room became a "must-stop" on the itinerary of international dignitaries visiting Washington. The CIA cleared each person ahead of time, each visit was limited to ten minutes and no photographs were permitted. If she was there, Christina tried her best to be gracious, but as time went by, the visits increasingly took on the air of "paying last respects" and this further depressed her. Susan and Anna were her support system and Alan, who drove up from Florida every few weeks and called her regularly, took on the role of devoted father-in law.

Day after day, Christina sat in Bobby's room. Frequently, she slept on a cot next to his bed and sometimes she'd squeeze in right next to him at night. She would talk to him animatedly and read to him, hoping he could hear her and that somehow her voice would lead him back to consciousness. Massaging his arms, legs, feet, and hands, she would kiss his forehead, whispering in his ear, "Come back, Bobby. Don't leave me."

Two months into the coma, the doctors were increasingly skeptical. As they advised the president, "The longer the coma continues unabated, the less likely he'll come out of it. The mind becomes accustomed to the vegetative state and it settles in."

Looking out the hospital window, Christina thought how pretty the hundreds of candle lights were, twinkling silently in the night. The vigils were always there—even in the bad weather. For the first few weeks, there were thousands of candles, glimmering their beacons of hope in the darkness. Now there were fewer—but she was still amazed that they were there, every night. The same thing was happening all over the world. People weren't forgetting what Bobby had done for them. "You see, little one," Christina said as she patted her protruding belly, her eyes streaming with tears, "Your daddy was a great man. A very great man."

"Don't say 'was.'" Susan put her arm around Christina. "He is a very great man."

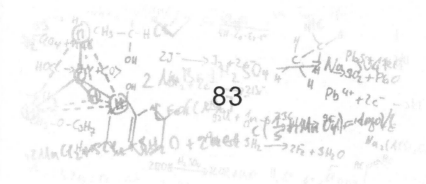

83

A BLACK SUBURBAN PULLED UP IN front of 550 Park Avenue and parked in front of the "No Standing Anytime" sign. Thompson, McKenna, Perrone, Bick, and two uniformed armed Federal Marshals piled out of the vehicle. They walked quickly into the building, flashed badges and told one of the security guards to take them up to the floor on which they could find Colum McAlister. The guard reached for the phone, saying he'd call upstairs to announce them.

Agent Thompson removed the receiver from his hand, "That won't be necessary. Let's go."

When the elevator doors opened on the sixty eighth floor, the first thing seen by the two beefy Bushings security guards positioned there were the marshals.

"Holy shit," mumbled one of them.

He was told to go downstairs and wasted no time in complying. The other was asked to escort the troop to McAlister's office, which he did. As the group entered the private reception area of McAlister's office suite, they encountered the aquarium's sharks, which were sullenly gliding through the water of the massive tank, their dead eyes peering through the wall of glass at the visitors.

Perrone walked up to McAlister's two breathtaking secretaries and asked, "Is he in?" While one of them was in the midst of saying, "Mr. McAlister is in a meeting" —Perrone flung open the oversized mahogany doors and led the group into the office. The size and opulence of McAlister's lair took them by surprise and most of the law enforcement team seemed momentarily distracted as they looked around the palatial surroundings. Perrone muttered to Thompson, "You sure can live large leeching off of shareholders —geez look at this."

McAlister's face purpled at the intrusion. Rising from his desk, he shoved his chair back as he bellowed, "Who the hell are you?"

Six badges flashed in answer to his question. McAlister's tan seemed to disappear instantly.

Bick stepped toward McAlister as he reached into his jacket pocket, removing a piece of paper that he unfolded. His six feet four inches towered over McAlister and his icy stare conveyed a disdain more effective than words. Bick spoke slowly, his patrician Beacon Hill drawl imbuing every word with extra gravitas. "I'm Jonathan Bick, chief United States Attorney for the Southern District of New York." He stopped and put on his reading glasses.

McAlister shifted from one leg to the other, poker faced.

Reading from the paper in his hand, Bick continued. "Colum McAlister— you are under arrest for multiple violations of the Securities Exchange Act of 1934, the Economic Espionage Act of 1996, the Cyber Security Act of 2002, extortion, blackmail, and conspiracy to commit the murder of Dr. Robert James Austin. You have the right to remain silent. Anything you say can and will be used against you in a court of law. You have the right to speak to an attorney, and to have an attorney present during any questioning.

If you cannot afford an attorney, one will be provided for you at government expense."

McAlister looked around at the assembled public servants and began to laugh. It was a hearty spontaneous laugh that didn't sound at all contrived. "You've got to be kidding. You're all nuts." He turned his head from side to side as he stretched his neck forward, like a prize fighter loosening up before a bout. Removing the white and blue striped silk handkerchief from the breast pocket of his Saville Row suit, he patted his forehead lightly and then dabbed the corners of his mouth. Inserting the handkerchief back into its pocket, he took care to ensure that it protruded exactly two inches. McAlister's eyes became snake slits as he looked over each of the men in succession. The street fighter kid who climbed from the slums of Brooklyn to the sixty eighth floor of Park Avenue wasn't easily intimidated.

When he spoke, his voice had a hoarseness to it that belied his anger, but his words weren't loud. "When my lawyers get through with you monkeys, you won't even be able to get a job flipping burgers. You're finished. All of you. You have no idea who you're dealing with." One of the marshals yanked McAlister's arms behind his back and attached handcuffs. McAlister craned his neck around. "Hey buddy—don't scratch my watch. It cost more than you make in five years."

As they left the reception area, McAlister barked orders to his assistants, whose disoriented expressions seemed to reflect their realization that it might be time to update their resumes. "Call Rosenberg at Cravath. I don't care what he's doing. Tell him to meet me downtown right now. He'll know where."

The procession filed into the elevators and no one seemed to notice the news alert that silently scrolled across the bottom of the

TV screen in the reception area: *Dr. Robert James Austin wins his ninth, tenth and eleventh Nobel Prizes for TB cure, revolutionary bacteriophage techniques, and arteriosclerosis breakthrough making statins obsolete. Full report to follow.*

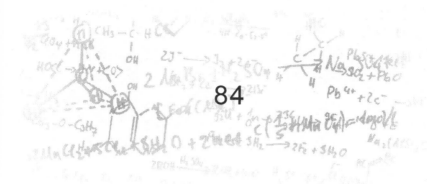

84

After four months, Bobby showed no signs of regaining consciousness. Susan had inadvertently created a public commotion when, during an interview, she said that Bobby was on the threshold of an AIDS cure. This gave the media's talking heads something to debate and prompted endless internet noise about why Bobby's doctors weren't doing enough to bring him out of the coma. The president called Bobby's team of doctors, which included the world's two greatest coma experts, to the White House so they could brief him.

While a few of the physicians present lobbied for an aggressive regimen of experimental drugs, it was quickly knocked back as being too risky. Similarly, a method called "DPS," in which electrodes are planted deep within the brain to deliver stimulating electric shocks, was rejected as too dangerous. The consensus was — 'this brain is not the brain for us to experiment on' and 'let nature take its course.' They advised the president that the prognosis for recovery was very poor.

Five months into the coma, Christina had finally come to grips with the situation. While she visited Bobby every day, and often spent the night, she wasn't there all the time. She was receiving grief therapy and also attending Lamaze childbirth classes for the single mother. As Washington D.C. lumbered into the holiday season, it was shaping up to be an uncharacteristically cold and snowy winter. The monuments and public buildings that Bobby had first seen when he was summoned by Varneys for an ultimatum at the age of twenty, looked majestic and magical in their illumination. Christina was invited to the president's Christmas Eve party at the White House. She declined to attend, but changed her mind when the First Lady called her and said, "You may not be aware, but every year the doctor was invited—not just by us, but by our predecessors. He never came and we understand why. But please share this night with us. We're going to say a special prayer for him. Bring whomever you want. They're all welcome here."

Alan, Susan and Anna never thought that they'd be sitting in a government limousine as it was waved through the North Gate entrance to the White House.

As they walked past Marine guards in full dress uniform, and entered through the North Portico, Anna whispered to Christina, "I could get used to this kind of thing."

Looking rather distinguished in the first tuxedo he had ever worn, Alan began to softly hum, "If they could see me now."

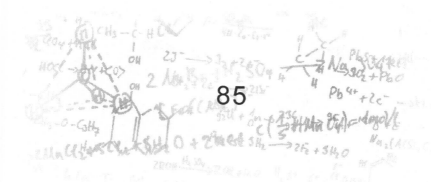

85

ON CHRISTMAS EVE, THE HOSPITAL had a skeletal staff and the smattering of worn holiday decorations made the vacant halls particularly depressing. Two CIA guards watched the small TV in Bobby's dimly lit room. A nurse's aide came in to collect some items. She busied herself at the other end of the room and then looked over to see what program the agents were watching. She didn't notice Bobby's eyelids flutter, or his right hand move to scratch his nose. Nor did she see his head move slowly from side to side, or his neck gradually crane backwards.

He cleared his throat very softly—once with considerable difficulty, and then several more times. The aide was now laughing with the agents as they watched the antics on TV. Bobby's hands moved uneasily, but finally found his eyes. His hands rested covering the lids. He then very gently began to rub them. Then, slowly his eyes began to open. Even though the lights in the room were low, a searing pain shot through him as the light overpowered eyes that had been closed for over five months. His body jerked in response to the pain. Shutting them tightly, he decided that he'd have to acclimatize them to the light over a period of time.

His voice was soft, hoarse and halting as he said one word, "Nurse."

The aide heard nothing and neither did the agents.

"Nurse." A little bit louder, but it was still very soft. "Nurse." Is anybody there?" The words came slow but they were intelligible, his voice still deep in his throat.

Nobody heard anything. Finally, the aide came by Bobby's bed. Now he was still. As she checked his intravenous feeder, the wires to the monitors, and the electric muscle stimulators, he said it again.

"Nurse." She thought she heard something. "Nurse. Is anybody there?" Bobby's eyelids were fluttering again and he moved his left hand to scratch the side of his head.

The aide jumped away from the bed as if she had seen a corpse rise out of a coffin. After a moment, she hesitatingly approached and leaned over the bed. "Can you hear me?" she asked.

"Yes. I'm thirsty," Bobby replied.

She started to yell, "He's up! He's up!" and ran out of the room, screaming down the hallway, "He's up! He's up! Where's a doctor?"

The agents by the TV bounded over to Bobby's bed and cautiously leaned over it. "Are you there? Can you hear us?"

"I'm so thirsty. Can I get some water?"

One of the agents whipped out his cell phone and dialed Varneys' direct office line. It was 9:15 Christmas Eve. Varneys sat at his desk and looked at the caller ID. He saw it was one of the agents at the hospital. They had never called him before. He just stared at the phone as it kept ringing. His eyes welled-up with tears. He picked up the receiver.

"Hello," was all that Varneys said, his voice soft and tired.

"Sir, it's Collins at the hospital."

"Yes, agent," replied Varneys, resignedly. He noticed that his hands were trembling and he had a hollow sore feeling in his gut. "You're calling about Austin I presume." Varneys moved the phone further from his ear, as if he didn't want to hear what the caller had to say.

"Yes, sir. He's up."

Varneys looked at the receiver incredulously, and then placed it hard against his ear. "What did you say?"

"He's talking. He wants water. Says he's thirsty."

Varneys dark eyes danced, the corners of his mouth turned up and his face glowed like he was four years old and it was time to open his birthday presents. "Well, goddammit. Give him some water. I'll be right over."

Varneys put the phone down. He knew he had to call the president but he sagged back in his chair. He sat there motionless with his eyes closed for a few minutes and then leaned forward, elbows on his desk, his chin pinioned on his clasped hands, his eyes shut tightly. "Thank you. Thank you for saving my boy," he murmured. He remained in that position for a few minutes, silent and still, his wet eyes sealed. After awhile, he began to breathe in deeply, and slowly exhale. A few minutes later, he stood up, wiped his eyes roughly with the back of his hands, pulled his vest straight, tightened his tie, and called the White House.

"It's Orin Varneys. Please put me through to the president."

"Hold on, sir." It seemed like an eternity, but two minutes later, the president's chief of staff got on the line. "Merry Christmas, Orin. The president is in the middle of his party. Can this wait?"

"No it can't. Please get him for me."

A few minutes later, the president got on the line. "What's so urgent Orin?"

"He's up sir."

"What are you talking about?"

"Austin came out of the coma a few minutes ago. He's talking. He's thirsty."

"God almighty. I can't believe it. It's a miracle. And Christina's here. We'll meet you there in ten minutes."

The president hurried back to the party room, made a bee line for Christina, interrupted the conversation she was having and took her hand. "I just got a call," he said as he began to quickly lead her toward a quiet corner of the room. Christina's emerald eyes flooded and her face went pale. Her feet felt like they were encased in lead as she struggled to cross the room with him. She had prepared for this moment. The president stopped and turned toward her, placing his hands on her trembling shoulders. She felt faint and tried to cement in her mind that if she fell, she had to be sure she didn't fall on the baby. "He's up, Christina. Robert's talking."

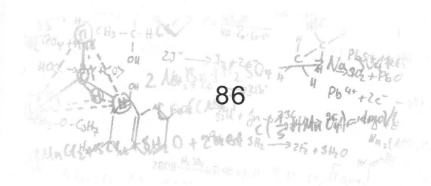

86

WHEN CHRISTINA AND SUSAN ARRIVED at Bobby's room with the president and two SUVs full of secret service guards, Varneys was already there, as were a throng of doctors. The doctor in charge announced that Bobby could only have one visitor at a time.

Smiling broadly, Varneys announced to the presidential party, "I said hello. He remembers me."

Susan rolled her eyes.

Christina entered the room. At first Bobby didn't see her because he was looking toward the windows. As she rushed to his bed, he turned his head and his eyes locked with hers. He held out his arms to her as best he could, his muscles weak and the intravenous tubes still attached, and when she bent over him, kissing him all over his face, her eyes streaming tears, he pulled her on top of him. "My beautiful girl. My Christina," he said, weaving his fingers through her hair as he kissed her forehead.

"I never thought I'd hear your voice again," she said, unable to stop crying.

It didn't take Bobby long to notice Christina's belly. He didn't say anything, but the look on his face did. "No it's not Twinkies," she chuckled.

"Mine?" he asked, eyebrows raised.

Christina punched his arm playfully. "Of course it's yours, you fool."

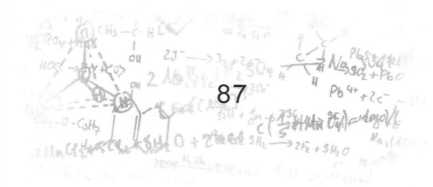

87

FOR THE FIRST FORTY-EIGHT HOURS, Bobby was coddled like a newborn and his doctors ruled out his being subjected to any questioning, but as soon as that period elapsed, the interrogations began. Perrone was the first.

"Doctor Austin, what's the last thing you recall happening in your lab?"

"I was deeply engrossed in working. I had achieved some kind of break-through and I was writing in my journal and typing on the computer. Then I felt this terrific crushing pressure against my head, and the next thing I knew, I was propelled into the air. I don't remember anything else."

Next up were the team of neurologists. Dr. Michael Miller, the world's leading coma specialist, showed Bobby a partially charred notebook. "Does this look familiar Dr. Austin?"

"It's the type of notebook I use in my research. Where did you get it?"

"It was found in the wreckage of your lab, buried under a mountain of debris. It's filled with equations and formulas. Your assistant, Susan, says it's your handwriting. Take a look."

Bobby opened the notebook and slowly viewed a few of the pages. After about a minute, he closed the book and pushed it away. "That's my handwriting."

"Is that your work on AIDS from that night? Dr. Austin—is that what you were working on?"

"Could be. I don't know."

"Please take another look at it." Bobby opened the book again and appeared to be concentrating very hard. He flicked through a few more pages.

"I'm sorry. It means nothing to me."

"You don't recognize the formulas?"

"No."

Miller stood up and gently patted Bobby's shoulder. "That's all for today, Dr. Austin. Get some rest. Regain your strength. We'll talk again tomorrow." The notebook was left on Bobby's bed stand. He felt very tired. He closed his eyes and drifted into a deep sleep.

The next day, the neurologists visited when Christina was there. One of them was holding a shopping bag containing all five volumes of the special edition of the *New England Journal of Medicine* that introduced Bobby's autoimmune disease theories to the world— the historic breakthrough that earned Bobby two Nobel prizes at age 25. After some polite chit chat, the physician pulled out a few of the volumes and asked Bobby to peruse them and "refresh his memory." Christina stood by Bobby's bedside while he began to read. She noticed how slowly Bobby was reading. He was laboriously plodding through each of the introductory paragraphs of the first volume, tracing his finger under every line.

While only at the end of page two, Bobby looked up, his face flushed and his eyes glassy. "Could you please come back later after I've had some time?" he said to the doctors.

"Of course, Dr. Austin. Take all the time you need."

Bobby noticed the glances the physicians cast each other as they exited the room and he could hear their animated conversation begin as soon as they cleared the doorway. Christina opened volume three which contained many of Bobby's equations and formulas. She held the book in front of him.

"Do you have any idea what any of this is?"

He looked at the page and then looked away. His eyes grew teary. Christina squeezed his hand. "It's alright Bobby."

88

I N THE ENSUING WEEKS AT the hospital, Bobby regained his physical strength. Tests regarding his intellect were administered by a parade of renown specialists—neurologists, psychologists, educators, hypnotists, amnesia experts—even Dr. Uhlman was summoned from retirement.

When Uhlman walked into Bobby's hospital room, he paused just inside the door. Bobby looked over at the old man, his head still shaved, but not as neatly as it had been years before, nor was it as shiny as Bobby remembered. The oversized hands were now wrinkled and marked by numerous liver spots, and the once powerfully built scientist with military erect posture, was thin and bent over, supporting himself with a cane.

"You must hate me," said Uhlman as he approached Bobby. "When you needed me the most, I wasn't there for you."

Bobby didn't respond. Uhlman felt like he was being skewered by Bobby's eyes as he slowly made his way over to Bobby's chair. He extended his hand, but it wasn't accepted. Just as he was drawing it back awkwardly, Bobby grasped it.

"I could never hate you. I was hurt, but I knew you were caught in circumstances beyond your control. It's good to see you Doctor. It's been a very long time."

A smile appeared on Uhlman's face as he slowly lowered himself into a chair next to Bobby, placed his hand on Bobby's knee and patted it. "You validated my life's work, Robert. How do I thank you for that?"

Uhlman leaned over toward Bobby. "They've asked me to tell you what you probably already know."

Bobby's eyes instantly teared up, but he forced a smile. "It was always just a matter of 'when.' I was lucky I kept it as long as I did."

Uhlman raised his eyebrows. "Lucky? Were you really?"

Bobby stared vacantly at the wall.

Uhlman continued, "I wish I had been a better friend to you, Robert. There was no acceptable excuse for my behavior, but after awhile, I was too embarrassed to contact you."

Uhlman didn't know if Bobby had even heard what he'd said. After a few minutes of silence, he leaned against his cane as he began the arduous process of standing up. His first attempt wasn't successful and he noisily flopped back into the chair. That sound seemed to snap Bobby out of it. He put his arm under the old man's shoulder and gently lifted him up.

"You did enough, doctor. You found Joe for me."

Eyes glassy, Uhlman bent forward and whispered into Bobby's ear, "I failed you in more ways than you know. I'm sorry." He squeezed Bobby's hand as hard as he could and made his way to the door.

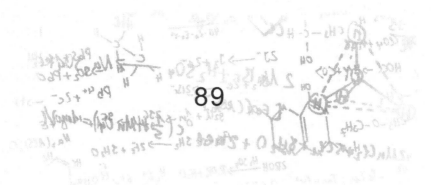

89

WHILE CHRISTINA FOLLOWED THE GOVERNMENT'S prosecutions, Bobby wasn't interested. Key testimony and leads from Martin Turnbull, Vincent Amaratto, Neil Foster, Randall Lindsay, Graham Waters, and Michael Petersen resulted in Colum McAlister's conviction on thirty-one violations of securities, economic espionage, extortion, blackmail, and money laundering laws. He was sentenced to nineteen years in federal prison, but there was insufficient evidence to bring him to trial for conspiracy to commit murder. Gunther Ramirez went unidentified and uncharged.

The FBI's success in infiltrating RASI resulted in the convictions of five RASI members including Kurt Osmond and Ashfaq Bashir on charges of attempted murder for the apartment explosion, and conspiracy to commit murder for the planned attack on the lab. They were acquitted of attempted murder relating to the lab attack, as the jury found that there was insufficient evidence to prove that the attack ever got beyond the planning stage.

But Bobby had no doubt about the source of the lab's destruction. He told Christina and Susan, but they discouraged him from sharing his view with others. Nevertheless, Bobby wrote the following letter to Varneys:

Dear Director Varneys,

I know you have your own theories as to what happened in my lab that night, but I would be remiss if I didn't share my thoughts with you.

As you know, I was fortunate for many years to possess a special intelligence. Or should I say, it possessed me. Through it, I came to understand certain fundamental truths that perhaps are uncomfortable.

You see, Orin (I guess it's time I called you that) —-there is a force of negativity and destruction in the universe. Highly efficient and infinitely resourceful, it empowers and leads. It gives diseases their resiliency, their tenacity, their propensity to reinvent themselves, resist treatments, regenerate and defensively mutate. It propels them. This force is not a neutral physical phenomenon. It's an evil —an active and pervasive evil. Are you surprised by this? Don't be. There is balance in the universe. That is the immutable law that governs what otherwise would be chaos. Everything has its reciprocal, its opposite. Do you believe in God? I do. Well, you can't have just that.

Throughout my life, I felt this force oppose me. It sought to disorient and distract me and undermine my health— physically and mentally. And then the day finally came as I always knew it would. I had cracked the code and it didn't want to lose that. AIDS is one of its greatest achievements you know.

I understand it will be hard for you to get your mind

around this. You're a man of action. You like to make files and close files, put the bad guys away. But the universe plays its own game. We can only do so much.

Sincerely yours, Robert

———————————•••••———————————

Feeling that he could make one last contribution, Bobby asked Susan to arrange for Uniserve to disseminate an online media statement, with accompanying links to the newspaper coverage that told the "Dumpster Baby" story. Within less than a day, this story became a viral sensation and proliferated throughout the world media, as did the short quote from Bobby which accompanied the press release, "Human life is never expendable. The implications of its loss cannot be predicted no matter how humble its origins or unlikely its promise."

The revelation that a child possessed of such unprecedented gifts had his provenance in circumstances so appalling started an avalanche of speculation in religious circles. Many began to view Bobby as a spiritual rather than a scientific phenomenon.

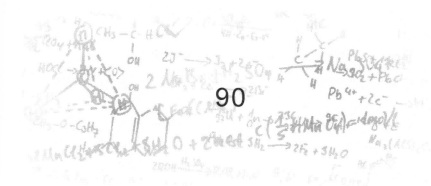

90

IT HAD BEEN ALMOST TWO years since Christina and Susan had last seen Varneys. When they walked into his massive office at Langley, they didn't notice a frail looking Dr. Uhlman slumped in a corner of the large sofa. Varneys introduced them to the aged scientist and then executed the obligatory small talk.

"So how's Robert doing?"

"Fine," said Christina. "He's relaxed. He and Susan are running Uniserve. He spends plenty of time every day with the baby. We're like a normal family now."

Varneys smiled. "And how's the little one?"

Christina's face lit up. "Getting bigger every day. He's beautiful. He reminds me of Bobby in so many ways."

"It's those eyes of his," Susan said, beaming. "The clearest light blue you ever saw. They go right through you, like little lasers. Even more so than Bobby's."

"A chip off the old block intelligence wise?" Varneys asked.

"I knew it wouldn't take you long to get to that," said Christina. "Is that was this meeting is about?"

Varneys stopped smiling and cleared his throat. "Not at all. Here, make yourself comfortable on the sofa."

Varneys pulled one of the guest chairs over to the coffee table, plunked himself down and leaned in toward them. "We—I mean Dr. Uhlman and I —thought it would be in Robert's best interests if we had a discussion."

Uhlman spoke up, his weak voice straining to project. "It's for Robert's good."

Varneys continued, "I'm doing this on condition that what you hear in this room remains between us. Do I have your agreement on that?"

Susan and Christina nodded.

"I don't think that either of you have a full understanding of Robert's history," Varneys said.

"He's told us a lot about his upbringing if that's what you mean," replied Susan.

Varneys dismissed Susan's comment with an almost imperceptible shake of his head.

Uhlman looked up and mumbled, "That's not what he's talking about."

Varneys nodded to Uhlman, signaling that he should proceed.

Uhlman scratched an eyebrow, then pulled on his ear lobe. "I first met Robert when he was four and a half. At the time, I was chief of Psycho-Neurological Development at the Mayo Clinic, a position I held for many years. Director Varneys was then head of the OSSIS—the Office of Special Strategic Intelligence Services. I was asked to examine the boy. He came to the attention of the state and ultimately federal authorities when his foster parents sought medical help with certain problems he was having. It wasn't long after I completed my examination that Robert began to live full time at the Institute for Advanced Intelligence Studies in Newton, and he was under my supervision until he left at age 20."

Varneys interrupted. "To the Doctor's credit, he correctly diagnosed Robert from the beginning."

"Based on what his foster parents told me and my examination, it was apparent to me that starting at age three, Robert was exhibiting the early stages of psychosis marked by strong paranoia and reality detachment—-all very unusual for a child of that age. It's always hard to predict how these conditions develop or regress in children because changes in body chemistry caused by puberty and aging can have a big effect. I was hoping that as Robert got older, he would improve but unfortunately, that wasn't the case. I also believe that his problems were exacerbated by a succession of catastrophic events."

"Did you try to help him?" Christina asked softly, her eyes watery.

Uhlman looked down at the floor.

"We monitored him constantly," Varneys said. "The Institute had a full-time psychiatrist."

Uhlman nodded. "Verjee. Doctor Riaz Verjee."

"Did Verjee treat him?" asked Susan.

Varneys shook his head. "At the time, we didn't think it prudent."

Uhlman continued. "Early on, we recognized that Robert was at his intellectual peak when he would detach from the present. In his semi-conscious dissociative state—what you call 'trances', he was at his highest level of creative thinking and problem solving."

"And you didn't want to interfere with that by treating him, did you? Because it was useful to your program," Susan said.

Varneys spoke up. "It's not that simple. You have to understand that we had no experience dealing with a mind at Robert's level.

No one did. We didn't want to dull him down with medications that were designed for ordinary people, or subject him to analysis that might backfire. We were dealing with a unique situation."

Uhlman's voice turned professorial. "I believe that a series of events accelerated the progression of Robert's illness—the sudden death of his parents, soon followed by Joseph Manzini's death and then shortly thereafter, Robert's learning the horrible details of his abandonment at birth." Uhlman cast a glance over to Varneys. "And then, immediately after that last trauma, Robert was required to leave the Institute. In retrospect, we know that this was a serious mistake. It heightened his isolation and paranoia. For all intents and purposes, he had no friends or family for years—until, of course, he met the two of you. So he lived solely in his own head— a dangerous place to be. His feelings of abandonment, rejection and betrayal were intensified by certain sensitivities— what we in the psychiatric field call 'over-excitability factors.' They're proportional to one's intelligence. In Robert's case, his intellect being so extraordinary, this heightened sensitivity was particularly acute."

Slouching in the sofa, Christina's eyes were closed as she shook her head slowly and murmured, "And he worked too hard. He put so much pressure on himself. It was just too much."

Uhlman nodded eagerly. "Yes. Exactly right. Adding to all of the other problems was the constant stress which he imposed on himself with his obsessive compulsive work ethic. But that, of course, was also a symptom of his illness."

"And as the years went by—neither of you did anything?" Christina asked.

"Not true," said Varneys. "As soon as I was in a position to— when I became Director of the CIA, Robert became a priority for me. I did everything I could to protect him."

Christina glared at Varneys. "But you didn't do anything to help him. You just wanted to keep him working, just like you did at the Institute. Just to maximize his output. That's all you cared about," said Christina.

Varneys' face turned red. "It was more than that."

"I'll bet," muttered Susan.

Uhlman continued, "The final destabilizing events were Robert's apartment being destroyed, and you, Christina, revealing your entanglement with the CIA. As Robert's disconnection from reality became more frequent and prolonged, his personality became increasingly dissociative. This is what was happening when I came to see him a few years ago at Prides Crossing and he had reached the point that he couldn't recognize anyone or even acknowledge their presence." Uhlman looked directly at Christina. "It was a miracle that you were able to bring him back and keep him on track for as long as you did."

The four of them sat in silence, none making eye contact, each lost in their own thoughts. Finally Varneys walked over to his desk and picked up an envelope that was inside a thick file folder. He opened the envelope and passed its contents over to Christina. "This is a letter I received from Robert."

Christina read it and then gave it to Susan.

After Susan put the letter down on the coffee table, Varneys said, "It's an unusual letter don't you think?"

Christina shook her head. "It's nothing new. Bobby often said there was some kind of force that was trying to stop him from curing diseases. He told us his view of how the lab was destroyed, but I didn't know he sent you a letter about it."

Susan jumped in. "Yeah—years ago —soon after we moved to the Prides Crossing lab—that's the first time he told me there was some 'supreme evil'—that's what he called it—that was interfering with his research and out to get him."

Varneys began to pace alongside his wall of windows, his steps as measured and precise as always. After awhile, he said, "You know, I was never satisfied with what came out of the prosecutions. When I got Robert's letter, it started me thinking. I couldn't get it out of my mind. I began to re-read all of the trial testimony and investigative reports. Things weren't adding up for me. And then I decided to do something that nobody else had done." Varneys looked over at Uhlman.

"What was that?" Christina asked.

"I ordered up copies of the surveillance tapes on the Prides Crossing lab. And I studied them. It took me months."

"But the tapes had been examined before, hadn't they?" asked Susan.

"Yes, but not going back three years prior to the explosion. And the investigators were only looking for one thing."

"What was that?" Christina asked.

"Intruders, co-workers, service providers. That kind of thing," replied Varneys.

Uhlman was pulling on his unevenly shaved chin with one hand, while the other tightly gripped the head of his cane.

Varneys picked up a remote control that was sitting on the coffee table. "I made a compilation of the relevant portions of the surveillance footage. Doctor—please walk us through the tapes."

As the footage played, Uhlman said, "Notice how Robert appears to be moving more slowly than normal, almost robotically. Director—please zoom in closely on his eyes."

Varneys manned the remote.

Uhlman continued, "You see how vacant he looks. His eyes are dead. Look at the expression on his face—there is none. He's in that semi-conscious state. He's functioning methodically but he's not in the present. When he returns to normal consciousness, he'll have no recollection of what he's done."

"Oh my God," Christina said as they witnessed Bobby working on the explosive devices.

"On and off, for over two years, late at night, in the confines of his locked office, he assembled the bombs. Of course, no one checked what he brought into the lab and needless to say, he was extremely adept at designing and building them," said Varneys. "And here—in this section of the video— you can see in the last year, how he sabotaged his own computers, wiping hard drives clean and destroying back-up memory."

Uhlman took the floor. "As Robert's illness progressed, it manifested itself in the creation of a self-loathing alternate personality whose goal was to frustrate his achievements and destroy him. That 'force of evil' that he spoke of —that he was so sure was opposing him and that tortured him in his nightmares— was internally generated. As he became sicker, it became more dominant. It took center stage when Robert didn't have full control over his mind—-when he slept or when he was in one of his trances. In the end, it did what it needed to do to try to stop him."

"So Bobby blew up the lab," Susan said.

Varneys nodded.

Tears streaming down her face, Christina asked, "So where does this leave us?"

Uhlman leaned in toward Christina and rested his heavily veined hand on hers. "He's stable now and that's good. He may stay like that indefinitely. I hope so. You and he deserve that."

"And this meeting. What was the point? Why did you feel you had to tell us?" Susan asked.

Uhlman leaned into his cane as he began the process of trying to stand up. "We were concerned for everyone's safety—Robert, the two of you, even the little boy."

"What does that mean?" Christina asked, her face flushed.

"I'm quite certain that Robert's intellect never really left him, but he thinks it did—and more importantly, so does his alternate self. So, for the time being there's no internal conflict. But if Robert's genius ever reasserts itself, it won't return alone."

THE END

William R. Leibowitz practices law in New York City and lives in the village of Quogue with his wife, Alexandria, and his dog, George.

Dear Reader: I hope you enjoyed *Miracle Man*.

Please email me at wrlauthor@gmail.com and it will be my pleasure to send you a personalized gift to welcome you to the *Miracle Man* family. The saga of Robert James Austin <u>will</u> continue and I'd be delighted to hear your thoughts and answer your questions. Please also visit miraclemanbook.com where you can hear/read my media interviews and access other content.

And if *Miracle Man* was special for you, then please tell your friends about it and post a review at: http://amzn.to/1wJgOtk

Many thanks -WRL